ANY RICH MAN WILL DO

Also by Francis Ray

Trouble Don't Last Always
I Know Who Holds Tomorrow
Somebody's Knocking at My Door
Someone to Love Me
Rockin' Around That Christmas Tree
Like the First Time
You and No Other

Anthologies

Rosie's Curl and Weave
Della's House of Style
Welcome to Leo's
Going to the Chapel
Gettin' Merry
Let's Get It On

ANY RICH MAN WILL DO

Francis Ray

St. Martin's Griffin New York

 For information, address St. Martin's Press, 175 Fifth Avenue, New York, N.Y. 10010.

www.stmartins.com

Library of Congress Cataloging-in-Publication Data

Ray, Francis.
Any rich man will do / Francis Ray.—1st ed.
p. cm.
ISBN 0-312-32431-6 (pbk.)
EAN 978-0-312-32431-5
1. African American women—Fiction. 2. Divorced women—Fiction. 3. Poor women—Fiction. I. Title.

PS3568.A9214A59 2005
813'.54—dc22

2005046582

P1

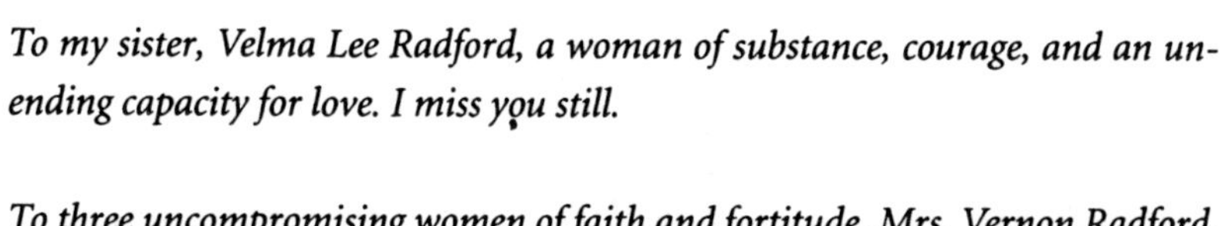

To my sister, Velma Lee Radford, a woman of substance, courage, and an unending capacity for love. I miss you still.

To three uncompromising women of faith and fortitude, Mrs. Vernon Radford, my mother; Mrs. Mattie Edgar, my mother-in-law; and Mrs. Robbie T. Byrd, past Director of Women's Ministry of Concord Missionary Baptist Church. These three amazing women look at the hearts of men and women and leave judgment to a higher power.

Special Thanks

Dr. Karen Hollie, noted Dallas psychologist, radio hostess, and columnist, who answered numerous questions as I worked on this book. My utmost thanks.

The Linen Gallery, Peacock Alley, and Hotel ZaZa for helping me research the sublime pleasure of sleeping on luxe linen. The experience was awesome.

1

Jana Franklin was out of luck and running out of time. She'd always believed she had more than her share of both. She'd been wrong. She had less than ninety-seven cents in her evening clutch and if she didn't come up with the rent for her motel room tonight she'd be out in the streets tomorrow.

What she needed was what she'd always used—an accommodating and generous man. She'd crashed a charity gala in a three-story Georgian mansion in the most exclusive area of Dallas to find one. But this time desperation, not greed or the allure of being in control, drove her.

Even as the frightening thought materialized, Jana fought to deny it. Desperation was not a word she had ever associated with herself. Why should she? She'd lived a privileged life and was accustomed to having whatever she wanted, whenever she wanted, and she'd always wanted the best.

As for need, by the time she was twelve her parents' disinterest had taught her never to need anyone. Her mother had taken the lesson one step further and drilled into the head of her only child to need men least of all.

Jana had learned that lesson well.

Since she was fifteen she'd carelessly used men as the whim struck, then moved on to the next gullible fool. If life had taught her anything it was that need made you weak and love was a joke for those stupid enough to believe in happily-ever-after. People who thought otherwise were asking for their hearts to be trampled on. Jana had always prided herself on being too smart for that, but somehow she'd taken a wrong turn and no matter what she did she couldn't seem to get her life back on track.

Tonight was her last chance.

Life was no longer an amusing game where she made the rules, then bent them for her own satisfaction and enjoyment. Her safe comfortable world was gone, perhaps forever.

Her trembling fingers clenched the stem of the champagne flute as she glanced around the formal living room of the palatial mansion. For the first time in her thirty-two years, she had no place to go and no one to turn to. Her black clutch held loose change, lipstick, and the key to a bug-infested motel room. Friends and family might be an option for some, but not for her. She'd never bothered to have friends and her parents had never bothered with her.

Another cursory glance around the elegant room filled with the wealthy and elite, and those who desperately wanted to be, increased the jittery feeling in Jana's stomach. She'd been here for twenty-five minutes, and although she'd shared good times and a bed with a couple of men in the room, neither had approached her nor spoken.

She felt uncomfortable in her own skin, restless, too keyed up to even enjoy her favorite drink. She was too aware of what would happen to her if she didn't accomplish her goal tonight.

Hope surged as she caught the eye of Dan Jefferies, a wealthy restaurateur and one of several men in the room who had once pursued her relentlessly. She'd rebuffed him and chosen a man ten years his senior and twenty times as wealthy. She hadn't been subtle in her rejection. Dan's sixty-foot craft couldn't compare to a luxurious yacht with its own helipad. As if remembering her very public put-down, he turned away, just as the other men in the room had done that evening.

A hint of color bloomed in Jana's pale cheeks. Her hand fluttered to the plunging neckline of her ill-fitting purple gown. It was a hideous dress, but it was the only appropriate attire she had left. If she had on one of her Armani or Valentino couture gowns, her nails and hair done at Neiman's salon . . . her thoughts trailed off. Somehow she knew those superficial trappings wouldn't help. Nothing had gone right since she'd fled Charleston in disgrace almost a year ago. Corrine Livingston had made sure of that.

"How the mighty have fallen."

"And it couldn't happen to a more deserving bitch."

Jana heard the snide comments of the nearby women as she was meant to and barely kept from tucking her head and leaving. Once they wouldn't have dared cross her and if they had, she'd have given it back to them in spades. What kept the harsh words locked behind her teeth was the vision of the small, cramped space that was now her home . . . at least for now. She could stand their abuse. What she couldn't stand was the possibility of never regaining her position in society.

A rich man would change that. But what if . . .

Her fingers tightened on the stem of the flute. She refused to let herself think about not succeeding. With an unsteady hand she tilted the crystal flute and drained the glass. The vintage wine tasted flat and left her feeling the same way. Once the thought of the chase, of seducing any man to her will, would have made her feel alive. Now it made her stomach roll.

She hadn't eaten all day. The women standing nearby laughed as Jana's stomach grumbled. She flushed with embarrassment.

Apparently tired of their little game, Priscilla Haynes, the hostess who had been standing with the two other women, confronted Jana. "I didn't know you were in town."

Priscilla was flawless in a black silk Armani gown that hugged her trim figure. A million dollars' worth of pure pink sapphires surrounded by oval-cut diamonds hung from her ears and circled her throat. The matching bracelet on her right wrist completed the one-of-a-kind suite. The diamond wedding ring was ten carats and flawless, as was the ten-carat diamond tennis bracelet on her other wrist.

Priscilla was a class-A snob and bitch. The slow drawling words were a none-too-subtle swipe that that knowledge would have precluded Jana being invited to the charity ball, since Priscilla was chair, in her home.

Unable to think of a quick comeback, Jana waved the empty flute in a dismissive gesture, then watched the other woman's hazel eyes narrow and grow even colder. Jana remembered, though now too late, making the same careless gesture shortly before leaving a party in Vail several years ago with Priscilla's fiancé.

Jana hadn't wanted the rich oilman. She'd simply wanted to show Priscilla, who thought she was all that, that she could. She'd sent him back to Priscilla the next day. Apparently his wealth far outweighed her humiliation because they had married six months later as scheduled.

"I . . ." Jana began, but couldn't quite come up with a witty remark. Smart comebacks had once been her staple and trade, that and getting any man she wanted. Saying she was sorry to Priscilla would have been a lie, but then when had Jana ever been bothered with the truth? Her prime objective was self-gratification, but look what that had gotten her.

Mitsy and Sherilyn, the two women who had spoken earlier, flanked Priscilla, bolstering her. A show of strength that said Priscilla had friends and Jana had nothing and no one. She never had. She hadn't thought she'd ever need them.

"Jana, you must have missed your salon appointment. I've seen better hair and nails on my cleaning woman," Mitsy said gleefully.

"We hear you're missing a lot these days." Sherilyn dared to flick the limp, ruffled sleeve of Jana's out-of-season gown. The bright purple design clashed garishly with her cinnamon-hued completion. "Where did you get this? The Salvation Army?"

"She earned it on her back like she has everything else," Mitsy answered.

"Not anymore," Sherilyn said. "Payback's a bitch."

Jana could have stood laughter better than the malicious glee in their eyes, the knowledge that Jana Louise Carpenter Livingston Murphy Franklin, the thrice-married woman who had once ruled those around her, especially men, was almost destitute with no friends, no family, and no place to go.

And it was her own fault.

Jana's brain urged her to leave, but the thought of what would happen to her if she left without accomplishing her mission kept her rooted on the Oriental rug. Without finding a wealthy man to support her she'd be out on the street tomorrow. The motel manager had already said she could "work it off." That she had been scared and desperate enough to momentarily consider his offer made her ill. There had to be one man here who still wanted her.

"I lost weight and didn't have time to shop." Jana carefully set the glass on a nearby table. "Excuse me. I see someone I know."

"We all know you, Jana. That's the problem," said Priscilla.

Jana flinched at the undisguised contempt in the woman's voice, then she continued past the hostile stares of the other people in the room. Most of them as gleeful as the women she had left. It wasn't difficult to read their thoughts: bitchy, man-stealing Jana was finally getting what was coming to her.

Jana's hand trembled as she grasped the brass knob of the powder room down the hallway. Thankfully it opened. Entering, she shut the door, then slid down until her bottom hit the cool black marble floor.

She'd called her mother for help, but she had said that she was having problems of her own. Jana's father had hung up on her. Neither had ever been there for her. Her mother has always been busy with the current lover: her father with his telecommunication firm. Why should now be any different?

Yet she couldn't help hoping that one day things would change.

She'd never worked a real job in her life. First there had been her wealthy father, who gave her money instead of his time, and her mother, who gave her lessons on handling men instead of handling the ups and downs of life, then a succession of men, each one wealthier than the last one. Five months ago that had stopped. Now she had to fend for herself, and had absolutely no idea how to do so.

It seemed that a beautiful face and a shapely body only worked for so long. She had been reduced to selling her clothes and jewelry, even her shoes, and moving to less and less expensive places to live until she had ended up in a dump that, a few months ago, she wouldn't have recommended a dog sleep in.

She lifted her head and leaned it back against the door. She'd read about the charity event tonight in the newspaper at the McDonald's where she had been able to con the young man behind the counter into letting her have breakfast while she only paid for coffee. But this week he was on vacation and the woman behind the counter wanted cash, not flirtatious smiles and a glimpse of cleavage.

With the elite in attendance—brown, black, white—she had been sure she'd find a man. She'd lived abroad long enough to have crossed the color line before, and saw no reason not to take the opportunity if it presented itself. Dallas was in the South, but the city had a cosmopolitan attitude about relationships.

But the opportunity hadn't presented itself. She wasn't five feet inside the great room where everyone was gathered before the buzz of whispers began to follow her like a bad scent. Her reputation and downfall had preceded her. Women who once cowered before her now smirked. Men who had once begged to be with her now barely looked at her.

No man wanted a woman no one else wanted.

That was the first lesson her mother had taught her when she was fifteen. They'd bonded as much as possible over discussions of men and sex when they had nothing in common to link them but blood. Her mother had taught her how to get a man, but she hadn't bothered to teach her daughter how to keep one. Jana had been taught that there wasn't a man she couldn't get. She found out too late that not all men were ruled by their zippers and now she was paying the high price, and so was her mother.

The brisk knock on the door made Jana jump. "I need to get in."

No please, no excuse me. Whoever was knocking knew Jana was inside, knew she was hiding.

The knock, more demanding, came again.

Jana struggled to her feet and swayed. Two glasses of champagne shouldn't have made her tipsy. She'd been drinking since she was fourteen. First in hiding, then after her mother had finally started to pay attention to her, they'd drink champagne and cosmopolitans when her father wasn't around. They'd done a great deal behind her father's back.

None of it good.

Jana made herself look in the mirror. She winced at the dark smudges beneath her eyes, the gaunt face, and the dull shoulder-length hair she'd tried to cut into a semblance of style with a pair of scissors she'd borrowed from the hotel manager. Her eyes looked old and defeated. She'd lost weight and the gown she'd bought on a wild shopping spree last year sagged on her. Not eating tended to do that to a person. She couldn't remember a day in the past three months when she hadn't gone to sleep hungry.

"Jana, open this door!" Priscilla demanded.

Jana flinched, swallowed, then rubbed her damp palms on her dress and opened the door. She wasn't surprised to see several women crowded into the hallway. They presented a united front against one. Once she would have been included, if only superficially, but that was before Charleston, before her life began its descent into hell.

"I don't want you in my house. A cab is waiting for you," Priscilla said.

Jana almost laughed. She had come by bus. Million-dollar residences needed a barrage of people, preferably at minimum wages, to keep them maintained and the occupants happy. The bus line was essential in bringing much of that help.

If only Jana could say her car was waiting or name a man who wanted to take her home. *Home.* Had she ever really had one?

"What's the matter with you? Are you so dense that you'd stay where you're not wanted?" Priscilla walked closer. "Get out of my house. Your presence offends me and every decent person here."

The verbal thrust made Jana cringe and come out fighting. "Since I know of your affair with a certain doctor in New York last year, and the rest of the women standing around you are just as bad, except Mitsy who prefers women, I'd say I'm in good company."

The slap across Jana's face snapped her head back and caused her to stumble against the wall. Stunned, she rubbed her stinging cheek. The attack was so unexpected that Jana simply stared at Priscilla as the verbal hatred poured from her mouth. Then, the male guests and a servant were there.

"Get this trash out of my house," Priscilla said, her voice and body trembling with rage. Everett, her husband, his face as closed as that of the other men with him—as if he'd never begged Jana to run off and marry him—put his arm around Priscilla and curtly nodded his head in Jana's direction. The stiff-backed butler stepped forward and grabbed Jana none too gently by the bare arm and led her past the watchful crowd.

It was all Jana could do not to hang her head in shame. By tomorrow news of her humiliation would have reached from one end of the country to another. Her fall from grace was complete. Opening the door, the servant kept walking until they were on the sidewalk. The garbage disposed of, he reentered the house.

For a long time Jana simply stared at the closed, recessed door, the light spilling from the many windows of the three-story home. The poorest to the wealthiest person inside had a home, maybe family and friends, waiting for them. What wouldn't she give to have as much? She'd never realized how desperately she wanted both until it was too late.

Trembling, Jana swallowed the knot in her throat, then turned, looked up and down the wide street bordered by million-dollar homes and flawlessly manicured lawns. Luxury cars and the Texas elite's newest darling, Hummers, lined both sides of the exclusive address, but there was no taxi. Jana glanced at her wrist, then felt a tear slide down her cheek. The 18-carat white gold Rolex with a mother-of-pearl face surrounded by two rows of diamonds, given to her by a very generous lover, had been sold weeks ago at a grocery parking lot to a man who had given her a tenth of what it was worth, but more than a pawn shop would have.

Opening her small clutch purse, she pulled out a wad of toilet tissue and dabbed her eyes. Pay-by-the-day motels didn't have Kleenex. But crying wouldn't change things. If it would have, she'd be back inside snubbing the hostess and selecting the lucky man to take her home. In the morning she'd have breakfast—mimosa, freshly baked flaky croissants, and waffles piled high with plump, juicy strawberries and fresh whipped cream.

Her stomach growled again. She should have eaten at the party when she had the chance, but she had been afraid that once she started she couldn't have stopped. Or worse, she might have thrown up the rich food. She was learning that hunger was manageable if you kept starving it. Feed it and your body wanted more.

She turned toward the bus stop, thinking as her steps quickened on the deserted street that she should have checked to see when it stopped running. The wealthy might want help during the day, but at night the servants went home unless they were working.

"Hey, beautiful, need a lift?"

Jana almost stumbled, then jerked around and saw Douglas Gregory in a $75,000 Mercedes. Salvation! She felt almost light-headed. Douglas was a second-string player for a Dallas sports team that was last in their division. At the party he'd been loud and obviously out-of-place and trying to fit in. He had probably been invited because of his connection to the team, but he wasn't accepted into the upper ranks. Each time he had joined a group, it splintered off.

"I'll take you anyplace you want to go." He glanced over his shoulder and behind him, then shoved open the passenger's side door.

Where he planned to take her was to bed. She hesitated. She hadn't been with a man in five months and frankly, for the first time in memory, she wasn't looking forward to it.

"Come on," he urged.

She took a step closer. In the dim light coming from the car she saw his angular, clean-shaven face. He wasn't much to look at, but she'd been with unattractive men before. Money, not looks, was important. Another lesson her mother had taught her.

Douglas glanced over his shoulder again. "Come on, get in."

Jana quickly understood what was going on. He didn't want anyone at the party to know he had picked her up. That was all right with her. He wasn't the type of man she usually chose either. The men she allowed her favors were charming, sophisticated, connected, and very wealthy. They had to be to be able to afford her. If she woke up at three in the morning and was hungry, there had better be a chef in residence or a hotel with twenty-four-hour room service to accommodate her.

"You coming or not?" he asked, impatience in his voice.

Jana quickly stuffed the tissue back in her purse then rounded the hood of the gleaming black car and got inside. She had barely closed the door before the vehicle took off. The smell of the new leather mingled unpleasantly with his heavy, woodsy cologne, causing Jana to feel queasy.

"I'm Douglas."

"Jana." First names meant sex for a night and good-bye in the morning. She'd played the game before, but this time she needed more than a night.

Bringing a smile to her face she turned toward him, thankful that the dimness of the car's interior showed only profile and cleavage as they passed the street lights, not the ravages of the past five months. "Thanks."

He chuckled. "I aim to please."

I just bet you do, Jana thought. Another man who thought he had the right moves to bring any woman ecstasy—which usually meant he didn't. But that was all right. Jana was a pro at faking it. Sex was a device to control men. Occasionally she found pleasure in the act, but she wasn't bothered if she didn't.

What she cared about was his paycheck. Since he'd been invited to the gala, it must be substantial which meant he could afford to keep her in the style she'd grown accustomed to.

"I just flew in for the charity event. I'm supposed to fly back out in the morning, but who knows. . . ." She let her voice trail off seductively.

He gave her a quick grin, then let his beefy hand fall heavily on her thigh. She wanted to shove his hand off. Instead she chatted, her edgy feeling returning as time passed. He didn't ask for her address.

A short time later she frowned as he pulled into the darkened theater parking lot of Highland Park Village. The upscale shopping center strip had single-level shops that rivaled those on Rodeo Drive.

Parking in a dark corner of the lot, Douglas cut the motor and reached for her. Jana inched back against the door. She didn't want a quickie, she wanted someone to take care of her. Someone to fix things and make her life right again.

"Why are we parked here?"

"My wife is home and I can't risk going to a hotel where I might be recognized," he told her impatiently.

Jana almost felt cheap and ashamed. "You could give me the money and I could rent the room, then call you on your cell," she suggested.

"I'm not going to risk it. From what I heard about you, this can't be your first time in a car," he said snidely.

It wasn't, but it had never been in these circumstances and never so crudely initiated. Jana stared at the disgruntled man and realized she had finally hit rock bottom.

All these years she'd told herself that she was using men. With startling clarity she realized they'd been using her. Her mother had been wrong. The man glaring at her wouldn't mind taking her in the front seat of his car, but he wouldn't want any of his friends to know, except the few he'd later brag to. He'd probably already bragged to at least one man at the party that he was going to score with her.

How could she have been so blind?

With a quick turn, she opened the door and got out. She heard the curse behind her and deftly evaded the hand grabbing for her. The chiffon ruffle on the back of her dress wasn't so fortunate. Her curse joined his at the sound of the fragile material tearing, but she didn't dare pause. Some men didn't take no. Her heels clicked loudly on the pavement as she headed toward the beckoning light of the shopping center.

"Get back in this damn car!" he yelled.

Although she felt light-headed, she increased her pace, fearing any moment she'd feel his rough hand on her arm. Instead she heard the slam of a door, then another. She dared glance over her shoulder to see the big car back up, then roar out of the parking lot. Panting, she slowed to fight off another wave of dizziness, unsure if it was from not eating a full meal in the last week or the intense heat. Even at night, the temperature in Dallas hung in the low nineties at this time of the year.

Catching her breath, her steps measured, Jana emerged from the parking lot and started toward the street at the other end of the shopping center. She was too wary to even glance into the store windows as she passed St. Johns, Gucci, and Cartier. Her focus was the street ahead. Hopefully a bus would be there, but the way her luck had been going, she doubted it.

A few steps later another wave of dizziness forced her to stop and press her hand against a plate glass window to steady herself. Eyes closed, she waited for her head to clear, painfully aware that each time the dizziness came it was more difficult to fight.

What wouldn't she give to be able to lie down on cool, clean sheets or for a cool glass of water. She didn't think she'd ever been as tired as she was now. If she didn't rest and get something to drink, she was afraid she wouldn't make it to the bus stop. Worse, she might pass out on the bus. And if she sat down on the sidewalk, she wasn't sure she'd be able to get back up.

Opening her eyes, she lifted her head and stared into the store. Directly in front of her was a king-sized brass bed piled high with luxurious linens and pillows. On the chrome nightstand was a silver pitcher, two silver flutes, and a small bouquet of fresh-cut flowers. Some might see the humor in the situation, but humor had never been Jana's strong suit.

As her gaze tracked around the store filled with colorful linens and bath products, she saw a tall, well-built man sitting behind a French country desk, his long legs, encased in jeans, stretched out in front of him. He wore a white shirt with the cuffs rolled back. His long-fingered hand slowly turned the pages in front of him.

As if suddenly aware he was being watched, he looked up and their gazes met. His dark eyes narrowed behind wire-rimmed glasses. For some odd reason his direct gaze made her want to step back into the shadows. She attributed the pounding of her heart to fear that he might recognize her. Priscilla and her friends would have a good laugh on hearing that Jana had passed out on the sidewalk.

Jana glanced toward the busy street that was a block away. She'd never make it if she didn't rest for a moment. There was only one choice left.

Before she lost her nerve, she reached for the crystal doorknob.

2

Tyler Maxwell was at the end of another long day. He'd just flown in from Chicago and had been up for the past twenty hours to ensure the updated computer system his team had installed to link Sterling Bank's 1,500 branches across the country was error free. The company before them had flubbed the job when the system overloaded, leaving thousands of tellers across the country with the very unpleasant task of telling their customers they were unable to access their accounts.

By attempting to save money the bank had lost millions *and* the goodwill of customers. Stockholders weren't happy. Tyler hadn't minded stepping in and correcting the problem. His success only served to further his reputation as a system analyst engineer and the owner of Prime Objective. His team was one of the best in the country.

On the way home from the airport, he'd called his sister Olivia, to let her know he had landed. He'd learned she had returned to her linen boutique, Midnight Dreams, to meet a couple whose special order had come in.

Instead of going home, he'd stopped at her store. Security was excellent during regular store hours in the upscale shopping complex, but scattered afterwards. Crime didn't have any borders. Since Olivia prided herself on customer satisfaction and service, she wouldn't have dreamed of telling the customers to wait until morning.

He'd arrived at the same time the anxious couple had. They were smiling broadly as Olivia led them to her office in the back. Grabbing a bottle of water from the refrigerator in the lounge, he'd made himself comfortable at the desk on the sales floor. His mouth twisted wryly at the seductive woman in a black negligee on the cover of the lingerie catalog in front of him.

It had been a long time between women and it wasn't likely to change anytime soon. Olivia thought he was still hung up on Courtney, but he'd simply decided he didn't have time to cater to another woman who wanted to make him over to suit her needs. He liked the way he was. Sliding the catalog aside, he began to look through the papers he'd removed from his attaché case.

Then something made him look up. A woman was staring back at him. He couldn't tell much about her except that she wore an evening gown. People often window-shopped after the movie or other events, so he wasn't particularly surprised. That changed when she opened the door and came in. He chastised himself for not making sure the door was locked.

His eyes narrowed as he got a better look at her. She appeared tired and had dark smudges beneath her eyes. Her shoulder-length black hair was uneven and looked as if someone had cut it blindfolded. Her movements were slow and deliberate.

He wasn't into fashion, but the evening gown looked outdated and worn. Most of the women who shopped the stores in the complex had money to burn, but he'd learned long ago not to judge people's financial status or their character from the way they looked. Many times he had been on the receiving end from Courtney about his shortcomings.

"I'm sorry, miss, but the store is closed."

Jana stopped at the sound of the deep Texas drawl. She stood a few feet inside the store as the man rose easily and stepped around the desk. His chest was broad, his legs long and muscular. He wasn't handsome in the traditional sense, but he had a kind of potent maleness that probably had women falling over themselves for him. For once, Jana was more interested in the cool air and sitting down for a moment.

Frowning he took a step closer. "Are you all right?"

"I . . ." was all Jana was able to say before her legs gave out. She felt herself falling. She thought she whimpered in protest, but wasn't sure. In the next instant she was lifted and gently held against a wide chest. Opening her eyes she stared up into a pair of intense black eyes and shivered.

"Tyler, what happened?"

Out of the corner of her eye, Jana saw an attractive petite woman rushing toward them. In her late twenties, she was wearing a pale yellow linen suit. Her arms were full of bedding. Behind the woman was a stylishly dressed couple of about the same age. They carried bed linens as well. Unlike the woman, they made no move to come closer.

"She fainted," Tyler answered calmly, as if it were an everyday occurrence. He never took his eyes from Jana. "Can you stand?" he asked her.

Jana managed a nod and readied herself to be dumped back on her feet. She hoped she wouldn't keel over.

"Put her here, Tyler," the woman instructed, then proceeded to move a stack of sample books from a Queen Anne chair in front of the desk where Tyler had been sitting.

Tyler placed her in the rose silk-covered chair, then turned away only to return with her scuffed and worn olive suede Manolo Blahnik mules. His carefully assessing gaze ran over her again. Jana's bare toes curled beneath the gown. Thank goodness her feet were hidden. It was all she could do to not shrink back in the chair.

Her mother had always maintained that a fashion faux pas was as bad as any other transgression. She'd been able to hide the fact that she was down to her last two pairs of Manolo Blahniks, neither of which were evening shoes, with her floor-length gown. It was too hot to wear hose even if she had a pair, which she didn't. Wordlessly, she reached for her shoes.

He gave them to her, then plucked a bottle of water from the desk, broke the seal and handed it to her. "Take a few sips of this."

Gratefully, Jana's hands closed around the cold bottle of water and lifted it to her lips. She would have guzzled it if he hadn't taken it from her.

"Not too much," he said, then allowed her another couple of swallows. Jana thought of snatching the bottle, but didn't think she had the strength. She swallowed convulsively. *Please don't let me throw up.*

"It's probably the heat," said the woman who had spoken earlier. "Can I get you anything or call anyone?"

With them watching her, Jana knew she had to say something. She couldn't decide what she wanted more, to slink away in shame or to close her eyes and rest. "If I could use the restroom?"

"Of course," the woman said. "I'll show you the way."

"She'll need her shoes, Olivia." Before Jana could protest, Tyler plucked the shoes from her lap, hunkered down, then held out his hand expectantly for her foot.

She moved her feet back further beneath her gown. "I—I can do it."

He stared at her a few minutes longer as if he might challenge her, then came easily to his feet. Envying him his easy strength, Jana slipped on one shoe, then the other, grateful that the dizziness cleared when she lifted her head.

As soon as she straightened, Olivia reached for her, but it was Tyler whose calloused hand curled around Jana's arm and helped her to her feet. He didn't let go, she was sure, until he was satisfied she could stand by herself. "Thank you."

"Bathroom is this way," Olivia said, taking slow steps as they moved toward the back of the store. "Are you sure there's no one I can call?"

"No." *No one who cared.*

"Here we are." In the back of the store Olivia opened the door to the surprisingly large bathroom. "Feel free to use the towels to freshen up. I'll be back shortly to check on you."

"Thank you," Jana said, then walked inside the spotless white and chrome bathroom, closing the door behind her. She hadn't said thank you so many times in such a short span of time in longer than she could remember.

The crowd she used to run with thought only of themselves first and always, just as she had. She'd lived a selfish, worthless life and it had finally caught up with her. If she died tonight no one would mourn her or care. Her head fell forward as misery swept through her.

She was alone.

This time when the dizziness came she didn't try to fight it. She embraced the peaceful oblivion that she had never been able to find when awake.

"I hope she's all right," Olivia said as she reentered the showroom.

"That awful dress she wore was torn in the back," Cynthia Ingram said, her green eyes rounded in shock and excitement. "And those shoes! Even if they were Manolo Blahnik. Suede in the summer! And so scuffed and worn. Perhaps you should call the police."

"Police?" Olivia's brows bunched in puzzlement as she took a seat at the desk.

Cynthia's brunette head nodded emphatically. "My guess is a man ripped her gown. He might come looking for her."

Olivia's worried gaze sought her brother. He leaned casually against the door jamb separating the shop from the back room. "Tyler?"

He smiled in reassurance. He'd noticed the rip as well, but he didn't think anyone was coming after her. As weak as she was they could have easily caught her if they'd wanted. "Mr. Ingram and I can handle him if he does."

Dennis Ingram, Cynthia's husband of three months, laughed and slung his arm around his wife's slim shoulders. "Tyler is right, honey. Don't you worry. Besides, she could have just as easily caught it on something."

"I suppose." Cynthia appeared somewhat disappointed. "Our speaker at the Junior League luncheon today was a woman from a local women's shelter. Guess all the horror stories are still with me." She wrinkled her pretty mouth. "Although I must admit I can't see how any woman would stand to let a man use her as a punching bag. The things women put up with and the lies they tell themselves just to have a man, it's pitiful."

"I'll get your receipt," Olivia said, then began writing up the sale.

Tyler kept his attention on the door of the bathroom. He didn't want to worry Olivia or alarm her customers, but he'd worked in enough hot spots around the world to be able to sense when something was off. The woman looked as if she were on her last leg. It might have been a coincidence that she just happened to come into Olivia's store or it could have been planned. Once she came out of the restroom she could leave or try to run a scam. He wasn't taking any chances. Olivia, with her trusting nature, would instinctively reach out to help in any way possible.

Olivia was the most trusting and unassuming person he knew. Her ex-husband had used her naïveté to ensnare her in a marriage that was doomed from the beginning. The heart-wrenching ordeal of her divorce a year later had almost destroyed the laughing, generous girl he had grown up with.

Tyler had been out of the country most of the time during her sham of a marriage and hadn't known the full extent of the problem until the divorce was almost final.

He'd kept his anger hidden and concentrated on helping Olivia rebuild her life instead of going after her manipulating and underhanded husband. With the help of her family, she'd survived and flourished. If humanly possible, he planned on making sure no one ever took advantage of her again.

Olivia finished writing the sale receipt and handed it to the Ingrams. "Thank you and enjoy."

"We will," Dennis Ingram shoved the slip of paper into the inside pocket of his tailored sports jacket. "We fell in love with Frette sheets when we stayed at the Ritz in Paris on our honeymoon. When we got your call this afternoon that our order had come in, we couldn't wait until tomorrow. Thank you for staying open."

Olivia smiled. "My pleasure. Your bed linens are the ultimate in luxury. I understand completely how anxious you must be to try them out."

The couple looked at each other and grinned.

Tyler noticed that his sister grinned back. Her smile was for a different reason. The set cost close to $4,500. He'd rather invest that kind of money, but others saw the purchase of luxe linens as an investment in itself, either for sheer indulgence or as heirlooms. Either way, they had made his little sister a wealthy woman in her own right. That she'd done it almost single-handedly, establishing her independence and bolstering her self-esteem, was priceless.

"Remember, if you need laundry service you have only to call for pickup and delivery. I included a pamphlet on caring for them if you wish to do it yourself."

"You think of everything."

"I try." Olivia came around the desk. "I'll show you out."

The couple didn't budge. "We'll wait until she comes out. If you hadn't waited on us, you wouldn't have had to let her in," Mr. Ingram said.

"I'm glad we were open," Olivia said, her brow creased in concern. "She looked worn out."

"She looked unsavory to me," commented Mrs. Ingram. "I wonder what she was doing in this neighborhood."

"You can bet it wasn't shopping, the way she was dressed," her husband answered.

Tyler noticed Olivia barely kept the smile on her face. Neither of them liked narrow-minded, snobbish people. Unfortunately, on occasion, their work demanded they associate with them. "Olivia, maybe you better go check on her."

"Please, excuse me." Olivia started walking to the back with Tyler close behind. She knocked gently on the restroom door, realizing as she did that she didn't know the woman's name. "Miss? Miss? Are you all right?" No answer. She knocked again. "Miss?"

Tyler stepped around her, his hand going to the doorknob.

"Tyler, wait." Olivia placed her hand on his.

"If she's not answering, she might have fainted again." Jana's worn, out-of-season shoes had a designer label and the torn gown had fit poorly, but her voice had been educated. Perhaps she had hit on hard times. But that didn't explain why she was wandering the shopping village when the stores were closed.

Olivia withdrew her hand and stepped aside. "Do what you think is best."

Tyler didn't take her unwavering trust lightly. He pushed the door open a few inches before it stopped. He cursed beneath his breath when he saw the woman's slim arm, her palm down. Slowly, not sure of what he'd find, he eased the door open a little more. There hadn't been any track marks on her arm, her pupils hadn't been dilated, but there had been a wild desperation in her face when she asked to use the restroom that had made him uneasy.

When the opening was wide enough, he slipped inside. Olivia was right behind him. By the time he'd done a cursory examination, his sister was kneeling by his side with a damp washcloth. Lifting the woman up, he took the cloth and ran it lightly over her pale face. Despite the obvious ravages, she was beautiful, her features delicate.

"Should we call an ambulance?" Olivia asked.

Tyler shook his dark head. "No. There are no broken bones or bumps."

"You better make sure. If she's hurt, you're liable," Cynthia said from the doorway.

"She could be running a scam," added her husband.

Olivia shook her head. "I don't think so."

Tyler agreed, and kept running the cloth over her face. She felt so light, his arm gently tightened around her as he tenderly bathed her fine-boned face.

The woman's lids fluttered, then opened. "W-what happened?"

"You fainted again," Tyler told her, helping her to sit upright. "Do you have any medical problems?"

She started to shake her head, then paused when the dizziness returned and said, "No."

"You better have her checked out just to make sure," Mr. Ingram said from the doorway. "People say that then sue later."

"Dennis is right, Olivia, I'd have her checked out," his wife commented. "You don't want any surprises down the road."

Tyler watched the woman lower her head and was afraid she was going to pass out again. "Miss?"

"I won't sue," came the soft whisper.

"If I had a dollar for every client that was told that, I could retire tomorrow," Dennis said.

Tyler didn't have to think long to recall the recent newspaper article touting the success of Midnight Dreams. "Perhaps it's best that we have a doctor check you out."

"I don't want to go to the hospital, and you can't make me." She closed her eyes for a moment, then reopened them. "I'll be on my way."

Tyler came to his feet bringing her with him, then released her. Almost immediately her legs buckled. His hand closed around her forearm. "I don't think so."

She glared at him. "You—you did that on purpose."

"It's either the hospital or the police. Your choice."

Her eyes widened. She paled even more. "I haven't done anything."

"That may be, but you're in no condition to go anyplace by yourself."

"I'm not your responsibility."

"I'd say that was true until you came into the store and fainted, which made my sister's store liable if you suffered any injuries. Or did you already know that?" Tyler asked, watching her closely.

She held his gaze. "Believe what you want, but you can't make me go to the hospital."

Tyler's eyes narrowed. All that bravado, yet she was trembling like a leaf. He admired courage, but not stupidity. Releasing her arm, he stepped back. "You know the way to the door, but this time, instead of reviving you, I'll notify the police. They'll take you to the hospital whether you want to go or not."

Her reaction was swift. "You bastard."

"I've been called worse." He nodded toward the door.

Jana took a step and the room swirled. She felt the soft hands of a woman and knew it was Olivia.

"Perhaps you should go to the hospital," Olivia suggested gently.

Jana decided to stop this nonsense in one surefire way. "I'm not paying."

"I don't recall asking you to." Tyler took her by the other arm and gazed at his anxious sister. "I suppose you want to go?"

"I'd like to make sure that she's all right."

Jana snorted, then turned her head away. "If you're so worried then you could call me a cab and pay him to take me to my place. Because if you think you'll stick me with the bill, you're in for a surprise."

Olivia's expression saddened. "I'll be responsible for the bill. Do you think you might be pregnant?" Shock raced across the woman's face. Olivia glanced at the woman's left hand. There were no rings. "I'm sorry if I insulted you."

"Save the apology. The only reason you care is because you don't want me to sue." No one had ever cared about her except her first ex-husband and she had blindly killed that love.

"The way you look, you can hardly blame her," Mrs. Ingram said from the doorway, looking down her nose at Jana.

Tyler felt the woman flinch. "Mr. and Mrs. Ingram, thanks for staying and for the advice. I'll see you out." He turned to Olivia. "Lock up. I'll wait for you outside, follow you home, then you can ride with me to the hospital."

"You just got back. I'll take her," Olivia protested.

Tyler was shaking his head before she even finished. Olivia was too easy a target. He was ninety-nine percent sure the woman wasn't running a scam, but the one percent bothered him. "We do it my way."

Olivia stared at him a few moments, then nodded. Tyler wasn't the type to change his mind once it was made up. "I'll just go inside to check on Griffin, then I'll come back downstairs."

"Let's go." His steps slow, Tyler started for the front door, his hand still around Jana's slim upper arm. His hand easily circled her arm. He wondered if she was fashionably thin on purpose.

Outside, he bid the Ingrams goodnight, then started for his truck. He felt Jana's resistance when he neared the vehicle. He glanced down and read the apprehension in her strained features. "You have nothing to fear from me."

"I'm not scared of any man," Jana told him. As if to underscore that point, she moved closer, letting her breasts brush against him, her free hand gliding suggestively down his chest. She should have thought of this sooner. "Why don't we go someplace quiet and I'll show you."

"Tyler?" came Olivia's hesitant voice.

Jana jumped, snatching her hand back, stumbling in her haste. Tyler caught her before she fell, his hand like a vise around her arm. "It seems your patient is recovering."

Jana felt heat surface to her face, but she held her head high. They were going home to a clean bed where they didn't have to prop a chair against the rickety door or listen to roaches, and heaven only knew what else, scuttle across the floor and fear they might get into the bed.

"Then I guess introductions are in order." Smiling, Olivia stuck out her hand. "I'm Olivia Sanders, and this is my brother, Tyler Maxwell."

Jana glanced from the extended hand to the small woman in front of her. *Play this for all it's worth,* a voice told her. She might get enough out of this to change hotels at least for a few days. She clasped the woman's small hand, but wasn't taking a chance in case they knew anyone in Priscilla's crowd. "Janet."

"What's your last name?" Tyler asked.

"Street," she replied.

"You live near here?"

"No."

"You ever fainted before?"

"No. Look, you're so anxious to go, let's go."

"Of course," Olivia said, pulling her car keys from her purse. "I'm sorry, introductions could have waited until later."

"A few minutes won't hurt, Olivia," Tyler said, his annoyance at Jana plain.

His sister nodded, then hurried to a white Lexus SUV parked a few spaces away and got in. Tyler waited until his sister backed out, then led Jana to his truck and opened the door. She started to get inside, then glanced back over her shoulder when he didn't release her.

"If I were you, I'd try to remember that Olivia is on your side. Lose the attitude."

He wasn't going to bully her. "I told you, men don't scare me."

"Maybe you haven't met the right man." None too gently he helped her into the cab of the truck, then slammed the door.

Twenty minutes later they entered the emergency room of Presbyterian Hospital. People spilled from the waiting room to outside on the sidewalk. The wails of small children and the moans of adults created an edgy cornucopia of sounds, and attested to the reason the clerk had said Jana might have to wait up to six hours to be seen. Jana had no intention of waiting that long.

As soon as they put her in a room and the nurse left, she planned to be right behind her. The only reason Tyler and Olivia were playing the Good Samaritans was fear of being sued. They needn't have worried.

Lawsuits took time, and in her case, she'd have to find a lawyer who'd work pro bono, which wasn't likely to happen. She was more concerned with returning to the motel and trying to get an extension on her rent. She'd seen a bus, but didn't know if any still ran to her side of town.

Somehow Jana's scheme didn't work out as planned. An hour after she was finally admitted and placed in a small cubicle, her two watchdogs were still with her. At least her head had stopped swimming as she sat on the side of the gurney in an ugly hospital gown.

She was pretty sure she could have gotten rid of Olivia without any problem or talked her into a "loan," but Tyler was another story. He stared at her with those cold assessing eyes of his, giving away nothing. She stared right back. Not for anything would she reveal how his rejection had made her want to crawl under the covers.

"What's taking them so long?" Olivia glanced at her watch. "We've been here almost two hours. It's been over an hour since they put us in here."

"Why don't you two go get some coffee or something?" Jana suggested.

Tyler merely lifted an eyebrow and continued to lean against the wall on the far side of the room, a position he had assumed when they entered. He had a capacity for stillness that was unnerving, whereas Olivia was almost always in motion.

"I'm sorry, Janet. Would you like some coffee?"

What she'd like was food and for them to leave. "No."

Olivia glanced at her watch again. "I'm going to see if I can find out what's keeping them."

The door had barely closed before Jana said, "On second thought, I would like that coffee."

"Is that right?" Tyler said, not moving an inch.

Her mouth tightened. "Yes, it is."

"Olivia would never forgive me if I left and you ended up on the floor again." He kicked up the brim of his Stetson. "I'll wait."

Gritting her teeth Jana turned around too quickly. A wave of dizziness hit her and she had to jerk back to keep from falling on the floor. It was too much to hope he hadn't noticed. Taking it slower, she lay down and turned her back to him. Her bad luck was holding steady.

3

Julian Cortez strode through the crowded emergency room corridor of Presbyterian Hospital, his long-fingered hands stuffed in the pockets of his white lab coat, his gaze locked on the revolving door leading outside to freedom. That morning he'd been awakened from a sound sleep shortly before six by a phone call from a doctor in the emergency room saying that he was needed. The call had come more than sixteen exhaustive hours ago.

Julian was used to those calls. Even during his internship in surgery at Parkland Hospital, renowned for its trauma center, it had been clear that he had been gifted with the skill, dexterity, instincts, and sheer nerve to operate on mangled bodies and save lives.

He'd barely finished that case before there had been another. That time an idiotic young man who had learned the hard way that speed and alcohol don't mix. Julian had fought with death many times in his thirteen years as a doctor, first as a surgical resident, then in private practice. Today he had won. Tomorrow, who knew. He'd learned to take victories where he could.

He didn't notice the stares and wishful looks of the women, both employees and visitors, any more than he took note of the beating of his heart. Since medical school he'd been teased by classmates because women were drawn to his dark, sensual looks.

Julian wasn't conceited, but he knew women found him attractive. There weren't many days that he didn't find at least one phone number stuffed in his lab coat pocket or on the windshield of his car.

If only they knew he thanked God that he bore a striking resemblance to his Cuban-born grandfather and not his father. Julian couldn't have stood looking daily into the mirror and seeing the face of the man who had made the lives of his family hell, the man who had let Julian's mother die needlessly.

Julian's hands clenched. He fought to push the old, bitter memory away. Velma Radford Cortez wouldn't have wanted him to blame or to hate. Her love had been boundless. Too bad she had loved a man who couldn't love her or his children the way they deserved. His mother was the reason he had gone into medicine, the reason it would always be his first passion.

He saw the petite woman in the middle of the hallway, turning around as if she was lost or looking for someone. Perhaps he noticed because she was wearing yellow and looked so fresh. When he neared she turned and saw him . . . and went still.

Then she started toward him. He'd been boldly approached before. He was too tired to even think about a woman, but tomorrow was another day. He was trying to decide what his response would be when she came to a stop in front of him.

"Dr. Cortez?" she said, her gaze going from the name written in black cursive on his lab coat to his face.

"Yes?" She had a sweet, almost breathless voice that was intriguing. Perhaps he wasn't as tired as he had first thought.

"I know you probably have a lot of emergency cases, but could you please take a moment to see Janet?" The woman bit her lip. "She walked off the street and fainted in my store's restroom. She's still unsteady. It's probably the heat, but I'm not sure."

For a moment Julian just stared. "You want me to see a patient?"

Her large brown eyes sparkled. "Could you, please? She's just down the hall."

Julian didn't know whether to laugh or be affronted. "Miss—"

"Dr. Cortez isn't on the ER staff, Mrs. Sanders. He's in private practice," said the charge nurse, a willowy brunette. "I've already told you that you have to wait. There are more pressing cases."

"How do you know Janet isn't one of those pressing cases? No one has even taken her blood pressure," Mrs. Sanders replied.

The nurse's eyes narrowed. "Be glad that she got a room."

Mrs. Sanders's mouth tightened, then she turned to Julian. "If you're in private practice, then you can see patients, can't you?"

Before Julian could answer, the charge nurse spoke again. "He's a trauma surgeon."

"Oh," Mrs. Sanders said, her shoulders drooping. "Forgive me."

Julian watched the woman turn away, her gaze searching the hallway again. She wasn't giving up. He admired her spunk. If there was a Mr. Sanders he was a lucky man.

"Sorry, Dr. Cortez. Have a good evening," the nurse said.

The nurse's eyes said she'd like to be going with him. His face expressionless, Julian nodded and continued on. Just as he passed Mrs. Sanders, she looked at him again. Worry shone in her eyes. His steps slowed. "Your friend is probably fine," he told her.

Mrs. Sanders crossed her arms over her soft, rounded breasts and shook her head of short auburn curls. "Neither Tyler nor I had seen her before she came into the store tonight. Two of my clients cautioned me to have her checked out to ensure she didn't claim she was injured when she passed out, but I just want to make sure she's all right."

Julian wondered who Tyler was. "Not many people would be that considerate."

She sighed, causing her breasts to rise again. Julian's interest peaked. "I learned long ago to live by my own standards and not other people's."

Julian's hand was lifting out of his pocket before he realized it. He balled it instead of brushing it across her face in reassurance. What was the matter with him? Too many long days were finally getting the best of him. "She'll be seen soon."

"I just have this feeling that she's had a difficult time," the woman said softly.

Julian didn't know what to say. He healed their bodies. Their minds were not his problem.

Her hands dropped to her sides. "Excuse me." She started to walk away.

"On the hunt for another doctor?" he asked impulsively, wondering why he didn't just leave.

"I may have better luck this time."

Her compassion moved him. The unspoken plea in her eyes, the unmistakable sadness tugged at him as few things in life ever had.

After his mother's needless death, he'd sworn he'd be the best doctor possible. He'd succeeded. His skills were almost legendary. So was his bedside manner. It was abominable. He was impatient, curt. Some said driven, and he was. His job was to heal their bodies, not be their bosom buddy. Yet, for some reason, he couldn't turn away from the woman in front of him.

"Perhaps you hit pay dirt the first time."

Her eyes widened as she realized he was going to help. "Thank you." Grabbing his arm, she pulled him down the hall and into the room. "I'm Olivia Sanders and this is Tyler Maxwell. Tyler, this is Dr. Cortez, a trauma surgeon, but he's agreed to see Janet."

Tyler came away from the wall and extended his hand, a half-smile on his lips. "Thank you, Dr. Cortez."

"I haven't done anything yet." He walked to the gurney with Olivia beside him. There was no reason for him to be upset that a man was with her, but he was.

Reaching out, Olivia gently touched Janet's arm. She lay on her side with her back to them. "Janet? Janet? Dr. Cortez is here."

Jana glanced over her shoulder. Her eyes widened with interest. The man was gorgeous. He had the face of a fallen angel with jet black hair, and the most beautiful golden eyes she had ever seen. She reacted automatically, her lashes dipped flirtatiously, her voice took on a seductive tone. "Aren't I the lucky one?"

"That remains to be seen," Dr. Cortez said, his voice clipped.

Jana's smile froze. She'd done it again. Even half starved and bone weary, she still reverted to type. Unerringly her gaze went to Tyler. His face was expressionless, yet she felt his disapproval as though he'd spoken it aloud. She made herself smile despite wanting to slink back under the covers.

"I'll get a nurse to assist me." Dr. Cortez went to the door and called. "Nurse." A pert brunette wearing scrubs appeared almost instantly. "Take her vitals."

"Yes, sir." The nurse removed the blood pressure cuff from a wall unit and placed it on Jana's right arm.

"Please excuse us," Dr. Cortez said to Olivia and Tyler.

Jana kept the smile on her face with an effort. She didn't care what any of them thought of her, she told herself as her nails bit into her clenched hands.

"Just relax," the nurse instructed.

"My sister and I will wait outside." Tyler curved his arm around a frowning Olivia and ushered her outside.

Sister. Ridiculously pleased, Julian turned to the patient.

Dr. Cortez's examination was quick but thorough. Five minutes later he lifted his head and draped the stethoscope around his neck. Finished with the nurse, he walked her to the door, then beckoned to Olivia and Tyler who waited just outside. "You can come in now."

Olivia saw Dr. Cortez's angry expression and rushed into the room. She hadn't missed Janet's attempt to flirt. Perhaps she had tried it again. Olivia couldn't blame her. The doctor was gorgeous. But he was the type of man she'd never look at twice. She never wanted another pretty man. "What is it?"

"There's nothing wrong with her that eating won't cure," Dr. Cortez snapped. "Next time you're on a crazy diet don't waste my time or the staff's," he said to Jana. "At least be woman enough to admit the problem."

"Must have slipped my mind," Jana said, but her voice wobbled.

"Don't be flippant!" he snapped, nearing the bed.

Olivia deliberately stepped between them. "I thank you for your help, but that's no way to talk to a patient."

"What?" Dr. Cortez's dark gaze zeroed in on her. "She knew why she fainted and kept this farce going in spite of seeing how concerned you were."

"Perhaps." Olivia stuck out her hand. "Thank you. I signed the admit papers to be responsible for the bill. If you'll let the admitting office know you saw Janet, I'll send you your fee."

Dr. Cortez was dumbfounded. He shook her hand as if in a daze. "Don't you understand she deliberately misled you?"

"Dieting is a very personal matter to some people," Olivia said. "Thank you for helping. As soon as Janet is dressed, we'll be leaving."

"You're taking her with you?" With each of Olivia's statements, his disbelief grew.

"Yes," Olivia said. Her ex-husband had taught her that things weren't always what they seemed. "Thank you again, Dr. Cortez. If you're ever in Highland Park Village, stop by Midnight Dreams."

His brows bunched. "What?"

She smiled. "It's a luxe linen shop."

Julian's frown only cleared marginally as he looked at Tyler. "You approve of this?"

"Against my better judgment."

"You sister is too naïve."

"Compassion doesn't mean I'm naïve," Olivia said, her mouth pouting becomingly.

Julian spoke to Tyler instead of addressing Olivia. "Is she always like this?"

"Always," Tyler answered easily.

Dr. Cortez glanced at Jana in irritation for taking advantage of Olivia, irrationally annoyed at Olivia for allowing it. "Mrs. Sanders, I hope you never trust the wrong person."

Pain shone briefly in Olivia's chocolate brown eyes, then it was gone. Instinctively, Julian knew a man was the cause. Inexplicably he wished he could take that memory away and replace it with . . . what?

Not understanding his protectiveness toward a woman who had decided to make herself the champion and guardian all rolled into one of a woman she'd just met, he decided it was time to leave. "Good-bye."

Tyler caught the door before it swung shut behind Julian. "I'll wait in the hall while she gets dressed, then we can take her home."

Olivia picked up the evening gown. "Are you comfortable with me helping you?"

Jana stared at her. First Olivia had helped, then defended her. Neither made any sense to Jana. No one did anything without hoping to get something in return. There had to be a reason Olivia was helping her. Jana just hadn't figured it out yet.

"Janet?"

Janet, not Jana. Now she understood. Olivia didn't know about her past. No one would help Jana. Pulling off the hospital gown, she reached for her dress.

Tyler didn't say anything as Olivia and Janet, arm in arm, emerged from the room. After a brief stop at the business office, they went to his truck. This time Tyler helped Janet into the seat in the back. Starting the truck, he pulled out of the parking lot. "Where to?"

"Any bus stop." Arms folded, Janet stared out the window.

His gaze caught hers in the rear-view mirror. "It's late. Where to?"

Shrugging her shoulders she glanced out the window. "Interstate Motel on 1–35 at Kiest."

Tyler exchanged a look with Olivia and headed toward the freeway. He was familiar with the moderate- to low-income area. The woman sitting in the backseat didn't strike him as a resident of a motel for transients, but it was also used for clandestine meetings. She'd tried to come on to him *and* the doctor. Maybe she was meeting a man there. It was her life and none of his business. Once he got her home she was no longer his or Olivia's responsibility.

Jana wanted time to stand still. If that happened she wouldn't have to get out of the comfort and safety of the truck.

"Which unit?"

When had any of her wishes come true? "Number eight."

Tyler parked directly in front of the unit. The strong beams of the headlight clearly showed the paint-chipped door, dingy windows, and dying shrubs. It was the last stop for those on a road to nowhere.

Jana saw Tyler and his sister trade glances. They probably wanted to get away from there as fast as they could. Jana had felt the same way when she'd walked from the bus stop to the cheapest place to stay she'd been able to find. Some kind of crazy pride reared its ugly head. She didn't want them to know how much she hated this place. "Can't say it hasn't been interesting."

Jana reached for the door handle. By the time she was out of the car, Tyler was standing beside her.

Without a word he handed her the take-out bag of food. The aromas made her mouth water, her stomach growl. Her hands closed tightly around the sack. She'd been surprised when he'd stopped to pick up take-out and included her without Olivia prompting him to do so. "Guess I can always restart the diet tomorrow."

His eyes said he knew she lied. She told herself she didn't care. Looping three fingers through the plastic handle, she walked to the door and took the key from her clutch. Sticking it into the slot, she waited for the green light to appear. It blinked red the third, then the fourth time she reinserted the key.

Her eyes closed. This couldn't be happening to her. Her head fell for a moment, then she turned and almost bumped into Tyler. Olivia was beside him.

"Problem?" he asked.

Although Jana's knees were shaking with fear, pride made her smile. "This happens all the time. I'll just go have them make another key."

"We'll just wait," Olivia said, her gaze going to the unit across the way where the music blared and three men lounged outside the door.

Clutching the key and her purse, Jana went to the office. Tyler held open the unpainted door for her and Olivia. The area was cramped with cheap furniture and pots of plastic plants covered with layers of dust. A few steps inside Jana saw her Gucci case by the waist-high counter. Her throat dried. "My key won't work."

The night clerk, a balding man with a beer belly and tobacco-stained teeth, grinned. "Rent was due at twelve. Maid packed your stuff."

She refused to look behind her to see their reaction. "I'll have it tomorrow. I promise."

His eyes roamed her body like greedy, silent fingers. He licked his dry, chapped lips. "Let me take care of the people behind you and then we can discuss it."

"Let's discuss it now." Tyler moved to stand beside Jana.

The man pulled his drooping pants back up over his stomach. "Just because you're anxious to get between the sheets, ain't no need to go off." His gaze cut to Jana. "Can't say I blame you though. After you leave I plan to have a little fun myself. Some women you can tell by lookin' at them that they're gonna give you a good time."

A sound like a growl came from Tyler. The grin slid from the manager's beefy face. He took one, then another cautious step backwards, as if fearing any sudden move would make Tyler come over the counter.

Tyler snatched up the suitcase. "Let's get out of here."

Olivia took Jana's arm and led her back to Tyler's truck. "Is there someone you want us to call?"

Jana looked away. "No. No one."

Olivia squeezed Jana's trembling hand in reassurance. "There is now."

Jana came to an abrupt halt. "What?"

"You have us." Steering Jana to the truck, Olivia opened the back door and ushered her inside. She quickly went to Tyler. "Janet needs a place to stay. Can she come home with us for a few days."

Tyler had known it was coming. "You know nothing about the woman."

"She'll be homeless if we don't help," Olivia reasoned.

"I'll get her another hotel room."

"I think she needs someone who cares just as much as she needs a place to stay."

Tyler stared at his tender-hearted sister. Olivia should have had a dozen kids to love and spoil instead of just Griffin. She had played the mother to her dolls from the time she could walk. Her nurturing instinct was strong. She'd just chosen the wrong man.

"I couldn't sleep at night if I turned my back on her," Olivia said softly.

Neither could he.

Tyler yanked the Stetson down on his head. He had been afraid of this, but he didn't voice his objections. Once Olivia got something into her head it was almost impossible to get out. "Just for the night."

Laughing, Olivia rushed to the truck and got inside. "Janet, you're going home with us."

Jana had already pegged Olivia as a do-gooder, the type of woman who picked up strays and tried to heal the wounds of those around her. Her brother was a different story. He'd immediately sized Jana up as someone he didn't want to know better. He was a good judge of character.

Her wary gaze followed Tyler as he put her luggage in the bed of the truck. "Does he know?"

"Of course." Olivia smiled brightly. "We live together. It's his house as well."

Fear of a lawsuit might have Olivia ensuring herself that Jana was all right, but it wouldn't extend to offering her a place to stay. There had been no mention of a husband nor was there a ring on her finger. She'd given no sign that she wanted anything from Jana except friendship. Jana couldn't remember a time that she was wanted simply for herself.

"You want me to come home with you?" Jana repeated, still disbelieving.

"Yes. It's about time the redecorated guest bedroom was used."

Jana's throat clogged. Relief swept through her. She didn't know what to say. Finally it came to her. "Thank you."

The Greek Revival–style home near Highland Park was beautiful and comfortably decorated. A skylight with intricate decorative plaster surround illuminated the entry. Olivia chatted gaily as she led Jana up the circular wrought-iron and marble staircase that extended upward two floors from the patterned wood flooring in the entry hall. "An elevator offers access to all three floors, but we seldom take it. Tyler thought of including it into the building plans so our parents won't have to take the stairs unless they want to when they visit."

On the second floor, she stopped and opened the last door on the east wing. "You should have everything you need."

Jana stepped cautiously inside and almost sighed with pleasure and relief. All the way there, she'd been afraid Olivia would change her mind.

The walls in the high-ceilinged room were buttery gold with deeply carved crown molding. A wood-burning fireplace with an oak mantel was directly across from the king-sized bed that was covered with a pale gold damask duvet with soft pastel undertones. On top of the bed were mounds of decorative pillows with lace accents and gold velvet stripes. Coordinating draperies arched and swayed over tall, narrow windows.

Crossing the polished hardwood floor, Olivia removed the decorative pillows and placed them on the striped velvet bench at the end of the bed, then turned the duvet back to reveal hand-embroidered ivory sheeting with golden embroidery. The last time Jana had been this close to such luxury was five months ago in Seattle, the last stop on her downward slide into hell.

"Janet, are you all right? I asked if you needed anything else."

Jana stared at Olivia and realized she had been talking to her. "I'm sorry. No."

Olivia plumped the already fluffy pillows. "Here I am babbling and you need to eat and rest. I'll bring up a pot of tea, but please don't wait to eat." Straightening, she crossed the room and opened a door. "Bathroom complete with toiletries and the most luxurious towels made."

Jana didn't know what to say, what was expected of her. No one had ever given without expecting something in return.

Olivia crossed back to Jana and pressed her hand against her arm. "Eat and I'll bring the tea."

Jana's gaze followed Olivia and saw Tyler standing in the doorway. Her hands tightened on the plastic bag of food. He unnerved her. It was as if he could see right through her and what he saw he didn't like. He had helped her, but no one had to tell her he did so because of his sister.

Crossing the room, he put her suitcase on the edge of the bed. "I know you don't want me here, but . . . thank you," Jana said.

"I'm sorry for your problems, but know this, I won't have my sister hurt or taken for a ride because she expects everyone to be as open and honest as she is. We both know that that isn't the case."

What was there for her to say? He was right.

"You're here for tonight only," Tyler continued, "and then you're gone. I'll help you get a place."

In spite of herself thinking of the insect-infested motel room she'd just left made her shudder. She couldn't prevent the shiver that raced over her body.

"Someplace you won't be propositioned to pay the rent even if you're willing."

Jana flushed. Again, what could she say? She had been desperate, but she was so used to doing what came so easy to her, what had gotten her what she wanted since she was fifteen until five months ago when everything started to unravel.

"Here you are." Entering the room, Olivia sat the porcelain tea service on a small table by the French doors. "I didn't know what type you preferred with your meals so I brought several."

Jana preferred champagne. She could almost feel Tyler's condemning gaze boring into her. "I'm sure it's fine."

"Well, good night." Olivia affectionately looped her arm through Tyler's. "If you're an early riser or get hungry during the night the kitchen is to the left of the stairs. Griffin can attest that Wanda keeps it well stocked."

"Is Griffin your husband?" Jana asked and watched a shadow cross Olivia's face, and Tyler's lips thin.

"My son, and the most important person in the world to me. Good night."

"Good night," Jana said.

Tyler looked over his shoulder just before closing the door after him. There was a promise in those riveting black eyes of his: *Mess with my family at your own risk.*

Jana wished she could call his bluff, but she'd read another man wrong and it had cost her dearly. Licking her lips, she sat in the Queen Anne chair in front of the table and opened the containers. Picking up a fork she practically shoved the chicken parmesan, salad, and bread sticks into her mouth.

She'd eaten in the most exclusive restaurants in the world, but no food had ever tasted better. Even the English tea was good. She didn't stop eating until only fragments were left. Wiping her hands on the linen napkin, she looked around for a phone. Seeing one on the nightstand she walked over, glad the dizziness was gone.

Her hand hovered over the phone for a long moment before she picked it up and dialed. As the phone rang for a third, then a fourth time she bit her lips. It was almost midnight here and close to ten in San Francisco. Her mother didn't go to bed early, but she might be out on a Saturday night.

"Hello."

Jana sank onto the bed in relief. "Mother, it's me."

"I thought it was Raymond. He's out again with that woman. I know he is."

"Mother, I need your help." Jana's hand clenched on the receiver. "Please. I was locked out of my motel room because I couldn't pay the rent."

"Jana, I taught you to handle men to get what you want."

Sex was always the answer with her mother. Once Jana had thought the same way. "Mother, if you could just send me enough money to come home—"

"No."

"Mother, I fainted tonight—"

"You weren't stupid enough to get pregnant, were you?"

"No, I hadn't eaten because I didn't have any money," Jana said, shame washing over her.

"That's nonsense," her mother scoffed. "Men fall all over themselves for you. I should know, I taught you."

Jana sighed. "Ever since I left Charleston last year, things haven't been going well for me. I told you Gray's grandmother turned everyone against me."

"It's your own fault for trying to win your ex-husband back. He couldn't stand the sight of you after what you did to him." Jana's mother tsked. "You shouldn't have gotten caught."

Jana dropped her forehead into the palm of her hand. "Mother, I need your help."

"Jana, you're thirty-two years old. You can take care of yourself. Raymond and I need to be alone to work out our little differences."

"I wouldn't have to live there. I cou—"

"I think he's back. I have to go."

"Mo—" she began, then heard the dial tone. Her mother had hung up on her. Jana swallowed repeatedly until the lump disappeared from her throat. Slowly she replaced the receiver, then picked it up again and quickly dialed.

The phone was answered on the second ring by a drowsy male voice. "Hello."

"Father, I need—"

"I told you not to call me ever again."

"I don't have a place to stay."

"Call one of your men." The phone crashed down.

Her hand clutching the phone, Jana felt tears prick her eyes. "I called my father and my mother. Why can't you forgive me and she love me?"

She hung up the phone and glanced around the room. She had a place to stay for the night, but what about tomorrow? There was nothing left to pawn. Except for a few pieces, her couture wardrobe and all of her jewelry was strewn from Seattle to Texas. Dallas had not been a random choice. She was here because her father was less than thirty miles away . . . with his new wife and stepdaughter.

Jana had seen them once in Richmond when she'd gone home three years ago after her scandalous divorce from Gray. She hadn't been welcomed. Her mother had been with husband number three in Milan and hadn't wanted to be bothered. Jana, true to form, had crashed a dinner party her father was having for his wife and had left with her stepmother's sister's husband. Jana had foolishly done it out of spite, but it had proven to be another bridge burned. Neither her father nor his wife would ever forgive her.

She hadn't thought she cared until she'd faced death only months ago and realized there would be no one to mourn her if she died.

Getting up from the bed, she went to the window and brushed the heavy damask drapery aside. She was in the heart of a big city, people surrounded her, yet she was alone as she'd always been. She hadn't realized how friendless she was until five months ago when she'd almost died in an electrical fire in a night club.

Peter Wilson, her lover at the time, had shoved her aside trying to save himself. She'd fallen and bumped her head. Dazed, she'd lain there as the posh night club filled with smoke and the frantic screams of people trying to flee the greedy flames. If a man hadn't rescued her and carried her to safety, she almost certainly would have died. As it was, she was kept overnight in the hospital for smoke inhalation.

When she was released the next morning she went back to the hotel to find that Peter and the crowd she'd been partying with for the past month had flown to New York. No one had called to check on her nor had Peter left a plane ticket. He had paid for the hotel room for the balance of the week. Two days.

Angry and irate, she'd called people who ran with them, expecting them to be incensed on her behalf. In each instance they were on Peter's side. They all believed his lie that she had gone off with another man at the club and that Peter thought she was safe. Her pattern of leaving one man for another as the whim struck was well known. As always, the story told by the person with the most money and influence was deemed to be the truth.

Peter's family was very wealthy. On the other hand, Jana's father had disowned her. In a matter of days she learned she had badly miscalculated her appeal. Peter's lies coupled with the threat of her ex-husband's grandmother made Jana persona non grata.

Slipping off her shoes, Jana lay on the bed and curled into a tight knot. How was she going to survive? She'd thought she was so smart. She'd tossed away her life with both hands and had no idea how to get it back.

Her gaze fell on a distinctive figure on the beside table. A Fabergé Egg, intricately crafted with 24-carat gold, Austrian crystals, and hand-enameled guilloche. Slowly she sat up. With unsteady hands she carefully lifted the top to reveal a removable silver swan swimming on an aquamarine lake with water lilies.

She'd seen enough of the pieces to have a good idea of their worth. This particular egg probably cost close to three thousand dollars. Even a tenth of that would give her some breathing room. The thought that formed in her head made her tremble. *Take the egg.*

She hesitated. She'd never stolen anything in her life. But she'd never been this desperate either.

With the money from the sale of the egg she could possibly catch a red-eye flight to San Francisco. Her mother would help her once she saw how badly Jana needed her. Her mother was just so worried about Raymond and her marriage that she couldn't think straight.

Getting up, Jana went to her suitcase and knelt down. Even as she unlocked the case and carefully wrapped the Fabergé Egg in a blouse, she felt her throat sting with tears of regret. Angrily she dashed the useless tears away and closed the case.

Olivia was stupid to let a stranger in her house. It was as much her fault as Jana's. Suddenly Jana recalled the promise of retribution in Tyler's eyes if she played Olivia. He'd show no mercy.

Jana got to her feet. She just had to make sure he never found out. After all, she was very good at games.

4

Tyler awoke early as usual. Almost instantly he recalled the woman sleeping a few doors down, which wasn't odd since he had spent a restless night thinking of her. She was oddly familiar, but he couldn't place her. He would. He never forgot a face, and hers was beautiful.

With a snort of disgust, Tyler tossed back the covers and headed for the shower. Janet was hiding something. And he'd bet his portfolio that she hadn't given them her real name. Pointing that out to Olivia wouldn't have mattered. Her only concern would be that Janet needed help.

Turning the shower on full blast, Tyler stepped beneath the six pulsating jets, his thoughts still on Janet. Not for an instance had she let the food go once he'd given it to her. She'd been half starved, but she hadn't bartered her body for food or the rent. Her fear and shame had been obvious at the motel. He had wanted to ram his fist in the clerk's smirking face.

Shutting off the water, he dried himself, then shaved. Her come-on to him and Dr. Cortez had been smooth and practiced, which was at odds with the shame and embarrassment he'd glimpsed in her eyes when they'd rebuffed her. He didn't like puzzles and Janet was certainly one.

Dressed and determined to put the woman out of his mind, he left his room for the kitchen and a cup of coffee. His time would be better spent working out the specifications for his next client.

Entering the gourmet kitchen with its barrel-vaulted ceiling, he came to an abrupt halt when he saw Janet, her back to him, standing in front of the large island. This morning she wore a straight, sleeveless sundress with faded pink flowers sprinkled over a dingy white background. The dress stopped several enticing inches above her knees and fit better than the gown she had worn last night, but it too showed she was having a rough time of it.

Again, he wondered what had brought her to this low point. And who was the real woman? The vulnerable one he caught glimpses of or the hard, manipulative woman who seduced with practiced ease?

He took a step closer, then halted when he saw Janet put something in the open suitcase in front of her. He stiffened with anger. "You didn't listen, I see."

Janet slammed the suitcase shut and spun around. He easily saw the fear in her large brown eyes.

He didn't hit women, but he was too furious to tell her that. "It takes a pretty low person to steal from someone who kept them from sleeping on the streets."

"It's just a couple of apples."

He quickly closed the distance between them. "So you're a liar *and* a thief."

She swallowed, glancing around the kitchen as if searching for an escape route. "I'm not a thief."

"Then you won't mind if I see what's inside." He reached for the case, just as she started to drag it down. The struggle was over almost before it began. He easily overpowered her, taking the case.

"Give that back to me!" she shouted. "You have no right."

Tyler fended her off with his hand on her chest, careful not to touch her breasts, but it was becoming increasingly difficult with her trying to regain control of the case. "Stop it before you get hurt."

"Like you care."

She made the statement with such aching loneliness he almost felt sorry for her. "You don't make it easy to care."

Suddenly she stopped, crossed her arms and looked away. "Go ahead and look."

There it was again, the vulnerable woman. He placed the suitcase back on the island, but made no move to open it. Perhaps he should let it go. Whatever she'd taken from the house could be replaced. They were insured. He might steal too if he was faced with sleeping in the streets.

"What are you waiting for?"

He opened the case. On top was a nearly empty bottle of Joy, a neatly folded set of bath towels, toiletries from the guest bath, granola bars Olivia kept in the cookie jar for Griffin, two apples and an orange from the fruit bowl on the counter. He stared at her.

She flushed, then stalked over and reached for the items. Tyler brushed her hands aside and snapped the suitcase shut. "I've stayed in a few places where I wanted a towel that wasn't so rough it tore off a layer of skin or so stained I didn't want to use it." He placed the case of the floor and went to the refrigerator. "How about bacon and eggs for breakfast?"

Now it was she who stared at him.

His head tilted to one side. "Don't believe I can cook?"

"That you'd offer me breakfast," she answered frankly.

"Consider it my way of apologizing." He took out eggs, milk, butter and bacon. "Cups are in the cabinet above, if you want coffee. It's on an automatic timer." Pulling out a skillet, he placed the bacon inside. "You sleep all right?"

Jana eyed him a bit warily. She couldn't understand why he was being so cordial this morning. "No."

With his back to her, he began cracking eggs in a bowl. "You'll get there. Juice and yogurt in the fridge if you want something before I finish."

"I already had a yogurt." She couldn't very well carry that in her case, she thought as she poured coffee into a pretty rose-patterned cup. Passing up a meal would be stupid.

"Good, then have a seat."

Jana sat at the round oak table for six and and watched him cook on the six-burner cook top while she sipped her coffee. She'd thought she had him figured out. She'd been sure he'd get angry about her stealing the towels and the toilet articles. Instead he was cooking her breakfast. It would have been a different story if she'd taken the Fabergé Egg. But somehow she couldn't. She would have sworn she didn't have a conscience. Perhaps there was hope for her yet.

"Where are you from?"

Her hand jerked on the handle of the cup. "No place in particular."

He stopped tending the bacon and looked at her. "Everybody starts out someplace."

But few had probably started as high as she had and fallen so low. "Richmond."

"Do you still have family there?"

"I have no one," she said, trying to be blasé about her announcement, but from the slight catch in her voice she knew she hadn't been able to quite pull it off.

"By their choice or yours?"

Her head came up. No wonder she was uneasy around Tyler. He was too perceptive. "It doesn't matter. Is the food ready?"

"Almost." He turned back to the skillet and lifted out the meat, then grabbed another skillet and forked in butter. "Scrambled all right?"

"However I can get them," she answered, then tensed. She hadn't intended for her answer to be so revealing.

"Can you handle the toast?"

Her eyes widened. "You want me to make toast?"

He turned. "It won't make itself."

"All I did was ask," she said, getting to her feet. He could irritate her faster than anyone she could remember. "Where's the bread?"

Tyler went back to his eggs. "In the bread box."

Jana felt foolish. Of course it was in the bread box, but she'd never bothered with cooking. She'd taken pride in always having someone to do the most menial tasks for her. And look where that had gotten her.

"You all right?" He was frowning at her.

"Of course." She quickly popped bread in the four-slice toaster, then seeing that the eggs were almost ready, reached into the cabinets and got two plates.

"Thanks." Tyler finished dividing the eggs just as the toast popped up. "I'll take care of this. You have a seat."

Jana looked at Tyler busily buttering the toast and realized he must have thought she was getting dizzy again. Every time she thought she had him pegged, he'd change. "I feel fine." She put their plates on the table and sat down.

Just as Tyler joined Jana at the table Olivia and a young boy entered the kitchen. Olivia had her arm around the boy's shoulder and she was smiling down at him. He grinned up at her. The love between them was glaringly obvious. Jana couldn't remember a time either of her parents had put an arm around her.

"Good morning," Olivia said. "Janet, this handsome young man is my son, Griffin. Griffin, this is Janet Street."

The young man, clad in dress pants and a blue oxford shirt, stuck out his hand. "Pleased to meet you, Ms. Street."

Jana hadn't had much dealing with children so she followed Griffin's lead. "Pleased to meet you, Griffin."

Olivia brushed her hand affectionately across Griffin's neatly cut hair. "Come on, help me make French toast. You two want any?"

"None for me," Tyler said. "Janet?"

She did, but didn't have the courage to say so. "This is fine."

"My mama makes the best French toast in the whole wide world. She lets me put strawberries and whipped cream on top," Griffin said enthusiastically to Jana.

Olivia laughed. "We both love breakfast so I let us indulge every now and then. You might as well join us, Janet, so I won't feel like a glutton by myself."

"I want two slices," Griffin piped up as he got the whipped cream and strawberries from the refrigerator.

"Janet?" Olivia paused with the bread in her hand.

Temptation won. "I'll have a slice if it's not too much trouble."

"We have a system, don't we, Griffin?"

"Yes, ma'am." Griffin removed the cutting board and whisk from the drawer.

"Go ahead and eat," Olivia said, opening the refrigerator.

Jana reached for her fork just as Tyler lowered his head and blessed their food. She snatched her hand away, not knowing if she was to say anything or not. Her family had never bothered with saying grace, but then they seldom ate together either. Her father was always at some meeting and her mother had her friends, her clubs and her men.

Lifting his head, Tyler picked up his fork. "Dig in."

Jana didn't need to be told twice. It might have been because she was hungry, but the food was delicious. By the time she'd finished, Griffin personally served her French toast liberally sprinkled with powdered sugar and topped with strawberries and whipped cream. "Thank you."

"My mom said you didn't feel well last night. Grandmother says food always make a person feel better," he offered.

Jana's hand tightened on the fork. She wondered what else Olivia had said. "Your grandmother was right."

Griffin went back to help his mother, but Jana's appetite was gone.

"Do you really think Olivia would have discussed what happened last night with a seven-year-old boy?" Tyler asked quietly.

She didn't know what to think. Everything about Olivia was foreign to Jana so she chose to say nothing. It shouldn't have mattered that a child knew she hadn't been able to pay the rent in a seedy motel and had fainted from hunger, yet somehow it did.

Olivia frowned on seeing Janet's untouched French toast. "If you aren't feeling well I could fix you a tray."

"If you're getting hot like Grandmother I know where she keeps her little fan," Griffin announced, then cut into his toast.

Tyler stifled a laugh as did Olivia. "Griffin, I don't think your grandmother would like for you to mention to others about her need for a fan."

He swallowed a mouthful of food before speaking. "All right, but I'm glad I don't get too hot. I'd miss all the fun in the pool and the games with my friends. We're going to Water World this afternoon."

Olivia smiled indulgently at her son. "Have SUV, will travel."

Jana realized two things at once: Olivia hadn't discussed her, and Griffin was a lucky boy to have her for his mother. What might her life have been like if her mother had taught her about love and compassion instead of deceit and sexual prowess.

"Janet, if you're finished eating, we can go."

Jana froze. Her head whipped around to find Tyler standing. She didn't want to leave. "I . . ." She swallowed and tried to think of a reason to prolong her stay.

"I won't leave you stranded," he told her. "I'll put you up in a reputable hotel suite where you can cook and I'll give you enough money to buy groceries for a couple of weeks. By that time you should have found a job."

Doing what? she almost asked. She had no skills . . . at least not any you'd admit to on a resume. Jana slowly rose from the table. For a little while she'd felt hope. Now there was nothing except a deep yearning in her gut. "Goodbye, Olivia. Thank you."

Olivia came to her feet as well. "Goodbye, Janet, and good luck."

Luck hadn't been on her side for some time now. She tried to smile, but her facial muscles felt stiff.

Tyler grabbed her suitcase and headed for the front door, his strides long and purposeful. He didn't look back. Another man who didn't want her around. She couldn't blame him. Jana had no choice but to follow. Olivia and Griffin trailed behind them.

Outside the sun was shining. There was a gentle breeze in the morning air, bringing with it the scent of roses in the well-tended beds on either side of the house. It was going to be a beautiful summer day. Jana stepped off the curved steps and started toward Tyler's truck parked on the circular driveway. He stood a bit impatiently with the passenger's door open.

"Mom, why is Ms. Street so sad?" Griffin asked.

"Because she's alone in the world," Olivia answered, her grip on her son just a little bit tighter as she said a prayer that he would always have family and friends who cared about him.

"No mother or uncle or grandparents or friends?"

"No one."

"I wouldn't like that."

She resisted the urge to kiss the top of his head. He was getting to that age where he didn't want public displays of affection. "Neither would I," she said, but she recalled a time when she had felt so very alone and isolated. She'd been a young bride and so much in love. Then her world had shattered into a thousand tiny pieces and she'd felt the same way. There'd been no one to turn to, no one to tell her shameful secret to.

She'd been so gullible, so stupid to have been duped by her ex-husband. Those had been the worst days of her life. She hadn't started to pull her life back together until she'd felt the first flutter of life in her stomach. The life growing inside her had pulled her out of her depression and self-pity and given her the courage to confide in Tyler the real degrading reason she had filed for divorce.

Instead of anger at her stupidity, he'd held her. Everyone needed someone sometimes. Yet Janet had said she had no one. From the dire circumstances of where she lived, she was right. No one should have to go through difficult times alone.

"Wait!" Olivia came off the porch and rushed to Janet.

The relief in Janet's face was obvious and made what Olivia had to say easier. Olivia wasn't a gambler, she'd tried once with disastrous consequences, but somehow she felt what she was about to do was right. "My regular sales person is quitting in a week. I was going to hire someone in any case because business at my linen boutique is growing. If you're interested in the job you can stay in the apartment over the garage for as long as you want. How about it?"

"It's already settled, Olivia. Get in, Janet."

"A woman can always change her mind," Olivia said, keeping her gaze fixed on Janet.

"If you don't want to live in a suite, I can take you to a hotel downtown and pay the rent in advance for a month," Tyler said.

Jana faced him. A month. It was a generous offer. Too generous. He wanted to make sure she left. She couldn't blame him for that. She didn't like herself very much either.

But if she took his offer what would happen to her when the month was up? Men weren't lining up at her door as they once had. Her mother was right about one thing. No man wanted a woman no one else wanted. Besides, with the amount of time she'd spent in beds, she knew bedding at least. Her life wasn't working the way she had been living it. Perhaps it was time to change it.

But could she trust someone when she herself had never been able to be trusted? "You're not just saying that? You'd really give me a job?"

"I'm a woman of my word."

"Olivia. Think about what you're doing," Tyler said ominously.

Olivia's gaze flickered to her brother, then back to Janet. "I am. All I ask is that you be honest, dependable, and courteous."

Jana was none of those things. Never had been. Didn't know if she could be.

"You can start Tuesday."

"Why not tomorrow?" Jana heard herself ask. Everyone had to start sometime.

"You'll need that time to get the garage apartment in order," Olivia explained. "No one has lived there since the gardener retired two years ago."

Olivia was offering a place to stay and a job. More than that, she was offering Jana a chance to get her life together. Perhaps it *was* possible to start over. "My name isn't Janet Street."

Tyler rolled his eyes. "We already figured that out."

Jana looked from one to the other. She'd thought she was so smart. Another reality she had to face. They'd known she was lying, yet they had still opened their wallets and their home to care for her. Her so-called friends hadn't done the same. In fact, they'd rejoiced at her fall from grace.

Yet this step was frightening. But even more frightening was the prospect of where she'd end up if she didn't turn her life around. She was at rock bottom. If she wanted to climb out of the pit she'd dug for herself, she had to start fresh. "My name is Jana Franklin."

There was no flash of recognition in their eyes, no stepping back in distaste.

Olivia extended her hand. "Pleased to meet you, Jana. Now, we have to get to Sunday school. Unpack, relax and make yourself at home. There's a pool in back. We'll be back around six." Smiling, Olivia returned to where Griffin waited and they entered the house and closed the door.

Jana wasn't looking forward to facing Tyler. He didn't want her here. Why that should hurt her she didn't know. She turned in spite of her trepidation. "I want this chance."

Tyler picked up her hand, held it despite her attempt to pull it back. He studied her palm. "Soft, not a callous anywhere despite the chipped nails." His dark eyes captured hers. "What's your story, Jana? You probably never worked a day in your life. That gown didn't go with your coloring, but the shoes fit and the few clothes in your suitcase have designer labels. What happened to you, and will it harm Olivia?"

She opened her mouth to lie, but moistened her lips instead as she gave herself time to think. If she wanted to change it had to be complete. "I don't know. I only know that this may be my last chance and I have to take it." She pulled her hand free and for a moment felt a wave of loneliness.

Once she had prided herself on not needing anyone because they always let her down. That was one lesson she wasn't going to forget. At best this was temporary. Taking the suitcase from Tyler, she reentered the house.

Eyes narrowed, Tyler watched her. There was buoyancy in her steps that generated a sway of her hips. It hadn't been there last night.

She was a strikingly beautiful woman with an innate sensuality that was almost palpable. She was trouble. He'd known that from the first moment he'd seen her. He'd been able to remain unmoved by her attempt at seduction because he'd known she was using it to distract him. If it had been real, he wasn't sure how he would have responded. He'd just have to watch himself.

Jana woke from her nap to hear someone knocking on her door. For a frightening moment she was afraid she was still in the motel and had only dreamed she had a job and a place to stay. She sprang upright in bed, then relaxed when she saw the tastefully decorated bedroom. Relief swept through her. Standing, she crossed to the door. Olivia stood there, her brow puckered in a frown.

Fear leaped into Jana's heart again. "You've changed your mind."

"No," Olivia quickly assured her. "I should have guessed you might be sleeping when you didn't answer the door. I'm sorry."

Jana tunneled a shaky hand through her hair. "It's all right."

Olivia's smile returned. "I just wanted to show you the apartment over the garage. Griffin is going to Water World with a friend and I'm joining them later. I thought we'd take a look together and see what's needed to make it habitable. I hope it's not in too bad a shape. Keats was a character."

"It's better than where I was sleeping."

Olivia scrunched up her face. "You haven't seen it yet."

"You didn't see my room," Jana returned and barely kept from shuddering.

"You have a point." Olivia held up an elongated key on a brass key ring. "You might want to change into something that you don't mind getting dirty."

"There isn't much else," Jana confessed, swiping her hand self-consciously over the Prada sundress she'd picked up on Rodeo Drive while on a shopping spree with one of the many men in her life. He was rich enough not to miss the several thousand dollars she'd spent that day. All the while, she'd kept telling herself she didn't care that her father was getting married that day and she hadn't been invited. That night, when her father was honeymooning in Hawaii with his new bride, she'd made sure her generous benefactor had gotten his money's worth.

Thinking how stupidly she'd behaved, Jana briefly shut her eyes.

Olivia mistook the reaction as embarrassment. "Don't worry. I have an idea." Taking Jana's arm, she headed down the wide hallway. "I should have thought of it right away. We're pretty casual at the shop." She glanced at the Manolos on Jana's feet. "We stand on our feet a lot."

"I can stay in these shoes for hours." In fact, she had last winter in Rome while shopping at the Spanish Steps. She'd frittered away her life in pursuit of pleasure and ended up with misery and despair.

Halfway down the hall Olivia stopped in front of a door and knocked. "You decent?"

Jana stiffened and stepped back, instinctively knowing this was Tyler's bedroom. "Why are we here?"

"To get you a shirt," Olivia said just as the door opened. "None of my clothes would fit."

Tyler filled the doorway. His white shirt was open, revealing rock-hard muscles and a flat stomach. "Yes?"

"Do you have a shirt Jana can put over her clothes while we get the apartment in order?"

His gaze tracked from Jana's face to her feet. She barely kept from squirming. "Sure." Turning, he went to the chest of drawers in the large room and came back with a folded light blue cotton shirt and handed it to Jana.

"Thank you."

He nodded. "Thought you were going to Water World?" he asked Olivia.

"I'm meeting them there, but I wanted to help Jana get settled," she said, taking the other woman's arm.

"Couldn't Wanda tackle the apartment?" he asked.

"Her arthritis has been bothering her lately. I hate to ask her to take on extra duty," Olivia explained. "I'd hire someone to help her if it wouldn't hurt her feelings."

He tapped his sister's pert nose. "You softie."

"She said you told her not to bother with your room," his sister told him, a smile on her lips.

He shifted uncomfortably. "Well."

Laughing, Olivia pulled Jana down the hall. "See you later."

Jana risked a peek over her shoulder. Tyler had walked into the hall, his hand propped on the door. Damn he had a body on him, hard with muscles that made a woman yearn. With all that intensity she bet he could drive a woman wild in bed. She tripped over her feet and flushed in embarrassment.

"You all right?" Olivia asked.

A man was the last thing she needed to be thinking about. "Better than I've been in months."

"Good, then let's go see your new home."

The Jana Franklin of three months ago, even three weeks ago, might have turned her nose up at the two-room apartment. The Jana Franklin who'd suffered degradation, humiliation, hunger, and eviction the night before stared at the room with hope shining in her eyes.

"The walls need a fresh coat of paint. The green tweed sofa has to go and so does the matching side chair," Olivia said. "Mother is a pack rat so you can look through the things in the attic for whatever pieces you need. We might even be able to find a replacement for the sofa and chair."

"Perhaps I'll just keep a dust cloth over it," Jana said, heartened that she could joke.

Olivia laughed. "Let's see about the bedroom. At least we know you'll have sheets."

The bedroom was considerably better, with a wide window and a full-sized sturdy oak bed, dresser, and nightstand. The bedspread was a nondescript plaid. The lamp was Tiffany. The area rug was Oriental.

"This has possibilities. There's linen in the house." Olivia put her hands on her hips. "You want to start in the kitchen?"

"You have to meet Griffin," Jana reminded Olivia.

Olivia glanced at her watch. "I have an hour to give you. Let's get the cleaning supplies out of the closet."

Jana touched Olivia's arm as they passed though the large, open area that served at the living area and connected to the kitchen. "I have a confession to make."

She stopped with her hand on the knob of the broom closet. Jana breathed a little easier to see patience, not weariness. "Yes?"

"I've never cleaned a room in my life."

"Well." Olivia opened the door and pulled a broom, bucket and a mop and set them aside to reach for a package of sponges from beneath the sink. "That's going to change as of today. You game?"

Jana didn't hesitate to reach for the broom. All she had to do was remember the seedy motel room. "I can learn."

"I know you can." Olivia put the pail under the faucet and turned on the water. The cell phone clipped to her pants rang. Shutting off the water, Olivia pulled the phone from her pocket, saw the number and smiled.

"They're probably calling to tell me to hurry. Hello." The smile slid from her face. "You're sure he's all right?" She plopped down in a chair at the kitchen table only to quickly stand again. "Griffin, yes, baby, I'm on my way."

"Is he all right?" Jana asked, unsure why her heart rate had sped up.

"Yes. Thank God. But he sounded so frightened." Olivia swallowed hard, bit her lip, then started for the door. "He was horseplaying with his friends in the water and went under. It scared him enough that he wants me to come."

"Then you should go."

"I'll help you when I get back." Olivia raced out the door, and hurried down the stairs.

"Maybe you should get Tyler so he can drive," Jana called from the top of the stairs.

"I'm fine." Jumping into the SUV, Olivia backed out and took off.

Jana debated only for a moment before she raced down the stairs and into the house. She started up the stairs without slowing her pace.

"What's the rush?"

She whirled. Tyler was lounging against the door, his arms folded. Her stomach got that crazy feeling again. "It's Griffin."

Unfolding his arms, he quickly crossed to her. "What is it?"

"He's fine," she quickly told him. "He went under while horseplaying in the water. He wanted his mother and Olivia took off. She said she was fine, but she was shaky. I'm worried about her."

He whipped out his cell phone on the way to the front door and punched in a number. "Where are you?" he asked as he went down the steps toward his truck. "Pull over and I'll be there in five. I can make better time and I won't have to worry about you and Griffin."

Jana chewed on her lower lip and followed on his heels.

"All right, then we'll play it the hard way." He hung up the phone and jumped in the truck.

"She's not going to wait?" she asked, already knowing the answer. Olivia wanted to get to her son as soon as possible.

"You got it." Starting the motor, he backed up and took off.

Jana watched the truck disappear, then went back to the apartment. Griffin was lucky to have a mother like Olivia and an uncle who loved him just as much. Jana had a few relatives, but she'd never been close to any of them.

Jana went back to the apartment to lock the door. She couldn't possibly do this by herself. She'd just wait for Olivia. Yet even as the thought came, she was crossing the room to get the cleaning supplies. This was hers, at least for the time being. It wouldn't hurt to clean up the place just a little.

Late Sunday night Tyler pulled into the four-car garage beside Olivia's SUV. Luckily, he'd overtaken her when she'd stopped for a red light just before Stemmons Freeway. He'd gotten out of his car and walked over to hers. Her hands had been clenched around the steering wheel.

She'd kept brushing the heel of her hand against her eyes. All he'd said was Griffin needed his mother as much as she needed him and then he'd asked her to pull into the service station across the street. Fortunately she hadn't argued. He understood her terror. Hearing that Griffin was all right and actually seeing for herself was a world of difference.

She didn't breathe easier until she saw Griffin. They raced to meet each other. Griffin had tried to be brave in front of his friends, but hadn't been quite able to make it when his mother had pulled him tightly into her arms, chastising him and telling him how much she loved him, then banning him from the water park for life if he pulled anything like it again.

It had been difficult for her to let him go back into the plunging pool of water, but she'd done it. She didn't want to baby him. Trying to balance between not being too strict and being too lenient was difficult for any parent, but especially for a single parent who had gone through as much as Olivia had.

"I'm hungry, Mother."

Olivia brushed her hand across Griffin's head. "You ate less than an hour ago."

"Feels like it was days," Griffin said as he got out of the car. "I bet Uncle Tyler is hungry too."

He wasn't, but he thought of Jana. He had thought of her a great deal since she'd come to him out of concern for Olivia. He'd gotten the impression that she was all about self. "Can't help you out this time."

Griffin's shoulders slumped. "How do you expect me to go to sleep hungry?"

Olivia smiled down at him. "You can have a glass of milk and a graham cracker, but that's all."

He looked up at her and grinned. "I was thinking more of cookies and ice cream."

"Nice try." She wiggled her finger on his chest. "Let's go inside and get you into bed."

Tyler went inside with them, then headed for the stairs. He told himself he just wanted to thank Jana and let her know Griffin was all right, but he couldn't deny that something about her puzzled him as much as it drew him. He hadn't missed the calculating way she had tried to come onto him last night, but she'd been genuinely worried about Olivia. It was almost as if she were two people. Shaking his head, he knocked on the door, then knocked again.

He glanced at his watch. 8:39. He frowned, turning away to check the family room downstairs as a thought struck. Wheeling around he reached for the doorknob. He started to open it, then lifted his hand. He'd been wrong about her once.

"Is Jana all right?"

Tyler turned to see his sister, her hand on Griffin's shoulder. "She didn't answer."

A frown flitted across her brow. "Perhaps she's still working in the apartment."

Tyler recalled the soft hands and broken nails. "I doubt it."

"She's not downstairs. Where else could she be?"

"Good question," Tyler said. The thought that leaped into his head of her with another man wasn't comforting.

"Would you please go check the apartment? I didn't notice a light when we came in."

Neither had he. From now on he was going to keep tabs on their houseguest until he had her completely checked out.

"I could go with you," Griffin offered hopefully.

"Your uncle can handle things. You're going to bed." Olivia turned him firmly toward the opposite wing.

5

Tyler started back down the stairs. He'd check the apartment, but he didn't think Jana would be there. She'd fallen too easily into trying to tempt first him, then Dr. Cortez. More likely she had changed her mind and decided to strike out on her own. That thought bothered him more than he wanted to admit.

He went up the stairs to the garage apartment and knocked. "Jana." He didn't expect an answer and he didn't get one. This time he didn't hesitate to open the door. The scent of pine-scented cleaning solution greeted him. He flicked on the light.

The room was immaculate. There were even rose cuttings in a water glass on the kitchen table. Closing the door, he moved further into the open room, then into the adjoining bedroom and clicked on the light . . . and forgot to breathe.

Wearing only his shirt Jana was stretched out on her stomach, asleep. The tail had worked itself up her long legs to just below her hips. Legs he could easily imagine locked around his waist. He drew in a shuddering breath.

"Jana." His voice was husky, rough.

She smiled, snuggling deeper into the bed. Walking over he gently shook her shoulder. His hand wanted to linger on the soft skin, to explore. Resolutely he kept his gaze on her face. She had to get some clothes on before he lost it. "Jana, wake up."

Sooty lashes lifted, her eyes beckoned, her lips smiled a siren's smile. Her body arched sensuously as she reached up and curved her hand around his neck and brought his head down. Seconds before their lips met and he gave into temptation, he jerked his head back. "Jana!"

She blinked. Her eyes widened. She shrank back in the bed.

No one had to tell him that she'd done this countless times. He pushed the anger and the image away. "Olivia was worried about you."

"I . . . I'm sorry."

He didn't know if her apology made him feel better or worse. "I'll wait in the other room while you dress."

Jana watched Tyler leave the room and closed her eyes. The image of his shocked face remained. She'd been so tired after cleaning the apartment she'd lain down and promptly fallen asleep. Tyler had awakened her from a dream, a dream in which they were lovers. Her response had been automatic and calculated to keep him enraptured of her. What she'd done was show him again how easily she could use her body.

Sliding her legs off the bed, she took off his shirt and draped it on the footboard. She slipped her dress back on, then stepped into her heels. She glanced into the mirror over the dresser and tried to bring some order to her hair, but gave up when finger-combing only made it worse. She laughed, then pressed both hands over her mouth, afraid the laughter would turn into tears. She looked a mess. She'd probably repulsed Tyler more than anything.

"Jana?" he called from the other room.

Impatience was in each syllable. She couldn't blame him. Well, she wasn't going to hide. Head high, she left the bedroom.

Tyler stood with the apartment door open. She continued toward him without a word. So he couldn't stand to be in the same room with her. It wasn't the first time a man had thought that. Her heel caught on something and she stumbled.

Tyler reached out to steady her, then just as quickly let her go as if he couldn't stand to touch her. That wasn't a first either.

Jana bit her lip and closed the door behind them. Tyler started down the stairs, leaving her to follow. She did, slowly, her thoughts on her ex-husband, Gray Livingston.

Gray was handsome, charming, and wealthy. She'd consciously sought him out because her father admired him. By marrying Gray, she had hoped to gain her father's love. It hadn't happened.

Her father had claimed he was ill on the day of her wedding. A family friend had walked her down the aisle and given her away. Gray had done everything in his power to make up for the hurt that day and every day of their short marriage.

Angry at her father's abandonment, and that she couldn't get back at him, she had made Gray her target. She'd taken a lover barely three months after they were married. She'd even planned to get caught. What was the purpose of cheating if it didn't get back to her father, hurt him as he had hurt and humiliated her?

She'd been so sure she could manipulate Gray just as she'd done every other man, but his love and devotion had turned into hatred. She hadn't been able to accept that he had moved on, that she couldn't get him back. Her return to Charleston a year ago to show him he still loved her had started her on her downward spiral. Her ex was the first man beside her father that she couldn't control. She had a feeling the third one was walking in front of her.

Tyler opened the front door to the house and stepped aside. He was far enough away so they wouldn't touch. "Come into my office."

Jana didn't even think of disobeying him. She stopped just inside the office door he'd left open. There were three computers on a long table, a massive desk with two phones and a fax machine, a stone fireplace with a picture of Tyler, Olivia and what must have been their parents, and Griffin as an infant over the mantel, a dark brown leather sofa, side chairs, and wall-to-wall bookshelves reaching to the high ceiling.

"Close the door," he ordered from behind his desk.

She tried to think of something, anything to explain her behavior and take that look of disgust from his face, but nothing came to mind. She closed the door and faced him, her hands clenched.

"Olivia is a respected businesswoman. She's worked hard to establish that reputation and make a success of Midnight Dreams. You try to crawl into the pants of every man that enters the store and her business will suffer," he said bluntly.

Jana flinched despite having a good idea of why he'd asked her into his office. "I must have been dreaming."

"Were you dreaming last night when we were outside the store or when you first met Dr. Cortez?" he asked, his voice tight with anger.

She thought briefly of trying to explain, then realized if she did she'd be out the door even faster. Tyler indulged Olivia, but if he knew about Jana's past she'd be out of the house in a heartbeat. "I was just flirting. It won't happen again."

If anything, his expression hardened. "It if does, you're history. No second chance, no financial help."

She nodded and turned to leave.

"Don't underestimate me, Jana," he warned.

Opening the door, she left. He had given her fair warning. She believed him.

Why should she care what Tyler thought of her? She had a job and a clean place to stay. The opinion of a man shouldn't matter. She paused on the bottom of the stairs and looked at the closed door of his study and realized that it did.

Another first.

Jana didn't have much of a choice of what to wear so by seven-thirty she was dressed in a black boat-neck top and a slim black skirt. She hadn't slept well lately so it had been easy to get up. Since the apartment was clean there was no reason not to go to work. Besides, the quicker she started working, the sooner she'd feel as if she had some control over her life.

Stepping into her shoes, she glanced at herself in the full-length cheval mirror in the room in the main house and grimaced. It was plain tacky to wear the little black skirt without stockings. It couldn't be helped. Grabbing the small Fendi bag, she slipped the thin strap over her shoulder and headed downstairs.

She smelled the coffee at the bottom of the stairs. She paused briefly, then continued walking. It wasn't likely Tyler was up cooking breakfast again. Yesterday had probably been a fluke. His calloused hands indicated he was used to manual labor. His new truck told her nothing. In Texas every other vehicle on the road was a truck.

Entering the kitchen she saw Olivia in a pretty blue suit talking with a slender black woman who was at the stove. The older woman wore a white uniform and spotless white thick-soled shoes. Jana couldn't imagine her mother laughing with the cook, but then Jana couldn't imagine her mother doing anything that didn't revolve around self-indulgence and men.

Like mother, like daughter.

Olivia reached for her cup on the counter and saw her standing there. "Jana, good morning."

"Good morning," Jana said, watching Olivia closely in an attempt to gauge her reaction to the way she was dressed.

Picking up the delicate cup, Olivia wore a welcoming smile on her face. "Jana Franklin, please meet Wanda Simmons, friend, cook, and housekeeper. She takes care of us. We couldn't get along without her."

Wanda beamed. "It's not hard doing for people you care about." She nodded in Jana's direction. "Nice meeting you, Miss Franklin."

"Pleased to meet you." Unsure what to do next, Jana stayed where she was.

Olivia solved the problem. "Please have a seat and I'll get you a cup of coffee. Breakfast will be ready in a minute." Opening the cabinet, she removed a cup and saucer that matched hers. "You must be tired after cleaning the apartment by yourself."

Wanda turned to look at Jana again. She barely resisted squirming. "You cleaned that place all by yourself?"

"Once I got started I didn't see any reason to stop," Jana said, which was the truth as far as it went. She hadn't expected to feel pride and satisfaction with each task she'd completed. Deep down she'd been afraid of not being able to take care of herself.

"Know what you mean." Wanda placed the eggs she'd been scrambling in a chafing dish, then brought the dish to the table. "Sit down, Olivia, and keep your friend company."

Jana was so startled by the cook's announcement, she simply blinked. She couldn't recall anyone she knew actually being a friend.

Olivia sat with a smile. "Wanda bosses all of us."

Wanda placed a large platter of bacon, link sausage, and hash browns on the table. "Got grits if you want them."

"No, thanks," Olivia said, spreading her napkin on her lap.

"More for me," Tyler said, entering the kitchen.

"Me too," Griffin said from beside him.

Jana froze in reaching for her cup. If she hadn't been so hungry she might have gotten up and left.

Greetings were exchanged. Griffin took a seat next to his mother, leaving the seat beside Jana for Tyler. She could have sworn he hesitated.

"Here you are." The cereal bowl Wanda sat in front of Griffin was lightly sprinkled with brown sugar. Tyler's was brimming with butter and a liberal coating of brown sugar.

"You do know how to tempt a man."

Jana tensed. Then Wanda giggled like a schoolgirl and swatted Tyler on the shoulder with the ease of a long and dear friend and Jana knew that he hadn't just taken a swipe at her.

"You want something else, Miss Franklin?"

Jana quickly shook her head. She didn't want to draw Tyler's attention. "No."

"I'll say the blessing." Olivia bowed her head to do so. Afterwards she picked up the serving dish to serve Griffin, then handed the dish to Jana. "You sure you want to come in today?"

"Yes." She made herself take a smaller portion than she wanted. She passed the dish without looking at Tyler. She did the same thing the next time Olivia handed her the platter of food. "I feel fine."

"You must have slept well. You look better this morning, doesn't she, Tyler?" Olivia asked.

Jana couldn't help it. Her head lifted. He was staring at her, his black eyes narrowed, his mouth tight. "Maybe it was her dreams."

Jana flushed and concentrated on finishing her breakfast. Tyler had her number all right. Smart man.

After dropping Griffin off at a day camp, Olivia parked at the end of the short block where Midnight Dreams was located. It was a quarter past eight and only a few cars were in the shopping center.

Grabbing a large insulated bag from the back, Olivia started toward the store at a brisk pace. "I like to get a jump on the day so I usually start out early. If you want to come in later once you've been here a while, you can."

"This is fine," Jana said, lengthening her strides to keep up with Olivia. She didn't mind. She was anxious to get the day started as well.

Opening the front door, Olivia headed toward the back of the store. "I'll put our lunch in the refrigerator and be right back."

"Thank you again."

"Think nothing of it," Olivia reassured her. "I've always eaten lunch at the store. When I first started out five years ago it was to save money and because I didn't have any help."

"But that's changed now, hasn't it?" Jana asked, stopping at the entrance to the back when Olivia went into a room across from the restroom. If Olivia was cutting off the alarm Jana didn't want to see it. She didn't want to give Tyler any ammunition to throw her out.

"Business is fantastic. Now I don't have the time or the inclination," came the laughing answer. A few moments later Olivia appeared with the insulated container still in her hand. "Come on, I'll show you the lounge. It's rather small, but it is well equipped."

Olivia was right, the area was tiny, but the thriving greenery and window curtained with white sheers over a white porcelain sink made the room welcoming. On the dot of counter space next to the sink were an automatic coffee maker and a smoothie machine. Beside it were a refrigerator, a cart with a microwave, and a toaster oven.

Opening the refrigerator, Olivia wedged the bag between a jar of pickles and mayonnaise. To Jana it was a miracle, because it was stocked so well. All that food had been so close and she hadn't known.

"I know it's overkill, but I like to be prepared when Griffin or Tyler drop by or I'm running late and leave the house without bringing anything. Then too, since I like to handwrite receipts and it takes longer, I like to offer clients refreshments." She closed the door. "Now, let me show you around."

"Does Tyler drop by often?" Jana asked, trying to keep the anxiety out of her voice.

"Unfortunately, no." Olivia stopped in front of the cherry writing desk on the sales floor. "He's busy with his own company."

Jana felt instant relief. She didn't have to worry about him popping up and checking on her.

"I guess I'll start from the beginning." For the first time Olivia paused, and the perpetual happiness disappeared from her eyes. "You've been considerate enough not to ask, but I'm divorced."

"I was too busy trying to figure out why you wanted to help me," Jana answered truthfully.

"Because you needed help."

"Tyler doesn't think so," Jana blurted.

"Tyler is very protective of me. He'll do anything to keep me from being hurt again," Olivia said with unexpected bluntness of her own.

Jana now knew the reason for the brief flashes of hurt and pain in Olivia's face when she asked the other night if Griffin was her husband . . . a man. Jana envied her because she'd gotten her life back on track. Jana wanted to do the same. "You survived."

"Yes, because of Griffin. Because of my family."

Jana had nothing and no one. As if realizing that, Olivia briefly pressed her hand to Jana's shoulder. "You have us now."

Not Tyler, Jana thought, but left the words unsaid. "So how did you get started?"

The smile returned to Olivia's face. "When Griffin was six months old I was flipping through a magazine when he was down for a nap and saw an article on a boutique in Manhattan that sold Porthault linen. It was the only outlet in the United States for the French manufacturer and most of their clients were from Texas. A hand-embroidered custom set can cost as much as twenty thousand dollars."

Jana was familiar with the brand. "It's the bedding of choice for the royal Windsors."

"You know about linens?" Olivia asked, surprise and delight in her face and voice.

Jana didn't know whether to laugh or hang her head in shame. "A bit."

"I just knew this would work out! Come with me." Olivia went to a twelve-foot-high wall of shelving near the front of the spacious store. "These are Frette sheets, favored by Italy's royals and the Pope. The couple the other night purchased a set. We also carry Yves Delorome, another French manufacturer, and Pratesia sheets from Italy that are manufactured from the top two percent of the world's Egyptian cotton, which helps give them an extra long life span of fourteen to twenty years, and Rivolta, the bedding of choice for the Mansion on Turtle Creek, the only five-star hotel in Dallas."

Jana noted that the Pratesia king-sized set detailed with handmade lace went for five thousand dollars. "The sheets I slept on last night were identical to these."

"The sales rep let me have them for almost nothing when I told him they were going in my guest bedroom." She chuckled. "He was hoping he'd get another sale from whoever slept on them."

"He's out of luck."

"We won't tell him," Olivia said in a confidential tone. "For many people, fabulous linens are the splurge of choice, which is understandable since so much time is spent in bed, relaxing or sleeping."

Or other activities, Jana thought. "They're also another status symbol."

"Exactly—and self-indulgent." Olivia ran her hand across the luxurious sheet. "I love the feel of them against my skin, and admit to having a collection, but it wouldn't make sense to put them on Griffin's bed and Tyler would have a fit if he knew that Wanda and I sneak them onto his bed when he's out of town."

"Why does he mind?" Jana asked before she could stop herself.

"Wasteful, he said. He'd rather put the money to better use. Tyler can be very practical."

"I hadn't noticed." Jana's tone was droll.

Olivia's mouth twitched. "Let me show you the rest of the store. I've recently added bathroom accessories, candles, and soaps. Bliss is one of my favorite manufacturers of bath and body products and a favorite among customers." Olivia picked up a red and black box and held it out to Jana. "This is one of their candles in pear-vanilla. It's so soft and wonderful. I have one in my bedroom as well as the bath."

Jana tensed at the mention of Bliss. It was the firm Gray's wife had started with two of her friends. Not only had she taken Gray from her, she was also successful in her own right and had the support of his family, especially his grandmother, Corrine Livingston. From the first time they'd met, Corrine had barely tolerated Jana. It was Corrine's threat of retribution that had started Jana's life on a downward spiral while Gray's new wife had a charmed life. She had the man, the prestige, the wealth, the love and respect while Jana had nothing.

"Jana, what's the matter?"

She couldn't answer. Too many conflicting emotions, none of them good, raced through her.

Putting the candle back on the shelf, Olivia took Jana by the arm and helped her to a seat in front of the desk. "Maybe you should go home and rest."

Rest wouldn't help. She didn't have a home. Her life was a shambles while Gray and his new wife were happy with a baby on the way.

"I'll get my keys."

"Wait." Jana grabbed Olivia's arm. "Give me a moment."

Olivia hunkered down beside her, for once as unmoving as her brother, but Jana saw the concern. Would Olivia feel the same way if she knew about her past?

"Let me get you some water."

Jana released Olivia's hand because she sensed the other woman felt the need to do something to help. She took the bottled water because Olivia needed Jana to. The water was trickling down her throat when another realization struck. She'd been thinking about Olivia, not herself, when she'd accepted the water. A small insignificant act to some, but to Jana it was a milestone. If it was possible to do one unselfish act, she could do another and another.

She realized something else. Her own huge ego and disdain of the woman

Gray was seeing had set her on a path of self-destruction. She'd let her own vanity overrule common sense. During the last five months her ego had been trampled underfoot, the anger toward Gray's wife and his grandmother hadn't. She still thought of them and they probably never gave her a thought. It was time to put the past behind her once and for all.

She came to her feet. "I'll put this back in the refrigerator and then you can show me the rest of the store."

"You're sure you're up to it?"

"Positive." Jana turned, her hand clamped around the bottle. She was taking her life back no matter how difficult.

A few minutes before the store was to open Olivia's sales associate came rushing through the door. The leggy young woman was dressed in black and white pinstripe pants and a white blouse with short sleeves. Several silver bracelets jingled on her left wrist.

"Sorry I'm late, Olivia. The car was running on fumes. I had to stop and get gas." She swept strands of thick curly blond hair behind her ear. Large hoop earrings dangled from her lobes.

"That's all right, Stella. It gave me time to show the new sales associate around. Jana Franklin, meet Stella Banks."

The two women shook hands. "You're going to love working here. Olivia is the best boss I've ever had and I'm not just saying that since I'm late."

"I've already found that out," Jana said.

"Now, I won't feel bad about leaving so abruptly, but this is a once-in-a-lifetime opportunity to go backpacking through Europe with friends." Stella almost danced with glee. "I can't believe in less than two weeks I'll be in Paris."

"Paris is beautiful this time of year," Jana said.

"Olivia told me. She's been there on buying trips." Stella sighed and hugged her large bag to her chest. "I'll go put my things up or I'll never stop talking about my trip."

"Have you traveled extensively?" Olivia asked Jana when Stella disappeared into the back.

"Yes," Jana answered, hoping she didn't ask for any more information.

"One day I hope to do more, when Griffin can go with me." Olivia went to the door. "It's ten. I better turn the closed sign over."

Jana breathed a sigh of relief. Honesty was draining. It was so much easier to lie, but Olivia deserved the truth . . . up to a point.

Jana sold exactly one item her first day at work and that was because it was to a repeat customer who knew exactly what she wanted. Fearing someone she knew might come into the store, she'd been tense all day, tending to hang in the background. Thankfully, no one had recognized her.

"You survived your first day," Olivia teased as they took the curved stone walkway from the garage to the house. Griffin raced ahead of them.

"Thanks to you and Stella for being so patient with me," Jana told her.

"We all have to learn." Olivia opened the back door to the kitchen for Jana, then followed. "Griffin, come out of that refrigerator. I'll have dinner on the table in just a minute."

He closed the refrigerator. "But I'm hungry now."

"When aren't you hungry?" Olivia handed him her attaché. "Please put this in my room, wash your hands and come back down to help set the table. Wanda mentioned she was cooking lasagna."

He raced over to get the case, then ran out of the room.

Olivia laughed, washed her hands, then put on oven mitts. "He loves any kind of pasta."

"Can I help?" Jana asked, feeling awkward. In this new role, she didn't know what was expected of her.

"Please get the salad out of the refrigerator." Olivia slid the lasagna out of the oven, then set it on a metal trivet on the table. "Wanda and I coordinate time so dinner will be ready when I get home. Tyler becomes so wrapped up with his work that he wouldn't remember to check on the food even with a timer. Believe me, we've tried. It's not unusual for him to forget to eat at times."

Jana removed the tossed salad in a clear bowl. She didn't want to talk about Tyler. "Wanda is a great cook."

"She sure is," Olivia answered just as the doorbell rang. "Please get that. It's probably the painter for the apartment."

Jana spun around. "I can't afford a painter."

Olivia paused with a pewter basket filled with breadsticks. "It's my responsibility as the landlord to ensure that the apartment is in good shape."

"No. You've done too much already."

"You need a nice place," Olivia said as she placed the bread on the table.

Griffin raced back in the room and to the drawer for the flatware. "I washed my hands."

Olivia smiled. "Thank you."

The doorbell sounded again.

"I'll tell him we don't need him," Jana said and turned, almost bumping into Tyler. Her heart raced. She backed away. "Sorry, I—I didn't see you."

"Tyler, please tell Jana that the apartment hasn't been painted in years," Olivia requested. "The cabinets might need to be refinished as well."

"No." Jana tried to ignore Tyler's silent presence. "The apartment looks fine the way it is." Making a wide arc around Tyler, she went to the door and opened it.

A good-looking man in his mid-thirties, neatly dressed in dark slacks and a blue striped cotton shirt, stood on the step. On seeing Jana, his eyes widened with undisguised interest. Belatedly, he tipped his cap. "Good evening. Don Jeffries to see Mrs. Sanders, please."

"I'm Mrs. Sanders." Olivia stepped around Jana, extending her hand. "Please come in."

He stepped inside, his gaze flickering to Jana before going back to Olivia. "You have a beautiful home."

"Thank you. I'm afraid I might have wasted your time." Olivia glanced at Jana. "We may not want the apartment painted. Could I please call you tomorrow?"

"Of course," he said. "Would you like me to look at the place and give you an estimate?"

"No," Jana quickly answered. The only way she could afford a painter was if he was free.

His appreciative gaze settled on Jana again. He pulled out a card and handed it to her. "Call me if you want me to come back out. I'm available anytime."

Jana knew when she was being checked out. The tingling in the back of her neck warned her that Tyler was listening to every word. "Thank you, but your services won't be needed." She opened the door. "Good-bye."

He left, but not before he gave her a long measured look that said, "I'm available."

"I still think you should have the apartment painted," Olivia said on the way back to the kitchen.

Jana didn't say anything. She was too aware of Tyler watching her with unmistakable disapproval.

6

She had done it again. Confused him.

Tyler had always known women were a mystery to him, but none had ever been as complicated as Jana. She hadn't taken advantage of Olivia and she hadn't taken the painter up on his blatant invitation. Tyler thought she'd do both. He'd thought she'd take the easy way out. He'd been wrong about a woman before, with devastating consequences. He didn't plan on it happening again.

"Thank you for dinner. I'm going to get my suitcase and go to the apartment." Jana started to rise. "Excuse me."

"No," Tyler said.

She had avoided looking at him through dinner, but now her head snapped around, her eyes widening. She sank back in her seat. He wanted her to leave.

"Look. Olivia's right. The place does need to be painted," he told her. "There's no sense moving until it's done."

She closed her eyes in relief and swallowed.

The sight tore at Tyler. He didn't want to care that she looked vulnerable and alone, but he did.

Her lids fluttered upward. "I can't—" She glanced at Griffin.

Tyler sensed her embarrassment. Griffin was paying more attention to his lasagna than them. "Olivia was right. It's the landlord's responsibility."

Jana's back straightened. "If it needs painting, then I can do it."

He never would have pegged her as stubborn. Trouble was, he kept trying to pigeonhole her and she wouldn't fit. "Do you know how to paint? Strip and varnish cabinets or the floor?"

Fury leaped in her dark eyes. She'd like to take his head off. Good, Tyler thought. He much preferred anger to vulnerability. "No."

"A professional can do it quicker and correctly the first time." He picked up his fork. He had been thinking about Jana so much that he hadn't eaten very much. "Painters tend to get an early start. You're welcome to go over and learn. Do you have a color preference?"

"No."

He frowned. He didn't care for her one-word answers.

"How about a deep rose?" Olivia asked. "Mother has some beautiful rose pieces in the attic. I distinctly remember an ottoman and a lamp. There may even be a pretty patchwork bedding set with multiple rose tones and patterns. We can go up and look at them after we finish dinner. There's a home-improvement store nearby where we can check out paint samples."

Jana looked at Olivia, not at Tyler. "Thank you. I'd like that."

Seems the lady carried a grudge, Tyler mused.

Jana might have liked it better if Tyler hadn't driven them to the home-improvement store. At least she was in the back with Griffin. She was still too aware of Tyler and his warning not to take advantage of Olivia. He didn't have to worry. Olivia's innate goodness more than Jana's fear of Tyler assured that that wouldn't happen.

While they were checking paint colors, a man introduced himself as a painter. He had finished a job that day and was looking for his next client. That he was in his early sixties and had his wife with him probably helped get him the job. Jana hadn't missed Tyler's disapproval of the other painter, but she had to agree with him. The man had been too flirty.

The next morning when the painter, Arnold Blair, arrived at seven with his two-man crew, Jana was there with Tyler. Tyler stressed that he wanted the job done right, but he wanted it completed as quickly as possible. Jana linked her fingers together. She would not be upset that he clearly wanted her out of the house and soon.

"You still want to learn?" Tyler asked, catching her off guard. They'd said very little after dinner last night and had only spoken this morning. "You have some time before you leave for work."

"All right." She was going to learn everything she could. She didn't like feeling helpless.

Tyler turned to the painter. "Do you mind a helper at zero pay?"

Mr. Blair caught on. "Miss, you might want to put on something over your clothes. Paint has a way of going where you don't want it sometimes."

Jana bit her lip, then went to the bedroom where she'd left Tyler's shirt. Slipping it on, she couldn't help feeling an inexplicable sense of intimacy. Shaking off the feeling, she joined the men. "Ready."

Mr. Blair handed her a paintbrush and pointed to the paint in the pan. "Go for it."

Bending, she slowly dipped the tip of the brush into the paint, then spread it across the wall, then repeated the motion. The lush rose color was beautiful. The furniture pieces she and Olivia had looked at last night in the attic would be perfect.

Pleased, she glanced over her shoulder at Tyler. Her heart stopped, then beat wildly. Tyler was smiling at her. This new, supportive Tyler could be trouble.

Julian Cortez was a decisive man. He had to be. Hesitation, even for a second, in the operating room could cost a life. Julian had wrestled more than one patient back from the jaws of death with his legendary skills as a trauma surgeon. So when he made up his mind to seek out Olivia Sanders, he did so at his earliest convenience.

Shortly after twelve Wednesday afternoon Julian parked in front of the Ralph Lauren store and got out of his Maserati. The door closed with a satisfying thump. He'd stood over enough mangled bodies that had to be cut from pretty sports cars to want a solid frame around him. Pretty packaging only went so far.

The same could be said, he supposed, of a woman. Olivia Sanders was pretty, but it was her unbendable spirit, her loyalty, even misplaced, that captured his interest.

His dark eyes narrowed behind his sunshades as he stared at Midnight Dreams across the street. He must have been in the shopping center at least a dozen times and had never noticed the shop. Pity. He would have liked to have met Olivia under different circumstances.

Checking the traffic, he crossed the busy one-way brick street. He wasn't sure of the reception, but he was sure he could get what he came after. Julian wasn't conceited, but he recognized his appeal to women. They had flocked to him for as long as he could remember. His mother hadn't thought that was necessarily a good thing.

She had told him more than once that people who only looked at the surface were only surface themselves. To find a person's true self, one had to look deeper. His mother had known what she was talking about. She'd married a man that made women's heads turn wherever he went, but he had been autocratic and cruel, ruling his wife and two sons with an unbending hand instead of love.

Julian stuffed his hands into his pockets as an old anger surged through him. His mother had died senselessly because an incompetent doctor had misdiagnosed her appendicitis for gastroenteritis, and because of his father's unwillingness to seek another opinion even though Julian begged him to do so. Julian would never forgive him for the pain his mother suffered.

Drawing his thoughts from the past, Julian opened the door to the boutique and pushed his shades atop his head of thick black wavy hair. The spacious store smelled faintly of a citrus scent he couldn't name, probably because to his immediate left was a glass étagère filled with candles, sachets, and soaps.

"Good evening. Can I help you?" asked a young woman.

"I'd like to see Olivia Sanders, please."

"She's at lunch. Is she expecting you?" asked the young woman, her warm gaze flickering over his face with blatant appreciation and interest.

"No, but it's important," he said. Once he made up his mind he didn't like wasting time. "My name is Dr. Julian Cortez. Do you know where she's having lunch?"

"She's in the back," the woman said. "If you'll wait here, I'll get her."

"Thank you," he responded.

Stella walked normally when she wanted to run. The instant she brushed the half-louvered doors aside, she raced into the lounge where Olivia and Jana were just finishing their salads. "Olivia, the most gorgeous man in the entire world is outside wanting to talk to you."

Olivia paled. Her hand went to her racing heart. "He . . . he couldn't be."

Jana shot up from her chair and rounded the small table. "Olivia, what is it?"

The smile slipped from Stella's face. "Dr. Cortez seems like a nice man. . . ."

"What?" Olivia said, jerking upright in her chair. Jana straightened.

"I'll get rid of him," Jana said.

"Wait," Olivia called, trying to get her heart to stop racing. She had thought Stella had been talking about her ex-husband Aaron. The man with the face of an angel and the soul of a devil. "I'll take care of it."

"I'm going with you," Jana said.

"Me too," Stella said.

Olivia looked from one to the other. How could she explain that she'd thought it was her ex-husband without opening herself up to more questions, questions that could ruin Griffin's life if they were answered? "If you want, but I'm sure it's not necessary. I was just surprised."

Getting up, Olivia went into the store with Jana and Stella close behind. Dr. Cortez looked up the instant she entered. He placed the bottle of perfumed ironing water back on the shelf. Oddly, her heart raced even more on seeing him. "Dr. Cortez, what a wonderful surprise. I'm happy you decided to visit the store."

"Hello, Ms. Sanders," he greeted, then his dark eyes widened on seeing Jana.

"Please call me Olivia." She crossed to him, still puzzled why he was there.

"Making house calls, Doc?" Jana asked, her arms folded, her hip cocked.

Julian wasn't easily intimidated. His father had tried. "Olivia, if I could have a few minutes of your time I'd appreciate it."

"We can use my office."

Julian followed Olivia past the two watchful women and into her office. She waved him to a seat in front of her desk, then sat. "What can I do for you?"

"Have dinner with me Saturday night?"

She blinked. "I beg your pardon?"

He almost smiled at the surprise on her face. "Have dinner with me Saturday night. You choose and I will make reservations."

"You're kidding."

Ok, the situation was no longer comical. "Why is it so difficult to believe I want to take you out?"

She flushed and Julian knew he had said the wrong thing. He tried to backpedal. "It isn't often that someone surprises me. And you did Saturday when you stuck up for a complete stranger. I'd like to get to know you better."

"I'm sorry. I have plans for Saturday night."

She didn't look sorry. "What night do you think you might be free?"

She placed her delicate hands on the desk and lightly laced her fingers together. "The truth of the matter is that I don't date."

For a moment he was the one who was stunned. "Ever?"

"Not in years." She turned a picture in a crystal frame around for him to see. In the photo she was grinning into the camera, her arms locked securely around a young boy whose grin was just as broad. "Between my son and the store I don't have time for anything else."

There had to be a very strong reason a woman stopped dating. He recalled his statement in the emergency room. "I guess you did trust the wrong man."

Olivia flinched and came to her feet. "I don't mean to be rude, but I have work to do."

Julian had no choice except to stand. He placed his business card in the center of the neat desk. "Just conversation and dinner. No strings."

"The answer remains the same."

"Then I don't guess I have any choice but to change your mind. Goodbye for now, Olivia." Julian left Olivia's office. What gave him hope was the brief flare of interest he'd seen in her face just before the door closed.

He wasn't surprised to see Jana pacing just outside the door.

"Why did you want to see Olivia alone?" she asked.

"I don't think it's any of your business."

She clamped her hands on her slim hips. "You might not tell me, but her brother will make mincemeat out of you if you hurt his sister."

"You mean like you tried to do?" he said, then instantly regretted the words as she paled. "I'm sorry. I shouldn't have said that. Guess I'm not in a good mood."

"Are you ever?"

"Occasionally." He flicked his sunshades back over his eyes. "Until the next time."

"There might not be a next time."

"I'd bet on it." Brushing past her, he nodded to the other sales clerk as he left the store. Olivia might not know it, but she'd presented him a challenge he couldn't resist.

"He asked me to have dinner with him and I said no. End of story."

Despite the arrogance of the man and his quickness to come down on her, Jana had to admit he was one handsome package. "I bet he was surprised."

Olivia's hand paused over the keyboard of the computer. "I'm not sure. Anyway, it's over."

"Well, *I'm* not so sure."

Olivia lifted her head. "What do you mean?"

"I got the impression he wasn't giving up." Jana folded her arms.

"He was just talking." Olivia gave her attention back to the computer. "Drop-dead gorgeous men don't date women who look like me."

Jana was so surprised by the statement that for a moment she didn't know what to say. "Women like you? What's wrong with you?"

Olivia's hands paused briefly, then continued typing. "Jana, please see if Stella needs any help and remind her to let you write up the next sale. She'll be off tomorrow and it will be just the two of us."

It was a dismissal. Clearly Olivia didn't want to talk about Dr. Cortez's interest in her. The old Jana would have considered it was no skin off her nose and not given it another thought. She might even have tried to get the man for herself, but that was before Olivia had stood up for her when no one else would.

Olivia needed someone, a friend, something Jana had never been to anyone. Jana didn't know how to do what Olivia did so effortlessly.

"Is there anything I can do?"

"I'm fine."

Then why are your hands trembling? Why won't you look at me? Unsure if she should voice the questions aloud, Jana quietly left the office feeling as if she'd let Olivia down. Being a friend wasn't easy.

It took Jana most of the day to try and work up her courage to ask Olivia for an advance on her salary. She'd done so much for her already. The painters were due to finish today. Last night when she'd gotten home she'd gone to check on their progress. The transformation was amazing.

Jana had gotten a kick out of sanding a small area on the cabinet. This morning she had applied varnish to the spot. But she still had a long ways to go before she was in control of her life. The fact was evident by her need to ask for an advance.

She'd waited until the store was closed and Stella gone. Olivia was at the desk in the showroom going over the day's receipts.

Jana rubbed her sweaty palm on her short skirt, trying to rehearse a speech. She who had once spent with wild abandon only had a dress, two tops and a skirt to her name and she was wearing the skirt.

Olivia glanced up before Jana could get the words past her dry throat. "Another day in retail. How does it feel?"

"Fine." Jana tried to work up moisture in her mouth. "I . . . er . . . know I haven't earned very much and you had the apartment painted, but could you possibly give me an advance on my salary?" She flushed. "I don't have anything else to wear." She'd worn the faded sundress the day before.

"Of course, and I know the perfect place to shop." Closing the books, Olivia stood. "I'll ask Tyler to pick up Griffin while I'm in back grabbing our purses and setting the alarm. Unfortunately, my son is very male in that he hates shopping."

Jana stared after Olivia, unable to believe it had been so easy. Perhaps she shouldn't have been so surprised. Olivia was the most unselfish person Jana had ever met.

In minutes Olivia was back and they were on their way. It didn't take them long to pull into a shopping center filled with a mixture of upscale shops. "We can try a regular store, but I used to get some real bargains at Secrets," Olivia said as she parallel parked.

Jana's eyes widened in surprise. "You shop resale?"

"At one time I was going to two or three social events a week and needed a different dress each time. Secrets saved my sanity and my banking account." Olivia emerged from the SUV. "Now I send a check to charity functions and stay at home with Griffin or just relax."

"I used to go out every night," Jana admitted.

"I'd rather be at home." After a car passed, they crossed the street.

Jana easily recalled the loneliness of being alone every night. The loneliness was the worst part of her being ostracized. "Don't you get lonely?"

"Occasionally, but it beats the alternative."

"What's that?" Jana stopped in front of Secrets' stained-glass door.

"Falling in love with the wrong man."

From Jana's viewpoint falling in love with *any* man was disastrous. She never stayed with any man for that very reason. She wasn't going to be miserable like her parents.

Olivia opened the glass door of the store. "Let's see what we can find."

They found two summer dresses, two pairs of pants, three tops, and a pair of heeled sandals. The next stop was a grocery store. Jana was lost, but Olivia guided her. It was after nine when Olivia pulled into the garage.

Tyler came out of the back door of the house to greet them. "Been shopping?"

Jana's arms around the sack of groceries tightened. Why did Tyler always catch her when she least expected to see him? Last night he hadn't been at dinner. Olivia said he often became involved in his work and lost track of time. Jana wished that was the case now.

"Yes." Olivia handed him the bag of groceries she carried. "Please help Jana. I'm going upstairs to see Griffin and see how long he can pretend to be asleep."

"You don't have to help," Jana said.

Tyler plucked the bag of groceries from her arms. "Lead the way."

Deciding the quickest way to get rid of him was to do as directed, she reached back in the car for the handled shopping bag from Secrets and started up the stairs, very aware that Tyler was behind her and of the snug fit of her short black skirt.

She pushed the door open. Faint fumes from the paint remained. Tyler brushed by her, tickling her senses with the citrus fragrance he wore.

"You can just put them on the sofa," she told him.

Tyler kept walking toward the kitchen. Jana gritted her teeth and closed the door. Determined to ignore him, she put the shopping bag of clothes on the counter. "Thank you. I can manage from here."

Folding his arms, Tyler leaned against the cabinet. "So, how did today go?"

"Fine." What he wanted to know was had she tried to seduce any men. He'd probably be surprised to know that men had plummeted to the bottom of her list. Turning her back to him, she began pulling perishables from the sack and putting them in the refrigerator.

"I see you went shopping."

The refrigerator closed with a loud thump. "So that's it. You just want to know how much I fleeced Olivia for." Opening the bag, she thrust the grocery receipts toward him. "$58.79 for the groceries and $78.96 for the clothes. Olivia is going to take it out of my check. Fifty a week for the clothes, seventy-five for rent and another twenty for the painter." When Tyler made no move to take the receipts Jana tossed them on the table and reached for the handled bag of clothes. "You want to check?"

His silence caused her anger to escalate. Without a second thought she upended the bag over the table and ticked off the items inside. "Any more questions?"

"Yes." Tyler nodded toward the pile of clothes. "What about those?"

Jana looked down and gasped. Laying on top of the pile were several sets of lacy bras and matching panties. She distinctly recalled looking at the new items at Secrets and silently bemoaning the fact that she didn't have money to buy them. She was so tired of washing the pitiful few she had every other day.

"No answer?"

Her frantic gaze went back to Tyler. "I didn't steal them. Maybe the sales woman didn't see them in the bag," she said. Even to her own ears it sounded implausible.

Tyler hooked one long lean finger through a pair of black thongs. "It would be a wild coincidence if these fit, wouldn't it?"

She snatched the panties from his hand, ignoring her racing heart. Picking up the bag she put the undergarments inside. "I'm telling the truth."

"Then this might explain it." He bent and picked up a white sheet of paper from the floor. "It fell out when you emptied the bag."

Jana didn't see how, but she took the paper anyway. Although there were only three words written on it Jana had to read them twice. *A gift. Olivia.* Slowly Jana lifted her head. "She must have purchased them when I was in the dressing room. She's already done so much to help me. Why?"

"Because that's the way she is," Tyler answered easily.

"But that's crazy," Jana said, a bit dazed.

"Not to Olivia's way of thinking," he said with a wry twist of his mouth. "The more she gives, the happier she seems to be."

"People will take advantage of her," Jana said, angered by the thought.

"Not anymore. Not if I can help it," he answered, his voice tight.

Jana didn't doubt him for a moment. He'd do whatever it took to keep his family safe. Perhaps if her parents had cared as much . . . her thoughts trailed off. It was time to stop blaming her parents for her problems and concentrate on being the kind of person who'd inspire the kind of loyalty Olivia inspired.

Reaching for another bag she began putting the groceries away. "I told Dr. Cortez as much when he came by the store this afternoon."

"Why was he there?"

"To ask Olivia out." She turned to get the next items from the sack and found Tyler holding two cans of tuna. He was much too close. Silently taking the items, she put them on the shelf. "She turned him down, but I don't think he's giving up."

"I suppose you think she should have taken him up on his offer?"

Jane accepted the box of cereal and the can of coffee before answering. "He's gorgeous, young, and rich."

"Is that all you require in a man?"

The question was voiced as mildly as the first one. When she glanced over her shoulder at Tyler, his expression was unreadable, yet her heart thumped. Time seemed to stand still.

Why did she have to be attracted to a man after all these years, and worse, to one who didn't trust her? She opened her mouth to give him a flippant answer, but somehow the words wouldn't come. "At one time."

"What changed your mind?"

"Doesn't matter." She moved to the next bag. Once again Tyler helped until all the groceries were stored. "I can finish the rest by myself."

"You do that very well."

She frowned. "Do what?"

"Push people away."

He saw too much. "Apparently not you."

"It just makes me wonder why." He reached out and grazed a finger down her cheek.

Desire raced though Jana. She jumped and staggered back. "Why did you do that?"

"Curious I guess." Folding his arms Tyler leaned back against the counter. "It's in my nature to try to solve puzzles. It's also how I make my living."

"You're a private investigator?"

"Computer system analysis," he told her. He grinned at the look of astonishment on her face.

"A computer geek?"

The smile widened. "And proud of it."

"It's hard to imagine you into computers," she said.

"What can you imagine me doing?" he asked, aware the question was leading.

From her sudden intake of breath, he guessed that her imagination was right on target with his. Her beneath him wringing cries of ecstasy from her lips.

So the attraction wasn't one-sided. He wasn't sure if that boded good or bad. She was hiding something. "Are you sleeping in the house tonight?"

"Yes. Olivia suggested I wait to move in to let the paint fumes completely dissipate," she told him, her voice unsteady.

"Makes sense." He lifted the handled bag. "Ready?"

She hesitated, then nodded. She jumped when his hand closed on her upper forearm. Acting as if he hadn't noticed her reaction he continued to the door. Neither spoke as they went down the steps and into the house. He handed her the bag at the bottom of the stairs. "Good night."

"You're not coming up?"

"I want to put in a few more hours on a program I'm working on."

She nodded, turned, then whirled back, her hand gripping the bag. "I know you have no reason to believe me, but I wouldn't take advantage of Olivia. I needed these things."

"You aren't used to asking for help, or getting it, are you?" he ventured.

"No."

"If you stick around here you will be."

"I don't understand you."

He smiled lazily. "A lot of people feel the same way. Are you hungry?"

For once she could answer that question truthfully. "No. Olivia and I grabbed a bite earlier. Good night."

"Night." Tyler watched her climb the stairs and wished he was climbing them with her. He took a slow, deep breath and another until he could feel the desire lessening. He didn't understand his attraction toward Jana, but he planned to keep it in check.

7

Thursday morning Jana woke up thirty minutes earlier than usual, dressed, and went downstairs to the kitchen in the house. If she planned to be self-sufficient and take care of herself she needed to learn how to cook. As she expected, Wanda was already in the kitchen. "Good morning, Wanda."

The cook turned from the double sink with a potato in one hand and a potato peeler in the other. "Good morning, Ms. Franklin. Can I get you anything?"

"Please call me Jana," she said, trying to work up her courage. As Tyler had guessed, she wasn't used to asking for help. "I can't cook. I've never even used a can opener. If you have time and it wouldn't interfere with your schedule, could you please teach me how?"

Wanda's thin face softened. "Of course, child. I taught Olivia's mother and Olivia, too." She motioned Jana over with the potato peeler. "Ain't nothing at all to cooking. You just got to have patience and practice. I don't suppose you've ever done this?"

"No." She couldn't recall ever peeling anything with a knife.

"This is where the practice comes in. Just hold the potato in your hand and start at one end and go to the other. Just like combing your hair." She demonstrated what she meant, then placed the potato in a bowl on the granite counter and reached for another. "Tyler likes fried potatoes for breakfast with his biscuits and sausage."

The thought of surprising Tyler with foods she had helped prepare had an unexpected appeal. "Can I try?"

"Sure." Wanda handed the potato and peeler to Jana. "You can do that while I start making the biscuits."

Jana tucked her lower lip between her teeth as she concentrated on sliding the instrument just beneath the potato skin. The cut wasn't as clean or as straight as Wanda's, but the peels mounted on the counter. "Finished."

Wanda looked over and nodded her approval. "While I roll out these biscuits you can peel and slice those onions on the counter in front of you, sauté them in butter and add the sliced potatoes." She dumped the dough on a floured cutting board. "Peel the onion under running water and your eyes won't tear. Together we'll have breakfast ready in no time."

Jana wasn't so sure, but she was willing to give it a try. She reached for the onion.

"You sure you cooked these potatoes by yourself?" Tyler asked, polishing off his second helping.

Pleased and proud, Jana couldn't quite believe it herself. "Next time I won't scorch them."

"They taste fine to me." Tyler leaned back in his chair and picked up his glass of orange juice. "What do you plan to cook for breakfast tomorrow?"

"What?" Jana's eyes widened.

"Don't you go teasing her, Tyler," Wanda admonished from across the room where she was stuffing pork chops for dinner. "Jana is going to be a fine cook. She's got patience and she's a quick learner."

Jana had heard the same praise from Wanda earlier and it meant just as much the second time. There were few times in her life she had been praised for anything that didn't have to do with the bedroom. Her parents certainly hadn't. "Thank you, but it's because you're such a wonderful teacher."

"She certainly is," Olivia agreed. "No matter how many times I burned the green beans, she never became angry or impatient with me."

Chuckling, Wanda shook her head of graying hair and placed the meat in the refrigerator. "Seems like every time Olivia cooked green beans there was a program on TV she wanted to watch more than she wanted to watch her cooking."

"I'm glad she can bake chocolate-chip cookies without burning them." Griffin smiled at his mother. "I'd sure like some tonight."

"We're having fruit salad." Olivia placed her napkin on the table and stood. "You two ready to go?"

"Yes, ma'am." Griffin finished his juice and rounded the table.

Jana came to her feet as well. "Ready."

Tyler stared up at her. "I'm still waiting for my answer."

"What would you like?" she asked. The words were barely out of her mouth when she realized how flirtatious they were.

Tyler's expression was interested more than annoyed. "Surprise me."

Relieved that he hadn't misinterpreted her answer, the tension seeped out of her. "I just might do that." Feeling more in control of her life than she had in months, Jana left the kitchen very much aware that Tyler was watching her every step of the way and annoyingly pleased that he was.

That day at work was considerably better than the first for Jana. She'd finally stopped tensing for fear of being recognized every time a customer entered. Instead, she'd greeted customers as warmly as Olivia and Stella did. It wasn't a coincidence that the majority of the customers she approached were women. Even without Tyler's comment, she'd already decided to steer clear of men.

That wasn't too difficult as most of the men who came into the store were dragged there by their wives or girlfriends. They generally made a beeline for the seat in front of the desk as soon as possible. In between helping customers she watched the men check their watch or frown at the women with them, who in turn threw them annoyed looks. It was obvious that neither were enjoying the shopping experience, which could mean a lost sale for Olivia.

Successful businessmen hated to waste time. That afternoon, when it happened again, she decided to intervene.

"Excuse me, sir, but would you like anything to drink while you wait? We have wine, coffee, tea, or sparkling juice. Or perhaps the *Wall Street Journal*?"

The well-dressed man in a gray pinstriped tailored suit who had been drumming his fingers glanced up at her. In his mid-fifties, he was distinguished looking with manicured nails and polished wing tips. "The *Journal* would be great. There's an article I wanted to read."

"Coming right up. With or without a drink?"

He glanced at the leggy blonde in deep conversation with Olivia. "With a white wine, please."

"I'll be back shortly." Jana was good as her word, setting the wine within easy reach on the desk and handing him the newspaper. "Please let me or the other associate know if there is anything else we can do."

"Thanks." He took a sip of wine. "You may have saved my sanity, and my wife from becoming even more annoyed with me."

"We want the shopping experience to be pleasurable for everyone." Jana moved away. Glancing around to see if there was a customer who might need her assistance, she caught Olivia giving her a thumbs-up. Jana inclined her head in acknowledgement. The next man who came through the door she wasn't so sure how to approach.

"Tyler, I didn't expect to see you here." Was he checking on her again or was she being paranoid?

He shrugged and glanced around the shop. "I'm stuck."

She frowned. "I beg your pardon?"

His gaze settled back on her. "The computer program I'm working on. When I'm stuck I go for a drive. How are things going here?"

When people went on drives they did just that. He *was* checking on her. This morning's lighthearted banter hadn't meant anything to him. She could be offended or give him the information he wanted. Seeing Olivia pass with two sets of sheets for the woman customer helped Jana reach a decision. She felt she had contributed in some small way to the sale.

"Wonderful," she finally answered. She nodded to the couple at the desk and told him everything.

Tyler rubbed his chin. "I know how he felt. I detest shopping."

"Most men do," Jana agreed, straightening the towels on a display.

"I have an extra laptop and Palm Pilot. It wouldn't take much to set up a little work sta—"

"No." Jana held up her hand to punctuate her statement. "A woman might not mind her husband looking at the newspaper, which is easy to put down, but I think we'd create more problems if he's in the middle of checking e-mail or other data and she wanted his opinion on anything and he didn't want to be interrupted."

"You might have a point. I tend to get lost when I'm on a roll."

"So Olivia tells me." The door behind them opened and two women entered. "Please excuse me." Jana went to greet the mother and daughter, who wanted to browse. Tyler appeared to be waiting for her, and since Olivia was still working with the couple, Jana went back to Tyler.

"Good luck in getting unstuck," she said, hoping to get him to leave.

"I already have. I just have to do a reconfiguration of the mainframe."

"Sounds reasonable to me."

He flashed her a grin that caused her stomach to do a flip-flop. "You don't know what I'm talking about, do you?"

"I understood what you said, I just don't know how it's done." She smiled. "Checking e-mail is about the extent of my computer knowledge."

"Then I'll have to teach you," Tyler said. "Can't have you living with us and not know about computers. See you at home."

"Drive safely." Jana watched him leave, a warm glow inside. *Home.*

"Would you like to go to church with me tonight?" Olivia asked as they sat around the table at dinner that night.

Jana choked on the lemonade she'd just drank. Tyler's broad hand slapped her between the shoulder blades.

"Jana, are you all right?" Olivia asked.

Holding up her hand for Tyler to stop beating her with what she thought was entirely too much enthusiasm, Jana took a small sip of the lemonade, trying to gather her thoughts. She could count on both hands the number of times she'd been in a church, and that had been for weddings and a funeral. "Church? Tonight?"

"Yes. I'm working with a group of ladies, putting together gift baskets for victims of domestic violence," Olivia explained.

"The children's Sunday-school class is collecting toys for their children." Griffin speared his last wedge of pineapple. "We have some great stuff."

"But those things won't make up for not having a home where they don't have to be afraid," Olivia said quietly.

"It's so they'll know that other people and God care about them," Griffin said. "I didn't forget, Mama."

"We could use an extra pair of hands," Olivia said. "But if you're tired I understand."

Jana considered lying, at least until she remembered being afraid and ashamed in the motel's office and having no place to go, remembered where she'd slept a week ago. Maybe a lightning bolt wouldn't strike her for what she was. Maybe the women would see her for what she was trying to be now. "Not any more tired than you are. Count me in."

"Can you be ready to leave in ten minutes?"

"Sure." Jana took her plate to the sink before coming back to slide her purse over her shoulder. "I'll be back as soon as I drop off my suitcase at the apartment."

"Need any help?" Tyler asked.

Jana lifted a brow. He knew very well that a five-year-old could carry her half-empty suitcase.

"Did you have time to change the linen on the bed or get fresh towels?" he asked her.

She hadn't. "That didn't even cross my mind."

"Wanda is way ahead of you." Olivia came to her feet, picking up Tyler's plate. Griffin followed with his. "She put your linen in a big plastic tote in the utility room. Tyler, could you carry it over for her, please?"

"No problem. I'll meet you back here." He rolled to his feet with that easy strength of his.

Aware it was a waste of time to argue, Jana hurried to get her suitcase.

"Haven't spent much time in church, have you?" Tyler sat on the eight-gallon tote just inside Jana's door.

"What a brilliant deduction." She placed the suitcase beside the tote and came back outside.

His brow knitted. He'd never heard that particular snide tone before. He studied her closely. She was trembling. "You're scared."

"Olivia is waiting." As soon as he came through the door, she closed it and started down the stairs. He caught her arm midway. "Let me go."

His response was to catch her other arm. "I'm no great biblical scholar, but I do know the one place where you don't have to be scared to go is church. People might judge you, but God doesn't. Thank goodness, I finally learned that."

That got her attention. "What could *you* have done?"

"Plenty. At least according to Courtney." His mouth in a narrow line, he released her arms. "God forgives our sins. All you have to do is ask. He doesn't keep throwing them up in our faces. Any person who has a true relationship with God will do the same. The rest don't matter."

"This Courtney woman judged you?"

"As you said, Olivia is waiting." Taking her arm, he started back to the house. He'd said too much already.

Jana had planned on staying in the background once they met with the group of women at the church, but that didn't happen. Olivia was too well respected and liked. Jana was welcomed with friendly hugs and warm handshakes. She couldn't remember all the names or who was related to whom, but one thing she was certain of, there wasn't a Courtney among them. Jana was curious about the woman who had seemingly thought Tyler didn't measure up to her standards.

Initially Jana worked with Olivia filling the baskets, then she volunteered to take them to the end of the large open area where they were to be wrapped. On her second trip she cringed on seeing the uneven paper, the tilting, misshapen bows.

"They're all pretty pitiful, aren't they?"

Jana's head snapped up to see a very pregnant young woman with her hands on her bulging stomach staring at the crooked bow she'd just tied. "God will have his way, but I sure hope this is a boy."

"If not?" Jana asked.

The woman grinned. "I'm going to buy every type and color of barrettes I can find." She extended her hand. "Maggie Palmer."

"Jana Franklin," she said, smiling without thought.

"Pleased to meet you, Jana. Are you a visitor to our church?

"Yes, Olivia invited me."

"There's a special place in God's kingdom for Olivia. She gets such a joy out of helping. This was one of her many community project ideas." Maggie moved her hands to the small of her back. "I hate to send these out to women who have already gone through so much."

Jana wasn't surprised that Olivia hadn't mentioned that this was her special project. Olivia generally cared about people. Jana sensed in the pregnant woman the same compassion Olivia seemed to have in such abundance. "Maybe we could fix them."

Maggie's eyes widened. She moved from around the table. "Please."

"We'll have to cut the ribbon," Jana said cautiously.

Maggie picked up the scissors on the table and clipped the bows away. "Now what?"

Jana studied the crammed wicker baskets. They had been stuffed with the idea of getting in as many items as possible. Presentation hadn't been a consideration. However, presentation, as her mother had taught her, *was* everything. Perhaps one lesson her mother had drilled into her head would finally help.

Removing all the items from the basket nearest her, Jana began rearranging the bath and body products and all the other items chosen to make a woman feel pampered and special. She paused only briefly when she saw the Bliss label. Finished, she gathered the clear wrap and held it for Maggie to tie a knot. Picking up a roll of red satin ribbon, Jana coiled it over her hand, secured it with a wire, then attached it to the basket.

"It's beautiful," Maggie said and hugged Jana. "You're a lifesaver. I defy anyone to say God doesn't send someone to those in need."

Jana started to dispute the claim, thinking of her life in the last five months, then she recalled standing in a motel office almost broke, with no hope. "Even if you don't believe He'll help," she said softly.

Maggie stared at her. "Yes. God's mercy and unconditional love is for everyone."

"Amen." A tall, dark-skinned man in his mid-thirties came up to them. He curved his long arm lovingly around Maggie and extended his hand toward Jana. "Pastor Palmer. Welcome to Concord."

Realization hit Jana. Maggie was the pastor's wife. She glanced upward quickly, wondering about that lightning bolt. "Jana Franklin."

"Didn't she do a beautiful job on the basket?" Maggie reached for the basket, but her husband moved her hands aside. She made a face. "He thinks I'll break."

"I think you're eight months pregnant with our child." He held up the basket, then looked at Jana. "You did a wonderful job. We want to do two hundred of these. We plan fifty a night. If you don't mind I can have the other women in charge come over and you can teach them."

Jana wondered if he would want her help if he knew her past? Probably not.

He must have sensed her hesitation. "You'd be helping women, many of whom have lost hope," he said softly.

A woman like she had been just a short week ago. And since lightning hadn't struck, maybe there was hope for her yet. "Make the call."

Jana once had prided herself on her ability to enter a room and draw the gaze of every man there. It didn't matter if he desired her or not, it mattered that he had looked and for that space of time, she had more power than he. Yet somehow, as she listened to Olivia tell Tyler what had happened that night at the church, Jana wanted to squirm.

"You should have seen the beautiful baskets she created. Everyone was raving over them."

"So you're a hit?" Tyler leaned back lazily in his chair and smiled at Jana.

Jana moistened her lips. That man had a killer smile. "I just helped."

"She's being modest," Olivia said. "But the baskets started me thinking. Jana could do a few up to offer as gifts and see how they go. If they prove successful, we can offer them seasonally beginning with the Christmas holidays. What do you think, Jana?"

Jana was too stunned to think anything except Olivia's offer of help wasn't temporary. "I don't know, Olivia."

"I'm counting off the days until Christmas," Griffin said. "I've already started on my list."

"Why am I not surprised?" Olivia rubbed her hand across his head. "Think about it, Jana, and we can talk later. For now, it's bedtime for Griffin."

"I want to tell Uncle Tyler about what we did." Griffin started for his uncle.

Olivia caught him by the shirt collar. "You can tell him tomorrow. Good night." She herded her son out of Tyler's office.

Jana stared after them.

"Surprised?" Tyler pushed up from the chair.

"Yes," she answered without trying to guard her answer. "I haven't made any long-range plans in a long time."

"Well, now you can. But what about my surprise for breakfast?"

The realization slowly sank in that she had a job, a place to stay, but most importantly she was wanted. "You'll just have to wait until the morning. Night."

"I'll walk you to your place."

"You can't walk me out every night," she told him. "If you don't mind, I'd rather go by myself."

"I'll walk you to the back door and wait until you're inside."

Knowing that was as good as she was going to get, she accepted his offer. At the back door of the kitchen, she sprinted across the lawn. She'd never hurried anyplace except to spend money. Laughing, she went up the stairs, opened the door and stepped inside.

Her place. She allowed herself to bask in that knowledge for all of thirty seconds before she recalled she had promised Tyler a surprise for breakfast. Whatever it was, it wouldn't be the erotic scene she'd dreamed the day after they met.

Sternly chastising herself, she took her suitcase and the tote into the bedroom. She'd sworn off men, and Tyler was at the top of that list.

Tyler came downstairs the next morning unsure what Jana's surprise for breakfast would be. When Jana had asked him what he wanted, it was a good thing he'd been sitting down or she would have known exactly what he wanted. The two of them naked in bed. If he wasn't careful he'd be in just as much trouble this morning.

Nearing the kitchen he caught the scent of coffee. He sniffed the air, trying to see if he could detect what she'd cooked. Somehow he couldn't imagine Jana as the homemaker type, but he could easily imagine them wrapped in moonlight and in each other's arms.

Annoyed that he couldn't stop thinking about the two of them in bed, he entered the kitchen and saw Jana, Wanda, Olivia, and Griffin huddled together. They all looked like the cat that swallowed the canary. "Good morning and where is my surprise?"

Griffin giggled. "Good morning, Uncle Tyler. You're really going to be surprised."

Tyler pulled out a chair and sat. "Well?"

Olivia pressed her fingertips over her mouth. Wanda folded her arms. Jana turned away from him, then turned back. In her hands were a cup and a small porcelain pot.

"Tea?"

"Perhaps." Jana sat the cup in front of him and poured.

He looked from the rich chocolate streaming from the sprout to Jana. "You're kidding, right?"

"You're surprised, aren't you? After all you didn't *specify*."

Griffin laughed. "You always have to be specific when you want something. I learned that from watching the genie cartoons."

"I stand corrected and chastised." Tyler picked up his cup. Steam curled upward. "You made this by yourself?"

"Yes, and since you're being such a good sport, you can have your second surprise."

"Marshmallows?" He'd never seen that sparkle in her eyes before. It intrigued him and beckoned, and he was pleased he was the cause.

Smiling impishly, she opened the lid of the creamer in front of him with a flourish. It was brimming with miniature marshmallows. He promptly put several in his cup, fascinated by the becoming change in Jana. She could definitely be trouble if he wasn't careful.

Later that morning Olivia paused in making the bed on the showroom floor with hand-embroidered linen and thought she shouldn't have a care in the world. Griffin was healthy and happy. She had a wonderful family who loved her. Business was booming. Jana was settling in nicely.

Yet Olivia continued to be restless, especially at night. She couldn't ignore any longer the very annoying reason. Dr. Julian Cortez.

She snapped the sheet tight and tucked it in. She was attracted to him, and no matter how busy she kept herself, thoughts of him would slip into her mind when she least expected them to. Worse yet were the wildly erotic dreams that each morning left her body yearning and tangled up in the sheets.

The cold, brisk showers weren't helping. It was becoming more difficult to keep a smile on her face and concentrate on the conversation at home and at work. Last night at the dinner table, Tyler and Griffin kept having to repeat themselves. That was unacceptable. Nothing could come between her and Griffin, least of all a man.

She was aware that Tyler was becoming concerned about her, but how could she admit that she was almost afraid to go to sleep for fear she'd dream about a man she'd met twice. It was Dr. Cortez's fault for disrupting her orderly life. She'd been content without a man. One heart-stopping smile from Julian and that had changed. She picked up a neck roll, but instead of placing it on the bed, simply held it to her chest.

"Are you all right?"

Olivia glanced around to see Jana staring at her with a puzzled frown on her face. "Did you say something?"

"I asked if you were all right. You've been staring into space, clutching that pillow for over a minute. That isn't like you."

Olivia placed the pillow on the bed. "Just thinking," she said, trying to stick as close to the truth as possible, but Jana didn't look as if she believed her any more than she had the other times she'd asked during the day. "How does the bed look?"

"Comfortable and inviting," Jana told her. "I'd certainly drop the three thousand dollars to take the complete set home with me."

Olivia looked at the wide bed with the covers turned back. On the nightstand was a pear-vanilla candle in a crystal holder, a book of poems, and a crystal lamp. The scene was set for lovers. Her thoughts veered to Dr. Cortez and her body heated. She clenched her hands again.

"You're thinking about him, aren't you?"

Olivia whirled around. "Yes." It was almost a relief to say it.

"I'd think something was wrong with you if you weren't," Jana said. "You probably threw him when you refused to go out with him. He's probably not used to women saying no."

Olivia smoothed her hands over the already neat bed. "Then he shouldn't come back."

"Is that what you really want?"

Olivia straightened, opened her mouth, then closed it. "Yes, especially after the dreams I keep having."

"That bad or that good?"

Olivia blew out a breath. "Depends on how you look at it. They're very erotic."

"Those are the only kind to have."

"Not for me. I'm a mother."

"You're also a woman. You're young, pretty. It's reasonable to be attracted to a man."

Olivia was already shaking her head. "I won't go through that again."

"Through what?"

Olivia started as if just realizing what she had said. "Nothing. I need to make a few phone calls."

"Olivia, I'm probably the last person in the world to try and give advice about men, but don't let one bad experience turn you off from all men," Jana told her.

"I need to do some work in the back." This time Olivia made good her escape.

The door opened and a middle-aged woman came in. Her bag was Hermès, her suit Dior, the pearls at her throat large and lustrous. Her hair was perfectly coiffured, her posture finishing-school correct. It had taken only seconds for Jana to size the woman up as being able to afford anything in the store many times over.

Most of her sales thus far had been low-ticket items. This customer could change things dramatically and pay Olivia back a little for all she'd done for Jana.

Smiling her brightest, Jana went to the woman. "Good evening, and welcome to Midnight Dreams. Can I help you with anything in particular or would you like to browse?"

"I was just . . ." Her voice trailed off, her eyes narrowed, "Excuse me, but have we met?"

Jana felt as if her heart had dropped onto the floor. She didn't remember the woman, but she'd never paid that much attention to the women, only the men. She kept the smile on her face with an effort. "I don't think so. I seem to have one of those faces."

"You look so familiar."

"Mrs.—"

"Fulton. Mrs. Robert Fulton."

Jana recognized the name, but thank goodness had never been involved with the real estate developer.

"Mrs. Fulton, what an honor. I'm sure I would have remembered meeting you. I haven't been in Dallas long, but Mr. Fulton is very well known throughout the country," Jana gushed. She might not have played the game, but she knew how it was done.

Mrs. Fulton preened. "I'm involved in a great many charities. We believe in giving back."

And what's the sense of giving money if no one knows about it? "The community is fortunate to have two philanthropic patrons such as you and your husband. If there is anything I can do to make your shopping experience at Midnight Dreams more enjoyable, please don't hesitate to let me know."

"Robert recently purchased a yacht and I understand Frette sheets can be custom-made with monograms," Mrs. Fulton said.

Only because Jana was used to the extravagance of people and had been indulgent herself was she able to keep from showing her excitement. "Frette sheets are sublime and can be made in a wide range of fabrics and colors to complement the yacht interior. If you'd come this way and have a seat, I'll get the owner, Olivia Sanders, and she can show you the sample book."

"That would be wonderful." Mrs. Fulton took her seat, setting the ten-thousand-dollar bag in her lap.

Jana plucked a little table from a display and set it beside her. "Would you like Perrier, wine or sparkling juice?"

"White wine, if you have it?" She placed the bag on the table.

"We do. I won't be but a moment." Jana headed for Olivia's office, closing the open door behind her. "Mrs. Robert Fulton is outside. She wants Frette monogram sheets for the yacht her husband recently purchased."

Olivia's eyes gleamed. She immediately came to her feet. "Then she's come to the right place."

"Same thing I thought. I'll get her wine." Jana said, heading to the lounge. By the time she placed the glass of wine on the small table next to the handbag, Mrs. Fulton had several swatches in her lap.

"Thank you," she said. "You've been very kind. I didn't get your name."

She hesitated a beat too long.

"Jana Franklin," Olivia supplied.

"Thank you, Jana," Mrs. Fulton said, then returned at looking through the sample book.

Jana left the two women alone. She'd dodged that bullet, but what about the next time?

She bit her lower lip. The people who traveled in the wealthy circles where she had once been welcome were relatively few. Many of them were self-indulgent, bent on one-upmanship and reigning supreme as the wealthiest of the wealthiest. Midnight Dreams catered to that need to say "Hey, look at me. I dropped sixty thousand dollars on sheets for my yacht." Sooner or later a customer would walk through the door and recognize her.

And when that happened, she'd have to leave.

8

Jana did her best to join Olivia in the impromptu celebration of the sale. Mrs. Fulton had come prepared with the measurements and used her black American Express credit card that cost ten thousand dollars a year for the privilege to carry it to pay for the order. But Jana couldn't shake the worry that time was running out for her.

"You're the reason for the sale," Olivia said, touching her glass of sparking juice against Jana's. "She told me just before she left that she was impressed with your friendliness and knowledge."

"It was nothing," Jana mumbled, taking a small sip, thinking of all the times sales associates had stroked her ego and she'd fallen for it.

"You're too modest. I've already called in the order and put a rush on it since she wants them for the launch party in a month." Olivia finished the juice and began rinsing the glass. "I better get back out there."

"I'll go." Jana finished her drink and took over rinsing both glasses.

"All right, but you don't seem very excited about the commission."

"Commission?" Jana turned around, her eyes wide.

Olivia laughed. "I thought that would get your attention. I didn't mention it because some people I've hired have tried to pressure customers. This way, it's a nice surprise and we both see if the fit is right."

Jana's heart raced. "How much?"

"Five percent of this." Olivia held a piece of letterhead paper.

For a moment Jana couldn't catch her breath. The sale was more than she had estimated.

"Sit down." Olivia helped her to a chair. "I'm sorry. I thought you'd be happy."

"I am . . . it's just . . ." Jana shook her head.

"I heard the front door. Will you be all right?"

"Go." Eyes closed, Jana took one slow breath after the other. She had money. She wasn't destitute any longer.

"Does good news always affect you this way?"

Her eyes snapped open to see Tyler, tall, lean, and male. The pulse that had been trying to settle sped up again. Would there ever be a time he didn't affect her? He crouched down in front of her. "A customer came in with me or Olivia would be back here with you. You all right?"

"I have money," she said, her voice shaky and filled with wonder.

"Yes, you do." His hand swept her hair back from her face. "What's the first thing you plan to do with it?"

She shook her head, swallowed. For so long she hadn't had the freedom to have choices. "I don't know."

He smiled gently at her. "That's a first coming from a woman."

Before she knew it she was smiling back at him. "I can't believe it myself."

From one moment to the next Tyler became aware that they were holding hands, their breaths mingling, her lips close to his. His breath snagged. The desire that was never far from the surface when Jana was near emerged. Her smile dissolved and he knew she was as aware of him as he was aware of her. He forced himself to release her hands and come to his feet. "I better let you get back to work."

"Y-yes." Jana stood, some of the happiness she'd felt earlier gone. Tyler might be attracted to her, but he wasn't going to follow through on it. And she knew it was because he still didn't trust her.

Olivia had just finished writing up the sales of several bath and body products to a repeat customer when she heard the front door open. "Thank you, Elaine. As always it was a pleasure helping you."

"Thanks, Olivia. Goodbye." The woman turned and stopped dead in her tracks.

Olivia looked beyond the woman and saw the reason. Julian Cortez was back. He looked mouthwatering and sexy in a white shirt, navy blue blazer and slacks. He would attract admirers wherever he went just as her ex-husband had. She wanted to believe he was just as superficial, but somehow she couldn't.

"Hello, Olivia," he greeted, then nodded at the customer.

"Well, hello." The woman extended her hand. "I don't think I've had the pleasure. I'm Elaine Parsons."

"Julian Cortez." The handshake was brief, although it was obvious Elaine wanted to prolong it. "Let me get the door for you."

Olivia saw Elaine's quick frown. She hadn't expected that. Elaine was single and beautiful, and one of the new breed of women who didn't wait for the man to make the first move.

"Thank you." As she passed him, she shoved her card in the pocket of his coat. "Call me sometime and we'll have drinks."

"That would be nice. Goodbye." Julian closed the door and turned to see Olivia frowning at him. "I told you I'd be back," he said with a slow smile.

"Since you just made a date with Elaine, I can't imagine why."

Now he was the one frowning. "No, I didn't."

"I heard you say 'that would be nice.' You can't deny it."

"I don't intend to," he told her. "It's a nice way of saying thanks, but no thanks. I only want to go out with you."

Olivia flushed with embarrassment.

"Dr. Cortez, who is taking care of your patients while you're here?" Jana asked, entering the room from the back, with Tyler behind her.

"I'm between appointments," he told her. "Ms. Street. Mr. Maxwell." He didn't know why they all traded a look. He just hoped they weren't going to gang up on him to keep him from dating Olivia. He was having a hard enough time without their interference.

"Call me Tyler." Olivia's brother took Jana's arm. "I'll be going. Walk with me to the door."

She resisted for a moment, then allowed him to lead her away. At least the brother was on his side, Julian thought. "I thought I might buy some new sheets for my bedroom."

Olivia flushed. He hoped that meant she had imagined him sharing the bed with her. "What size?"

"King." Wouldn't she be surprised to know he'd never made love to a woman in his bed? And only a handful had ever been in his penthouse apartment. He didn't like tearful good-byes.

"This way please."

Julian followed, noting the sway of her hips, the shapely body. He'd never thought of a woman as being cuddly, but Olivia was and it wasn't because she barely came to his shoulder. It was something innate about her that made him want to hold her, keep her safe, and keep that beautiful smile on her face.

"Are you trying to coordinate with any particular color or theme?" She stopped in front of a shelf filled with sheets ranging in different hues and patterns.

He hadn't thought that far. "I like yellow."

She frowned up at him. He smiled, wondering if she recalled that she had on yellow when they'd first met. "But I'm open to suggestions."

"I'd say stick with a neutral tone to make them more visual and less tiring." She opened a package of sheets. "These are Yves Delorme. They are one hundred percent Egyptian combed cotton. Feel."

He'd rather feel her and she him. Her hands were small and dainty. It didn't take much effort on his part to imagine them on his body or his on her. His hands joined hers on the sheet, noting the difference, his hard to her soft, just like their bodies would be when they came together and blended into one.

Olivia knew he had intentionally touched her. She snatched hers away. His remained on the sheet, deliberately gliding over where hers had been.

"I don't think I've ever felt anything as soft."

She swallowed, linking her fingers together in front of herself. "This set is fifteen hundred dollars."

He blinked. "I beg your pardon?"

She smiled, a slow heart-stopping smile, for the first time. "Shall I get you a glass of water?"

He looked back at the king-sized set and shook his head. "Guess I forgot where I was."

"Don't feel bad. I've been in business for almost six years and Tyler still has the same reaction," she said.

"Thanks. That does make me feel somewhat better."

She moved to another shelf. "These are from the same manufacturer, but plain. They retail for three hundred dollars." She opened the package. "If you close your eyes you won't be able to tell the difference. The weave is what makes the other set costlier."

"I'll take these."

"Please come with me and I'll write you up." She pulled the sheets from the shelf.

Julian caught the other end. "I'll take them."

"I'll need them for the stock number."

"You won't be writing the number now," he said reasonably.

It seemed silly to argue over who would carry the sheets. Besides, men had offered to carry things for her before and she hadn't thought a thing about it. That was the problem with Julian, she thought too much about him. "Thank you."

Stepping around her desk, she waved him to a seat. Dutifully he placed the set on the far corner of the desk. "Please have a seat. Can I get you anything to drink? Wine, tea or water?"

"Yes," he said still standing.

"What would you like?"

"I'd like wine tomorrow night with our dinner."

She took her seat and reached for the receipt book and pen. "I've already given you my answer."

"One I refuse to accept."

Her head came up. "Arrogance is not an endearing quality."

"It's not arrogance to go after what you want," he told her. "If I gave up every time there was an obstacle, I wouldn't be a doctor."

"How so?"

Julian didn't like talking about his past. Even his friends and associates knew very little about him. It had been a slip of the tongue. "It's unimportant."

"Sorry, I didn't mean to pry." She went back to writing the receipt.

"Why don't you have a computer?" he asked, oddly irritated with her.

"Because it's too impersonal," she said, still looking down. "I apologize if it's taking too long."

"It's not taking too long," he snapped.

Her head came up again. "Which one of us are you angry with?"

The question was so blunt and dead on, he was speechless for a moment.

"Well?"

"I don't like to talk about my past or remember it," he admitted to her.

"Then we have something in common." She tore off the receipt, picked up the sheets and slid them into a white shopping bag strewn with poppies. Rounding the desk, she gave him the bag and receipt.

"Thank you. Improper laundering can shorten the life of sheets, so I've included laundering instructions or you can return them to us and we'll have them done for you."

"I need proper care too."

She folded her arms across her chest. "Women probably fall at your feet like ripe fruit."

"They see this face and not the man. I thought you'd look deeper than that," he said, unable to hide his annoyance with her. "How would you like to be judged on what others thought?"

She didn't have to think long for the answer and recall that she had been. "I wouldn't like it."

"Then why are you judging me that way?" he asked.

If he hadn't looked so frustrated, she might have evaded the truth. "Because it's safer."

"But is it fair? You struck me as a fair woman."

"Why are you pushing this?"

He started to shrug, then stopped. "You intrigue me."

"Because I said no?" She needed the answer and hoped he was honest enough to give it to her.

"That just made me more determined. Almost from the moment I saw you in the emergency room, I wanted to ask you out." He smiled. "I was tired and on my way home, but seeing you made me feel . . . I don't know. Refreshed."

He frowned and Olivia knew he hadn't meant to say the word. More importantly it meant he was telling the truth. "Why haven't you tried to persuade me to go out with you by reminding me that you helped me at the hospital?"

"Because one had nothing to do with the other."

The front door opened and a couple entered. Jana, who had been trying to look busy, moved to greet them. Olivia turned back to Julian. He appeared sincere, but so had her ex-husband. Her hands dropped to her side. "The answer remains no. Now, if you'll excuse me."

Julian stared at her a long time, then he nodded abruptly and spun on his heels. He reached the door the same time the customer who had just come in was leaving. The door had barely closed before Jana rushed over to Olivia. "Please say you accepted this time?"

Olivia wrapped her arms around herself and watched Julian jaywalk across the street. "It wouldn't have worked."

"How do you know if you don't give it a chance?" Jana asked. "Men like that don't have to go to this much trouble to get a date. And purchasing bed linen is not high on the list for single men."

"He almost had a coronary when I quoted fifteen hundred dollars for a set." Olivia glanced at Jana before looking back at Julian. He opened the back door to his car, tossed the package into the seat, then slid inside. She didn't expect the pang of regret to hit her so fast or so deep.

Jana watched him as well. "As I said, I'm probably the last person to give advice about a man, but if Tyler trusted him enough to give you two time alone, I'd say go for it."

Olivia bit her lower lip. "I won't be used again."

"Despite his ticking me off, I'd have to side with Tyler. Dr. Cortez is not playing with you. Believe me, I can tell," Jana said.

"I guess you've had a lot of experience with men."

"Enough," Jana answered, finding it easier to be more open each time she talked with Olivia. "If you want Julian, go after him."

Olivia started for the door. Julian backed out and sped off. "It's too late." She couldn't keep the misery from her voice.

Jana came to stand beside her. "Call his office."

Olivia was already shaking her head. "It's probably for the best." She firmly turned away from the window. "Enough talk about Julian. After we close I'll drive to my bank on the way home for your money. Have you decided what you plan to do first?"

"Pay my hospital bill and the painter. And I don't want an argument out of you about the painter."

A pleased smile washed across Olivia's face. "You sure? It will take a big chunk out of your money."

Jana sighed. "Yes, and I better take care of them before I weaken. I've been sneaking peeks at the black leather dress in the Gucci window every time we pass."

"I've learned not to look, but I've had more practice," Olivia said.

"You have a way of making me feel normal when I'm not sure I've ever been," Jana confessed. "If you hadn't helped, I don't know where I'd be today. You saved me."

"I'm just glad I was there."

The door opened and Julian rushed into the store. "I'm double-parked. How about drinks?"

Olivia saw the Maserati parked directly in front of the store. "The police are very diligent and unforgiving in this area," she warned him.

Julian took a step closer. "How about a walk in the park?"

"I'll be in the back," Jana said, and hurried away.

Neither Julian nor Olivia took their eyes from each other. "You'll be towed."

"Coffee before work at Starbucks in the morning?"

His handsome face was etched with determination. Jana was right. Perhaps it was time she stopped remembering the past and started living in the present. She did want to go out with him. All men weren't like her ex-husband and it was unfair of her to keep thinking so.

She took a deep breath. "I distinctly remember you asking me out to dinner and I'm holding you to it."

A slow grin spread over Julian's face. Olivia barely kept from sighing dreamily. "How about eight tomorrow night at Chamberlain's?"

"Sorry, I promised Griffin we'd go to a carnival. Is next Saturday all right?"

"It will have to be, but feel free to call me if you and Griffin want company or you want to go out earlier," he told her.

"I'll keep that in mind." Quickly going to the desk, Olivia scribbled her address and phone number on the back of a business card. "Now get going before you get a ticket. Here are my address and phone number, in case something comes up."

He would have liked to say it wouldn't, but he knew better. Emergencies didn't care what doctors had planned. He clutched the card in his hand. "You won't regret it."

"If I thought that, I wouldn't have said yes."

He laughed. "You're something. Until next Saturday night."

Olivia watched him through the window as he hurried to his car and drove off. She'd done it now and she couldn't wait to see how it turned out.

Tyler couldn't concentrate. He kept making stupid errors on the program he was working on. His team was scheduled to meet in a week to compile data for the systems program for one of the largest manufacturing firms in the country. Errors were unacceptable. He knew that, yet he couldn't clear his mind and work.

Finally accepting he wasn't going to do any more for today, he hit save, then exited the program. He was a man who saw solutions when others saw chaos. So why was he having so much difficulty trying to figure Jana out? And why was he worried that with the commission she might leave?

Tyler rubbed the back of his neck and admitted what he'd been trying to ignore. He was seriously attracted to the woman. Perhaps because she was such an enigma. Bad girl one moment, vulnerable the next. With a commission of almost three thousand dollars, she wouldn't have to stay in a garage apartment or buy secondhand clothes. And that's what bothered him. The possibility of her leaving.

He heard the front door open and got up and walked out of his office. Olivia and Jana were laughing and talking like old friends. "I thought you two would be home an hour ago."

Both women wiggled their hands, then held out one foot, then the other.

On their feet were jelly flip-flops. "We stopped by this little salon on Preston," Olivia replied. "Jana insisted on treating us to a pedicure and manicure."

"She has to be ready for her date," Jana explained.

"Dr. Cortez?" Tyler guessed.

Olivia's smile slipped a fraction. She stared at Tyler. "We're going to Chamberlain's for dinner next Saturday night."

"He double-parked to come back and ask Olivia again." Jana grinned at Tyler. "He was so desperate he suggested a walk in the park."

"A man who looks like Julian isn't nor ever will be desperate," Olivia said.

"We'll let Tyler decide," Jana said. "When is the last time you asked a woman to go for a walk in the park?"

"I can't recall ever doing so."

"We'll take that as a no." Jana went to the front door. "Good night."

"You aren't staying for dinner?" Tyler asked.

Jana held up a handled bag with the logo of a popular restaurant. "I stopped on the way. Good night."

Tyler was reluctant to let her go. "Will it keep? I told Wanda about your sale and she made a special dinner."

Jana stopped and stared.

"Shrimp étouffée," he said. "Of course Griffin wanted his shrimp deep fried."

"You're kidding, right?"

"Why don't you come see for yourself?" Feeling inordinately pleased, he took her arm. "Olivia, Griffin is in the media room playing computer games."

"I'll get him and be right back." She took the bag from Jana. "Let me put this in the refrigerator."

"Thank you," Jana said as Tyler swept her along. "This isn't the way to the kitchen."

"I thought we'd eat on the portico."

She stopped again the moment she stepped on the terrazzo floor and saw the table draped with an ecru linen tablecloth and lotus candles. The backyard was lush with blooming flowers and dense greenery. The tranquil blue water of the pool was twenty feet away.

He felt her tremble. She looked up at him. His heart clenched at the glimmer of tears in her eyes. He had never felt so helpless. He'd never before felt anything so right. "It's just a celebration dinner."

She swallowed and swallowed again. "I guess I'm still excited about everything. Don't mind me."

It was more than that, but he let it slide. "Have a seat and I'll get you a glass of wine."

He popped the cork and filled her glass, then his. Griffin and Olivia came out and he filled their glasses as well. Griffin would have cranberry juice as usual. Hoping he wasn't too obvious, Tyler took a seat beside Jana, blessed their food, then lifted his glass. "To more great sales and commissions."

Glasses clinked, and they drank. Picking up the serving dish, he served Jana.

"That's enough," she told him.

"Wanda's feelings will be hurt if this is in the refrigerator in the morning." He intended to make sure she ate and took care of herself.

Jana frowned at the large chunk of French bread he put on her bread plate. "I won't be able to fit into my clothes if I keep eating like this."

"Adding a few pounds never hurt anyone." He passed the dish to Olivia.

"Spoken like a diplomatic man," Jana said with a smile.

"Mama, did you know children in France drink wine?" Griffin speared a giant, batter-fried shrimp. "Rene in my class is from Paris and he says his mother lets him have wine with the grown-ups."

Olivia picked up her fork. "When we move to France I'll give it all the consideration it deserves."

"That means no," Griffin said to Jana.

Jana paused in eating, the happiness of moments ago muted as she recalled drinking with her mother. No matter how she tried, she couldn't remember them eating together. They had never shared the deep bond Griffin and Olivia shared. What might life have been like if an adult had stepped in and tried to help her?

"The food taste all right?" Tyler asked, his brow puckered in a frown.

"It's fine." Jana caught Griffin's attention. "You're very fortunate to have a mother who loves you. When you're grown you'll learn that drinking before you're old enough isn't that much fun."

"Did you?" he asked with wide-eyed curiosity.

"Griffin, don't ask personal questions of adults," Olivia admonished.

Jana refused to look at Tyler. She made her tense body relax. "It's all right, Olivia. Yes, I did, but I wish every day that I hadn't. You'll be happier and have more friends if you wait."

Griffin screwed up his face. "I like having friends. I guess I'll wait." He turned to his mother. "Wanda fixed a chocolate cake for dessert."

"And since I know you're going to stop playing with your broccoli and carrots and eat them, you can have a slice." Olivia smiled sweetly.

Griffin pierced a floret. "My team won the soccer game today. I scored right between Anthony's legs." He giggled. "It was great."

The conversation soon revolved around Griffin's day at camp. No one looked at Jana differently. Slowly, she started to eat again. Tyler and Olivia weren't condemning her, but they might if they knew what else she had done.

How do you explain to a seven-year-old boy that his mother is going on a date? Olivia had thought about the answer to that question all afternoon and now that they were finished with Griffin's bath, his prayers and story time, she still hadn't come up with an answer. She saw no reason to put off telling him.

She tucked the covers under his arms and smoothed her hand over his head. Her heart swelled with love. She'd do anything, go through anything to keep him safe and happy.

"Griffin, I want to talk to you."

"I'm not going to drink wine until I'm older, I promise," he told her.

"It's about something else." She took a deep breath and decided to go for it. As long as he didn't have to go to sleep Griffin would happily let her sit there half the night. "Do you remember when Uncle Tyler was dating Courtney last year?"

His face scrunched up. "She wanted you to take away my video games."

Olivia had forgotten that. Courtney hadn't approved of video games or much else as Olivia remembered. Tyler might have been serious about her, but she was too rigid in her Christian beliefs. "Remember they went to the movies, to dinner, church? When a man takes a woman out by themselves it's called a date. A man has asked me on a dinner date with him next Saturday night."

Griffin sprang up in bed. "He's not going to want you to take away my video games, is he?"

Olivia briefly wondered if her son was too deeply involved in his games, then recalled him giving up the money he had been saving for a new game to the children with their mothers in the shelter. "No."

He stared at her a long time. "Cindi in my class said a boy stood up her big sister and she cried herself to sleep."

When Olivia had been seven, she and her friends had talked about dolls and tea parties. "Julian, Dr. Cortez, is a doctor. There's always the possibility that he'll be needed to help someone who is sick, but otherwise he won't stand me up."

"Cindi said the boy who stood her sister up said he was sick, but their cousin saw him at the movies with another girl."

Olivia felt on firmer ground. "Then Cindi's sister is better off. Anyone who would lie is not worth her time."

"Will I meet him?"

Smiling, she hugged him. "Yes."

"Does Uncle Tyler know him?" he asked, apparently still a bit apprehensive.

"Yes, and he likes Dr. Cortez," she said, hoping to ease the concern she saw on her son's face.

"If Uncle Tyler likes him, I guess you can go out with him," he said, lying back down.

Olivia almost expected him to give her a curfew. "Thank you, Griffin, but if you don't like him I won't go out with him."

"You must like him since you've never gone on a date before."

Brilliant child and I wouldn't have it any other way. "We're just getting to know each other."

"He better not make you cry."

"He won't. Now, close your eyes and go to sleep." Olivia didn't have any doubt she could keep the promise. She'd never cry over a man again. Kissing Griffin on the forehead, she turned off the lamp on the nightstand and tiptoed out of the room.

Saturday morning Jana was showered and dressed by seven thirty. Last night Tyler had received a phone call while they were clearing the table and she had helped Olivia with the dishes. She had been glad. She hadn't wanted him asking questions about her past. Olivia was too well mannered. Tyler was too inquisitive not to want to know more.

In the kitchen she prepared toast and scrambled eggs, congratulating herself even though a good portion of the eggs stuck to the skillet. She'd do better the next time. Wouldn't her mother be surprised, she thought as she munched on the toast.

Jana had left a message about the commission on her answering machine and told her not to worry. Her mother hadn't called back. Jana hadn't been surprised. Her mother seldom called. She always said she was so busy.

The knock on the door caused her to frown. She glanced at the clock on the stove. 8:04. Olivia didn't usually leave until 8:10. They'd gotten into the habit of leaving early and had stuck with it.

Opening the door, she saw Tyler in his usual dress of shirt and jeans. "Can I come in?" he asked.

She hesitated, then stepped back. They may as well get the drill over. "Of course."

"You sleep all right out here?" he asked, stepping inside. "The fumes all gone?"

"Yes." Tyler made her nervous. "Would you like a cup of coffee?"

His mouth twitched. "No chocolate?"

"No." She started for the kitchen and sensed him following.

"You make it?"

"Unless there's a genie somewhere that I'm not aware of." She opened the cabinet and took down a mug. "Have a seat. I'd offer you breakfast, but I haven't got the hang of making eggs yet."

"Coffee's all right."

Pouring him a cup, she took it to the table where he was seated. "Black?"

"Fine." His large hands wrapped around the mug.

Jana stared at his long fingers. A week ago, the first thing she would have thought about was how they might pleasure her.

"Something wrong?"

She almost jumped, annoyed that that was *exactly* what she had been thinking. "Not at all." She picked up her cup. "Now that we're finished with the small talk, what is it you want to tell me?"

"For starters, I want to thank you. You didn't have to tell us about your past to help Griffin."

Jana was taken aback. She shrugged to cover it. "He's a good kid. Someone should learn from my mistakes."

"Olivia can't stop singing your praises. Seems you have a knack for satisfying customers," he said, watching her over the rim of his cup.

She flinched in spite of herself. She didn't doubt Tyler had seen the reaction. Very little got past him. "I hate to rush you, but I don't want my boss thinking I'm getting lazy."

"Can't have that." Getting up, Tyler rinsed the cup in the sink. "I'll walk you down."

"That isn't necessary."

He cocked his head to one side. "I didn't say it was. Get that little purse of yours, and let's go."

He was bossy and pushy, but she did as he requested. As soon as she returned, he took her arm and started out the door. His touch was light, but she felt the imprint of his strong-fingered hand almost as if it were a brand, and smelled the citrus cologne that made her want to investigate. She couldn't deny that he excited her. Men had only been useful in the past if she could use them to her benefit. It was strange, but Tyler appealed to her because she couldn't.

Just as they reached the bottom of the steps, Olivia and Griffin came out of the house. "Good morning. I see you're ready to go."

"Morning, Ms. Franklin," Griffin said.

"Good morning, Griffin, Olivia." Jana shoved the strap of her purse higher on her arm. She turned to face Tyler and found him much too close and too tempting. "Goodbye."

"See you tonight."

There was a promise, almost a caress, in his deep voice, in the way his hands slowly trailed from her arm. Jana couldn't stop the shiver of awareness that raced through her. She'd never been attracted to the brainy, studious type. She'd considered them boring and suspected they'd be the same way in bed.

Somehow she knew that wouldn't be the case with Tyler . . . if she let things get that far. He didn't know who she was and, if he did, he wouldn't be staring at her with need just beneath the surface. He was possibly the only man who'd ever wanted her for her, and not just because of her bad reputation.

And he was the one man she dared not become involved with.

9

Throughout the day, Jana tried to remember that Tyler was off limits, but it was difficult. They were too aware of each other. As soon as they arrived home from work, Jana escaped to her apartment. She didn't want to see Tyler. Caring about any man was asking for trouble.

She'd barely entered the bedroom before there was a faint knock on the door. She tensed, fear and anticipation pulsing through her. She caught herself checking her lipstick and hair in the mirror over the dresser. Annoyed with herself, she went to the door. Instead of Tyler, Griffin stared up at her. She tried to convince herself she wasn't disappointed.

"Mama said dinner is ready. Uncle Tyler had to go out of town, so it's just us." Griffin grinned up at her. "I can have his slice of chocolate cake."

She smiled down at the child. It was so easy to like him. "I think your mother will have something to say about that."

His smile disappeared, his head lowered. "You're probably right," he said, then he looked up again with a grin on his face. "But it won't hurt to ask her." Then he turned and ran back down the stairs.

Jana followed. What wouldn't she give for his enthusiasm and optimism.

Jana decided later on that night that Olivia should have been a politician as she watched Olivia and Griffin riding in the box cars of the slow-moving train around the track at the small carnival in a field near their church in Oak Cliff. The happy sounds of children's laughter, the beckoning spiels of barkers, and the screams of those on more adventurous rides filled the air.

Jana hadn't stood a chance of staying home alone and working on getting her apartment in order with the pieces from the attic. That could wait, Olivia had said. She and Tyler could help her with that later. She hadn't wanted Jana to be home by herself. Jana hadn't put up too much of an argument.

Jana didn't like being alone or that Tyler kept intruding into her thoughts. No man had ever done that before. But then, she'd never known a man as complicated and as unpredictable as Tyler.

"Hi, Jana," Griffin called as he and Olivia passed her.

Smiling, Jana waved. She'd finally convinced Olivia to let him call her by her first name.

"Excuse me. Don't I know you?"

Jana tensed. Slowly she looked at the man who had spoken. Thankfully she didn't recognize him. "No." She turned back to the ride, which was coming to a halt.

"Then I'd definitely like to. You here with anyone?"

She threw him a disinterested look. "Yes. Have a great night." Then she walked over to meet Olivia and Griffin. She hadn't even sized the man up to figure out if he could afford her. Jana smiled. What had once been automatic was no longer that way.

"What's next?" she asked Olivia.

"Home," Olivia answered.

"Mama, can I ride the mini roller coaster?" Griffin asked. "I promise I'll get up the first time you wake me up for Sunday school."

Olivia's mouth twitched. "The *first* time? You mean I won't have to come back and drag you out of bed by your feet?"

He giggled. "You never do that."

"I might if you don't get up in the morning." She handed him the tickets to the ride a few feet away. "No running."

Griffin didn't run, but he did a fast walk. Olivia and Jana followed. "Hold tight," Olivia called out to Griffin, stopping at the rail.

"He's a great kid," Jana said, meaning it. Olivia had a right to be proud. Briefly she thought of her own childhood. "He's lucky he has you."

"Thanks, but I'm the one blessed." Olivia kept her eyes on Griffin as the roller coaster climbed twenty feet in the air before swooping down again. The joyful screams of the children followed.

Jana knew Olivia wasn't just mouthing words. Despite the pain of her divorce, she'd turned her life around. Jana was determined to do the same.

"You want to go with us to Sunday school in the morning?" Olivia asked. "Afterwards we're going to the shelter to distribute the baskets."

"I really need to get the apartment in order," Jana said. The more she went out, the more chance there was of being recognized. Then, too, no matter what Tyler said, if Olivia's congregation learned about Jana's past they might not like it that she'd brought a woman like Jana into their midst.

"Maybe next time." Olivia went to meet Griffin as the ride came to a slow halt.

Jana blew out a breath and stuck her hands in her pockets. She'd disappointed Olivia, but that was better than her friends turning against her. Jana was an expert on how people smiled in your face, then cut your throat.

She'd been one of them.

Jana didn't get out of bed until after ten Sunday morning. She'd suspected Olivia would invite her over for breakfast and she had. Jana had been able to truthfully say she hadn't gotten up yet. If Courtney had been critical of Tyler, what would she and those like her at the church say about Jana? It didn't bear thinking about.

Jana dressed and went to the house. She might as well make good use of the time and bring the things out of the attic. Unlocking the door with the spare key Olivia had left in a flowerpot near the back door, she went inside.

On the second floor, she couldn't help but look longingly down the hall toward Tyler's room. It was too easy to imagine them together. Shaking away the thought, she continued to the attic. The crammed space resembled an antique store. Oriental rugs, chests, tables, and lamps abounded. Olivia said the various pieces represented her mother's change in taste through the years.

Deciding the best way to go about transferring the things she had picked out was to put everything near the door, she began doing just that. The rose velvet ottoman trimmed with fluffs of ribbon fringe was first. Next came the sleek console table she planned to put behind the sofa. She admired the six-arm handcrafted wooden candelabrum lamp with scalloped shades, then picked it up, turned to add it to her pile, and bumped into someone.

She gasped, losing her grip on the lamp. Tyler moved quickly to take it from her. Her hand pressed to her rapidly beating heart. She wasn't sure it was entirely due to fright. "You scared me."

"Sorry." He placed the lamp on the floor. "I heard noises and came to investigate."

"I decided to finish with the apartment," she explained, wishing he had on a shirt. Apparently he'd been asleep. At least he'd taken time to pull on his jeans. Now if he'd just fasten them.

"I thought you might have gone to church with Olivia. They're distributing the baskets afterwards, aren't they?"

The guilt came hurtling back. "They don't need me."

"Everybody needs someone," he said softly.

She certainly couldn't argue that point.

"Want help?"

He wasn't going to make her feel guilty, but he was making her hot. "Don't you think you should finish dressing?" He was too distracting with his roped muscles and tempting mouth.

His smile was slow, lazy and sexy as hell. He had the audacity to absently run his hand across his muscled chest. "Sorry. Be back in a minute."

Jana discovered he was just as tempting from behind. He had a tight butt. She easily imagined her nails pressed into his flesh as they came together. Her pulse quickened.

She swiped her hand over her face. Tyler certainly was making it difficult to stick to her promise of no men.

"What do you want to move first?" he asked when he returned.

You to the North Pole. "Can you take the tufted area rug? I'll finish putting things together while you're gone."

He hefted the 8 x 11-foot flowered rug on his broad shoulder as if it weighed nothing. "Be back in a sec."

Don't hurry on my account, Jana thought. *Perhaps I'll cool down by the time you return.* Blowing out a breath, she went to get the patchwork bedding set.

Working together, they were able to get everything in place in less than an hour. The rose tones worked beautifully in the open room and were repeated in the bedroom. With the pieces she'd been able to add, the place took on a stylishness it had lacked before. She'd even been able to fashion blush pink draperies over the sofa and chair as slip cover.

"You certainly know how to spruce up a place," Tyler said. "But it's missing something. Be right back."

Jana frowned, then went to fluff the patchwork pillows on the sofa. They'd been a part of the bedding group and helped tie the bedroom to the living area.

"Here you are."

Jana looked up and her breath caught. He had a large bouquet of red and yellow roses.

"I remembered you had flowers on the table the day you cleaned the apartment."

Jana wondered if he also remembered her trying to seduce him. Her question was answered in the next second when his eyes narrowed, his gaze going to her mouth. Heat and desire shot through her. She swallowed.

"Where is the vase?"

Jana snapped out of her daze. "I'll get it." In the kitchen she took the vase from beneath the sink, with hands that refused to steady. When she straightened, Tyler was there to put the roses inside. Jana filled the tall glass cylinder with water.

"We work well together," he said.

Jana didn't want to think of what else they might do well together. She was not going to repeat the pattern of going to bed with any man she found attractive. "Thank you."

"Anytime. Now that the place is finished, you want to go grab a bite to eat?"

It hit her at once. "You haven't eaten, have you?"

"No."

She couldn't recall anyone putting her needs before their own, unless they wanted something in return. Could she do any less? No matter how busy she was, she couldn't stop thinking about Olivia. She'd done so much for Jana and asked for so little in return.

Jana took a deep breath. "What time do you think they'll deliver the baskets?"

"Around twelve."

She glanced at the clock on the stove. It was seven minutes after eleven. "If we grab something quick, maybe you could take me to church."

His smile made her breath catch. "It will be my pleasure."

"Thanks." She turned, then spun back. "What should I wear?"

"Doesn't matter," Tyler told her. "God looks at the heart."

"He might, but others might not share His or your view." She almost added that she'd bet Courtney wouldn't.

"The blue pinstripe blouse and black pants you had on Tuesday will work," he said.

That he remembered what she had worn caused warmth to curl through her. "I'll hurry." Jana went to get dressed, taking her roses to the bedroom with her.

Jana quickly discovered that thinking about something and doing it were entirely two different things. They'd arrived just as the two-story white brick church was dismissing. As Tyler had indicated, the parishioners' clothes ranged from simple to elegant. Jana hadn't seen so many hats since she attended Derby Day in London last year. When the match was over, she'd left with the winning team's captain, an Italian count.

"You all right?"

She could lie, but the death grip on her purse said differently. "I'll get there."

He nodded and they went inside. It became apparent immediately that Tyler was as well liked as Olivia. He was greeted repeatedly with handshakes, pats on the back and one-armed masculine hugs.

Jana noticed he also received his share of longing looks from women. She was the recipient of a few glares. It seemed she wasn't the only one dealing with issues. "I can't do this." She wasn't aware she'd said the words aloud until she felt Tyler's hand close gently around her arm. She couldn't bring herself to look at him. "I have to leave."

"Jana, I'm so glad you changed your mind!"

Jana lifted her head. Olivia and Maggie were making their way through the crowd toward them. She was trapped.

"You'll have another friend if you'll give Maggie a chance," Tyler whispered.

Jana bit her lip and said nothing. People like her didn't have friends. Did they?

Both women wore pleased smiles when they stopped directly in front of her. Greetings were exchanged.

"Jana, we had some last-minute donations. Do you mind making a few more baskets?" Olivia asked.

"I was afraid I might mangle them," Maggie said with a smile, her hand on her stomach. "I should have known you'd show up."

Jana recalled what she had said about God sending someone to those in need. If He did, it wouldn't be a woman like Jana.

Olivia frowned. "Jana, are you all right? You didn't hurt yourself moving stuff, did you?"

"Do you want to sit down?" Maggie asked, her voice just as concerned as Olivia's had been. "The lounge is down the hallway."

"Do you want to leave?" Tyler asked.

It was her choice. She could stay and help as she wanted to or let her past continue to trample deeper underfoot what little self-respect she had left. She opened her mouth to say she was leaving, then remembered something else: Tyler saying the one place she was always welcome was the church. The other was his and Olivia's home.

Jana made herself meet his gaze. His was filled with understanding and patience. If she had somehow gotten Tyler on her side, perhaps there was a chance for her not to mess this up as she had messed up her life.

Her gaze went back to Olivia and Maggie. "I'm staying. Let's get started on those baskets."

Each woman joyfully took her arm. "Let's go," Olivia said. "Men can't come because of the security of the shelter. Thanks, Tyler, for bringing her. We'll see you later. Bye."

"I'll be waiting," he said softly.

Jana couldn't help but think the words held a special meaning just for her. If she was right, what did she plan to do about it?

There were few dry eyes at the women's shelter by the time the last basket and toy had been given out. Olivia's effort made a lot of women and their children happy. During the presentations and the reception that followed, Jana noticed Olivia stayed in the background. If Maggie was right about God sending someone to those in need, He couldn't have sent a better person than Olivia to Jana.

"Olivia, you did it," Jana said on the drive home.

"God did it," Olivia said. "I was just a conduit. At least for a moment or two the women and children were able to forget they were in a shelter and why." She glanced in the rear-view mirror at Griffin dozing in the back seat. "Children understand the least and suffer the most."

Jana knew that firsthand. "But not today, thanks to you."

Olivia nodded and turned onto their street. "We were so busy I didn't get a chance to ask about the apartment. How much did you get done?"

"Everything." Excitement rang in Jana's voice. "Do you have time to come and see?"

"I'd love to." Olivia turned into the driveway and parked in the garage. "Griffin will probably be fully awake by the time we hit the back door. But if not, I'll get him settled and come right back out."

"Do you need any help?" Jana asked, unbuckling her seat belt.

"Thanks, but I can manage." Olivia reached for the door handle.

"See you in a bit." Jana got out of the SUV, waited until she saw that Griffin was walking on his own, then went to the apartment.

She was just as pleased with the results as she had been earlier. A moment of doubt hit when she saw the improvised chair covering. She heard someone on the stairs and went to the door. Griffin led the way. Behind him were his mother and Tyler.

"I came to make sure you don't start talking about decorating and lose track of time," Tyler said. "Griffin and I are hungry."

"Not after two pieces of cake and no telling how much punch," Olivia countered.

Griffin seemed resigned rather than surprised by his mother's announcement. "Grandmother Maxwell says mothers have eyes in the back of their head," he said to Jana. "Did yours?"

"No." Jana's mother had been too busy with her lovers to pay any attention to her only child. Jana stepped aside for them to enter.

"Oh, Jana, it's beautiful." Olivia's warm gaze took in everything. "It doesn't seem like the same place. I want to see the bedroom." She took off in that direction.

"Where's the television?" Griffin asked, his brows puckered.

Jana smiled with Tyler. "I've never watched much television."

"Then what did you do?" he asked innocently.

Her smile vanished.

"Anything she wanted to," Tyler answered for her. "I've told you you're only limited by your imagination. Come on, let's go light the fire."

Griffin took off in a flash, only to stop at the door and face Jana. "Jana, if Mama says it's all right you can borrow my portable DVD or my books."

Jana was stunned, touched and almost speechless. "Thank you, Griffin. I may take you up on the offer."

Smiling, he took off again. After a long look, Tyler went with him.

"He's never offered before to loan out his things." Olivia crossed from the bedroom door to Jana. "He likes you. We all do."

But would they if her past were revealed? "I like you too."

Olivia looped her arm with Jana's. "Come on, let's go laze by the pool and watch Tyler grill."

Tyler kept one eye on the steaks and burgers and the other on Jana. He hadn't missed the startled expression on her face when Griffin asked what she did, nor the uncomfortable silence that followed.

"Uncle Tyler, is it ready yet?" Griffin asked for the third time in less than a minute.

"Let's see." Tyler turned over the ground chuck patties. Smoke wafted up. Olivia and Jana laughed and he glanced in their direction. He went still as he looked at Jana though the smoke. He suddenly remembered where he'd seen her. Blood pounded in his veins.

"Uncle Tyler?"

"Sorry." Scooping up the meat with the long-handled spatula, Tyler slid the patty onto Griffin's bun. "Come and get it, ladies."

Olivia and Jana got up from the cushioned lounge chairs by the pool and started toward them. The pinched expression Jana wore earlier was gone. She appeared relaxed . . . until she caught him staring at her.

She went as motionless as a deer caught in the beam of headlights. "W-what is it?

"Just thinking. Grab a plate," he instructed. He was glad to see she did just that, but she kept throwing cautious looks at him.

To put her at ease, Tyler busied himself preparing his own plate. He could use his skill on the computer to find out about her past or he could let things play out.

At the table, Jana was the first one to bow her head for the blessing. Afterwards she lifted her head and stared across the table at him as soon as Olivia finished saying the blessing. Her eyes were filled with wariness. The sight tore at him and he thought, whatever her story, it was obvious she was trying to get her life together now. After all, everyone deserved a second chance.

"Ladies, since the men did the cooking, you're doing the dishes, right?" he said.

"That's right," Griffin said around a mouthful of food.

Olivia cut into her ribeye. "Women cook *and* wash dishes all the time. Why can't you two?"

"What do you think, Jana?" Tyler asked, loading his baked potato with sour cream, chives, cheese, and bacon bits.

For a moment he thought she was going to keep playing with her garden salad. "I think Wanda would appreciate Tyler and Griffin's help with dishes in the morning."

Griffin straightened in his chair. Tyler scowled. Olivia and Jana laughed.

"I don't think there's any need to go that far." If he could keep that smile on her face he wouldn't mind kitchen duty. "I'll handle the dishes."

"I'll help," Griffin offered, but clearly his heart wasn't in it.

"I'm doing the dishes," Jana surprised them all by saying. "It's the least I can do. If someone will show me how to work the dishwasher."

"I'll show you," Griffin volunteered. "Afterwards we can watch a movie. Have you ever seen *Aladdin*?"

Tyler and Olivia groaned.

"No, but I'd love to," Jana said.

"Great," Griffin said, finishing off his burger. "I'll show you how to use the DVD player, too."

"Thank you, Griffin."

Jana was smiling again. For that pleasure, Tyler could sit through the thousandth showing of Griffin's favorite movie.

Jana couldn't believe she was actually watching an animated movie and enjoying it. Or did her enjoyment stem from the people around her?

This is the way a family is supposed to be . . . warm, supportive, loving, tolerant . . . and for a while I'm part of it.

Jana snuck a peek at Tyler, slouched in the side chair next to her, his long legs stretched out in front of him, his hands linked over his flat stomach. Her lips twitched at the glazed look in his eyes. Obviously he'd rather be watching something else. He was there because Griffin had insisted the entire family watch *Aladdin*. Jana would never forget Griffin catching her hand and saying, "You, too, Jana."

She'd taken a seat on the sofa in the media room with Griffin next to her and Olivia on the other side of him. Griffin had accepted her. That complete trust coupled with that of Olivia was humbling. Jana would do anything to keep their faith in her.

Tyler was another story. He kept confusing her. This afternoon at the cookout when he'd looked at her, his eyes piercing, she had felt threatened. She couldn't explain why she sensed that emotion. She just knew she had.

Suddenly Tyler looked at her and winked. The apprehension that had begun to build again disappeared. She winked back, then sobered. Tyler wasn't for her. She returned to watching the movie, unable to deny that she was beginning to wish he was.

Tyler sensed Jana was watching him more than the movie, and that was all right with him. He was doing the same thing.

Too bad real life couldn't be wrapped up in a pretty package like a lot of movies. The good guys didn't always win. Often they were kicked in the teeth again and again, or went down for the count and never got up.

Without friends or family to help you through the rough times and be there with you to celebrate the good times, life could be vicious and cruel. It certainly had been to Olivia, but Griffin had been the result. No one had to tell him she'd go through it again because it had given her the most precious thing in her life, her son. It had also made her more self-assured.

He'd often heard the saying that "What doesn't kill you will make you stronger." He had to agree. Courtney walking out of his life had torn him apart at the time, but now he was a better man, a more tolerant man because of it.

On the fifty-one-inch screen he watched the wedding scene of a thief and a princess. Aladdin had been redeemed. Most people weren't all good or all bad. There were degrees.

"We can watch *Finding Nemo* next." Griffin took Jana's hand and went to find the DVD. "It's the story of a father fish that goes searching for his son who was kidnapped. My dad would do that if I got kidnapped, wouldn't he, Mama?"

Olivia's smile was strained. "Yes, he would and so would your uncle, your grandparents and all the people who love you, and most of all, so would I."

Tyler knew some people changed. Others, like Griffin's father, would be bastards until the day they died. Tyler threw a glace at Jana, who patiently sat on the floor with Griffin as he told her about the various movies in his collection. She wasn't the same woman she'd been a week, or even a day ago.

She'd have her chance.

Jana had never been nervous when a man walked her to the door. It was a foregone conclusion where they'd end up. With Tyler that wasn't going to happen no matter how her body yearned and heated when he was near her.

Opening the door, she moistened her lips. "Thank you for helping me with the apartment."

"You're welcome."

She swallowed. "Good night. I'll see you in the morning."

He shook his head. "I'll be busy working."

"Because you helped me and spent time with Griffin," she correctly guessed.

"And I'd do it again," he told her easily.

She didn't doubt him. Tyler was a man of principle.

"I better let you get to bed, but there is one other thing I need to do," he said, staring at her lips.

His head slowly descended toward hers. Jana quivered in anticipation. His warm lips touched hers. She simply melted in his arms. She didn't try to think of the best way to manipulate him, how to tease him until he was crazy with desire or how much she could get out of him. The truth was she couldn't think at all, but she could feel.

Wild emotions surged through her, heating her blood, deepening the craving in the junction of her thighs. The kiss was like nothing she had ever experienced before. Her hands curled in the fabric of his shirt, then moved around his neck to bring him closer, closer still. Her body pressed against his, needing, wanting.

His head lifted, his breathing harsh and labored. "I knew you'd take the top of my head off," he rasped, his voice rough and incredible sexy.

"I'm not sure mine is too steady," she said, trying to get her breathing under control.

He laughed, a wonderful sound that made joy dance in her heart. "Your beautiful head is still attached to your incredible body." He kissed her quickly on the lips. "Sleep tight. I'll be underground for a few days."

She didn't want to let him go. She had the incredible urge to ask him just to hold her again.

His eyes narrowed. "You all right?"

She drew her arms to her sides. "How can you ask after a kiss like that?" She'd meant it as teasing. He didn't smile as she'd wanted him to.

His thumb tenderly grazed her bottom lip. "My mother has a saying. Take joy where you can find it. Don't waste it looking for trouble."

Men didn't mention their mothers to her. Nor did they hold and look at her as if she were precious. "Don't forget to eat and take care of yourself."

That time he smiled. "Yes, ma'am."

"Good night," Jana said and went inside. She was turning back the floral duvet on her bed when she thought of another difference between the past men in her life and Tyler. He respected her.

Jana hadn't known she could miss a man as much as she missed Tyler. They'd only kissed, but a kiss like none other she'd ever experienced. She hadn't thought she was the type to go weak-kneed over a man. The second their lips fused Tyler had shown her how wrong she was. The revelation was frightening and exhilarating. She wasn't as jaded as she'd thought.

It was Wednesday and she hadn't seen him since Sunday night, but each day she'd found a note slipped under her door.

The words were simple, but telling. *Hope you had a great day,* on Monday. On Tuesday he'd written, *How about a non-animated movie when I come up for air?* Jana saved the notes like a schoolgirl and didn't feel silly for doing so.

At least she didn't have time to brood. The shop had been busy most of the day. Both she and Olivia were needed on the floor. She'd just finished writing the receipt for a customer who'd purchased two sets of towels when Priscilla Haynes walked in. Jana stiffened in shock and fear.

With Priscilla was Mrs. Robert Fulton. Both women's mouths were pinched. Priscilla's eyes were filled with hatred, Mrs. Fulton's with annoyance. Their gazes raked over her, then they moved toward Olivia, who was helping a couple select bedding.

"Hello, Olivia. We need to speak with you at once," Priscilla told her, not bothering to keep her voice down.

Jana began to tremble. Of all the scenarios she'd envisioned, she had never thought Priscilla and Olivia would be on a first-name basis.

Olivia's smile was strained. "Hello, Priscilla. Mrs. Fulton. As you can see I'm with a customer. I'll be with you when I finish."

"If you don't stop and hear what we have to say, you may not have any customers," Priscilla snapped, her gaze cutting back to Jana. Her threat brought activity in the shop to a halt. The young couple with Olivia edged away as if expecting an altercation.

"Please excuse me," Olivia said to the wary couple, then spoke to Priscilla. "I can tell you're upset, but whatever it is will have to wait. Please come back later."

Priscilla's chin lifted. "Perhaps I was wrong to come here and warn you about the slut you have working for you."

Jana wasn't sure if the gasp came from her or Olivia. Slowly, one by one, everyone in the shop followed the direction of Priscilla's hate-filled stare.

"Priscilla, please leave," Olivia said, her voice tight with anger.

Priscilla whipped back around. "You'd defend *that slut* after she's whored her way from one end of the country to another? Her first husband threw her out of their bedroom naked when he caught her with his business associate."

Jana wanted to sink through the floor in shame. She wanted to run, to escape, but her feet were glued to the floor.

"She'll go after any man with money. She doesn't care how old or how lewd the act. She shouldn't be allowed to be in the room with decent women," Priscilla ranted. "Last year she dared attend the funeral of a man she'd been mistress to, flaunting herself in front of the grieving woman and her children."

Olivia stared at Jana mutely, begging her to deny the claims. Jana couldn't, and she knew it was about to get worse.

"Her own father has disowned her. She and her mother are cut from the same dirty, amoral cloth." Priscilla took two steps toward Jana. "But she underestimated her appeal when she tried to get her ex-husband back. His grandmother let it be known that whoever was a friend of Jana was not a friend of hers. Since then Jana has been on a slow descent into the cesspool where she belongs."

"Jana?" Olivia finally managed to say. "Is this true?"

Jana's throat was so tight she couldn't speak.

"She'd as soon lie as look at you. You don't socialize much since you had Griffin, but don't take my word for it, ask any of our crowd. She's no good. She had the nerve to crash a party at my house. I had her thrown out." Priscilla spoke to Olivia. "No one is going to shop here as long as she stays. Isn't that right, Cynthia?"

Mrs. Fulton, who had ignored Jana since Priscilla spoke, didn't hesitate. "Unless she goes, you can cancel my order."

"No," Jana said, her voice choked. She stepped forward, finally able to move. "No. I'll leave. It's not her fault. She . . ." Jana felt the tears clog her throat and fill her eyes. To cry in front of these women would be the ultimate humiliation. "I'll go." She quickly walked into the back for her purse, then ran out the front door, knowing as she did that she couldn't run fast enough to leave her past behind.

10

Tyler beat his deadline by a hair's-breath. Kicking back in his chair, he called his team members, checking to ensure that they were all on schedule and ready for the job Friday in Las Vegas. They were.

He decided to drive to Midnight Dreams. He didn't try to deny that the reason was to see Jana. He'd missed her. When he came downstairs this morning, she had already left.

He was on the walkway leading to the garage when he saw Jana heading for the stairs leading to her apartment. She was sobbing. His heart jumped into his throat. He glanced wildly around for Olivia before running to Jana.

"What's the matter? Where's Olivia?"

Jana fought against his hold, shaking her head. Realizing she was hysterical, he shook her. "Jana, where's Olivia?"

She shuddered, her head remained downcast. "At the shop."

"What happened? What is it?"

She pushed against his hold. "Let me go."

"No! Not until you tell me what's going on."

"It's over. My past finally caught up with me," she said.

"You're not making sense."

She pushed ineffectively against him again. "Ask Priscilla Haynes. She would be happy to explain everything to you. She had everyone at the store hanging on every word."

His stomach knotted, but he didn't let her go. "I'm asking you."

She looked up at him, her dark eyes flared. "All right, I'll tell you. Any man with the right price can have me and I'm never cheap. You could never afford me, Tyler. I thought it was ironic, my line of work now, considering all the time I've spent in bed."

Tyler let his hands fall away from her.

Her laugh was ragged. "Didn't want to hear it after all?" She turned around. "It won't take me long to pack and you can fumigate the place." She ran up the stairs to her apartment.

For a long moment Tyler couldn't move. He'd always known she was hiding something dark in her past, but hadn't dreamed it was that. Sure, she'd initially come on to Julian and him, but not once since then had Tyler seen her act inappropriately with any man. If anything, she tended to avoid men when she first began working at Midnight Dreams.

His thoughts veered to Olivia. Priscilla was status-conscious and could be vindictive. He threw a glance toward Jana's closed door and started toward his truck.

He was halfway to the garage when Olivia pulled up. By the time he reached her she had gotten out of the SUV.

"You know," she said.

His gut clenched. "Jana told me."

Olivia placed a hand on her arm. "The person Priscilla described is not the woman we both know."

The knot in his gut eased. "You don't have to convince me. Come on. She's packing."

"She can't leave," Olivia said, her brow creased with worry.

"She's not," Tyler said, heading for the stairs. Without knocking, he opened the door.

Jana, her suitcase in her hand, stopped abruptly on her headlong flight out of the apartment when she saw them. "Come to fumigate already?"

Tyler ignored her baiting words. "Running away won't solve anything."

Jana tossed her head. "I'm just moving on. You couldn't have expected me to stay here. I'm used to better," she said, but her voice trembled.

"You didn't seem in a hurry to leave before now," he pointed out.

She shrugged carelessly. "Priscilla just made me move up my time schedule. Besides, you should be throwing a party."

"How about throwing one if you stay?" Tyler asked softly.

Longing darkened her eyes. She swallowed.

Olivia came to stand beside Tyler. "You don't have to go."

"Priscilla doesn't make idle threats. You'll lose business. If I go, perhaps Mrs. Fulton won't cancel." Her grip on the suitcase tightened. "Both women wield a lot of power. I've learned the hard way that you can't go against them."

"I've already given Mrs. Fulton a full refund despite her signing a sales receipt that said there was no refund on special orders," Olivia told her. "I don't want her business. No one threatens me."

"They woke the sleeping tigress," Tyler said, proudly grinning down at his sister.

Jana stared at them as if they had lost their minds. "You'll lose customers. Don't you understand that?"

"No one dictates to me who I can hire or who my friends are."

Tears streamed down Jana's cheeks. "Don't you understand? She was telling the truth. I don't inspire loyalty in anyone, not even my parents. And I've never had a friend."

"You do now," Tyler said, brushing the tear from Jana's cheek with his thumb.

Longing went through her. She wanted to accept the comfort he offered, but she couldn't. "I'm not worth Olivia putting her business in jeopardy. One of the owners of Bliss is my ex-husband's wife, Claire. If I stay, you won't get another product. I can't blame her."

Jana made herself look at Tyler. "He caught me cheating on him. When I didn't get the divorce settlement I wanted, I tried to hurt him by embellishing details of affairs with as many men as I could think of. I was vicious and mean and very convincing."

Tyler tried to absorb what she was telling him and he did to a certain point, but he was more concerned with the tears shimmering in Jana's eyes, the way her voice kept breaking. She was hurting. How could he condemn her? He hadn't lived the life of a saint.

"I've always done business with Brooke," Olivia said, referring to Bliss.

Jana hated what she had to do next, but she had to make them listen. "Brooke hates me just as much as Claire. I used the man she thought she was in love with to pass the time while waiting for my next victim." She swallowed the tears clogging her throat. "I'm no good. Men were playthings to me."

"*Were,*" Tyler repeated. "What changed your way of thinking?"

He deserved that much truth. "I finally realized that all the time I thought I was using men and being in control of my life, they were the ones in control. Worse, they were using me."

Tyler wanted to reach out to her, but sensed she'd fight like a cornered animal. "You learned. You told me you wanted a chance to start over. You have that here. You can be strong enough to face up to your past and accept the blame or you can run."

Tears she couldn't control no matter how hard she tried streamed down her cheeks. Angrily Jana brushed them away. "You don't know what you're asking. People look at me as if I'm filth on the bottom of their shoes, and they're right."

"I don't, and neither does Olivia," Tyler said, gently.

"Tyler's right. I'm going back to the store. The last time it closed in the middle of the day was when Griffin had the chicken pox and wanted me to come home and Stella had gone to lunch. I need you at the shop since Stella resigned." Olivia opened the door. "I'll be waiting."

"People won't shop if I'm there," Jana tried again.

Olivia's gaze didn't waver. "People make mistakes. I wouldn't be much of a Christian if I didn't understand that. I'll be waiting for you." Turning, she went out the door.

Tyler remained unmoved. "Are you going to let her do this alone?"

Jana took a deep shuddering breath. "She'll be fine once I'm gone."

"Do you honestly believe she'll let them think they've won?"

Olivia was sweet, but she wasn't a pushover. "No."

"At least you have that right."

Jana dropped the suitcase and paced in frustration. "You were right about me. How can you want me anywhere near you or your family after what I've told you?"

"Because not one of us is sinless, because you're not the same woman," he said quietly.

Her gaze cut to him. "I came on to you *and* Dr. Cortez."

"That you did." His head tilted to one side. "You were trying to get under my skin enough to let you go. I imagine most women try to come on to him because of the way he looks."

"You're just as handsome," she blurted. Her eyes widened at her blunder. "You're trying to make me out as this good person. You're wrong. I only look out for myself."

"If so, Olivia and I were wrong about you. Our mistake." Tyler stepped back and opened the door. "If you want to go back to your old life, I can't stop you."

Frustration welled up within Jana. "You're better off without me."

He left the door open and walked over to her. "Would the Jana you described have been concerned with other people's welfare? Would she have given back money?" Stepping around her, he picked up several large bills on the coffee table. "Your commission?"

She wrapped her arms around herself when she really wanted to wrap them around him, understanding at last the full extent of what her lifestyle had cost her. "The money wasn't mine any longer. The order has been canceled."

"But you weren't aware of that before Olivia told you. At least give yourself credit for not wanting to take money that you hadn't earned. It never would have crossed the mind of the woman Priscilla was talking about." He went to her. "I know it's not going to be easy. You hurt a lot of people and they aren't going to easily forget, if at all. All you can do is show them that that person is gone."

"They hate me." She couldn't stand it if he hated her.

"Can you blame them?"

"No. No, I can't."

"Then don't waste time or tears on something you can't change, use it on something you can fix and that's showing them the woman Olivia and I have come to know and respect. I'm going to the shop to help Olivia. You want to come with me?"

"I can't." Stepping around him, she picked up her suitcase. "Please thank Olivia for me. Goodbye, Tyler."

"I don't want you to go," he said softly.

She stopped, hesitated, then continued. He followed and watched her determined steps across the yard. "If you want to change, why are you running away?" *Why are you running away from me?* he wanted to ask.

She turned and stared at him with tortured eyes. "Can't you understand this is the first unselfish act in my life?"

Tyler thundered down the stairs to her. "Are you sure that's the reason, Jana? Or is it because you don't have the courage to face the people you wronged? Once again, you're taking the easy way out, leaving Olivia to be the brunt of snide remarks."

"I can't stay!" she screamed.

"Then go," he said. He pulled out his wallet. Angry at her refusal to stay and fight, he snatched up her hand and slapped the money into her palm, closing her fingers over the bills. "Take it. I don't want you sleeping in a rat trap."

Not waiting for her to say anything, he went to his truck and drove off. He refused to look back.

Midnight Dreams was eerily quiet. Olivia walked around the shop, rearranging, straightening where there was no need. This was her dream, her chance for financial independence. She'd started with a loan of five thousand dollars from Tyler. Last year she had grossed close to $2 million dollars. The downturn of the economy hadn't affected her business.

Priscilla's revelation could.

Olivia turned from smoothing her hand over the linen on the bed and glanced out the window. There were quiet periods in any business. Was this one of those times or had the grapevine already started? If so, so be it. Never again would she shy away from the truth to save face. She'd done that when she refused to tell anyone the real reason she filed for divorce from Aaron.

She sighed. She could just imagine the field day gossipers like Priscilla would have if they learned her horrible secret. She'd do anything to keep that from happening. Griffin would be safe at all cost.

The door opened and she looked around as Tyler came through the door. "Jana?"

"She's gone," he said, unable to keep the despair and anger from his voice.

Olivia went to him. "I wanted her to stay, but it had to be her choice. I think you were beginning to like her."

He shrugged, picked up a candle from a shelf in an uncharacteristic nervous motion. "Doesn't matter."

She curved her arm around his waist and leaned into him. "Relationships have never been easy for either of us."

"Seems that way." He held her away from him. "If this gets ugly, can you stay afloat?"

The corner of her mouth tilted. "With a penny-pincher for a brother, what do you think?"

He almost relaxed. "But money is only part of it. You've put so much into this place to make it successful. It's a part of you."

"You'd understand that better than most people." She looked around the shop. "If I can survive Aaron, I can survive this."

The door opened; both turned. An elderly couple entered.

"I thought it was Jana," Tyler said.

"I'm sorry," Olivia said before going to the couple.

Tyler looked though the plate glass window. "Jana, where are you?"

Jana sat on the concrete bench at the bus stop with her suitcase in her lap. On one side of her was a young woman with a baby asleep in a stroller. On the other was a robust woman in a white maid's uniform. Neither had said a word since Jana sat down between them twenty minutes ago. Why should they? They were strangers. Nothing connected them except they were all waiting for the same bus.

Jana swallowed the painful lump in her throat. She hadn't been foolish enough to not take any of the money. She'd left the money Tyler tried to give her and all of the commission except $100. Although it was considerably more money than she had the night she met Olivia and Tyler, it wouldn't last long.

I don't want you sleeping in a rat trap.

Tyler's words came back to haunt her. She'd taken enough from them. She just wished she knew what to do next.

A late-model convertible sports car cruised to a stop in front of the bus bench, ignoring the angry blasts of horns behind it. "A woman as gorgeous as you shouldn't be waiting for a bus. Hop in," urged the driver.

The full-figured woman sitting on Jana's right nudged her with her elbow. "He's talking to you."

"Why can't he be talking to me?" the young girl in a halter and shorts asked, her voice peeved.

"Because, although that baby might prove you don't mind what he has in mind, the car's a two-seater," the older woman said.

"I don't want him anyway," the young woman said, crossing her legs.

"Come on, honey. Let's go have drinks and talk," the driver cajoled.

The woman harrumphed and mumbled, "Who does he think he's fooling?"

"Well, go on," the young woman said. "But don't get caught like I did. Babies sure cut into your fun."

Jana looked down into the carriage. The baby was sleeping peacefully. She couldn't imagine Olivia thinking Griffin spoiled her fun.

"Screw it. You aren't the only woman in town." The car sped off.

Jana didn't even bother to lift her head. "How old is your baby?"

"Two months," the young mother sighed. "Mama has to spend the night where she works. She broke her glasses and I brought her extra pair." She pouted her deep red lips. "I had planned on going out with my friends tonight, but now I have to keep Yamika. It isn't fair."

"She probably feels the same way," the older woman said.

The young woman's head whipped around. "What's that supposed to mean?"

"Just what it sounded like." The older woman stood as the city bus pulled up.

"At least a man wanted me." The young mother efficiently broke down the carriage, ignoring the unhappy cries of the abruptly awakened baby that was tucked under her arm like a football. "You'd have to *pay* a man."

"That's what you think." The older woman tossed over her shoulder as she got on the bus.

Mumbling, the young mother and crying baby followed. For a crazy moment Jana wanted to snatch the baby from its mother. No child should have to grow up as she did, knowing they were unwanted, winding up so desperate for that love they'd do anything.

"You coming, miss?" asked the driver.

Jana came upright, but couldn't make herself get on the bus. She was afraid if she did she'd end up miserable, alone, and bitter.

"Guess not," the bus driver said. The door closed. The bus pulled off, leaving Jana staring after it.

11

Julian had called Dallas home since he'd been in medical school. He loved the city, but detested the heavy traffic, which seemed to grow worse with each passing month. On his way home from his office, he eased to a stop behind another car in the stop-and-go, bumper-to-bumper traffic on Preston. If he took a right at the next light he'd run into Highland Park Village. Perhaps he could talk Olivia into a latte. It was time for her store to close.

The traffic light changed and he pulled off. That might not be a good idea. He didn't want Olivia to think he was crowding her. One wrong move and he was history. He planned on being on his best behavior. He couldn't recall ever being so anxious for a date or so concerned about making a good impression.

Women had been coming on to him since he was old enough for the first adolescent urges. He'd never been bothered by the prospect of one leaving because there was always another to take her place. Inching up in traffic, he winced at how callous that sounded. He'd be very disturbed if Olivia walked away and he had yet to even kiss her.

He wanted to. Badly. Perhaps he'd catch her in a weak moment. Flicking on the signal, he took the next turn onto Mockingbird. No guts, no glory.

To help put her at ease about his unexpected visit, perhaps he'd tell her how much he enjoyed the sheets. On second thought that might not be wise since he didn't seem to be able to stop thinking about her on those sheets with him. His body reacted predictably. He shifted to ease the sudden uncomfortable fit of his pants and tried to think of anything to get his mind off Olivia, her arms open, her eyes hot and filled with desire as she reached for him.

He glanced around, trying to find anything else of interest. The condos, the flowers, the trees lining the two-lane street, the man and woman at the bus—he whipped his head back around to do a double take. That couldn't have been Janet with a suitcase. He looked into his rearview mirror, but the thick crepe myrtle bushes next to the street obscured his view. But what if it had been?

He was more anxious than ever to see Olivia. No one had to tell him that, if Janet had betrayed Olivia's faith and trust in her, Olivia would be deeply hurt. Like his mother, Olivia was a sensitive and compassionate woman. No one should take advantage of her. Even as the thought swept through his mind, he fought with the knowledge that whatever it was that drew him to her probably wouldn't last and he'd move on. Or would he?

"It was business as usual as far as I could tell." Olivia looked at the receipts for the day. "So you can stop worrying."

Tyler gave Olivia a thumb's-up although they both knew that that might change tomorrow or the next day, but there was no sense worrying about it now. "We better get home."

Putting the receipt book in the desk drawer, she came to her feet. "Are you going to look for her?"

"I wouldn't know where," Tyler said, frustration in his voice.

Rounding the desk, Olivia lightly touched his arm. "At least she knows where to find us."

He nodded, but the knowledge didn't help. Each time he thought of Jana having to go back to that hotel, his stomach clenched. He'd called twice. If she was there, she wasn't registered under either name.

"Let me lock the door and I'll get my—" All of a sudden Olivia went still and stared.

Tyler turned around. Disappointment hit him hard when he saw it was Dr. Cortez and not Jana.

"Hello," Julian said, thinking he should have followed his first instincts and kept on toward home. Neither looked pleased to see him. "I hope you don't mind me dropping by."

"I'm sorry, Julian." Olivia went to him. "I didn't expect you."

His gaze went from Olivia's unhappy face to Tyler's tight-lipped expression. "Guess I was right."

"Right about what?" Twin furrows raced across Olivia's forehead.

"The reason Janet was sitting at the bus stop with her suitcase," he answered.

"What? Where?" Tyler asked, striding toward Julian.

"Julian, please, where did you see her?" Olivia asked, her voice just as anxious.

"About five blocks up Mockingbird," he told them. "At least I think it was her. I only caught a glimpse of her when I passed. She had a suitcase . . ." His voice trailed off as Tyler raced for the door. Frowning as deeply as Olivia had earlier, Julian turned back to her. "Do you mind telling me what's going on?"

Olivia shook her head. "I'm not sure I can do that, although I appreciate you telling us about Jana. We were worried about her."

"Jana? I saw Janet," he corrected.

Olivia threaded her hand through her hair. "Jana is Janet."

"If you're trying to confuse me, you're doing a good job."

She signed, realizing there was little sense in not telling him everything. "All right, I'll explain, but on one condition."

"Name it?"

"That you listen objectively and keep an open mind."

He didn't hesitate. "All right."

Olivia glanced at her watch. "If I'm not home in ten minutes for dinner, Griffin will call. After dinner we're playing his new video basketball game."

Julian was as surprised as he was intrigued. He was also a man who took opportunity when he saw it. "Perhaps if I followed you home there'd be a few minutes for us to talk. Then, too, I could meet Griffin and let him know his mother will be in good hands since you said you haven't dated much."

Olivia tilted her pretty head to one side. "It sounds reasonable, but why do I get the feeling you have an ulterior motive?"

Julian grinned. "Because you're a perceptive woman. I already plan to wrangle an invitation to stay for dinner."

His honesty coupled with that engaging smile made her laugh. Perhaps Julian would be good for her. "Consider yourself invited."

Tyler didn't draw an easy breath until he saw Jana sitting on the bench at the bus stop. He whipped into a driveway of a neat pink brick home and slammed out of the truck. Her head down, her shoulders slumped, she looked to be a woman mired in hopelessness and despair. If she'd let him, he'd show her that her life didn't have to be that way.

"Jana," he called to her when he was several feet away.

Instantly she looked up. Her lips trembled. By the time he reached her, tears were streaming down her cheek. His arms went around her, holding her tight against him. "It's all right."

She held him just as tightly. "I didn't have anyplace to go."

"You do now." Ordering himself to let her go when he had been so afraid that he'd never get the chance to hold her again, he picked up her suitcase and started for his truck.

She was still sniffling when he gently urged her into the truck and gave her his handkerchief. Rounding the truck, he climbed inside and fastened his seat belt. When she made no attempt to fasten hers, he did it for her, then started the motor. "We're going home."

She glanced up with the remnants of tears glittering in her eyes. "The police passed twice and looked me over. I was afraid they'd stop the next time."

Tyler shifted the truck into reverse, backed out into the street and took off the way he had come. "How long have you been there?"

"Since I left the house." She crumpled the handkerchief in her hand. "I couldn't seem to make myself get on the bus."

"I'm glad." In a matter of minutes he turned the corner onto his street. "Julian saw you at the bus stop."

She swallowed. "After a while I stopped paying much attention to the cars passing by."

Tyler knew men often trolled the area looking to pick up coeds from nearby Southern Methodist University. Traffic was always extremely congested. "Turned them all down, huh?"

She looked up. "It never crossed my mind to do otherwise."

"Of course not," he said and pulled into the driveway that curved around the side of the house to the garage in the back. "Want to bet that car in front of the house belongs to Julian?"

Jana twisted uneasily in her seat. "I don't want to see anyone. Could you please let Olivia know I'm all right?"

Parking the truck in the garage, Tyler opened her door. "She'd feel better and believe it more if it came from you."

"I have to face people," she said.

"Exactly." His hands spanned her small waist and lifted her out of the truck. "Come on. You need some fluids after sitting outside for three hours."

"The bench was shaded."

Holding her hand, he continued into the house. "It was still in the nineties today, and the bench was stone."

She rubbed her posterior. "Don't remind me."

He stopped and looked down at her. "I'd be glad to do that for you."

Her mouth opened, but nothing came out. She blinked rapidly as tears formed.

"I'm sorry," he quickly said, using his thumb to wipe away the moisture. "I was trying to make you laugh. Courtney always said I had a weird sense of humor."

The tears stopped immediately. "You mentioned her before."

"So I did." He entered the kitchen and saw Olivia, Julian and Griffin at the table eating. "I see you started without us."

Olivia squealed and was up in a flash. She and Jana hugged and wiped away tears with the tissues Tyler handed each of them.

"Those are happy tears, right, Mama?" Griffin asked, rising as well.

With one last sniff, Olivia held out her arm and her son came. "Yes, they are."

"I'm glad," he said. "Jana can play the video game with us if she wants."

"Trying to get another victim?" Tyler pulled out a chair for Jana.

Griffin grinned. "I'm playing Dr. Cortez after Mama. He promised he can take losing."

Julian smiled and casually sipped his iced tea. "A bit confident, aren't you?"

"That's the only way to be, Mama says." Griffin rounded the table and took his seat. "But considering you're a guest and you're taking Mama to dinner, I'll go easy on you."

"Griffin!" Olivia admonished, but she was laughing.

Jana took the seat Tyler held out. This felt right. Her gaze went to Olivia, then Tyler sitting beside her, piling food on her plate. They cared. Hearing about her past hadn't made them care any less. "Griffin, thanks but I think I'll just watch."

"How about you, Uncle Tyler?"

Tyler filled Jana's glass with iced tea. He was sticking as close to Jana as possible. "I'll sit with Jana and watch."

Julian looked at the score on the wide-screen television, which made it all the more glaring. Griffin had decimated him. The media room was ominously quiet. Griffin, who wore a big grin on his face, apparently wasn't concerned with or cared that grown-ups were supposed to win, which meant double for guests.

"I tried to warn you."

Julian looked at the little boy sitting cross-legged in a pair of shorts and polo shirt, the instrument of Julian's destruction still in his small hands. Apparently Griffin wasn't concerned about rubbing it in either.

"Griffin." Olivia said her son's name softly, but he lowered his head as if in contrition.

Julian was close enough to see that the smile remained on the young boy's face. Griffin was fiercely competitive with a keen intelligence, nerves of steel and uncanny instincts. Julian had liked him immediately.

"I want a rematch," Julian finally said.

"Not tonight," Olivia said, talking over Griffin's protest. "It's thirty minutes past your bedtime. Protest and the next time you'll go to bed whether or not the game is over."

Griffin began putting up the video equipment. Apparently Olivia didn't bluff.

"Good night, Julian." Tyler stuck out his hand. "Griffin is a whiz with video games and seldom loses."

"Now you tell me," Julian laughed. "Good night."

"Good night, Julian, Olivia," Jana said, then to Griffin. "Perhaps you can teach me sometime."

His grin broadened. "I sure will."

"Good night, Jana. We'll expect you for breakfast in the morning." Olivia told her, her hands on Griffin's shoulders.

"I'll see you then." Jana left the room with Tyler by her side.

"Julian, we haven't had a chance to talk and getting Griffin down for the night during the summer can be an experience." Olivia lovingly wrapped her arms around Griffin and pulled him back against her. "Perhaps if you have time you can come by the shop tomorrow."

"I have surgery in the morning," he said as they slowly walked to the front door. "It would have to be late afternoon."

"You cut on people?" Griffin's eyes widened with awe and pleasure. "Wow!"

"Griffin!" Olivia shook her head. "I'm sorry, Julian."

"It's all right. I've a feeling Griffin is an unusual young man." Julian stopped at the front door. "Are you going to be a surgeon when you grow up?"

"No, sir. I'm going to be like my father," Griffin supplied. "He's a financial planner and owns his own company with my grandfather."

Olivia tensed, her hold on Griffin tightening possessively. Julian knew he had stumbled into forbidden territory, but he didn't know how to back out without causing Olivia any more discomfort or hurting Griffin's feelings by ignoring the comment.

"My dad couldn't make it for Christmas, but he sent me a ton of cool games I wanted." Griffin stared back up at his mother. "Didn't he?"

"Yes," Olivia answered, her face and voice strained. "Your father loves you very much."

"He sure does." Griffin's attention switched back to Julian. "He couldn't make my birthday last year, but he will this time because I'll be eight in September and I'm not a baby anymore."

It wasn't difficult for Julian to figure out that Griffin's father didn't have much, if any, involvement with his son. Julian's father had been the same way. The army had been his first priority, not his family. "You certainly aren't a baby," Julian agreed. "A baby couldn't have beat me so badly, but I'll do better next time."

"How about Saturday night when you pick up Mama?"

Julian glanced at Olivia, glad to see the tension gone from her face. "If your mother doesn't mind, I could come fifteen minutes early."

Griffin whirled around. "Could he, Mama? Please?"

She brushed her hand tenderly over his head. "I suppose."

"Yippee!"

Julian smiled, enjoying the enthusiasm and spontaneity of the young boy. "I'll call tomorrow and let you know what time to expect me. Good night." With his hands in his pockets, Julian strolled to his car. Olivia might want to tell him what was going on with Jana, but he was more interested in the story behind her divorce.

Tyler gripped the money Jana handed him seconds after they entered her apartment. "You should have taken this."

Jana linked her fingers together. "I couldn't. Besides, I didn't need it."

He tried to look at it the way she did, but couldn't. Things might have turned out differently if Julian hadn't seen her. Just the thought of her being alone and in need knotted his stomach. She was safely back, and he had to fight the urge to crush her to him and make love to her. He couldn't. Not until Jana saw the woman he saw. "I have to go out of town tomorrow. I don't expect to be back until Sunday. I'd postpone it if I could."

"Somehow I know that. Have a safe trip."

"I'll see you in the morning." He pulled her into his arms, giving in to the desire to taste her lips, to hold her again. "Good night."

"Wait." She touched his arm.

Tyler stopped immediately, becoming worried when Jana didn't say anything. "What is it?"

She shook her head. "Nothing. Good night."

His finger lifted her chin. "You can ask or tell me anything."

"I just . . . just wondered why Courtney thought you had a weird sense of humor."

That was the last thing he expected her to ask. "I suppose because we never laughed at the same jokes. Come to think of it, we never agreed on much of anything."

"Was she important to you?" Jana asked, knowing she had no right to, but unable to stop herself.

"I was very close to asking her to marry me when she broke off the relationship."

A myriad of emotions pummeled Jana. She tried to feel sorry that the relationship hadn't worked, but couldn't. "Do you still care about her?"

He swept a finger down the side of Jana's face. "No. It just took me a while to realize that it wouldn't have worked."

"Why?"

"We were totally different people. Courtney wanted a perfect man, a man who had no vices. I like to play nickel poker occasionally, drink a beer, laze on the couch, and watch the Sunday game on television."

Jana's eyes widened. She couldn't believe a woman had actually walked away for such minor infractions. "Then she'd crucify me."

"Probably." His mouth twisted wryly. "No matter how I tried I couldn't quite come up to the level Courtney expected of me. It made me more tolerant of other people."

"Like me?"

"Like anyone. No one is perfect in this imperfect world. The best you can do is try. Anything else?"

"No, thank you. And thanks for being there for me. I won't let you or Olivia down."

"Don't let yourself down." His lips brushed gently across her. "Get some rest. Welcome home."

Trembling fingers pressed against her lips, then she smiled and whispered when the door closed behind Tyler. "Thank you, Courtney."

12

Jana went to sleep feeling as if she could conquer the world. However, by the time she followed Olivia into Midnight Dreams the next morning, her knees were shaking, her hands sweaty. Not even remembering Tyler's unshakable support that morning during breakfast helped. "I'm not sure I can do this anymore."

"You can." Olivia took her arm and kept going to the back. "Take a deep breath, push it out slowly, and relax."

"I don't think that will help," Jana said, but she did as Olivia instructed. "Maybe I should have waited a couple of days before coming back."

"Nonsense." Releasing her arm, Olivia took a seat behind her desk and put their purses in the bottom drawer. "You're a friend and a valuable asset to the store."

Friend. Her very first one. "I didn't know what having a friend meant until I met you," she confessed. "As for being an asset . . ."

Olivia booted up the computer before she spoke. "You're staying. I have an eleven-fifteen appointment and I'm leaving you in charge."

Jana's eyes widened. "Me?"

"You'll do fine." Olivia's slim hands danced over the keyboard. "And you can always reach me on my cell."

Jana opened her mouth to argue, then closed it. It was about time she acted as if she had as much confidence in herself as Olivia and Tyler had. "All right. I'll start on dusting."

"Thanks. That's definitely my least favorite thing to do."

Smiling, the tension slowly ebbing, Jana left the office.

Moments after Olivia left, three fashionable women entered the store. Hoping fervently they didn't know her, Jana went to greet them. "Welcome to Midnight Dreams. Is there anything I can help you with or would you like to browse?"

All three gave Jana the once-over. "We'd just like to look," the one in the middle said.

"Please feel free." Jana kept her smile in place although she was sure they'd come to look her over and not the merchandise.

The women went through the motions of picking up a candle here, bath soap there, then inspecting the linen on the bed, all the time their gazes sliding back to Jana.

They knew.

Jana's first instinct was to duck her head in shame and embarrassment; her second was to ask them to leave. She dismissed both inclinations. Yesterday Tyler had asked her if she had enough courage to face up to what she had done. She realized until she did, she'd never put her old life behind her or have the new life she craved.

Putting on her brightest smile, she walked over to them. They crowded together like a covey of quails, apprehension replacing speculation on their faces.

"Are you sure there isn't anything I can show you? I can tell by the way you carry yourselves and those stunning couture outfits you have on that you are discriminating buyers with impeccable taste. Armani, Ralph Lauren, Prada?" Jana said, ticking off the designers. The Kate Spade handbags were almost identical and matched their outfits in hot pink, sun yellow and apple green. "I love Kate Spade bags. I've met her."

"So did we, at a private showing at Neiman's," the one in green, apparently the leader, said. The other two made sure Jana could see the logo on their bags.

"I just love Neiman's, but when it comes to pure indulgence in linen you can't go wrong shopping at Midnight Dreams." Jana ran her hand over the eight-hundred-thread count sheet. "Feel. Can't you just imagine slipping between these after a long day? This is one purchase your husband will thank you for." She'd also noticed the wedding rings. All were more than three carats, but they weren't A-1 colorless. Obviously they were still trying to belong.

One by one, the women brushed their hands across the sheets. Jana could almost hear their sighs. "At five thousand dollars this is the best investment you can make."

"We're just looking," the outspoken one said, but she kept looking at the bed.

"We also have D. Porthault sheets. I'm sure you've heard of the Paris manufacturer." From their blank looks Jana knew they hadn't. "Who in society doesn't know they're the choice of English royalty? Being able to say you have on your bed the same sheets as those Queen Elizabeth sleeps on is priceless. Oprah prefers Anichini. Those are so fabulous the company doesn't even put the thread count on the package. Once you've felt them, you'll know why. They're sublime."

"Where are they?" asked the one in yellow.

Jana almost rubbed her hands together. "This way."

Thirty-seven minutes later the three women left the store, each carrying a shopping bag with a set of sheets. Jana couldn't wait to get to the phone. She didn't want to disturb Olivia, but there was one person she could call. "Tyler, I did it!"

"I could join in the celebration better if I knew what's made you so happy."

Jana laughed out loud. "Three women came in to scope me out and they all left with bed linen."

"Good for you."

"After seeing the set on display for five thousand dollars they considered it a steal to buy a set for nine hundred, especially when they can name drop that Oprah buys the same brand."

"I'm proud of you."

Her chest felt tight. No one had ever said those words to her, but then she couldn't think of too many things she'd done in her life to be proud of . . . until she met Tyler and Olivia.

"Jana?"

"I'm here." She took a steadying breath. "Just thinking how different my life might be if I hadn't met you and Olivia."

"You did. That's all that matters."

"Yes, I did." The door opened and a middle-aged man entered. "Customer. See you when you get back."

"Count on it."

Jana's heart fluttered. "Bye." She hung up the phone, and walked out to meet the customer. "Welcome to Midnight Dreams."

Jana met Olivia at the front door of Midnight Dreams waving sales receipts. "$3,430.98." She was bubbling. "I can't believe it!"

"You have the proof in your hand." Olivia placed her attaché case and sample books on the desk on the sales floor. "With the sale I just completed, we're having a banner day."

"I actually enjoyed selling, even to the three women who came in to size me up." Jana quickly told Olivia everything. "I may make a copy of the sales receipts and frame them."

"You should. It will remind you that you're stronger than you think," Olivia said. "God has a way of reminding us of that from time to time."

Jana didn't know about that. She wasn't high on religion. The people at the church she'd met were nice, but it could have been surface just like she'd been. Gray's grandmother was reportedly a staunch Christian, yet she had tried to ruin Jana's life. "Some of the biggest churchgoers are probably the biggest sinners."

"God understands that all of us can backslide now and then. Regardless of the women's initial motives, you both won."

Jana frowned. "How do you figure that?"

Olivia's smile was patient. "They learned not to be so harsh or quick to judge others, and you learned that with God in the mix, good can come out of bad."

If Jana had ever met a person as optimistic as Olivia, she didn't remember. "You're incredible."

"Not by a long shot. It took me a long time to get where I am and every step was difficult." She leaned against the desk. "When my marriage disintegrated I felt as if my heart was ripped from my body. I couldn't understand why God had given me so much pain. I didn't even begin to understand until I felt Griffin move." Her hand briefly cupped her stomach. "Without the marriage, he wouldn't have been born. He more than makes up for anything I had to endure."

Jana's eyes hardened. "My life is in shambles. I can't see the good in that."

"I don't mean to belittle what you've gone through, but you're more blessed than many people." At Jana's look of disbelief, Olivia continued. "You're safe and healthy. You have a place to stay, a job, food, friends, and you're making more. The women we prepared the baskets for can't say as much," she said.

"Perhaps your defining moment hasn't come or, if it has, you don't realize it yet," Olivia continued. "Just ask yourself one thing, and you don't have to tell me: Would you rather return to your old life or continue to build this new one?"

Jana thought of her privileged and luxurious jet-set life and the people she'd met, most of whom were as superficial and shallow as she, a life where no one cared if she lived or died. "I want to build a new life," she declared firmly.

Olivia didn't act surprised by the answer. "Then, whatever the reason or person that started you on this path did you a favor."

Jana's first instinct was to argue. Corrine Livingston had meant to crush Jana. Wait. Maybe she had simply been trying to protect her family. Wouldn't it be ironic if Jana owed her new life to Gray's protective grandmother. "She probably didn't mean it that way."

"What did I tell you about how God being in the mix changes things?"

The pastor's wife thought the same thing. "Maybe for some people, but not for me."

"For everyone." The phone on the desk rang and Olivia picked up the receiver. "Hello, Midnight Dreams." Her gaze flickered to Jana. "Hello, Julian."

Smiling, Jana moved away.

"If you like we can have lunch here. I'll see you in thirty minutes." Hanging up the phone she told Jana, "Julian will be here in thirty minutes for lunch."

"That will give you enough time to run to the store and get a fresh bouquet of flowers for the table. The tablecloth and candles are already covered."

Olivia frowned. "That's going a bit far. I'm not sure if I want this to go past a couple of friendly dates."

"Yes, you are. You're just scared." Jana handed Olivia her purse from the desk. "Go. I'll set the table."

Olivia didn't move. "There's linen on the top shelf in the back room."

Jana escorted Olivia to the front door. "I know where everything is. Get going. You want to be back in time to freshen up your makeup."

"I wish I knew where this will end. How's that for optimism?" She bit her lip. "I prayed about it, but I just don't know."

"I've been a player long enough to spot another one. Julian is for real, but that doesn't mean things will last," Jana told her frankly.

"There's more to think about than just me. I hadn't considered how much Griffin would like Julian," she said, her voice troubled.

"From what I saw last night, Julian is just as taken with Griffin as Griffin was with him." Jana opened the door. "Scoot."

"All right, I'm going. I'll just have to play this through." Closing the door behind her, Olivia was gone.

"You didn't have to go to this trouble, but I appreciate it." Julian sipped his iced tea. On the ecru-draped table was a bouquet of fresh-cut flowers with roses, daisies and lilies and silver flatware. The air was gently scented with a vanilla candle.

"This is Jana's idea," Olivia admitted.

Julian lifted a brow. "You sure know how to burst a guy's bubble."

Dark chocolate eyes stared back at him. "But if I hadn't wanted the table to look nice, I wouldn't have let her talk me into it."

"You're such a mixture of courage and vulnerability," Julian commented, his fork poised over his salmon salad.

"I'm not vulnerable," she said, pushing her salad around on her plate. "Or very courageous."

Yes, you are, he wanted to say, but he let it slide. He had a pretty good idea both were because of her ex-husband. "I made reservations for eight at Chamberlain's. I thought I'd come by around half past seven."

Her head came up. For a moment there was fear in her eyes. "Griffin likes you. The game with you Saturday is all he talked about."

She'd fight a bear bare-handed to protect her son. "There haven't been many men in his life, right?" Julian said.

Lines radiated across Olivia's forehead. "Griffin has family who love him. My brother and his grandfather are all the men he needs," she said a bit defensively.

"And a mother who would give him the world if she could."

"Of course," she answered immediately.

"So simple and so complex, but then a mother's love always is." He smiled in remembrance. "You remind me of my mother." He chuckled at the shock on Olivia's face. "She loved us unconditionally, and wanted the world for us."

"You have sisters and brothers?"

"A brother." He picked at his salad. "He's a corporal in the army, stationed in Germany. My father is a drill sergeant and he's there as well."

"And your mother?"

His hand flexed. "She died when I was sixteen."

Her small hand covered his. "I'm sorry. That had to be devastating."

"She didn't have to die." He'd never discussed her death with anyone, but the quiet patience and understanding in Olivia's face drew the words from him. "We were on vacation and the doctor misdiagnosed her appendicitis. He sent her home with Maalox." His mouth tightened.

"I begged my daddy to take her to another doctor, but he didn't believe in coddling his soldiers or his family. She lay in bed for almost six hours in excruciating pain, then she seemed fine, the pain gone.

"We found out what was going on a month later when she became ill. The reason the pain subsided was that her appendix had ruptured. The last days of her life were spent in misery that didn't have to happen."

"So you decided to prevent other mothers and children from going through what your family had," she correctly guessed.

"Yes."

"You make her proud."

That had always been his goal. Feeling a little exposed, he pulled his hand back. "What about Jana?"

Olivia slowly put her hand in her lap. If he didn't want her comfort, it shouldn't matter. "I asked Jana if she minded me telling you. Remember your promise not to prejudge." At his nod, she told him of Priscilla's visit. "Jana is no longer that woman. She's proven that each and every day."

"So you keep Jana on despite a threat of losing business?" he asked.

She straightened. "I didn't say anything about losing business."

"You didn't have to," he said tightly. "It's no big jump to know the woman and her cronies wouldn't want around a woman known to go after any man she wants."

"I told you, Jana isn't like that anymore," Olivia defended.

"You've had a chance to see that. They haven't."

She leaned back in her chair. "You're right, but neither did they try to find out. They just assumed and crucified. She had the label, and they didn't look any further."

Julian stared at her a long time and she was afraid she'd revealed too much. "Is this all about Jana or something else?"

"I was just making an observation." Olivia rose and began picking up the plates. "I'm sorry to rush you, but I need to get back on the sales floor."

Julian gathered the flatware. "Despite my reputation as having no bedside manners, I'm a good listener."

She took the things from him and placed them in the sink. "I'll remember that if ever there is a need."

He wasn't going to push it. He had a feeling he might wind up dateless for Saturday night if he did. "You're very loyal. Griffin is a lucky boy."

"I'm the one who's lucky. I can't imagine how my life would be without him in it," she said.

She looked so sad. Julian wanted to hold her, take whatever worried her away. "See you Saturday night. Tell Griffin to get ready."

"I will. But he's already plotting your demise."

He'd gotten her to smile. "I better rent a game or two and practice." His beeper went off. He recognized the number. "Excuse me." He dialed the number on his cell phone. "Dr. Cortez." He listened, then said, "I'm on my way."

His face grave, he turned to Olivia. "I'm needed at the hospital. Care flight is bringing in a patient."

"Go." She briefly touched his arm. "I'll pray for both of you."

"Thank you." He headed for the door at a fast clip. From what the surgical resident had told him, they'd need all the prayers they could get.

Several hours later Julian sat in the doctor's lounge, his head bowed, his fingers laced together between his legs. Tonight their prayers hadn't been answered. Death had won.

For the better part of an hour for the second time that day he'd desperately fought to repair the broken body of a young woman cut from the wreckage of her car. She'd lost control when she tried to go around another car and skidded off an embankment.

He'd known before she was rushed into surgery the first time that the damage to her internal organs might be too severe, the blood loss too great. She'd made it through the first surgery, but had begun to hemorrhage in ICCU and was rushed back into the operating room. Her body had been too weak to survive. She'd never regained consciousness. She'd died while he was still trying to tie off bleeders.

"You did everything you could, Julian."

He lifted his head. Anger snapped in his dark eyes. "It wasn't enough."

Frank Jamison, the surgical resident who had assisted him, merely patted Julian on the shoulder and walked out of the doctor's lounge. They were taught in medical school that you couldn't save them all.

Julian wanted to rage, felt the words clawing at his throat at the senseless waste of life. The girl had been speeding home for her mother's birthday party. He'd had to tell her parents that their eighteen-year-old daughter wouldn't be coming home.

Too keyed up to remain sitting, he got up, paced. The mother had become hysterical. The father had looked dazed, utterly broken.

Julian walked to the window and looked out at the night skyline of downtown Dallas in the distance. Life went on, but not for Patti Ann Young. And for those she left behind, their lives would never be the same.

Changing out of his surgical scrubs into his street clothes, he left, got into his sports sedan and punched in a Sade CD. The singer's mournful voice and sad songs suited his mood. He thought he was driving aimlessly until he turned onto Olivia's street.

He stopped in front of her house. Lights shone from windows on the first floor and upstairs. Leaning his head back, he stared up through the moon roof. The night was beautiful. Death hadn't changed that. The day Julian's mother died the tulips she'd planted bloomed. He'd carried her outside to see them. An hour later she was dead.

Sitting up, he picked up the car phone and punched in Olivia's phone number.

"Hello." Just the sound of Olivia's voice somehow soothed the rough places.

"Hello," she repeated.

"Olivia, it's Julian."

"Julian?" There was a question in her voice, a slight hesitation as if she already knew.

"I wasn't able to save her."

"Oh, Julian, I'm so sorry. Are you still at the hospital?"

He rubbed his hand over his face. "No. I'm parked in front of your house."

"Would you like to come in?"

His getting through the night might depend on it. "Yes."

"I'll be right down."

Julian disconnected the phone and got out of the car. By the time he reached the front porch Olivia was there. He felt an almost overpowering need to hold her. Instead he stepped inside and closed the door behind him.

"Thank you." He rubbed the back of his neck. "As a trauma surgeon you expect the odds to be against you going in. We're trained to put our emotions on automatic."

"You value life, Julian. The person should be mourned."

He slipped his hands into the pockets of his slacks. "You never know the ones who will affect you. Young, old. They all want to live."

Gently she touched his arm. "Come into the kitchen. I'll get you a cup of coffee."

He nodded and followed. Taking a seat at the table, he watched her gather the things needed, her motions quick and efficient. She wore a long pink silk robe with three-quarter length sleeves. She looked adorable.

"I take it Griffin is asleep."

Olivia tossed a smile over her shoulders. "About ten minutes ago." Picking up the tray, she came to the table. Julian stood and helped her, then held out the chair next to him for her. She didn't hesitate to take it. "Thank you. Cream and sugar?"

"Black." He accepted the rose-patterned cup. "Sorry, I probably got you out of bed."

Olivia flushed prettily. "You didn't. I was working on plans for the store."

He nodded toward the pot. "You're not having any?"

The corners of her mouth tilted upward invitingly. "I'd be up half the night if I did."

He sat his cup down. "Yet you went to the trouble to fix coffee for me."

"It was no trouble." She sent him a teasing look. "Don't tell me you're one of those bachelors who can't cook?"

"My mother would have disowned me," he said. "She was from New Orleans and could cook like nobody's business. Her peach cobbler would make you drool. She taught me and my brother to cook and clean."

"Smart woman."

He couldn't agree more, except when she'd chosen her husband. "I take it you are doing the same with the Whiz Kid."

"Absolutely." She smiled at him. "One day a lucky woman is going to get a wonderful man."

"All trained." He relaxed in his chair.

She placed her folded arms on the table. "We're still working on putting the toilet seat down."

He grinned at her. "My money is on you."

She grinned back.

Somehow his gaze dropped to her lips, soft and inviting. He didn't think. He just leaned forward and brushed his against hers. She stiffened.

Before she could draw back, his hand cupped her head, keeping her in place with gentle persuasion instead of force. He felt the tremor that went through her body, felt his own heart rate increase.

Everything within him wanted to deepen the kiss, explore her sweet mouth. Instead he pulled back. Her eyes slowly opened. They were dazed. His weren't much better. The lady packed a wallop. When he really kissed her, it was going to be mind-blowing.

Slowly releasing her, Julian stood and stared down at Olivia. "That wasn't my intention when I arrived, but I'm glad it happened." He held out his hand. "Come on and lock up."

Olivia circled her lips with the tip of her tongue as if searching for the taste of him. Julian's hand clenched, then opened. "If you do that again, I may not be responsible."

Her eyes widened. She seriously thought of repeating the motion. Instead she took his hand and stood.

He squeezed it gently. Without a word he went to the front door. "I'll see you Saturday night. I'll be on my best behavior."

She wasn't sure she wanted him on his best behavior. She'd never known a kiss could empty your mind and fire your body like that.

"Good night and thanks." Opening the door, he closed it after him.

Olivia pressed her trembling fingers to her lips. Julian could turn her inside out, transform her brain into confetti, make her knees week. She grinned and raced up the stairs to her room.

What a man, what a man.

"What's the matter?"

Saturday evening, Olivia spun around in the kitchen with the telephone in her hand. "Wanda's daughter came up unexpectedly from Lubbock. She can't make it to babysit Griffin." Sighing, she hung up the phone.

"I bet she wanted to, and you insisted she not come," Jana guessed.

"Family is important." Olivia removed Griffin's favorite cookies, chocolate chip loaded with walnuts, from the oven and placed the pan on the cooling rack. "I'll just have to cancel. Tyler isn't due home until tomorrow."

"Whoa." Jana turned Olivia around to face her. "You are not canceling your date with Julian. I have the perfect answer."

"I'm open to suggestions." Olivia removed her oven mitts. "I was kind of looking forward to going out with him tonight."

"If you weren't, I'd check your pulse. He's a dish. I'll keep Griffin. Unless you don't trust me with him," Jana added.

"I'll pretend you didn't say that. You don't know how energetic he can be." Olivia thrust her hand through her hair. "He's never still for more than a minute."

"Like his mother."

She smiled. "I'm afraid so."

"Why don't we let Griffin decide?" Jana suggested. "He can teach me how to play the video game."

"With that as a lure, he'll be your new best friend."

"Never can have too many. Let's go find out."

The two women left the kitchen together and found Griffin sitting crossed-legged in the media room playing a video football game. Jana saw no reason not to be up-front. "Griffin, Wanda can't make it. Looks like I'm your sitter, if you don't mind. You can start teaching me how to play."

"Great!" He scooted over on the carpeted floor. "Those are your controls."

Jana threw a quick look at Olivia, then sat beside Griffin and picked up the controls. "I don't suppose you'll take it easy on me because I'm a beginner?"

He looked at her sideways. "I might if we can have cookies and ice cream once Mama leaves on her date with Julian."

Jana laughed. "Nice try. I already heard her tell you at dinner that you can have two cookies, but no ice cream."

He shrugged carelessly. "Uncle Tyler and Grandpa always say you don't get anywhere if you don't try."

Even a seven-year-old had learned that valuable lesson. She was playing catch-up. "What do I do first?"

Griffin proceeded to show her how to work the controls. She quickly caught on, but no matter what she did, Griffin kept her scoreless.

Several minutes later the doorbell interrupted Griffin's total defeat of Jana. Laying the controls aside, he was up in a flash and racing for the door. Jana caught up with him at the door, admiring his restraint when he asked who was at the door since he wasn't tall enough to look through the peephole.

"Is that you, Dr. Cortez?"

"Yes."

Griffin unlocked the door and grabbed Julian's hand, dragging him over the threshold. "Come on, I've been waiting."

He nodded in passing. "Hello, Jana."

Jana tipped her head. They were still unsure of each other and both were aware that Olivia was the only link they shared. "Doc."

"I've been warming up with Jana." Griffin didn't release the doctor's hand until they were in the media room.

Julian glanced at Jana lagging behind. "How did you do?"

"I didn't score one point," she said, taking a seat in the deep burgundy leather sofa facing the television. "Griffin might be unbeatable."

"We'll just see about that." Julian rubbed his hands together, hitched up his pants and sat.

"You want a chair?" Jana asked.

"No, I'm fine. You can get into the swing better sitting on the floor."

"Prepare to be crushed," Griffin said.

The challenge was on. Amid giggles and verbal sparring, the two played. Olivia found them that way, sitting side by side. Her heart twisted. Griffin so much wanted a father. Tyler and their father tried to make up for her ex-husband's absence, but couldn't really. And there was no way Aaron would ever be a real father.

"I won!" Griffin shouted.

Julian groaned. "I'll never be able to hold my head up." Griffin giggled louder. "I bet I know a game I can win," Julian said.

With that warning, Julian pounced on Griffin, tickling him. In a matter of moments they were rolling on the floor. Julian looked up and saw Olivia with a wistful smile on her face. He went completely still. Griffin took advantage of Julian's inertness to climb on his back, his arms going around his neck. "I won again."

Julian barely noticed the boy's weight. He was too busy absorbing the stunning impact of his mother. She wore a tangerine sleeveless sheath that made her flawless cinnamon complexion glow. "You look beautiful."

"Thank you," she said shyly.

"Oh, Mama, you can't take him now." Griffin unclamped his arms from around Julian's neck and stood.

"A man can't stand up a woman." Julian came to his feet as well.

"I know or they'll cry," Griffin said, his expression grave.

Julian frowned down at him, then looked at Olivia for an explanation. "He and his classmates have been discussing dating," she explained.

"I'm glad you're not like the boy who stood Cindi's big sister up. She cried," Griffin told him. "But Mama said Cindi's sister was better off without him."

"Your mother is right." He stuck his hand out to Griffin. "I'll take good care of her."

Griffin looked enormously pleased by the gesture. "It's all right if she gets two desserts."

They all laughed. "I'll remember that. You ready to go?"

"Yes." She went to Griffin and kissed him on the cheek. "My cell is on. Two cookie limit and once Jana puts you in bed stay there, and no cutting off the monitor or you'll have me to deal with."

"Yes, Mama," he said dutifully.

Smiling, Jana put her hand on Griffin's shoulder. "He'll be fine. Have fun."

"Good night." Julian's hand on the small of Olivia's back, he led her to the door. The heat of her body caused his hand to tingle, his body to want. Ruthlessly he brought his desire under control. If he wasn't careful, his first date with Olivia would be his last.

13

Chamberlain's, a four-star restaurant in a sprawling upscale shopping complex, has the best steaks in Texas, so Julian wasn't surprised when there was a wait for valet parking in front of the red brick structure. Three cars were ahead of them. "Sorry about this, but we won't have to wait for our table."

"If there wasn't a wait on a Saturday night, I'd suggest we find another place to eat," Olivia said.

Julian threw her a look. "Why do you always surprise me?"

"I'm not sure. Could it be because you expect so little from women?"

He frowned. She'd done it again. The women he dated were beautiful and charming, good in bed, and able to walk away from him as easily as he walked away from them. He hadn't thought of any of them last night when he was dealing with the loss of his patient. He'd called Olivia.

"The valet is motioning for you to pull up."

Julian eased up behind a Corvette. "You think I'm shallow, don't you?"

"I haven't formed an opinion past dedicated and determined. However, it wouldn't speak well of me if I dated a shallow man."

Julian stared hard at her. He couldn't tell if she was laughing at him or not. He'd never had this much difficulty gaining a woman's trust. Or was it that they hadn't interested him enough to think about them past the time they'd spend together.

He moved up. Perhaps he was shallow. "Have you ever been here before?"

"No." She smiled. "Griffin is more into places like Chuck E. Cheese's."

"You've done a great job with him," Julian said. "He's not shy about speaking his mind."

"No. No one will ever take advantage of him," she said, her expression set and determined.

"His father didn't send those games, did he?" he guessed.

Her brown eyes widened, then she glanced out the window. "No."

He placed his hand on hers clamped together in her lap, waited until she looked at him. "My father and I didn't get along. Without my mother's love, I wouldn't have made it."

"Thank you." Her hands beneath his relaxed.

Releasing her hand, Julian pulled up to the valet stand. Almost immediately two smiling attendants opened their doors. "Good evening, folks. Welcome to Chamberlain's."

Julian rounded the sports sedan and took Olivia's arm. Wearing the same friendly smile as the valet attendants, the doorman held open one of the double wooden doors. "Good evening. Enjoy your meal."

"Thank you," Julian and Olivia said simultaneously.

As Julian had predicted, they were immediately shown to their intimate table near a stone fireplace. On the pristine white tablecloth was a deep red hibiscus in a bud vase. The waiter appeared and took their orders. In minutes he was back with a small French loaf and the wine Julian had ordered.

"You aren't on duty tonight?" Olivia questioned.

"Nope. Tomorrow either." Julian sipped the red wine and nodded his acceptance. The waiter filled their glasses and withdrew.

Julian lifted his glass. "To becoming better acquainted."

Olivia touched her glass to his and sipped. "This is delicious."

"So is the food and the cheesecake is marvelous." He placed his glass on the white tablecloth. "You can have two desserts, remember?"

"Since I only had a few crackers for lunch, I may take you up on your offer."

Julian immediately signaled their waiter and ordered the appetizer sampler. "So business is good."

"Yes. Jana is the reason." She reached for the bread. "Do you want any?"

"No, thanks."

Olivia placed the sliced bread and then a pat of butter on her bread plate. "She's a natural at sales. She's friendly and knowledgeable."

The waiter placed their salads and appetizer of jumbo shrimp, scallops, and portobello mushrooms on the table, then left.

She frowned. "I think you might have overdone it. I hate wasting food."

"We'll ask for a take-away box." He picked up a skewered sesame shrimp and held it out to her.

Olivia eyed the shrimp, then Julian. He smiled. "It won't bite."

Cautiously she leaned forward and bit. "Delicious." She moaned in pleasure and Julian's body reacted to the sound, a sound he could easily imagine coming from her when they were in bed making love.

She offered him a shrimp. He didn't hesitate to take the food. Perhaps it would get his mind off making love to Olivia until neither one of them could lift their head from the pillow. Somehow his lips brushed against her fingertips.

Olivia's sharp intake of breath went through him. She stared at him. Julian smiled despite the need that rushed through him. "I agree. Delicious."

Olivia blinked and busied herself with her salad. "How long have you lived in Dallas?"

"Since medical school at UT Southwestern," he answered, willing to take it slow. Olivia was worth the cold showers. "You?"

"All my life. I went to college at UT in Austin." She glanced up at him. "So I guess that makes us college mates or something."

He knew what he'd like them to be. His expression must have shown as much because she dove back into her caesar salad. He almost sighed. If he kept this up, he'd be lucky to get her to go out with him again. He searched his mind for a safe topic. "Why luxe linen?"

Her head came up and Julian was determined that it remain that way. She explained how she'd read an article in a magazine. "Three years ago I relocated to where I am now. It's a prime location, near my home, and Griffin's school."

The waiter served their food, replenished the bread, topped off their wine, and disappeared.

Her eyes sparkled when she mention her son. Julian cut into his rare Kobe filet mignon. "He's something."

"He is, isn't he?" she laughed. "He doesn't know fear."

There it was again. Her deep need for Griffin to care for himself. Just the thought of her possibly being abused sent rage through him. "Your marriage—"

"Is not open to discussion." Her words were sharp, unconditional.

Instinctively he knew she'd leave if he pushed it. "Has anyone ever beat Griffin at video games?"

She relaxed. "Tyler. But no one has ever beaten him two games in a row."

"Figures," Julian said with just enough grumpiness to ensure Olivia would laugh.

"I must admit he likes playing with you." She bit into her asparagus.

"Because he beats me," Julian guessed.

"No," she said, her face troubled. "He likes you."

"And that worries you?" Julian paused in reaching for his wine.

"Yes." She looked across the table at him. "I didn't realize how much he'd be taken with you or think about how he'll feel when this is over."

Julian didn't expect his gut to clench. "This is our first date and you're dooming us already?"

She placed her fork on her plate. "You'll move on, Julian. It's inevitable."

He didn't like the calm way she'd said that. "You don't seem disturbed by the thought."

For a moment she looked incredibly sad. "I learned long ago to be realistic."

He suspected her marriage had taught her many hard lessons. He easily recalled the hell his father had put his mother through. Rage at Olivia's ex-husband swept through him. "Perhaps you learned the wrong lesson from the wrong man." He shoved his plate away.

Her eyebrow lifted at the harshness in his tone. "Perhaps."

Immediately contrite, his hand closed tenderly over hers. Olivia had been through enough. "I wouldn't hurt you or Griffin."

"Not intentionally." Withdrawing her hand, she smiled. "Now, about dessert."

She was pushing him away again. Julian straightened and signaled the waiter. He'd let it go for now. He'd just have to show her he wasn't going anyplace anytime soon.

Griffin was as difficult as Jana had anticipated in getting to bed and closing his eyes. There was always one more thing he needed to do: check his goldfish, get a glass of water, find his favorite book. Still, they were only thirty minutes behind schedule. Best of all, he'd fallen asleep almost immediately.

Making sure the monitor was on, she picked up the portable receiver and went downstairs to the pool. Placing the monitor out of harm's way and where she could see it on the glass table several feet from the pool, she turned up the volume and slipped out of her pants and blouse. Underneath was a black one-piece swimsuit she'd purchased the day before.

She dove into the tranquil blue water of the rectangular pool, barely creating a ripple, swam several feet away, and then back to the edge. She didn't want to get so far away she couldn't hear the monitor. Olivia couldn't possibly know how much it meant to Jana that she let her watch Griffin. She was trusted.

Reaching the end of the pool, Jana listened, then floated on her back, staring up at the huge half-moon above. It almost looked as if she could touch it. The sight made her feel small and miss Tyler like crazy. She hadn't realized how much his presence had come to mean to her until he was gone.

"Hello."

Tyler. Jana's pulse accelerated. She came upright, floating in place, and simply stared at Tyler, who stood at the edge of the pool. He had on snug-fitting jeans and a white shirt. He looked wonderful and sexy as hell. "Hello. We didn't expect you until tomorrow afternoon," she managed, her voice breathless.

"Finished quicker that I thought. I didn't see any reason for staying."

She didn't know what to say. He was hunkered down by the edge of the pool, the light from the house silhouetting his well-built body. He was a tempting man.

He stood, still staring down at her. "I think I'll join you." His hands went to the button on his jeans. Jana's eyes widened, but she couldn't look away. She told herself she was glad when he shoved his pants down his long, muscular legs that he had on a pair of brief black swim trunks.

So she hadn't quite stopped lying.

He grinned devilishly. "I saw you when I came home. I make it a practice to check the house when I get back."

"You checked on Griffin?" she asked, a safe subject.

"Sleeping." He slipped into the water. "He can usually talk Wanda into extending his bedtime."

Her pulse hammered like crazy. "Wanda couldn't make it."

His brow puckered, then cleared. "You?"

"Me," she said.

"It seems you're a woman of many talents."

Once she might have taken that as an insult. "It does." She swam easily beside him. "I made good grades in school until I learned I got more attention if I screwed up. I was very good at screwing up."

"A lot of children do that."

"I suppose, but at the time I was so angry with my parents for ignoring me, I just wanted to disrupt their lives and make them look at me. My mother finally did when I was fifteen, but it was to make me a clone of her." She reached the edge of the pool, hoisted herself out and reached for a towel to dry her face while she left her lower legs in the water. "I remember being so happy that she was paying attention to me, teaching me about boys, and how to always be in control."

Shock, then anger swept across Tyler's face. He'd never understand her parents. She wasn't sure she ever would either.

"My mother is one of the most beautiful women I've ever seen. Having her pay attention to me was the most important thing in the world. We became friends, or so I thought."

"What happened?" He climbed out and accepted the towel she handed him.

"She liked listening to my escapades, but we never shared anything if it didn't involve conquest. To her, control was everything and I was her willing pupil."

He sat beside her. "It's natural to look up to your mother. It's the parent's responsibility to teach the child right from wrong. You weren't taught."

"I was so busy racking up scores, I didn't care. The more my father ignored me, the worse I became." Somehow she found the courage to look him in the eye. "The night we met I'd been to Priscilla's house, looking for a man to take care of me."

"Did you find one?"

"In a matter of speaking." She told him about being tossed out of Priscilla's house and being picked up by Douglas Gregory. "In that car in the darkened parking lot, it finally hit home that I had sunk to rock bottom. I ran."

Reaching over, he squeezed her hand. She squeezed his back. "There hadn't been a man in my life for the past five months. To survive I sold almost everything."

"You're not the woman Priscilla or the others knew."

"I finally believe that. Perhaps my father will believe it too and stop hating me. Heaven knows, I've given him and his new wife reasons." She sighed. "I've done so many unspeakable things in my life."

"In the eyes of God, sin is sin. He's not going to keep throwing them up in your face, so neither should you. You won't get very far in life if you don't let go of the past and stop dragging it with you every step of the way."

"I don't want that life anymore, but I realize it will be difficult for some people to accept that I've changed."

"If you try to live for other people instead of yourself, you're doomed to be miserable," he told her.

"I think that's what I did with my mother. I imitated her in hopes she'd love me." Jana stared up at the moon again. "I wonder if she ever did. I called her the night I fainted and ended up at the hospital. She wasn't interested."

"So, what do you plan to do now?"

She looked at him. "Be the best that I can be. I was great today in the store. I don't need a man to take care of me or make me feel special."

"Well, that all depends on the man don't you think?" Tyler replied, his voice dropping to a husky pitch.

"Beside my ex, I've only known one kind," Jana said, regret making her voice strained.

"Then you're long overdue. It will be my pleasure to reacquaint you." His fingertip softly traced her lower lip. "If you'll let me."

Her body quickened, yearned. She was caught between desire and wanting more than sex with him. "Tyler, too many things in my life are unsettled now."

"I understand." He stood and tugged her to her feet. "I have a present for you." With his free hand, he lifted a rose print gift bag from the glass table.

Her eyes rounded. She'd been so intent on him, she hadn't noticed anything else.

"It won't bite," he teased.

Finally accepting the bag, she lifted the tissue-wrapped box out and gasped. Her gaze bounced from the bottle of Joy to him. She blinked, and then blinked again.

"If you cry, I'm taking it back."

She managed a shaky smile. For a practical man like Tyler to buy the expensive perfume was more precious than any gift she had ever received. "Thank you."

"You're welcome. How about that movie Monday night in the media room around eight-thirty? I'll bring the buttered popcorn."

For a moment Jana visualized them on the sofa, not making love, simply holding each other. "I'd like that. Good night."

"Good night, Jana. Sweet dreams."

Handing him the monitor, she walked away. With Tyler home, sweet dreams were the only kind she'd have.

Olivia hadn't meant to be quite so frank about the outcome of her dating Julian. Maybe because Aaron's dishonesty had been so devastating she'd overcompensated. Now, walking beside Julian to the front door, she wished she'd kept her mouth shut. Before and after her blunder, she'd enjoyed being with him.

She unlocked the door and turned, lifting her hand. "Thank you for a wonderful evening."

Julian looked from her outstretched hand to her face. "Thank you." His hand closed over hers and he pulled her into his arms.

His warm, persuasive mouth covering hers cut off her startled cry. This time there was no gentle brush of lips. This was a wildly erotic and bold taking of her mouth by a man who knew what he was doing.

His tongue ravished her mouth, the heat of his hand burned though her dress, his hard body excited her. She couldn't think and gave up trying and just enjoyed Julian driving every thought from her head except the incredible pleasure he was bringing her. Much too soon he lifted his head.

"Have you or Griffin ever driven bumper cars?"

It took a long moment for her brain to work, for his words to sink in. "No."

"Great. If you don't have plans for tomorrow afternoon, how about I pick you and Griffin up around five. We can eat before or afterwards, whatever works best for you," he said.

"You want Griffin to go on a date with us?" she asked.

"Yes." Julian smiled. "At least he won't beat me this time."

A knot formed in her throat. When he moved on it would be difficult for both mother and son, but not for anything would she deny either of them the prospect of being with Julian. "He'll be so excited. We'll be ready."

"See you then." He kissed her quickly on the lips, urged her inside, then closed the door.

Olivia heard him whistling. She smiled.

Sunday morning Jana stared in the mirror and assessed herself. Nothing about her hinted at the kind of life she'd once lived. After two weeks the dark circles were gone, her cheeks had filled out, her hair was styled, her nails manicured, her feet enclosed in heeled sandals. She wore a white silk blouse and black gabardine slacks. The look could have been improved with a jacket, hoop silver earrings and a silver chain necklace, but she hadn't made her decision until that morning.

She was going to church with Tyler and Olivia. She'd told them at breakfast. Olivia had hugged her. Tyler had given her a smile that she'd always treasure. That they could forgive her and want her around after what they'd learned about her past was nothing short of miraculous. Church was important to them and although Jana wasn't sold on it for herself, it wouldn't hurt to give it a try. She'd certainly screwed up on her own.

Picking up her purse, she went downstairs. They were waiting for her by Tyler's truck. "Sorry to keep you waiting."

"For this we'd wait all day," Olivia said, getting in the back seat of the vehicle. Griffin climbed in behind her.

"You look beautiful and smell wonderful." Tyler opened the passenger door for her.

"Thanks to you." She climbed inside. "But I have to admit I'm shaking in my shoes." She never wanted to lie to him.

"You'll be fine." He closed her door and went to the driver's side and got in.

Jana wasn't so sure, but she was willing to give it a try.

If you expect God to forgive you of your sins, you have to forgive others.

Pastor Palmer's words replayed themselves over and over in Jana's head long after they'd returned home from church. After lunch, she'd excused herself and gone outside to sit by the pool and think. Her motto had always been, "Don't get mad, get even." No one crossed her and got away with it. No matter how long she had to wait she'd eventually pay them back.

And because of the way she'd treated people, no one had helped her when she was down. Every person she'd wronged and those close to them had been standing in line to pay her back.

Their motto had been the same as hers.

"What are you thinking?" Tyler asked, sitting on the lounge chair next to her.

She sighed. "You reap what you sow." That had been in Pastor Palmer's message too.

"True, but you're fast racking up points in your favor." He took her hands in his. "Pastor Palmer thanked you from the pulpit."

She'd been surprised and a bit embarrassed to stand up. "I'm sure Maggie had a hand in it."

"Probably, but you deserved to be recognized for helping," he told her. "Some people only want to help themselves."

"I was at the head of that line," she reminded him.

"*Was.*" Standing, he pulled her to her feet, his arms going around her waist as he nuzzled her neck. "You always smell and taste sensational."

Boneless, she sank against him, arching her neck to allow him better access. "It's the perfume."

"It's the woman," he said, brushing his lips across hers again and again, teasing both of them before taking her mouth in a deep, hot kiss.

Their breathing was off-kilter when he lifted his head. "Want to go see a Rangers' game?"

Her hands on his wide chest, she stood easily in his arms. "Baseball, right?"

His sinful mouth twitched. "Right. We'll stuff ourselves with junk food since we don't have to set an example for Griffin. It will just be a lazy afternoon of fun."

She couldn't think of anything she'd like to do more. "It sounds wonderful."

Olivia and Griffin were waiting in the living room when Julian drove up. She couldn't deny she was anxious. Julian could make a woman throw caution to the wind. She didn't like to recall that she'd done that once with disastrous results.

Aaron had been a chameleon, sly and devious. He and Julian were worlds apart, but Julian could hurt her just as badly if she allowed herself to care for him too much.

"Julian is here." Griffin was out the door in nothing flat.

Olivia followed. Julian, in worn jeans that molded to his muscular thighs and a blue pinstriped shirt, emerged from the sports sedan and waved. "Hi, Olivia. Griffin."

Fifteen feet from the car, Griffin stopped dead in his tracks. "Wow!"

Julian smiled. "That was exactly my reaction when I first saw the car on the showroom floor." He put his hand on Griffin's shoulder and walked closer to the car, pointing out details. "The front has a chromed mesh-front grill and side vents."

Olivia hung back. How could she not care for a man who treated her son with such care and affection?

"Would you like to sit in the driver's seat for a moment?" Julian asked.

Olivia saw that Griffin was torn. Like most little boys he loved cars, but he was also excited about the bumper cars.

He looked at her. "Can I, Mama?"

She didn't hesitate. "Yes."

Griffin cautiously sat on the custom handcrafted ivory leather with bordeaux piping, the same color as the car, and wrapped his hands around the leather-covered steering wheel. His legs weren't long enough to reach the pedals and he could barely see over the gauge-filled dash, but he was grinning for all he was worth.

"How fast will it go?"

"With a V-8 engine it can take you from zero to sixty miles per hour in five point one seconds and reach speeds of one hundred seventy miles per hour." Julian hunkered down beside the open door. "But that's not why I bought it." He waited until Griffin looked at him. "It's one of the safest cars made. Driving fast is dangerous. Remember that when you start driving."

"I will."

Julian pushed to his feet and turned to Olivia. "Ready?"

"Yes, if we can get Griffin out of the driver's seat."

"I got it covered." He seated her and went to Griffin. "There's a Chuck E. Cheese's near where we're going. You think we can talk your mother into eating dinner there?"

"I bet we could."

"Great. Hop in the back seat and fasten your seat belt. Women don't like to be kept waiting and we want to make sure she stays in a good mood."

Griffin quickly got into the back seat and fastened his seat belt. "Mama, are you in a good mood?"

She looked at Julian next to her. "Yes, Griffin, I'm in a very good mood."

"And I plan to keep you that way," Julian whispered softly as he pulled away from the curb.

If only he could, she thought. *If only he could.*

14

By Monday Olivia was ready to move forward with her idea of having gift baskets available to customers. Theirs would be different and distinct. They'd put bath products with towels or bathrobes; pair perfumed ironing water with sheets.

Julian was even coming over later to help. Yesterday had been filled with fun. Griffin had enjoyed himself. He was so tired he had fallen asleep when his head hit the pillow. That had given her the opportunity to go back downstairs and kiss Julian goodnight. Several times as she recalled with remembered pleasure.

Olivia paused at the desk on the sales floor, her eyes going dreamy. The way Julian kissed and made a woman feel should be illegal. But she was grateful it wasn't. During their outing she had made up her mind to enjoy the time with Julian and let tomorrow take care of itself.

She went back to the list Jana had given her. As soon as they closed, she and Jana were going to the floral wholesale warehouse. They'd already loaded the merchandise in her SUV. She had a feeling this was going to be great for business.

The door opened and she looked up and saw Mrs. Fulton. Olivia stiffened. The woman hesitated, then came directly to the desk, her hand clenched around the gold chain strap of her Chanel bag.

"Mrs. Fulton."

"I, er . . ." Mrs. Fulton's voice trailed off, she moistened her lips. "I've come to give you another chance."

Her gaze direct, Olivia came to her feet. "I run my business as I see fit. Good day."

"I—" Mrs. Fulton stopped and took a step back.

Olivia heard the swinging door behind her and knew Jana had entered the room. "There is nothing more to discuss."

The older woman didn't move. "I'm sure we can work something out to both of our satisfaction."

Olivia stepped around the desk "There is nothing to work out." She glanced at her watch. "I'm sorry. We closed as of three minutes ago and we have an appointment."

"You'd take her over the kind of business I can bring you?" Mrs. Fulton asked, her chest puffed out in her pink and black mini-check Chanel suit.

"I'd close before I turn my back on a friend," Olivia told her without hesitation.

Mrs. Fulton stared at Olivia, then seemed to crumple in the Queen Anne chair in front of the desk. "You have to help me. My husband wasn't . . . wasn't pleased when I told him we wouldn't have the linen for the launch. He has some very important guests coming." Her grip on her bag tightened.

"You could try another store or another manufacturer," Olivia suggested.

"Don't you think I've tried? My husband wants Frette sheets, but since I canceled my order the company won't even attempt to finish the order unless I'm willing to pay triple because they have to push my order ahead of others."

Jana whistled softly.

"Robert won't pay such an exorbitant amount. Please, you have to help me," Mrs. Fulton pleaded.

"I'm sorry, Mrs. Fulton," Olivia said. "You put me in a terrible position when you canceled and I had to notify the company. The manufacturer prides itself on top-quality workmanship and customer satisfaction. I pride myself on customer satisfaction as well. Money and many man-hours were lost in cutting those custom sheets."

"What am I to do?" Mrs. Fulton asked, her face drawn as she battled tears.

"There are two possible solutions." Olivia folded her arms. "You can postpone the launch or have someone monogram regular sheets."

Tears crested in Mrs. Fulton's eyes. "I told everyone about the sheets. I'll be ruined."

And you brought it on yourself by bragging, Jana thought. Mrs. Fulton knew as well as Jana that women would be checking to see the Frette label. When they didn't see it, the news would spread that she had lied. Jana took satisfaction in the other woman's misery until she remembered the pastor's message the day before. Most of all, she remembered that Tyler and Olivia had forgiven her and what might have happened to her if they hadn't.

If you want God to forgive you, you have to forgive others. Jana didn't know if God had forgiven her or if it was He who had directed her to Midnight Dreams, but she was willing to give Him the benefit of the doubt.

"Olivia, if the sheets are ready except for the monogram could the company overnight them and you hire a seamstress to do the monogram?" Jana asked.

Mrs. Fulton perked up. "Could we do that?"

Olivia tried to hide her surprise at Jana's attempt to help a woman who had wanted to ruin her. She stared at Jana a long moment, then unfolded her arms, picked up the phone and dialed. If Jana could forgive Mrs. Fulton, then so could she. "Their rep is in New York this week," she said, then moments later. "Yes, Henri, Olivia Sanders. Fine, thank you. I need to speak with you about Mrs. Fulton's order."

Olivia hung up ten minutes later. "The sheets should arrive by Friday. It will be an additional ten thousand dollars. I assumed you wouldn't mind paying."

"Thank you." Mrs. Fulton fumbled in her purse, pulled out her American Express credit card, and handed it to Olivia. She didn't take it.

"The seamstress we use charges by the letter, the intricacy of the lettering, and the type of thread. A ballpark estimate would be an additional two to three thousand dollars," Olivia said.

"Whatever you say," Mrs. Fulton agreed, the credit card still in her hand.

"There is one other thing before the sale is written up. You owe Jana an apology."

Mrs. Fulton's eyes widened. She shrank back in her chair.

Olivia's eyes narrowed. "If you can't do that, then this conversation is over."

"I'm sorry," the woman whispered.

"Apology accepted," Jana said, seeing Olivia in a new light. Tyler had indicated she was a tigress and he was right.

Olivia took the card and gave it to Jana. "Jana will assist you."

Mrs. Fulton's lips pressed tightly together.

"Is there a problem, Mrs. Fulton?" Olivia asked.

"No." She quickly shook her head.

"Good, because this is to help you and not because I need the business," Olivia said. "I'll pull the old order from the back."

Jana sat and stared across the desk at the haughty, miserable woman who had been taken down a notch or two. "You didn't ask for it, but I'm going to give you some advice. Cultivate the friendships of those who could care less about the manufacturer of your linen or how much money you have."

Mrs. Fulton nodded slightly, then glanced away, dismissing Jana.

Instead of thinking what satisfaction snatching every frosted hair out of Mrs. Fulton's head would bring or dwelling on how ungrateful she was, Jana thought of Tyler. He always saw the best in her. "You better be glad I'm not the person I used to be."

Mrs. Fulton glanced around sharply. Fear leaped in her eyes.

"Don't worry. What I'm trying to build is more important than revenge." She picked up a pen. "But if I were you, I'd watch my back with Priscilla."

Working together that evening it didn't take long to wrap the baskets and load them in Olivia's SUV. Griffin wanted Tyler to see Julian's car and somehow talked them into going for a drive with the moon roof down and a stop at the Marble Creamery for ice cream. They took their ice cream outside where they could sit in the black wrought-iron enclosed patio in front of the store.

Olivia looked across the table at Tyler with his arm around Jana, her feeding him a mixture of fresh strawberries and vanilla ice cream with a spoon. She smiled.

"Next time we'll have to try that," Julian said softly.

Olivia glanced at Griffin beside them, licking his chocolate ice-cream cone. "I'll hold you to it."

"How about Wednesday night?" he asked, his gaze warm and full of promise.

Olivia didn't hesitate. "I'll be ready at eight."

"Hello, Tyler, Olivia," greeted a tall, slender man with graying hair. "You too, Griffin."

"Hello. Mr. Callier," Olivia and Griffin said.

Tyler stood and extended his hand over the three-foot railing. "Good evening, Mr. Callier. This is Jana Franklin and Dr. Julian Cortez. Lionel Callier."

The older man nodded to Jana and shook Julian's hand, but clearly his attention was on Tyler. "How are things going?"

"Great. Would you like to join us?" Tyler asked.

He held up the quart-sized white sack. "No thanks. I better get home with Courtney's ice cream before it melts."

"She and her husband are back from Africa?" Olivia asked.

There was a long pause. Mr. Callier glanced away then looked at Tyler. "She's by herself," Mr. Callier said quietly.

Tyler was not going to speculate on the reason. He took his seat, repositioning his arm around Jana's shoulder. "You must be glad to have her home."

"Yes, I am," he confirmed, a frown on his angular face as he studied Jana. "Well, I better get going." He continued toward the parking lot.

"Uncle Tyler," Griffin whispered when Mr. Callier was several feet away.

"Yes, Griffin."

Griffin watched Mr. Callier get into a late model black Cadillac, then asked, "You aren't going to start dating her again, are you, Uncle Tyler?"

"No, Griffin. She's married." He turned to Jana sitting quietly beside him and tightened his hold. "I'm interested in another woman."

Jana had rolled over her competition in the past. She'd used every sexual trick she could think of to get the man she wanted. Even if she thought that would work with Tyler, she had left that life behind.

"You aren't paying any attention to the movie." Tyler sat beside her in the media room later that evening. Olivia had put Griffin to bed as soon as they returned, then retired herself.

They'd chosen a comedy from the wide selection of DVDs. As she'd expected, it was nice just sitting beside Tyler on the sofa, his arm around her. But she couldn't relax. "Just thinking."

Tyler turned off the movie and dimmed the lights in the room. Her breath quickened even before he turned, his mouth unerringly finding hers.

He took his time driving her slowly out of her mind with need and pleasure. She couldn't get enough of his hot mouth, his inventive tongue that teased and beckoned. His large hand stroked her stomach, going higher and higher until he cupped her breast. She shuddered, then arched.

He groaned. She moaned.

Her hand swept beneath his shirt. His skin was smooth with muscled hardness beneath.

"You taste sweeter each time I kiss you," he said.

She wanted to. She wanted to be everything he had ever wanted in a woman. His mouth took hers again. It was a long time before he lifted his head. "If I don't stop now, I may not be able to."

She didn't want him to stop and almost voiced her objection aloud. "You're doing this for me, aren't you?"

He tipped her chin up with his finger. "You deserve to be cherished, and I'm the man to show you just how much."

She recalled his promise. "You already have."

"Honey." He pulled her back in his arms and just held her.

She snuggled closer, content to lie in his arms. This was the life she wanted. She just hoped and prayed, yes prayed, it wouldn't be taken from her.

"What about Courtney?" she asked, barely breathing as she waited for his answer.

He stared down at her. "It's over between us. I wouldn't lie to you."

The fear receded. Tyler was too honorable to lie to her. Her hand circled his neck and she pulled his head down to meet her lips.

Jana didn't notice Mitsy and Sherilyn were in the store until she handed the customer in front of the desk a large-handled shopping bag containing the gift basket she'd just purchased. Jana's smile froze. Frantic, she glanced around the store, searching for Olivia.

Jana located Olivia near the front of the store showing a matronly women the last of the five baskets Jana had made. They'd proven as popular as Olivia had predicted. The only other customers were a young couple in their mid-twenties browsing in bath accessories. There was only one reason for the two troublemakers to come into the store. It was exactly a week since the altercation with Priscilla.

"Can I please have my bathrobe gift basket?"

The woman's rather amused request snapped Jana's attention back to her. "Of course. I'm sorry."

"That's all right, dear," the older woman said, a twinkle in her dark eyes. "The older I get, the more I catch myself drifting, but you're rather young."

"I'm older than I look," Jana bantered. "Enjoy."

"Thank you. I will." The woman started for the front door.

Jana noted that Olivia had greeted Sherilyn and Mitsy but, aware that Jana was finishing up a sale, she had remained with the customer. Apparently Olivia didn't know the two women or sense the trouble they might cause. Jana thought of taking Olivia's customer, then dismissed the idea. She might as well let them get their jab in and get it over with.

Besides, Tyler said he'd drop by on the way to a project he and his team were working on. She didn't want him there if things got nasty. After being around Olivia and Tyler, Jana now understood what real friendship meant. They deserved their pound of flesh.

Taking a deep breath, Jana moved toward the two solemn-faced women. "Welcome to Midnight Dreams. Can I show you anything?"

Mitsy looked down her long nose at Jana and shoved the leather strap of her black Chloé bag over her shoulder. The chic black and white suit was also Chloé. The double string of pearls, a prerequisite for women in the Junior League, were perfectly matched and lustrous. "I want to see those towels on the top shelf."

"Which color?"

"Every color," she ordered.

"And style," Sherilyn added. She wore Prada, but the light blue designer suit couldn't make up for slimness that bordered on gauntness. It was rumored at one time that she had an eating disorder.

"Those are for display. I can get you a set from the back," Jana told them.

"I want to see *those.*" Up went Mitsy's nose again.

Jana hadn't thought it would be simple or easy, but they might as well learn that she wasn't running or hiding. She'd done enough of that. "Of course."

Glad she'd worn pants, she pulled the sliding ladder over and climbed up. She was reaching for the towels when there was a hard bump against the ladder. Almost toppling, Jana frantically grabbed the ladder to steady herself. Her heart racing, she looked down. Both women gazed innocently up at her. They wanted more than retribution, they wanted Jana broken and bloody.

"Hurry. We haven't got all day," Mitsy snapped.

Gathering a set of plush towel in berry to her chest, Jana carefully came back down the ladder. "Here you are."

"Are you dense?" Mitsy sneered. "I can't very well look at them with you holding them."

Jana's eyes narrowed, but she went to the bed and placed the towels on top. "They're Egyptian cotton and we offer free monogramming."

Both women snorted, but it was Mitsy who snidely said, "I could afford to have everything in this store monogrammed if I wanted."

"On the other hand, *you* couldn't afford to have a handkerchief monogrammed with your initials—b-i-t-c-h," Sherilyn giggled as if she'd said the funniest thing in the world.

Mitsy joined her. "I'd pay to see that."

Jana picked up the towels. "Mitsy, would that be cash, check, or charge?"

"What?" Mitsy's hazel eyes widened.

Jana didn't even try to keep the satisfied smile off her face. "You said you'd pay to see that. I have to ring up the sale first before I can send them out to be monogrammed."

"I'm not buying those," Mitsy huffed. "Bring me those satin slippers on display over there."

"Is there a problem?" Olivia, her brow puckered, came up to them.

Jana shook her head. "Nothing I can't handle." She turned to Mitsy. "Is there anything else you would like to see?"

"If there were, I would have asked you."

"Perhaps—" Olivia began, but stopped when Jana touched her arm.

"It's all right. Really. Why don't you see if that couple has any questions or are they still browsing?"

Olivia looked at Mitsy and Sherilyn a long time, then moved away. Jana now had friends. The knowledge erased the nasty thoughts running through her head. Once upon a time she would have made a point of enticing their husbands and making sure they later found out about it. But now, Tyler was the only man she wanted to be with.

Calmly, Jana faced the women. "I can take anything you dish out and you know why? Because I'm just beginning to know and treasure what real friends mean." She smiled and spread her arms wide. "So bring it on. You can run me all over the store until I have things ten feet high, but you won't break me. But I have to warn you, I'll only bend so much."

Her smile growing, she went to get the slippers and then returned, surprised to see that Sherilyn was leaving the store. She placed the slippers beside the towels. "Here you are."

Mitsy picked up the slippers. "I can't see the size."

"Seven," Jana told her.

"I'll see for myself." Slipping the bag off her shoulder, she placed it on the bed and took the slippers to the window, examining the embroidered shoe in detail.

Jana caught Olivia's gaze and smiled to reassure her. Another customer came in and Jana nodded her head for Olivia to assist her. Jana could handle Mitsy.

After a long two minutes, Mitsy returned, tossing the slipper down. "It's not what I want." She picked up her purse. "I'll take the towels."

Jana couldn't hide her surprise. She'd thought Mitsy would rather wear flannel in public than purchase anything from her. "If you'll come with me, I'll write the receipt." Rounding the desk, Jana sat down and reached for the receipt book.

"Where's my wallet? Where's my wallet?"

Jana looked up, a lump settling in the pit of her stomach like lead. Mitsy was looking directly her.

"You stole my wallet! Give it back!" she shrilled, the black Chloé bag gapping open.

Jana slowly came to her feet. "I don't have your wallet."

"What is it?" Olivia asked, rushing over.

"Your sales clerk stole my wallet!" Mitsy repeated. "It was in my purse when I came in here. She took it when I went to the window to check the slipper's size."

Olivia didn't even look at Jana. "You must have lost it someplace else."

"I distinctly remember seeing it after I came in here when I opened my purse to check my lipstick." Mitsy turned her angry gaze on Jana. "You're a slut and a thief!"

Jana clenched her hands instead of slapping Mitsy. "I don't steal."

She sneered. "I notice you didn't deny you have the morals of an alley cat."

"I don't have your wallet," Jana repeated. Then she saw something that made the floor shift beneath her feet. Tyler was entering the store. How much more could he hear about her and not be disgusted by the sight of her?

"Call the police," Mitsy ordered, staring hard at Olivia. "As the owner, you have a responsibility to your customers."

"My sister is well aware of her responsibility," Tyler said, coming to stand beside Olivia. "What's going on?"

Every eye in the shop converged on Tyler. Jana wanted to disappear. She didn't have any doubt the missing wallet was planned. Mitsy would play this out to the hilt and that meant Jana would soon be in handcuffs.

"Jana stole my wallet. I demand the police be called," Mitsy said.

"I agree," Tyler said.

Jana began to tremble. She hadn't realized how much she wanted his blind faith in her. She didn't bother with defending herself again. What was the use?

"First, however, I want to look at the tape from the security cameras," Tyler said, his expression thoughtful.

"W-what?" Mitsy asked, her fingers tightening on the handbag.

"Security cameras," Tyler explained, his voice neutral. "They're strategically located throughout the store. They'll tell us who stole the wallet."

Mitsy swallowed, but said nothing.

Tyler pulled out his cell. "I'll call the police, but maybe you should check your purse again before I do. Filing a false police report is a crime too. Jana could sue you for slander when the real culprit is discovered."

He pressed in one number. Mitsy grabbed his wrist. "I don't want to get anyone in trouble."

"If she stole your wallet, she deserves to be in jail. My sister has the reputation of the shop to consider," Tyler said. "Jana won't be able to deny what happened once we view the tape."

Mitsy released Tyler's arm and fiddled with the pearls at her throat. "Maybe, maybe I dropped it and my friend picked it up." She pulled out her own cell phone. "I'll call her."

"If you're sure," Tyler drawled, deactivating his phone. "I want you to get exactly what's due you."

"Sherilyn, do you by chance have my wallet?" Mitsy's face creased into a semblance of a smile. "Oh, good, I'll meet you at Hermès." She disconnected the phone and dropped it into her bag. "She has it. I was mistaken. I left it on the table where we had lunch. She forgot to tell me. I better go."

Mitsy started for the door and Tyler caught her arm. "Don't you think you owe Jana an apology?" Her mouth tightened. "I'd hate to see you sued for slander. Isn't your husband thinking of a political career?"

"That's the least you can do," said the woman Jana had helped earlier. "She certainly has grounds."

"Who are you?" Mitsy asked, her lips pursed in annoyance.

"No one you'd know. I'm just doing some shopping while my husband is in town. Perhaps you've heard of him: Winston Strong."

"The Fifth Circuit judge?" Tyler asked.

"Yes." The woman smiled. "You know Winston?"

"No, ma'am. Just heard of him," Tyler said, a thoughtful look on his face. "He has quite a reputation for integrity."

"Yes. I'm very proud of him." Mrs. Strong turned her attention to Mitsy. She was no longer smiling. "We both detest injustice of any type."

"Mrs. Strong, this is a pleasure," Mitsy gushed, extending her hand. "I'm a member of the Junior League. We're having a reception in the home of our president for you tomorrow."

The handshake was brief. "I was looking forward to it until now."

Mitsy eyes widened as the words sank in. She gulped and turned to Jana. "I'm sorry. Please accept my apology."

Jana was still looking with bewilderment at Mrs. Strong. "You don't know me."

Mrs. Strong smiled again. "It doesn't take me long to size up a person. You struck me immediately as a woman of substance."

Jana was touched. "Thank you." She turned to Mitsy. Being gracious wasn't as difficult as she once thought. "I accept your apology," she told Mitsy.

Relief swept across Mitsy's thin face. She faced Mrs. Strong. "I'll see you tomorrow. Good-bye." She hurried from the store.

Jana brought her full attention back to Mrs. Strong. "I deeply appreciate your help, but Mitsy has valid reasons for not liking me. At one time I wasn't very likable."

The elderly woman didn't bat a lash. "Many people have pasts they'd rather forget. To me, they are the most interesting and strongest. It takes courage to change. I don't suppose I'll see either of you ladies at the luncheon tomorrow?"

"No," Olivia and Jana said in unison.

"Too bad. It would have been interesting." She extended her hand. "Good-bye."

Jana closed her hand around the other woman's. "Good-bye."

The door had barely closed before Olivia gave Jana a brief hug, then went to help the couple that had stopped browsing to watch the drama unfold.

"You all right?" Tyler asked.

"Wonderful. It's a good thing Olivia has security cameras."

"She doesn't."

Jana blinked. "What?"

Smiling, Tyler lifted her chin to close her mouth. "I was bluffing."

Her throat tightened. "You believed me."

"Did you doubt that I would?" he asked, the smile gone from his face.

She considered lying, then said, "Yes."

"Then I'll have to work harder at getting you to trust me." Curling his hand behind her neck, Tyler pulled Jana closer for a brief kiss. "That's for starters. I'll be back tonight around eleven."

She trembled. "Would you like to come up?"

"Yes, but I better not." His thumb grazed across her lips. "You're too tempting. Stay safe."

Jana watched as Tyler waved to Olivia on his way out the door. Their relationship had definitely added another dimension and although it was scary she couldn't wait to see him again.

"Where are we all going on our next date?" Griffin asked the moment Julian came through the front door Wednesday night.

Olivia was sure the expression on her face was as stunned as Julian's. She'd let Griffin stay up to say hello to Julian because she'd known he wouldn't have gone to sleep otherwise. Helpless, she looked down at the expectant face of her son and didn't know quite what to say.

"I'm open to suggestions," Julian said, hunkering down so that he was eye level with Griffin.

"Well," Griffin drew the word out. "We could go to Game Works." He spread his small arms as wide as they would go. "It's this big arcade with two floors of video games." He giggled and folded his arms. "I bet there's one where you can beat me."

"Griffin," Olivia admonished, but since Jana, who was babysitting Griffin, and Julian were laughing, she didn't think her reprimand had done much good. "It isn't nice to brag."

Her son looked up at her with innocence shining in his eyes. "But Uncle Tyler and Grandpa Maxwell always said if it's fact it isn't bragging."

"I can't possibly pass up that challenge, especially since I'm trying to impress your mother," Julian said, the corners of his mouth tilted upward. "I suppose this place has a restaurant."

"A whole floor with different foods," Griffin said, some of his excitement subdued. "Since I had pizza Sunday I can't have any for a while now."

Julian put his hand on Griffin's shoulder and looked up at Olivia. "Any plans for Friday afternoon?"

"We don't have any, do we, Mama?" Griffin asked, his eyes wide and hopeful.

Seeing the two of them together, Olivia felt a lump lodge in her throat. "No," she finally managed.

"Yippee!" Griffin impulsively launched himself into Julian's arms, then laughed louder as Julian rose to his feet while still holding Griffin.

"I guess we have a date," Julian said as he set Griffin down. "I expect your mother to get a good report from Jana. I wouldn't want anything to stop us from going out Friday night."

Griffin headed for the stairs, then stopped midway and called, "Good night," before continuing up the stairs.

Smiling, Jana followed. "He'll be in bed by the time I get there."

A tremulous smile on her face, Olivia turned to Julian. "Thank you."

On seeing the tears in her eyes, the warmth in them, Julian felt tightness in his chest he'd never experienced before. "I care about him, too," he said, meaning every word. "Besides, it's bad form to let the son of a woman you're interested in always beat you."

Olivia's heart quickened. It would be so very easy to let herself care too deeply for Julian. "I'm far more impressed with a man's other qualities." She reached for his hand. "Come on. I'm ready for my ice cream."

Like teenagers, they'd shared a banana split loaded with chocolate syrup, strawberry and caramel topping, nuts, and whipped cream. Sitting at the far end of the patio at the Marble Creamery, they took turns feeding each other. They laughed and talked in between bites. Julian insisted on offering the plump cherry to Olivia. Opening her mouth, she leaned forward to eagerly accept the ripe fruit. The laughter died when she stared into Julian's hooded eyes. *He wanted her.*

She felt her body clench with the first faint stirrings of desire. Surprised, a bit embarrassed, and yes, pleased, because her ex-husband hadn't taken this away from her as well. She glanced away.

Strong fingers turned her head. "What is it?"

She felt her face heat and hoped he wouldn't know the cause. She didn't like lying, but the alternative was unthinkable. She leaned away from the disturbing warmth of Julian's hand when she had the crazy urge to turn her head and bite. "Just thinking."

"Thinking, huh," he said. "Wonder if it was the same thing I was thinking?"

Olivia flushed deeply, her eyes widened in alarm. Speechless, she stared across the small table at Julian. She didn't have to see the smoldering look in his dark eyes to know they had been, and still were, thinking the same thing. Her breath snagged. She didn't mind thinking about intimacy, but she wasn't ready to put action to those thoughts. "Jul—"

"It's all right," he said, standing and reaching for her hand.

Unsure of what he meant, she automatically placed her hand in his and walked beside him to where his car was parked. "I—" she started, but had no idea of what she meant to say.

Julian, who had been reaching for the door handle on the passenger's side, curved his arm around her waist instead, effectively trapping her body between his and the car. She trembled from the heat and hardness of his body, from the feel of his unmistakable desire.

His hand cupped her cheek. "It's not hard to figure out that since you haven't been dating, you haven't been doing other things either."

She would have tucked her head in embarrassment if his strong hand hadn't gently kept it in place. It didn't enter her mind to close her eyes. His gaze was too intent.

"We'll take this one step at a time."

She moistened her lower lip with the tip of her tongue. "What if we never get to step two?"

His grin was slow, sexy, and self-assured. "You let me worry about that."

Laughter bubbled from her lips. "You're as bad as Griffin."

"I like the sound of that." His thumb grazed her lips, making her tremble. "I like tasting your lips even more." His mouth boldly took hers, his tongue mating with hers, thrusting deeply. Trembling, she held on, kissing him back, feeling desire once again sweep over her.

He lifted his head, his breathing as labored as hers. Shivering in his arms, she knew what he already knew. One day they wouldn't pull back.

Tonight was the night.

Jana sensed it the moment she opened her door Friday night and saw Tyler. When they arrived home, Julian had been waiting for Olivia and Griffin. They'd quickly changed and left. Tyler had been in his office. Jana had stared longingly at the closed door before going to her apartment.

Now, seeing him, her pulse raced, her breath quickened in anticipation. The hot desire in his eyes ignited her own.

She'd never wanted to please a man as much as she wanted to please Tyler nor been so afraid that she wouldn't be able to. Before she'd met him, her actions toward men had been cold and calculated. Her emotions were never involved. With Tyler all of her senses were sharpened and attuned to him. With every breath she drew, every fiber of her being, she wanted him to be as caught up in their lovemaking as she.

"May I come in?" Tyler asked.

Fear and exhilaration swept through her. She had to swallow before she could answer him. "Yes." She stepped back on legs that trembled and refused to steady.

Coming inside, he closed the door behind him, his gaze still locked with hers. His hands tenderly cupped her cheeks, then slid to her shoulders and drew her into his arms. Warm lips skimmed along her neck. "I could kiss you all night."

Eternally grateful that she'd taken her bath early, Jana gave herself up to the pleasure of being held. "I'd let you too."

"Let's see." His mouth took hers in a hot, open-mouth kiss that stole her breath and made her body ache. She strained closer, her arms locking around his neck. Hungrily he feasted on her mouth and she on his.

Soon it wasn't enough. Her impatient hands went to his shirt and tugged it free. The muscled warmth of his skin only made her want to touch his more. Her lips brushed across his nipples. He shuddered, his hands clenching on her arm. She froze.

Had she offended him? Was she too bold? The one thing she dreaded was seeing distaste in his eyes. She couldn't bear that.

"Jana?" Her name was a hoarse thread of sound.

She didn't want to look, but she lifted her head. Oddly, Tyler's faith in her gave her the courage to do so.

Finally their gaze met. Tears sprang to her eyes. In his eyes she saw the tenderness and warmth she'd yearned for all her life. And something else: a burning desire that shook her to the core.

"Tyler," she whispered, a call that he answered. His mouth fused with hers, gentle at first, then ravenous. She was with him all the way. The terry cloth robe slipped from her shoulders. She wore nothing underneath.

His sharp intake of breath caused her eyes to open. His expression was filled with reverence. He didn't take time to unbutton his shirt, just reached for the tail and pulled it over his head. It was still in the air when he pulled her back into his embrace.

A bubble of laughter slipped past her lips at his impatience. It became a whimpering moan of pleasure as his mouth closed on her taut nipple and sucked. Her legs turned to water.

Tyler swung her up in his arms and strode quickly to the bedroom and placed her on the bed. With trembling hands she reached for the button on his jeans.

"I'll do it faster." He proved he was right. Kicking the jeans aside, he covered her body with his. It was glorious and arousing. She wanted more. A small, needy whimper slipped past her lips.

"I'm going to love every incredible inch of you, then start all over again," he promised.

He was good as his word, slowly driving her crazy with wanting him where her body ached the most. He lavished her body with kisses, took teasing love bites, stroked her until her skin was hot and sensitized. "Tyler, please."

He was relentless. Kisses trailed from the slope of her shoulder, past the thrust of her breasts to her stomach until he reached the essence of her. She cried out, arching off the bed, and shattered. When she was still coming down, he began to enter her.

"Jana."

She fought through the sensual haze and opened her eyes. She kept them open as he filled her completely. Then he began to move, a slow rocking at first that caused a coil of heat in her stomach to radiate outward. She locked her legs around his hips, her arms around his neck and gave herself up to his lovemaking. She gave him her all and he gave in return until they were both racing for completion. They finished together in a wild shout of exhilaration.

Tyler's breath was coming in spurts. He'd never experienced such ecstasy. He started to roll, but Jana's arms tightened around him. He brushed a tender kiss against her damp temple. "I'm heavy."

"You're not," she said, nuzzling the side of his neck.

He returned the favor. He couldn't seem to get enough of her. "Yes, I am."

"In a good way," she murmured, then nipped his earlobe.

His body that had begun to cool stirred. "I want you again."

"Then take me."

He joined them, then rolled. He stared up into Jana's flushed face. Her hair was mussed, her nipples pouting. He grew harder just looking at her, but looking could never be enough.

Her hands splayed on his chest, she began to move, a slow circular motion of her hips. He closed his eyes, enjoying her driving him to the edge of sanity. Like a blind man, his hands touched her wherever they could until one covered her breast and one hand slipped between her legs.

His finger sought the sensitive nub in her body and stroked. Her body began to move faster. His eyes opened. Her head thrown back, her eyes closed, her lips slightly parted, she gave herself to him holding nothing back.

He'd never seen anything more beautiful or more humbling. He tried to prolong their joining, but their bodies refused to be denied. Wrapping his arms around her, he kissed her and felt them go over together.

Later they lay facing each other in silence, content for the moment. "I don't want to leave you," Tyler said.

"Then don't," Jana whispered. "Stay with me."

"For as long as you'll let me." Kissing her forehead, he hooked his arm around her and drew her closer. "For as long as you'll let me."

15

Olivia and Jana weren't having a good night. They were used to being with Julian and Tyler, and used to talking with them frequently. Now they'd been alone for the past three days. Once Griffin had gone to bed, they'd given each other manicures. After their nails dried they watched a movie and ate popcorn.

"At least we'll see them tomorrow," Olivia said. "Tyler did say he'd be finished, didn't he?"

"Yes." Jana grabbed a handful of popcorn she didn't want. It was sheer torture having Tyler so close and being unable to be with him. He came to her almost every night. They'd make love, talk, then sleep in each other's arms. She'd never known such contentment. "Why didn't you go to the medical dinner tonight with Julian?"

"I wanted to." Olivia sipped her cola. "But Griffin's schedule is getting so out of whack. Plus I don't want him thinking Julian means more to me than he does."

"He's too smart for that." Jana tossed popcorn into her mouth. "He's crazy about Julian."

"Caring for Julian is easy," Olivia admitted.

"The same with Tyler." She turned to Olivia. "I don't want you to betray his trust, but this Courtney woman still worries me."

Olivia sat up, placing the glass on a coaster on the coffee table. "He's over her."

Jana closed her eyes briefly. "I guess it's payback time. I tried to take my first ex-husband away from the woman he was seeing."

"What happened?" Olivia asked quietly.

"He told me to get lost," Jana said, then sat up beaming. "Tyler has just as much integrity as Gray, maybe more so. He wouldn't run a game on me."

"Of course not."

Jana plopped back on the sofa. "We are two very lucky women."

"We're blessed," Olivia corrected.

"Blessed," Jana said. This time she believed.

Jana was an asset to Midnight Dreams. She loved the shop and helping customers. Olivia said she was a natural and Jana believed her. The store was bustling and she couldn't be happier.

"Hello, Midnight Dreams," Jana said into the receiver, a smile on her face.

"I want to see you."

"Father?" She almost screamed aloud. Happiness swept through her. "Of course. There's so much to tell you."

"Where can we meet?"

"Anytime. You can come to the garage apartment where I live or you can come to the place where I work. Whichever is best for you," she told him. She'd hoped and prayed, but never let herself believe he'd actually call her. She'd sent him two letters since she couldn't get him on the phone.

"I prefer the house," he said. "I'll be there at seven."

"I'll be waiting," she quickly said. "Father, I'm so glad you called. I want things to be different between us."

"They will be. Good-bye."

Jana felt like twirling around with her arms outstretched. *Her father had finally forgiven her.* She'd almost stopped hoping that that would ever happen.

"What put that smile on your face?" Olivia asked.

"I just got off the phone with my father. He wants to see me." Even saying the words made butterflies take flight in her stomach.

Olivia's smile almost matched Jana's. "That's wonderful. I'm so pleased for you."

"I owe it all to you and Tyler." Jana shook her head. "If the both of you hadn't stepped in to help me change my life it might not have happened."

"We simply gave you the opportunity." Olivia leaned against the desk. "You were the one courageous enough to turn your life around."

"For a while I didn't think I'd make it." Jana glanced around the shop. "I like working here. I like my life."

"Very few people can say that and mean it," Olivia told her.

"As much as Julian has been hanging around, I'd say I'm not the only one who can say that," Jana teased.

Olivia blushed. Jana laughed. "A handsome, attentive man can certainly make a woman's life interesting."

"Like Tyler?" Olivia bantered.

"Especially Tyler. To think I was scared of him. He's the most sensitive, honest man I've ever known."

"He thinks you're pretty special."

Jana sobered. "My past doesn't bother him. It's almost as if it never happened."

"To Tyler, it didn't. That was your life before."

"That what he says, but . . ."

"But what?" Olivia asked.

"What if one day something happens and he changes his mind? Or we're out and I meet one of the men I used to know? What then? Could he still look at me the same way?"

Olivia placed her hand on Jana's arm. "Tyler is rock steady. He firmly believes it's not what the person was but who they are now, just as I do. He won't change."

"No, I guess not," Jana answered, but deep down she wasn't sure. Tyler was dependable, but he had also stopped caring for Courtney. They'd made no promises. In any case, long ago Jana had promised herself that she'd never fall in love. It was too painful when they didn't love you back, and no one ever had.

"You're going to wear out your new shoes if you don't stop pacing and come back inside."

Jana glanced over her shoulder at Tyler and continued to pace on the sidewalk in front of the house. "He's late. What if he doesn't come?"

"He'll come." Tyler walked to her and slid his arm around her waist. "Traffic from Frisco is terrible this time of day."

"Maybe." Jana bit her lip.

"Stop worrying." Tyler tightened his hold. "If he hadn't wanted to meet you, he wouldn't have called."

"That's what I keep telling myself." She glanced up into Tyler's strong face. "I've waited so long for him to forgive me, for him to love me."

"He couldn't help but love you," Tyler told her.

Jana turned away without saying anything. Tyler's family was so different from hers. He'd grown up with loving parents. Hers couldn't or wouldn't love her.

"Here comes another car."

Jana whipped her head around. A white Mercedes cruised toward them. Her heart began to beat faster. She stepped out of Tyler's arms and started toward the car.

Tyler caught her arm. "Wait here, Jana."

Her stomach somersaulted as the sports sedan stopped directly in front of the curved walkway. The windows were tinted so she couldn't see inside.

The door on the driver's side opened. Her palms dampened. The moment the man came into sight, the years and harsh words tumbled away. "Father." She rushed to him, throwing her arms around him before he reached the sidewalk. "I missed you so much."

"Let's go inside." He pulled her arms firmly from around his neck.

"Of course." She'd forgotten that he had never liked public display of affection, perhaps because her mother was so demonstrative, especially with men. "Father, I'd like you to meet Tyler Maxwell, the brother of the woman I work for. Tyler, this is my father, Thomas Carpenter."

"Pleased to meet you, Mr. Carpenter." Tyler extended his hand. For a moment he didn't think Jana's father would shake his, then he slowly lifted his hand.

"Mr. Maxwell."

"Please come inside," Jana said, still bubbling. "I want you to meet Olivia Sanders, my boss and friend, and her son, Griffin." She laughed self-consciously. "Olivia insisted you stay for dinner. I tried to call you back, but got the machine."

"I've been busy. Can we go inside?" he asked tightly, his mouth pinched.

Jana's smile slipped. "Of course. This way." She started to take his arm, then thought better of it. She led the way up the sidewalk.

Tyler stepped in front of her and opened the door. "Please come in, Mr. Carpenter."

Olivia appeared almost immediately. "You must be Jana's father. We're so pleased you could make it and hope you can stay for dinner."

"Not if my life depended on it," came the harsh reply.

Jana was stunned. Anguish almost sent her to her knees. "Fath—"

He rounded on her, cutting her off. "Don't ever refer to me as your father again. I disowned you long ago."

"Mr. Carpenter, that's no way to talk to your daughter," Tyler admonished, his voice hard.

"You can't tell me what to do," he riled. "From that display I witnessed outside, it's plain to see why you let her stay. You're just like all the other men in her life."

"Father, please."

"With all the men your mother was sleeping with I don't know why I was the one caught. She's trash and you're just like her. Money and power only give it a classier name and address." He stepped toward her. "I came here to *tell* you to leave town. Because of the sordid past of you and your mother, I had to leave Richmond. I won't leave Frisco. I have a wife and daughter I respect. I can hold my head up."

With each condemning word, the ache inside Jana grew. "Fa— I'm sorry."

"Too little, too late." His hands clenched. "Do you have any idea how it feels to hear men discussing your wife and daughter like high-class tramps?"

Tyler had heard more than enough. "Mr. Carpenter, it's best that you leave."

Jana's father brought the full force of his anger on Tyler. "I had you checked out. You're not the usual type. Neither was her first husband. She nearly destroyed him. Don't let her do the same to you." He strode to the door. "I'm changing my phone number. If you come near me or my family, I'll have a restraining order put on you."

"Please!" Jana cried.

"If you're looking for forgiveness, you won't find it here." He looked first at Tyler, then at Olivia. "Did she tell you that she picked up my sister-in-law's husband at a birthday party she'd crashed? She did it to get back at me for not inviting her. I didn't because I was ashamed of her and with good reason, as she proved. If you know what's good for you, you'll kick her out." Opening the door, he left.

Jana stood there, trembling, aching, wishing she was numb instead of hurting so deeply. Her father had never loved her and he never would.

"Jana."

She jerked away from Tyler. She felt too brittle to be touched.

"Jana, why don't you come upstairs and lie down for a while in your old room?" Olivia asked gently.

How? She could never look either of them in the face again. She was trash. How had she let herself believe that she could change? She raced to the door. Tyler caught her before she had gone five feet. "Please," she begged, refusing to look at him.

"He was wrong."

She shook her head. "If only he was."

"Jana—"

"Please, I need to be alone for a little while."

His hands tightened, then Tyler released her and stepped back. "I'll give you an hour."

Jana continued out the door, across the lawn, then up the stairs into her apartment. She only went a few steps before heart-wrenching sobs tore from her throat. She crumpled to the floor. Her father hated her. Could she blame him?

She'd done things, had things done to her that would make a streetwalker blush. How had she thought she could be happy when her past would always be there, waiting to trip her up and bring her back down again?

She was what she was. She'd never be able to outrun her past or live a life good enough for people to see her and not the old Jana.

So why keep trying?

Pushing up, she went to her bedroom and stared at herself in the mirror. Tonight she was going to be just what her father thought she was, amoral and heartless. Turning away, she went to get dressed.

Tonight, she was going on the hunt.

Tyler tried to stick to his promise to wait an hour, but lasted only forty-seven minutes before he went to the apartment. Jana had sounded so broken it had torn him up inside. His fists clenched. It had been all he could do not to drag her father from the house. Each step Jana made away from the old life was difficult enough. She was still too unsure of herself.

He rapped on the door. "Jana. Open up. I brought you a tray. Jana?" No answer. "I'm coming in." Using the spare key, he opened the door and saw the bedroom door open. He walked quietly in that direction. If she was asleep he didn't want to wake her.

The room was empty. The perfume he'd given her wafted in the air. The mirror in the bathroom was foggy with steam. She'd dressed and gone out. She'd never done that before. He didn't like to think of the possible reason for her doing so now.

People were quick to pass judgment on her. He wouldn't fall in that category. Going to the kitchen, he put the plate of food in the refrigerator, then straightened. The roses he'd cut from the garden and given her that morning were on the breakfast table. One long finger touched the petal.

"Come home, Jana. Be as strong as I know you can be. Come home. Come home to me."

Nightlife in Dallas, like most big cities, didn't start to swing until midnight. Aware of this, Jana sat through a couple of movies, then went to lower Greenville Avenue where the trendiest of the private nightclubs were located. This was the most likely place to be patronized by the type of man she was looking for. She wouldn't get past the velvet rope without being on the list, but she planned to interest a man before he went inside.

Paying the cab, she got out. Late-model luxury cars lined the streets and crowded the small parking lot. She staked out a darkened corner of the parking lot and waited, ignoring the men who arrived in a Lexus, a Infinity. When the Porsche Carrera roared into the parking lot, she moved to a white Mercedes she had already picked out that was several cars from the end of the parking lot, and began digging through her purse.

"Is everything all right?"

She started and turned around, sizing up the man in one quick glance. Late fifties, wanting to be thirty, with a cream-colored Ralph Lauren sports jacket, tobacco-colored tailored slacks, Cole Haan loafers. She caught a whiff of Creed cologne that cost four hundred dollars for eight ounces.

She pressed her hand against the Hermès scarf she hadn't been able to part with that she'd worn as a top, exposing several inches of skin. The man's gaze lingered on her breasts, just as she'd planned, then dropped to the bare skin. She waited for his gaze to lift, trying to keep the irritation from her face as she did so. "I seem to have locked my keys in the car."

He stepped closer. She caught his arm. "Don't. The alarm might go off." She sighed, running her hand through her hair, tightening the scarf across her breasts. "To make matters worse, I left my cell phone charging at home. I can't even call service or go home since my house keys are on the key ring."

He pulled out his cell as she'd known he would do. "Please use mine."

"You're a lifesaver." The cell phone was top-of-the-line. She dialed a false number, paced, then sighed and left a frantic message that she was locked out of her car and where she was. "My brother must be out." She handed him the phone. "Thanks."

"You don't plan to wait out here, do you?" he asked.

"I don't have much choice. I need to be here in case my brother comes."

His gaze touched her breasts again. "I hate to leave you out here. Please, just come inside for one drink at least. Your brother would understand, and it's hot out here."

She couldn't take the chance of the real owner of the car coming out and driving away. "I'm afraid I can't. Although I'd love to. It's so refreshing meeting a courteous man like you."

"There are a few of us left. I've got an idea." He laughed self-consciously. "I guess we better introduce ourselves first. I'm Harry Former."

"Janet Street." The name just slipped out. She wasn't sure why she didn't want to use her real name. Wasn't she doing this so she could throw it in her father's face?

"Janet, why don't we leave a note on the car with my cell number. That way your brother could reach you," he said.

"That's sweet of you, but what if we get separated inside? It's always packed and jumping."

"We won't if we go to my place."

It was a bold move on his part, but hadn't she laid the groundwork for just that invitation? She took a cautious step back.

"Please don't take offense," he said quickly. "You'll be perfectly safe." Going into the breast pocket of his jacket, he pulled out his wallet and showed her his driver's license. "See, you can trust me."

Since she planned on going home with him, she refrained from pointing out that if he was an ax murderer her seeing his license wouldn't make a hell of a lot of difference. The address at the new W apartments meant he had money. The units started at half a million.

"You can trust me," he repeated.

"All right," Jana finally said, allowing him to lead her to his car. She started to get in, then stopped. She knew this would end in his bed as well as he did. Most people who went clubbing wanted sex for the night and no lingering good-byes in the morning.

"Just a drink and conversation," he cajoled.

She got in the car. This was what she came for, what she wanted.

The drive to Harry's place took less than fifteen minutes. He pulled into the underground parking lot and parked near the elevator, which quickly and silently took them to the penthouse floor.

Unlocking the door, Harry stepped aside so she could enter. The penthouse was beautiful and tastefully decorated with artwork, sleek furniture, and hardwood flooring. The more she knew of Harry, the more it appeared as if he could keep her in the manner in which she had once been accustomed.

He went to the bar and splashed whiskey in a glass she knew was Baccarat. "What would you like?"

For me to have lived my life differently. The words came to her so strongly that she thought she had spoken them aloud.

Frowning, he came around the bar. "You're not afraid, are you?"

"Not the way you think."

"Good. Drink this. It will help you relax."

And lose any inhibitions about tumbling into bed with him. She downed the whiskey in one gulp.

His smile was slow. "I like a woman who can handle her liquor." He took her glass. Let me get you another one." At the bar, he poured another drink. On the way back to her, he picked up a control on the glass coffee table. Lights dimmed, a fire started in the fireplace, soft music began to play. "That's better."

Jana didn't say anything as he handed her glass to her. Just don't think, she ordered herself.

"Why don't we sit down?" Taking her arm, he led her to an immense chaise with a carved wood frame near the fireplace. She didn't want to think of all the women who had been there before her and who would come after her.

They were barely sitting before his arm went around her, his lips pressing against her bare arm, his free hand on her knee and sliding higher.

Jana shut her eyes. *Just go for it. This is all you'll ever be.*

His hand reached the edge of her skirt and began to inch higher. His mouth moved to the curve of her jaw, the same place Tyler had brushed with his fingers.

"No!" she bounded up.

"What's the matter with you?" He stood, glaring at her. "You're old enough to know the score."

"Yes, but tonight I don't want to play the game." She started for the door.

"Then why did you come up here? You knew where it would lead."

Her hand on the doorknob, Jana turned. "Every man wouldn't expect sex for helping a woman." She knew one in particular. "If you hurry, perhaps you'll be able to pick up a more accommodating woman." Opening the door, she made good her escape.

The security light on the garage and at the corner of the apartment allowed Tyler to see Jana when she was a good distance away. He made himself remain on the third step leading up to her apartment rather than going to her as he badly wanted to do. She stopped when she saw him, then slowly continued until she stood over him. The wrapped top was just wide enough to cover her breasts.

"I picked up a man. He took me to his penthouse."

Tyler's gut clenched. So many emotions were running through him he couldn't sort them all out.

"I tried to shut my mind down to what was going to happen, but I couldn't."

He caught her hand. "You're a different woman now."

"I want to be," she said quietly.

"Your father threw you a curve, but you didn't cave in."

Tyler knew her so well. "I was going to show him that I was as amoral as he said. Then I realized that I would only be hurting myself again, just as I've done all these years." Her hand clenched in his. "All my life I've tried to make my parents love me. My mother's twisted sense of values became my own. I kept hoping my father would step in and stop me. After a while I didn't care. Being in control over such powerful men was its own lure, and I was always in control. I never let myself care too much for any of them."

His thumb grazed the top of her hand. He didn't want to hear this, but realized she had to talk about her painful past before she could put it completely behind her.

"I can't go back to that lifestyle. From now on, I'm going to live for myself."

Tyler came to his feet, his hand tenderly cupping Jana's face. "I knew you could do it. You're right. You have changed from the first time I saw you."

"I was deceitful, desperate, and a pain."

His thumb grazed over her lower lip, felt her shiver. "Not then. In Seattle at the nightclub."

Her eyes widened.

"I'm the man who carried you to safety. I was there with a client, unwinding after a busy day."

She was momentarily speechless. "Why didn't you ever say anything?"

"I didn't place where I had seen you until the cookout a week after you came. Then too, I was enjoying getting to know the woman you were becoming, the new Jana."

Her trembling hand covered his. No words had ever meant more. Her forehead touched his. "You are an amazing man, Tyler Maxwell."

"You're an amazing woman."

Her head lifted. "Not yet, but one day I hope to be. There's another reason why I came home. You."

He was momentarily speechless. "You make a man weak and feel like he can lift a mountain at the same time."

"You make me believe." She wanted so badly to make love with him, but not with some other man's cologne clinging to her. "Good night."

"Good night."

Halfway up the stairs, she stopped. "Thanks for waiting up for me. No one ever has before," she said, then continued up the stairs. Opening the door, she went inside. *The new Jana.*

She felt new and it was wonderful.

"Quick. Lock the door and turn over the open sign before anther customer comes in," Olivia said, hanging up the phone.

Jana laughed and did as she requested. "Is this the woman who wasn't sure about dating Julian a month ago?"

Olivia made a face. "As I've always said, a woman can change her mind."

"You won't get an argument from me." Jana followed Olivia into the back. "Where are you two going tonight?"

Olivia blushed. "He's cooking dinner for me at his place."

Jana's eyebrows slowly rose. Olivia's blush deepened. She ducked her head.

"I like Julian," Jana said. "I'd say go for it."

Olivia's head lifted. "He kissed me and my brain turned to fuzz."

"It's kind of scary knowing a man can do that to you." Jana grabbed their purses from the cabinet.

Olivia laughed. "It's kind of difficult to imagine Tyler that way."

"Your brother is the most complex man I've ever known." They started for the front. "He can be so laid back one minute, then dangerous and compelling the next. The minutes race when I'm with him and drag when we're apart."

"The same thing with Julian," Olivia admitted, digging in her purse for her keys. "That's why we're staying in tonight. Thank you and Tyler for babysitting Griffin."

"We enjoy him. With Tyler, I'm learning that staying at home has it privileges," Jana said, and then, "Looks like we have a determined customer."

Her hand still in her big purse, Olivia lifted her head and froze. "God, no!"

Jana looked from the angelically beautiful, well-dressed man to Olivia. Her face was pale, her entire body trembling. Instinctively, Jana wrapped her arms around Olivia and stepped in front of her to block out the angry-looking man. "The door is locked. Whoever he is, he can't hurt you. All we have to do is walk back to the phone and call Tyler and he'll be here in minutes."

"I—" Olivia began, then closed her eyes. "Why did he have to come back?"

"Come on. Sit down." Supporting Olivia, Jana started toward the back. The glass on the door rattled. Olivia flinched and stopped, seemingly as if her strength was gone. This Olivia frightened Jana. "I'm calling Tyler." Removing the phone from its holder, she hit the speed dial. He answered on the second ring.

"Tyler, we need you at the shop. A man frightened Olivia."

"Aaron," Olivia said softly. "Tell him it's Aaron."

Olivia looked back over her shoulder. "It's Griffin's father."

Tyler's curse said it all.

16

Hanging up the phone, Jana helped Olivia to the chair in front of the desk, thankful it was facing away from the door. "Tyler will take care of everything. I'll get you a glass of water."

"He can't see Griffin. He can't!" Her eyes widened. She fumbled for the phone. "I've got to call Wanda and warn her."

Jana stayed Olivia's nervous hands. "Griffin was going home with Xavier after day camp today. He won't be home until after seven."

Olivia relaxed immediately. "I forgot."

Those two words told Jana how much the appearance of her ex-husband had affected Olivia. "Griffin is probably trying to talk Xavier's mother into letting him have another dessert."

The strain around Olivia's mouth lessened. "Carol is a good mother. She won't let him get away with anything."

"Of course she won't. You'd never entrust Griffin to anyone who didn't have his best interest at heart."

Olivia sat upright, her nails digging into Jana's hand. "He couldn't have come back for my baby. I won't let him ruin Griffin's life the way he wanted to ruin mine." She rose to her feet and turned, the paleness gone and in its place fierce determination. "There's no way in hell I'll let him get close to my son."

"Tyler's here." Jana went to the door with Olivia directly behind her. Jana could hear the two men arguing before she unlocked the door. "Tyler, maybe it's best you come inside to Olivia's office."

Tyler's mouth tightened.

"If he wants to cause a scene, it's all right with me," Aaron said, picture perfect in Armani.

"It's all right, Tyler," Olivia said. She started for her office.

With a triumphant smirk, Aaron followed.

Tyler flexed his hands, a muscle leaping in his jaw. Jana caught his hand as he passed. "She needs you to stay in control and help her."

His sharp gaze sliced into her. Once it would have made her cower, now she squeezed his hand. "Go. I'll lock the back up."

"Sorry. Thanks." He caught up with Aaron. Both disappeared through the swinging doors.

Jana locked the front door and called Wanda. "We might be here awhile."

"That devil is back."

No translation was needed. "They're in Olivia's office."

"She never wanted him near her again. This must be hard for her," Wanda said. "You stay close by her in case she needs you."

"Wanda, what they're saying is private. I have no right to be in there."

"Olivia stuck by you. Tyler's sweet on you. Can you do any less?"

No, she couldn't. "You play dirty," Jana said.

"Don't waste any more time." The phone went dead.

Jana hung up the receiver, took a breath and went to the back, very much aware that it was going to get rough.

Olivia felt more in control behind her desk. Having Tyler by her side helped. So did Jana's presence. She'd just come inside, closing the door softly behind her.

"What do you want?"

"Not even a hello after almost eight years, Olivia? What happened to all that Southern hospitality and Christianity?" Aaron asked with a smirk on his face.

"Spit it out, Aaron, then get the hell out of my sister's life." Tyler took a threatening step from around the desk.

Aaron's light brown eyes narrowed. "It's not Olivia's life I'm concerned about, but that of my son."

"No!" Olivia shouted, coming around the desk to face her ex-husband. "You're not coming near my son."

"He's mine too or did you forget that?"

Her cold gaze held his. "No, but believe me I've tried."

The nasty smile slid from his face. "My lawyer will call tomorrow with a date, time, and place to meet. I advise you to be there."

"Why?" she asked "The divorce is final. I made sure all the papers were filed and I have the decree."

"Which might not have been granted if the judge had known you were pregnant."

"You couldn't have cared less!" Her fists clenched. "You were sleeping with Edward more than you were sleeping with me."

The nasty smile reappeared. "And enjoying it more."

Tyler moved fast . . . but Olivia was faster. The slap across Aaron's face echoed across the room. His hand lifted and swung. Tyler caught his hand, slinging it away violently, causing Aaron to stumble and fall.

Fists clenched, legs apart, Tyler stood over him. "Get up and get out."

Aaron slowly came to his feet. "You'll pay for this."

"Not as much as you if you raise your hand to anyone in my family again," Tyler promised.

Jana opened the door. "I'll show you out."

Aaron looked at her as if he were seeing her for the first time, then his eyes narrowed as if trying to place her. Straightening his tailored jacket, he left without another word. Jana followed him out, locking the front door behind him. Olivia not dating and her insecurity with men now made perfect sense. Such a betrayal would cut deeply.

Jana closed her eyes, but the picture of Gray's face filled with pain and shock wouldn't go away. She realized how deeply her betrayal of her first husband had wounded him. His grandmother had a right to hate her. In a sense she was no better than Aaron. They were both cheaters and liars, both had hid their deviousness from the person they married.

She turned as Olivia and Tyler emerged from the back. "Tyler and I are going to pick up Griffin. Can you drive my SUV home?"

"All right." Jana accepted the keys. "If there . . ." Her voice trailed off. Nothing she could do or say would help.

Olivia tucked her head. "Thank you."

Jana's hand clenched around the keys. She wished she hadn't listened to Wanda. Her gaze settled on the middle of Tyler's wide chest. "Drive carefully."

"You all right?"

Her head came up. Tears stung her throat. With all he and Olivia were going through, he still thought of her. Perhaps if she had met him years ago her life might have been different. "Yes."

His eyes narrowed as if he didn't believe her. "See you later."

"All right." Jana looked at them moving slowly, as if each step was an effort. Aaron's threat to Griffin was taking a toll on them both.

Griffin thought it was cool that his mother and uncle joined them at Chuck E. Cheese's for pizza and fun. He couldn't believe his luck when he was able to get another dessert and play all the games he wanted. He was having one of the best times of his life. But on the drive home he began to realize that his mother was quieter than usual.

"You feel all right, Mama?"

"Of course, honey." She turned to look into the backseat of the truck where he sat. "Just a little tired. I think I'll stay home tonight and you and I can play a couple of your new games."

"Wow." He almost jumped up and down in the seat. It was already past his bedtime. This day was coming close to the wonderful times of his birthday and Christmas all rolled into one. Her spotted Julian's car when they turned onto their street. Griffin giggled. "I'll beat him as usual."

"I thought it would be just the two of us," his mother told him.

He liked playing games with his mother, but Julian was cool. He never treated him like a little kid or acted if Griffin were imposing when he and his mother were sitting on the sofa together. "Sure."

Tyler pulled into the garage and cut the motor. "Are you positive you want to handle it this way?"

"Yes."

Griffin climbed out of the backseat of his uncle's truck. He'd learned long ago not to try and figure out what adults were talking about. "I'm thirsty. Can I have a soft drink?"

"Yes."

Before she changed her mind, Griffin raced toward the kitchen.

"You can't make it up to him by letting him have his way," Tyler said, gazing down at his sister.

"I know." She rubbed her temple. "I better go tell Julian I'm not going."

Julian stood when Olivia came into the media room. All Jana would tell him was that she was running late. He frowned and crossed to Olivia. She was trembling. Her eyes were red, her lids puffy as if she'd been crying. "Olivia, what is it?"

"I'll be going." Jana came to her feet. "Good night."

"I'll walk you out," Tyler said as she neared.

Jana's smile was brittle. "That's not necessary."

"I think it is." Without waiting for an answer Tyler laced his fingers with Jana's and left the room.

Julian took Olivia's cold hands in his. "Please tell me what's the matter."

She pulled her hands free, inexplicably feeling lonely already. "We can't see each other again."

"What?"

Olivia picked up a framed crystal picture of her and Griffin with his cap and gown on when he'd graduated from kindergarten. "It's best for everyone."

"How can you say that? Something's happened and I want to know."

"My ex-husband is back." She swallowed before she could continue. "I think he wants custody of Griffin."

"Honey, no." He tried to pull her into his arms, but she pushed away. Her rejection hurt.

"I hate to be rude, but I'm very tired."

He didn't move. "I don't get it. Your ex shows up and you're ready to turn your back on me, on us?"

She placed the picture back on the table. "There is no us."

That infuriated him. Catching her arms, Julian turned her around. "Look at me. What has this to do with us?"

"Just let it go."

"Not until you tell me."

Angry, more frightened than she had ever been, she shouted, "I won't make a fool of myself again."

"Just because he cheated on you with some woman is no reason to think I will."

A pained expression crossed her face. "If only he had."

"What?"

"My ex-husband is gay. Only he failed to tell me at the time of our marriage. I can see you're shocked. Imagine how I felt when I read his e-mail from his lover, his best friend and the best man at our wedding." This time she was able to push out of his arms.

"I was so stupid. If I hadn't seen those e-mails he never would have admitted his secret life. And you know what he said? That he only married me because I was so gullible and innocent. He never cared about me. He just used me."

"Olivia . . ." Julian began, then discovered he didn't know what to say to help her. She had a right to be angry and frightened.

"Leaves you speechless, doesn't it? Took me almost four months to tell my family. Then I had to be tested for AIDS, subject Griffin to the same tests, then waiting each time for the results." She closed her eyes momentarily. "The fear is indescribable. He put me and Griffin at risk for his own selfish pleasure."

"Olivia, no woman should ever have to go through what you had to endure, but you can't paint me with the same brush."

"He's almost as handsome as you are," she said.

"I'm not gay," Julian quickly told her.

"But you're beautiful. It's only a matter of time before another woman catches your attention." She looked him in the eyes. "I won't go through that again."

"You're not pushing me out of your life."

"Leave, Julian."

"I'm not leaving until you start making sense."

"You leave my mother alone." Griffin rushed into the room, his small fists balled.

"Honey, no!" Olivia wrapped her arms around her son before he reached Julian, holding his trembling body close to hers.

"Griffin, I'd never hurt your mother or you," Julian told the little boy, regretting that he had handled things so badly.

"You were yelling at her," Griffin accused.

"I'm sorry, but sometimes when grown-ups feel passionate about something they yell, like playing sports."

Griffin looked as if he didn't believe him.

"Good night, Julian."

With her arms wrapped protectively around her son, Olivia was close to tears again. Julian had no choice but to leave quietly. "This isn't over," he told her.

He left the room without another word, carrying with him the picture of Olivia's frightened face. He had a low opinion of men or women who weren't honest about their sexual orientation. Their partners had a right to know, but Julian was aware that gay men, more than gay women, sometimes led a double life.

Outside, he looked back at the house. He'd leave for now, but he had no intention of staying away. Olivia *and* Griffin meant too much to him to be shut out of their lives.

Tyler hadn't gotten to where he was by taking no for an answer. He'd overridden or ignored every one of Jana's objections to him following her inside her apartment. He didn't know if she was upset because of what she'd learned about Olivia's husband or some other problem. He just knew he was going to find out why before he left.

"You going to tell me what's bothering you, or do I have to guess?"

Her hand threaded through her hair, shiny and fashionably cut, vastly different than when he had first seen her. "Tyler, I'm rather tired."

"So you want me to guess." He took a seat on the sofa.

Jana blew out a breath. "Shouldn't you be with Olivia?"

Crossing his legs, he placed his arms on the back of the sofa. "She wants time with Griffin."

Twin furrows ran across Jana's forehead. "What about Julian?"

"Griffin has to come first." His mouth flattening into a thin line, Tyler pulled his arms from the back of the sofa and clasped them between his knees.

Jana went to stand in front of him. "You can't mean that she doesn't plan to see him again?"

"Olivia will make the right decision."

Jana started for the front door. Tyler caught her just before she could grab the doorknob. "It's her decision to make."

"But it's wrong. He cares about her," she said.

"Then he'll understand that she's reliving a lot of pain and heartache, and let her work through it." Tyler headed for the kitchen.

She shot him a look. "You wouldn't."

"I'm not as patient about some things." He opened the refrigerator. "Did you eat?"

"I wasn't hungry."

He reached in and pulled out a plastic-covered container. "We'll have ham sandwiches."

Jana reached around him for the mayonnaise, lettuce, and tomatoes. "Have a seat. I'll fix them."

He smiled.

"What?" she asked, placing everything on the spotless white formica counter.

Tyler took a seat at the small wooden table in the kitchen. "I distinctly remember the time you wouldn't have offered or known how."

Jana paused in reaching for a knife. "Sometimes that life seems so far removed from me, almost as if someone else lived it, then other times . . ." Sliding the knife out of the holder, she whacked the lettuce.

"Then other times . . ." he prompted

She opened the bread sack and paused. "I feel as if I'm only a step away from what I was." She went back to fixing the sandwiches. "Olivia's ex reminded me so much of myself, so selfish and arrogant in what I wanted no matter how it might hurt anyone. I always came first."

"The difference is, he's still the same prick."

She whirled back. "But he made me remember those times I carelessly ruined people's lives."

Tyler went to her, not touching, just looking deeply into her pain-filled eyes. "You're not the woman you were yesterday or even a day ago. Each day you learn more about yourself. Painful to look at, but if you don't, you won't become the woman I know you can be."

"And what kind of woman is that? One that picks up strange men and goes with them to their apartment?" she asked.

He touched her then. "A woman, like most of us, who's not perfect or blameless or sinless, but trying to find her way. A woman with enough courage to admit her mistakes and try to learn from them. A woman I'm glad picked Midnight Dreams to enter."

"It was the only store open."

"Guess we were both lucky." He pulled her into his arms, their bodies aligning.

Her hands trembled on his chest. "How is it that you always manage to smooth out the rough places in my soul?"

His eyes darkened. "Because you deserve happiness, you deserve to know you have value."

"As long as I'm in your arms, I believe."

"Then I'll just have to hold you more often."

"Please."

His mouth brushed across hers in a gentle kiss. Slowly he lifted his head. "You make my head swim."

She snuggled close, feeling strong and weak at the same time that she could bring a man like Tyler such pleasure. "Same here." She took a deep breath and took another precious step. "With you being in control no longer matters. With you, I can't wait for the mindlessness, the fluttering in my stomach when you're near." She lifted her head. "Strange, but it's liberating."

He groaned and pulled her closer. "You're making it difficult to turn you loose."

She didn't want him to, but Olivia needed him tonight more than she did. Slowly she pushed out of his arms. "Have a seat while I finish fixing the sandwiches."

"Why can't I nibble on your neck while you're doing it?" he asked, his mouth curved into a winsome smile.

"Because I wouldn't be able to think and there's no telling what I'd put in the sandwiches or how long it would take." She went to the counter.

"Just fix one for you. I already ate."

She glanced over her shoulder. "Taking care of me again?"

"Always."

The word went straight to her heart. Having a man like Tyler around almost made her believe in forever.

Olivia hadn't been able to eat more than a few bites since Aaron showed up on Saturday. Today was Tuesday. Her stomach was tied in knots. It didn't help that Griffin kept asking about Julian. Aaron had taken something else from them.

Seeing Aaron across the table with not a care in the world made her want to go over the table and wipe that smug smile off his face. He didn't care that he was disrupting his son's life. As usual, he only cared about himself.

"Thank you for coming, Mrs. Sanders," Aaron's lawyer, Ben Barnes, said. "You have your lawyer, so there's no reason for your brother's presence."

"There's every reason in view of the fact that, if not for Mrs. Sanders's brother, your client would have struck her," Brianna Ireland, Olivia's lawyer, stated.

"She slapped me," Aaron snapped.

"And your response was to hit back?" Brianna asked. Brianna was brainy, beautiful, and resourceful. And depending on the situation, she could be ruthless and relentless. She was the best divorce lawyer in the state.

Aaron opened his mouth, but his lawyer touched his arm and spoke for him. "Of course not. My client's emotions have been running high since he's been separated from his son."

Brainna's brow rose. "That's strange since Mrs. Sanders has not heard from him since she informed his parents of her son's birth as she was unaware of his whereabouts."

Aaron's lawyer laced his fingers on the polished cherry table in the conference room of Brianna's office. "Second-hand knowledge at best and unproven."

Opening a folder in front of her, Brianna removed seven Christmas cards and seven birthday cards, then shoved them across the polished surface. "As you can see from the return address, date on the envelope, and the writing on the cards, Mrs. Sanders did indeed notify her son's grandparents of his birth."

"We'll have those analyzed for authenticity of course." Aaron's lawyer barely glanced at the cards.

"Of course." Brianna turned to Aaron. "Mr. Sanders has expressed no interest in his son. Frankly, Mrs. Sanders is concerned that any association may be detrimental to the child."

"Because I'm gay?" Aaron asked sharply.

"Because you're a liar, a cheat, and have the morals of an alley cat," Olivia said, unable to remain quiet. "You knew you were gay with multiple partners and that your lifestyle put me and any children we might have at risk, yet you said nothing."

"Slanderous hearsay," Mr. Barnes said. "Might I point out that the divorce decrees cited irreconcilable differences?"

"Because I was too ashamed to tell anyone the truth," Olivia admitted.

"Don't say any more, Olivia," her lawyer cautioned.

"Please let her continue," Mr. Barnes said, his smile slick. "You admit to being ashamed. Might you also have been angry with Mr. Sanders? So angry that you failed to let him know that you were carrying his child?"

"Don't answer that," Brianna told her.

Aaron's lawyer smiled like a cat that just spotted a bird's nest on the ground. "She doesn't have to. Since both parties wanted the divorce it went through three months after papers were filed. Five months and two weeks later birth records show Griffin Maxwell Sanders was born, weighing seven pounds, eight ounces with an Apgar score of ten. He was full term and healthy. She deliberately kept the pregnancy a secret, depriving my client of almost eight precious years of his son's life. We want joint custody."

"No!" Olivia shot to her feet. "You're not taking my son."

"Olivia." Tyler wrapped his arms around her, but he felt the same. "Name your price. I'll pay it, whatever it is."

Aaron stood, managing to look offended. "How dare you think I'd put a price on my son's head. If that's the way you think, perhaps I should sue for full custody."

"You can't do this!" Olivia cried. "Hate me, but don't take it out on my son!"

"*My* son as well."

Mr. Barnes stood. "In anticipation that an amicable agreement could not be worked out I filed papers last week petitioning the court for joint custody. We'll let the courts decide. Good day." Mr. Barnes picked up his briefcase and left with Aaron.

The door closed behind them. Olivia trembled in Tyler's arms. "He can't take my baby."

Tyler looked over her head at the lawyer's solemn face. "We'll fight."

Olivia gazed at her lawyer. "Brianna, you don't look hopeful."

She placed the greeting cards in her folder before she spoke. "The Family Court's judge is not going to look at his sexual orientation as a deterrent to joint custody, because the court can't openly discriminate. And you can bet his lawyer is going to make sure the case is heard before a liberal judge. But any judge will want some very good answers as to why you kept your pregnancy a secret."

"I wasn't sure at first," she said slowly.

"And when you were?" her lawyer asked, watching her closely.

"I wanted to protect my child from a man who lied as easily as he breathed, an adulterer." Olivia straightened. "I still feel the same way."

"Because of his sexual preference?" Brianna asked.

"I'm not homophobic, if that's what you're asking. Some of my best clients are gay men." She shook her head. "It wasn't the fact he was gay, it was because he lied to me and used me."

"That was the answer I was hoping for." Brianna tapped the folders on the table. "But why did he come back now?"

"We've been asking ourselves the same thing," Tyler said. "He didn't suddenly feel paternal and get an urge to be Griffin's father. There has to be a reason, and I'm going to find out."

"Do that, and keep me posted," Brianna told him. "Be prepared for this to move quickly because a young child is involved."

Olivia swallowed the lump in her throat. "There's a chance he could win, isn't there?"

"I won't lie to you, but the court strongly favors the mother in custody cases. You're a wonderful, well-respected woman in the community with a spotless reputation and nothing to hide." Her eyes hardened. "If we have to, we'll fill the court with people who'll testify on your behalf."

"But that might not be enough," Olivia said, her stomach knotting when Brianna didn't disagree. She could lose her son to a selfish, disreputable man, and there was nothing she could do about it.

Aware that Olivia needed to keep her mind occupied, Tyler didn't object when Olivia insisted he drop her off at Midnight Dreams. While she was in the back putting up her things, he spoke briefly with Jana who assured him she'd keep an eye on Olivia. He didn't have a doubt she would. She'd changed from the selfish woman to a caring individual who thought of others first. He hoped he was one of those lucky individuals. Kissing her on the cheek, he drove home and went straight to his computer.

If one knew where to look there was a wealth of information to be had in cyberspace. He'd try to get it legally, but if he had to bend a law or two he wasn't going to lose any sleep over it. Tyler's fingers raced over the computer keys. First, he wanted to check to see if there had been anything about the earning status of Sanders, LLC, in the news lately. Aaron liked money and the privileged lifestyle it granted.

But the manicured nails, tailored suit and perfect diction couldn't hide the fact that he was a sleaze. He'd suckered Olivia into a marriage to hide his homosexuality. He hadn't cared about her then or later. The divorce had been quiet because he hadn't wanted knowledge of his sexuality to get out.

It had been almost eight years since Tyler had seen him, but he hadn't changed from the self-centered man he'd proven to be during his short marriage to Olivia. There had to be a reason for his sudden decision to seek joint custody.

Tyler located an interview in the *Washington Post* dated fifteen months ago. Harold Sanders, Aaron's father, had been interviewed about the growth potential of the private equity firm he'd started. They had taken a hit after 9/11, and like many companies were trying to come out of a tailspin.

Further digging revealed Aaron's father, the CEO of the firm, had been diagnosed with prostate cancer seven months ago. He'd gone into remission after chemotherapy and radiation. An article in *Black Enterprise* magazine four months ago revealed the cancer had reappeared in his lungs, then spread to his liver. He wasn't expected to recover.

Tyler leaned back in his chair. He'd only met Harold Sanders once, the day his son married Olivia. He had struck Tyler as a rather quiet man. His wife was the same way. They'd acknowledged Griffin after Olivia had notified them, sent birthday cards and Christmas cards with money, but nothing personal. They'd made no move to make him a part of their lives.

It was only after Griffin started asking about why his father didn't visit like his friends' dads and asking if it was his fault that his father didn't live with them that Olivia had begun sending gifts in Aaron's name. She'd wanted to spare her son the pain of knowing his father didn't care about him, but it had made Griffin idolize his absent father all the more. If there was the slightest chance for him to see his father, Griffin would take it.

And that would break Olivia's heart.

Olivia added not sleeping well to not eating well since Aaron's lawyer had called to tell them of the date to meet in the judge's chambers. It was set for Friday. Aaron was moving quickly. She didn't mind. She wanted him out of her life as soon as possible.

This time for good.

Sitting in the judge's chambers next to her lawyer, with Aaron and his lawyer less than two feet away, it was difficult to keep her anger and fear under control as Brianna had warned her to do. Her nails dug into the purse in her lap.

"Thank you, Judge Watkins, for agreeing to meet in your chambers to discuss the custody of Griffin Maxwell Sanders," Aaron's lawyer said. "You'll see by the papers before you that at the time of my client's divorce, he was not aware of his wife's pregnancy."

"Neither was my client, Judge Watkins," Brianna stated. "The divorce and the reason for it had put her under great emotional stress."

"We are not here to discuss the divorce, but the wrongful withholding of my client's right and privilege to share in the joy and pride of raising his only child," Aaron's lawyer said.

"He never wanted Griffin. He doesn't want him now."

"Olivia, please," Brianna cautioned. "I'm sorry. Your Honor, but, like any caring mother, my client loves her son deeply and wants what is best for him."

"Keeping him away from his father isn't best for him," Aaron's lawyer quickly pointed out.

"That's debatable," Brianna was just as quick to say.

Aaron came out of his chair. "What's that supposed to mean?"

"Sit down," Judge Watkins ordered. "I don't want another word out of anyone unless I ask you directly." Aaron glared at Brianna, but he took his seat.

"Mrs. Sanders, Mr. Barnes raised a good question. Once you knew you were pregnant, didn't you consider the child's father had a right to know?"

Olivia's hands tightened on the purse. "After I learned he was having an affair with his best man at our wedding along with several other men, I felt so stupid and gullible, that I tried to think of him as little as possible. My pregnancy was the only thing that sustained me during the darkest period in my life."

The judge didn't even glance at Aaron. "Did you keep the pregnancy from your ex-husband because of his sexual orientation?"

Olivia was glad Brianna had already posed the question and that she could answer it truthfully. "It wasn't that he was gay, it was because he'd lied to me and used me. After the divorce I didn't know how to locate him, so I contacted his parents. Since his birth, Aaron hasn't made any contact with Griffin."

Judge Watkins turned to Aaron. "Mr. Sanders, what do you have to say on your behalf?"

"I love my son. I want to make that clear, but I was afraid that she had turned him against me. Also, I didn't want to disrupt his life." Aaron briefly bowed his head "But my own father is ill and I see now how important the relationship is between a father and a son. I want to be a part of Griffin's life, to let him know his grandfather before it is too late. Nothing is as important to me."

Brianna pressed her hand against Olivia's to keep her quiet. "Mr. Sanders, according to the staff at the hospital, you seldom visited your father while he was hospitalized."

Aaron's cold stare drilled into her. "They're mistaken."

"Is the house staff mistaken as well?" she asked. "You've visited your father only twice in the past two weeks."

"I've been busy running the company and preparing to gain custody of my son," he defended. "My parents understand and support me in this."

"My client has a prosperous business and finds time for her son," Brianna put in smoothly. "He is and always will be her first priority."

"Not quite," Aaron's lawyer said.

"What are you talking about? I can have witnesses lined up within the hour that will collaborate what I've said," Brianna said.

"I wonder what those witnesses think of Mrs. Sanders hiring Jana Franklin, a woman known to live off the generosity of men and that's putting it nicely," Mr. Barnes said. "More importantly, why is this same woman living in the garage apartment on the grounds of Mrs. Sanders's home and allowed to be in daily contact with an impressionable child? Ms. Franklin's reputation is so debased that her own father wants nothing to do with her. In fact, he is only too willing to testify to the fact."

Olivia didn't need to feel Brianna's hand clench on her arm to know Aaron's lawyer had dealt them a setback. "Jana has changed."

"Not according to her father," Aaron's lawyer said. "Haven't some customers canceled orders or stopped patronizing your store because they don't wish to associate with her?"

"One customer canceled an order, then reinstated it," Olivia told him.

"Sales have gone up since Jana has come to work from me. I have the records to prove it. She's a valuable asset."

"From male customers, no doubt." He placed a folder in front of the judge. "You'll see that she has been married three times and moved from man to man with appalling regularity. She's also been seen embracing Mrs. Sanders's brother. There is no telling what else is going on before that young child."

"The only thing going on is what's in people's narrow and nasty minds," Olivia said. "Jana goes to church and has helped with community projects. My pastor and his wife, as well as other members of my church, will testify as much." She glared at Aaron. "Some people can learn from their mistakes, others revel in them."

"What about your client's lifestyle?" Brianna questioned.

"My client's sexual preference is and should not be of concern in this matter. Only his fitness as a parent, which, unlike your client's, is unquestionable. His only focus at this time is gaining joint custody of his child," his lawyer pointed out. "He is a responsible citizen and respected in the community. He has been deprived from watching his son grow up or developing a relationship with him." He faced the judge.

"In an effort to partially end the suffering my client has had to endure, I ask you to grant him visitation rights until a custody decision can be made."

"No!" Olivia came up out of her chair, shaking off Brianna's hand on her arm. "He doesn't want Griffin. He's incapable of loving anyone but himself."

"Mrs. Sanders, your objections have been noted, but studies have shown again and again that children raised with the influence of both parents grow up to be emotionally healthier and productive over their counterparts," the judge said. "Please take your seat."

Olivia responded to her lawyer's determined hand more than the judge's order. She dropped into her chair.

"Your Honor, might I reiterate that Griffin's paternal grandfather is gravely ill and is not expected to recover. He has expressed his wish to see his grandson before dying." Mr. Barnes placed another folder in front of the judge. "His deposition and his doctor's statement. The quick resolution of this matter is paramount."

Brianna leaned forward. "My client also asks a quick resolution because she doesn't want her son's life disrupted. It should also be pointed out that his paternal grandparents have contacted their grandson only with birthday and Christmas cards since his birth. On the other hand, Griffin's uncle, Tyler Maxwell, a respected businessman, and Griffin's maternal grandparents have had an integral and positive effect on his young life. He's happy and well adjusted."

"Mrs. Sanders," the judge said, "Has Griffin expressed an interest in seeing his father?"

Olivia didn't want to answer the question. Griffin would be over the moon if he knew his father wanted to see him, but he only knew the lies she'd told him, lies she thought would protect him.

"Mrs. Sanders?"

"He thinks his father loves him," she finally said.

"I do," Aaron piped up. "We deserve to be together."

Olivia turned on him. "You deserve to rot in hell for what you put us through. I had to hold him while he screamed in pain when they drew blood to make sure he wasn't HIV positive, then endure the agonizing wait for the test results."

"You b—"

"Aaron," his lawyer quickly cut him off. "Your outrage is understandable. She put Griffin through a lot of needless pain."

"Not according to studies at that time," the judge said. "It shows she was smart and concerned. Obviously she has done what she felt best for her child."

Olivia tried to take heart in what the judge said, but Brianna's hand remained clamped on hers. It wasn't over.

"I need time to go over what was presented before me today. In the interim, however, Mrs. Sanders, you will have Griffin available and ready to spend the weekend with his father. He can pick him up at twelve tomorrow. He will be returned no later than six Sunday afternoon."

Stunned, Olivia stared. "No."

"Griffin deserves to know he has a father who loves him," the judge said.

"Let me go with him," she pleaded. "Aaron is a stranger to him."

"That may be your fault," the judge said with disapproval. "Don't let your prejudices blind you to what's best for Griffin."

"You're the one who's blind," Olivia protested.

"Olivia," Brianna cautioned.

Judge Watkins stiffened. "Ms. Ireland, I advise you to instruct your client to conduct herself better when we meet again." She closed the folder. "All parties, including Griffin, will meet in my chambers a week from today for my final decision. And Mrs. Sanders, I suggest you spend your time wisely in preparing Griffin for the visit with his father. Don't even think of defying my order."

"He'll be ready, Judge Watkins," Brianna said.

Olivia said nothing as tears rolled down her cheeks.

Jana knew when she saw Olivia's pale face that evening the news wasn't good. She also knew her first concern would be her son. "Griffin is in the kitchen helping Wanda prepare dinner." Jana didn't add the cook had remained because she had wanted to learn what the judge had decided. Olivia was already aware that they all supported her.

"Are you Jana Franklin?" the woman who came in behind Olivia asked.

Jana got a funny feeling in the pit of her stomach. The attaché case denoted she was probably Olivia's lawyer, the Dolce & Gabanna white suit that she was probably very successful. "Yes."

"Why? What's going on?" Tyler asked, joining them.

The woman's gaze went to him. "So sources were correct."

"Make sense, Brianna," Tyler told her.

"Let's go into the library." Olivia led the way, as if every step was more difficult than the last.

Jana didn't move. Brianna stopped and looked back at her. "This concerns you as well."

"What is it?" Tyler asked again.

Jana already knew. Her past had caught up with her.

17

Less than five minutes later Jana realized how right she was and how much her father truly hated her. She felt chilled and wondered if she'd ever get warm again.

"Jana, I'm sorry."

Jana's head snapped up on hearing Olivia's softly spoken words. "They're trying to take your son away from you and using me to do it, and you're sorry?" Too keyed up to sit any longer, she stood. "You should be berating me and helping me pack."

"I won't turn my back on my friend," Olivia said. "I need to go see Griffin." Coming to her feet, she was gone.

Jana might have known that would be Olivia's response. It was up to her. "It won't take me long to pack."

Tyler stepped in front of her. "I thought we already had this conversation."

She wrapped her arms around her waist when she wanted to wrap them around him and weep. "They'll use me to take Griffin."

His knuckles caressed her cheeks. "They can try. You're not the same woman."

Tears clogged her throat. "My father thinks so."

Tyler's face filled with rage. "He's about as much of a father as Griffin's father is, and that's as nothing as it gets."

Jana turned to the lawyer. "You know I have to go. Tell them."

Brianna crossed her long legs and looked Jana in the eyes. "I've heard your name recently mentioned a couple of times, and it has never been good."

Jana didn't flinch, didn't hang her head. She'd done enough of that. This was the kind of woman, smart, successful, beautiful, respected, that Tyler could be proud of. She envied her when she'd never envied anyone. "How boring for you."

"Actually, it was," Brianna agreed. "Personally, I wouldn't get mad at the woman for taking my man, I'd try to figure out what he got from her that he wasn't getting from me and make sure he didn't stray again. Or hang him up by his balls."

Jana looked at the woman with surprise and a grudging respect. That's exactly what she would have done . . . if she cared enough, which she never had until she met Tyler.

Brianna leaned back in her leather chair. "If I thought you'd hurt this case, I'd help you pack. The fact that you're more concerned with Griffin's happiness than your own is in your favor. And sleeping in a garage apartment isn't exactly what you're used to, yet I don't get the feeling that you're unhappy about it."

"I'm not," Jana said. "Olivia helped me when I had no place to go."

Brianna nodded. "Olivia is well known for being a nurturer with a strong faith. The fact that, knowing your reputation, she still helped you turn your life around is a major point in her favor. You're father's unwillingness to forgive makes Olivia's kindness all the more commendable."

"See," Tyler said, sliding his arm around her waist.

Brianna's arched brows quirked at the motion. "Is there any point in asking if you're dating anyone besides Tyler?"

Jana flushed. "No."

Tyler smiled, his arm tightened.

"Well, Aaron's lawyer believes your relationship might affect Griffin," Brianna told them.

The smile died on Tyler's face. "He should be more worried about his client."

"His problem." Brianna looked from one to the other. "Then I take it you two haven't gotten hot and heavy in front of Griffin."

"What do you think?" Tyler asked, his body tense.

Holding up her hands, Brianna stood. "Just asking. I'll see myself out. The next forty-eight hours won't be easy for Olivia."

"We'll be there for her," Tyler said. "She's gone through enough."

"I couldn't agree more." Brianna went to the door. "Nice meeting you, Jana." It took Jana a moment to respond.

"Thank you." Nodding, Brianna was gone.

Tyler pulled Jana into his arms. "You are going to be sensible, aren't you?"

Jana asked a question of her own. "Will there ever come a time when people will forget my past?"

He had to be honest with her. She deserved nothing less. "For some, yes. For others, no."

She looked out the atrium doors to the gardens beyond. "I wish I had the power to change the past."

"You can't. You can only learn from it," he told her.

She faced him. "Some lessons are too hard." Her voice trembled as much as her body.

"Not if you don't have to learn them alone."

"Tyler, I . . ."

"What?" he asked.

"Nothing." She placed her head on his chest and curved her arms around his waist.

Needing to hold her as much as she seemed to need him, Tyler held her, hoping that was enough, yet afraid it wouldn't be.

Olivia had put off the conversation with Griffin as long as she could. In an hour Aaron would be there to pick him up. Tyler had offered to talk with Griffin, but she needed to do this herself. But it was going to be the hardest conversation she had ever had.

"Griffin, I need to talk to you." She put her joysticks aside. She had needed to be close to him, to touch him as much as possible. She refused to think that there might be a time when she couldn't.

He'd been overjoyed that she had stayed home from work, just as he had been last night when she'd allowed him to stay up an hour longer, reading to him until he fell asleep. He hadn't known that she hadn't left his room until that morning.

"Sure," he said, with his usual bubbling laughter. "I was creaming you anyway." He put his controls aside and turned to her. "I was thinking, since you stayed home today, we could go to the Chuck E. Cheese's for lunch. Maybe Julian could meet us there."

Her trembling hand ran over his head, then curved around his shoulder. Would either of them ever forget Julian? Probably not. He'd left a void in their lives. She'd tried not to care too deeply, but the pain of their separation proved that she'd failed. But now wasn't the time to dwell on it. Griffin's welfare was what mattered most. "You remember when I explained to you that even when two people are in love and get married, they might not stay in love like your grandparents and they get a divorce."

The animation left his face. "Like you and my father."

"Yes."

His fingers plucked at the hem of his shorts. "Some of my friends' parents are divorced, but they still see their fathers and get to do things with them."

Olivia's heart clenched at the hurt in her son's voice, the droop of his shoulders. Aaron had a lot to answer for. No matter how unchristian, Olivia hated him with every fiber of her being, but she wouldn't let those feelings spill over and hurt Griffin. "Your father loves you. He's just been busy, especially now since his father is ill."

Griffin's small head came up. "Granddad Sanders?"

Although Griffin had never met his paternal grandparents, he remembered them nightly in his prayers. "Yes." Olivia swallowed. "Your father wants to see you."

The spurt of joy on Griffin's face tore at her heart. "Like now? He's coming to see me even before my birthday or Christmas?"

She swallowed again. "He's in town."

"Wow!" Griffin took her hand and bounded up. "Come on, Mama, let's go see him."

Although she felt a giant weight on her chest, Olivia allowed herself to be pulled up. "He's coming here to pick you up."

His dark brown eyes rounded. "Here?"

Her hand ran over his head. "He'll be here at noon."

Griffin jerked his head toward the wall clock. "That's in thirty minutes."

And much too soon. "That . . . that gives us enough time to pack."

"He's taking us with him?"

Her hands fisted. "Just you. You two are going to spend some time together. He'll bring you back tomorrow at six."

Some of the happiness left his face. "You're not coming with us?"

Olivia hated herself for being glad then, as always, she thought of Griffin first as she had since she felt the first flutters in her stomach. "It will be wonderful with just the two of you getting to know each other. It will be just like a sleepover and I'll be as close as the phone."

She could see the appeal of the idea taking root in his quick-thinking brain. "Just the two of us having fun?"

"You could go to Chuck E. Cheese's with him."

"We could, couldn't we?" He grabbed her hand again. "Let's go pack. I want to be ready when my father gets here."

"Do I look all right, Uncle Tyler?" Griffin asked for the umpteenth time.

"Never better," Tyler said, sitting beside Olivia on the living room sofa. "Any man would be proud to call you his son."

Griffin went back to staring out the window. "You sure he has the right address, Mama?"

"Yes," Olivia mumbled.

"It's not twelve yet," Tyler pointed out. He almost wished Aaron wouldn't show up, but that would be too cruel. Whatever Aaron was, Griffin loved him and wanted him to be a part of his life. Trouble was, Aaron had proved that he didn't care about his son.

"Boy. A limousine just pulled up." Griffin glanced over his shoulder. "Do you think that's him?" He raced over and took her hand. "Come see if that's him."

Tyler took Olivia's trembling arm and went to the window. Aaron strolled up the walkway as if he owned the world.

"Is it him?" Griffin asked.

"Yes," Olivia said, one strangled word.

Griffin took off for the front door. Tyler didn't try to stop him.

Griffin opened the door and stared up at his father for the first time. He wasn't as tall as his uncle or Julian and his shoulders weren't as wide, but the smile on his face was all that mattered. He squatted down so they were eye level.

"Griffin?"

Too full to speak, Griffin nodded

Aaron opened his arms. "Come to your father, son."

Used to hugs and roughhousing from his uncle, and lately Julian, Griffin launched himself into his father's arms, expecting him to catch him and maybe swing him around as they did. Instead his father grunted and almost toppled over.

Griffin heard his father say a bad word a workman had used when he hit his thumb instead of the nail. The man had been angry. Tears sprang to Griffin's eyes. He'd messed up. He'd made his father mad.

He felt himself lifted and stared into his uncle's face. "Is he mad?" Griffin whispered, afraid to look and see for himself. The workman had gone to his truck and hadn't returned for a long time.

"No." Uncle Tyler said. "You're just as glad to see Griffin as he is you. Aren't you, Aaron?"

"Of course," Griffin heard his father say, but he didn't sound happy.

Griffin cautiously looked over his shoulder to see his father flicking his fingers over his suit. "I didn't mean to make you fall."

"You did nothing wrong," his mother said, but she wasn't smiling either.

"No one said he did." His father's smile returned. He held out his hand. "Are you ready to go?"

Griffin scrambled down, careful this time to curb his happiness. He took his father's hand. "Yes, sir."

"Where are his things?" his father asked.

Uncle Tyler hunkered down to Griffin, reached into his pocket and handed him a small cell phone. "The charger is in your backpack. Call anytime. You know how mothers worry."

His father looked as if he'd eaten something that didn't agree with him. "That isn't necessary."

Uncle Tyler ignored him and handed him the backpack. "Have him back tomorrow no later than six."

Without a word, his father started toward the waiting limousine. Griffin wanted to ask him to stop. He hadn't kissed his mother good-bye and she looked so sad. She started after them. Uncle Tyler put his arms around her.

"I love you, Griffin. Always remember that," she called.

Although he didn't like saying it in public, he didn't like seeing his mother cry either. "I love you too, Mother. I'll call." He held up the phone, just before his father opened the door and urged him into the limousine. The door shut. Through the tinted window he saw his mother leaning against his uncle with tears streaming down her cheeks.

"Something is wrong with my mother. I need to get out." He tried to reach for the door handle, but his father wouldn't let him.

"She's fine. Let's go," he ordered the driver and the car took off. "And you won't need this." He took the phone, slipping it into his coat pocket.

"I can't call my mother," Griffin said.

"Don't be a baby," his father chastised. "Maybe now she'll know how it feels."

Griffin didn't understand what his father was talking about. He just knew something was wrong with his mother. He clearly recalled the time she'd cried because she'd been worried about him at Water World.

Disobeying two rules he'd always been taught, Griffin didn't fasten his seat belt nor did he remain seated while the car was moving; instead he got on his knees and looked out the back window of the speeding vehicle at his mother and felt like crying too.

"He took my baby," Olivia cried.

Olivia wouldn't move until the limo disappeared. "I know it hurt." Tyler hugged her to him as they entered the house. He led her to a chair in the living room and knelt beside her. "It's hard, but he'll be back. You'll talk to him tonight."

Tears streamed down her cheek. "Aaron is too mean and selfish to let Griffin keep the phone."

"That's why I slipped another one in his backpack when neither of you were looking." He squeezed her hands. "Aaron isn't the type to help Griffin unpack. He'll call."

She hugged him. "Thank you."

"I love him too," he said, his voice suspiciously rough.

She stared down into his face. "In feeling sorry for myself I'd forgotten that."

Tyler brushed the last of her tears away. "You're entitled."

Olivia shook her head. "Feeling sorry for myself won't get Griffin back in my arms sooner. I better get to the shop."

Straightening, Tyler pulled her to her feet. "Jana and the new part-time clerk can handle things."

"It might make the time go by faster," she told him.

He didn't believe her, but let it go. "In the meantime I'll keep searching the Internet. Maybe the private investigator I hired has come up with a reason for Aaron's sudden interest in Griffin."

Olivia's eyes narrowed. "Whatever the reason it's for his own good. He's only out for himself."

Tyler nodded. "I agree. We'll find the answer and be ready for the next hearing."

"If the judge rules against—"

"She won't," Tyler interrupted.

"If she does," Olivia continued, her face set, "I'll do whatever it takes to keep Griffin away from his father permanently."

Tyler had already figured as much. There was no way in hell he'd allow Aaron more than temporary visitation of his nephew. "I'll make the arrangements."

She squeezed his hands. "I'll run upstairs to get my purse. Please let me know if you find out anything."

"You'll know the second after I do."

"Courtney was a fool to let you go," Olivia said. "Jana has more sense."

"But she's a whole lot harder to catch," Tyler said.

"My money's on you." Patting his arm, she went to her room.

Tyler stared after her, then went to his office, wishing he felt as confident about Jana. No matter how hard he tried, he knew that, in the back of her mind, her past still haunted her. He'd be the biggest liar in the world if he didn't admit it had given him some sleepless nights as well.

Sitting at his desk, Tyler turned on the computer and waited for it to boot up. What he had to remember, what he hoped Jana remembered, was that there were no little or big sins in the eyes of God. Sin was sin and once a person repented, in God's eyes, the sin was forgotten and cast into the sea of forgetfulness. Tyler was of the same opinion.

Jana was a different person, and he wanted her in his life. This time he didn't plan to lose.

Olivia had powdered her nose twice since she'd parked several car lengths down from Midnight Dreams. She looked at her reflection in the compact. There was nothing she could do about her red eyes and puffy lids. She couldn't stay in the SUV all afternoon, but she didn't want to alarm her clients.

Closing her eyes, she leaned her head back against the headrest, unable to keep her mind off Griffin. Was Aaron watching him carefully enough? Griffin was an inquisitive young boy. He needed guidance and perimeters set. Aaron had about as much parenting skill as a fly.

Opening her eyes, she reached for the door and got out. She'd go crazy if she kept thinking about it. Shoving the straps of the satchel bag over her shoulder, she strode down the street and into the shop.

Both Jana and the new clerk glanced around. Olivia smiled at them despite the fact she wanted to scream out her anger and pain. "I'll put my purse up and be right back out to help you."

Jana crossed to her. Her gaze didn't miss a thing. "You don't have to be brave. If you need to cry, cry."

Olivia blinked. "I don't seem able to do anything else."

"He's the smartest boy I've ever met."

"But he's just a boy." Biting her lip, Olivia went to her office and sat behind her desk. "Please, God. Take care of Griffin."

"I don't feel well." Griffin shoved what was left of his fifth large slice of pepperoni pizza across the table from him. He had thought it was so cool that his father had let him decide where they ate dinner. Griffin had chosen a pizza parlor where he'd proceeded to eat his way through a large pizza accompanied by three strawberry sodas.

Aaron frowned across the wooden table. He hadn't taken one bite of food. "What's wrong with you?"

Griffin's arms circled his waist. "I think I ate too much."

"Don't you have more sense than that?" Aaron snapped. "Didn't your mother teach you anything?"

Griffin's eyes filled with tears. This wasn't turning out like he thought. All his father did was fuss. Nothing Griffin did pleased him.

"Your mother turned you into a crybaby. Stop sniveling," his father ordered.

"Yes, sir," Griffin managed, but somehow a tear slid down his cheek.

"Let's go." Standing, his father grabbed him by the arm and almost dragged him to the limo. "Get in, and don't you dare throw up."

Griffin did as he was told. He wanted his mother, but one look at the angry face of his father and he knew better than to ask to go home. "Can I call my mother?"

The anger on his father's face disappeared. "We don't want to worry your mother." Scooting closer, he pulled Griffin to him. "You'll be fine."

Griffin snuggled closer. Maybe his father didn't dislike him after all, but he still wanted his mother.

Olivia was fighting a losing battle. Expecting the knock on her door to be Jana or Ann, the new clerk, she reached for another tissue. "Come in."

The door opened and Julian stood there, tall and more handsome than any man she'd ever seen. "Hello, Olivia."

Her hands clenched. "What are you doing here? I don't want to see you anymore."

"I can't stop thinking about you, worrying about you and Griffin."

Tears filled her eyes and ran down her cheeks. "Please go."

Julian strode across the room, blatantly ignoring her words. "You're not shutting me out. I care about Griffin, too."

She lost the battle against the tears and her determination to avoid Julian. "Oh, Julian."

"I'm here, honey. I'm here." His arms tightened. He never wanted to let her go. Worrying about Olivia and Griffin, not being able to see them, or comfort her, was a hell he never wanted to go through again. "We'll fight to keep Griffin where he belongs."

"I can't stop worrying about him," she confessed. "Aaron will be more concerned about winning Griffin's affection than in setting limits. You know how Griffin likes having his way."

Julian tenderly brushed the tears from her face. "He's also smart and loves his mother."

"Please tell me he'll be all right."

"He'll come home to you tomorrow and that's where he'll remain."

"I don't think I could stand it if he didn't," she told him.

Julian plucked tissue from the box on her desk. "Dry your eyes. You have a customer."

She did as he said. "I haven't been much help since I came in. I'll probably cry all over whoever it is."

Julian kissed both of her hands. "He won't mind."

"You?"

He looked a bit embarrassed. "I need another set of those sheets. I miss sleeping on the ones I bought since they are in the laundry."

Olivia felt a smile curve her mouth upward. "Oh, Julian, thank you."

"Good night, Griffin."

"Good night, Father," Griffin dutifully said from beside his father on the sofa in the sitting room of his father's suite in the downtown hotel.

"I'll see you in the morning," his father told him, making no motion to get up to help him get ready for bed like his mother did.

"Yes, sir." Griffin went to his bedroom and quietly closed the door. He supposed the room was all right, but he missed his own room with his books and games. He missed his mother most of all. She always helped him run his bath, listened to his prayers, and read him a story afterwards. Maybe he should tell his father.

Griffin took a couple of steps toward the door, then stopped. His father had called him a crybaby. He didn't want him to think he couldn't take a bath by himself. He wasn't a baby.

Going to his backpack, he began taking out his clothes. He pulled out his pajamas and was reaching for the next item when he saw the phone. He grabbed it, began punching in his home phone number. Suddenly he stopped and went into the bathroom and closed the door before continuing. The phone was picked up before it rang the second time.

"Griffin, is that you, baby?" his mother asked. Her voice sounded like the time he had become separated from her in the grocery store.

"Yes, ma'am."

"You're all right, aren't you?"

He didn't want her to think badly of him like his father did. "Yes, ma'am. I'm going to run my own bath."

"Where's your father?"

Griffin let the lid of the toilet down and sat on top. "I guess he's still watching TV."

There was a pause, then, "I don't want you running hot water. You can wait until you get home tomorrow night to take a bath."

He perked up a bit. "I can?"

"One night won't hurt. Have you eaten dinner?"

"Yes, ma'am. We had pizza for dinner and afterwards we came back to the hotel and looked at a couple of Disney movies. I didn't want to tell him I'd already seen them."

"Griffin, you sound different. Are you sure you're all right?"

He wanted to go home, but he didn't want his father mad at him. "Yes ma'am. I better get ready for bed." Before he started crying like the baby his father had called him.

"All right, just remember I love you, will always love you no matter what. I want you to remember that we can always talk about anything. If you find out you're not sleepy and want to talk, all you have to do is call."

"Good night, Mama. I love you."

"Good night, sweetheart. I love you too. I'll see you tomorrow. I made your favorite dessert."

Griffin rubbed his stomach. He didn't want to think about food. "Yes, ma'am. Good night."

"Good night."

Griffin disconnected the phone and went to change into his pj's. Tomorrow he was going home.

Olivia's eyes tightly closed, she clutched the receiver even after the only sound was the droning dial tone. Tears seeped from beneath her closed lids.

Tyler finally took the receiver from her. "Olivia?"

Shaking her head she turned, burrowing into the comfort and security of Julian's arms, but even as she did so she thought of Griffin alone. Ever since she had come home, she'd sat by the phone in the media room, watching the phone, waiting and praying for her child to call.

"He was trying to be so brave." She lifted her head because the people surrounding her loved Griffin as well and were just as worried about him. Tyler, Julian and Jana had waited with her since she came home from Midnight Dreams, doing their best to keep her mind off the silent phone.

"Aaron sent Griffin to get ready for bed by himself. Griffin says he's all right, but he wanted to get off the phone so he could go to bed." She wiped her eyes with the handkerchief Julian gave her. "Griffin has never willingly gone to bed."

"Wanna bet he reverts to his old ways tomorrow night?" Tyler said.

A slow smile formed on Olivia's face. "He'll probably have a thousand things to tell me."

Julian stroked her hair. "And you'll listen patiently to every one of them even if he's already told you twice before."

"Probably more times than that. That's Griffin's favorite tactic," Olivia said, her heart lighter. "He'll say, 'are you sure I told you this before?' with the innocence of an angel."

"He came by that honestly," Tyler said. "Both of us hated to go to bed."

"You're still a night owl," Jana remarked.

"I think better at night." Taking her hand, Tyler pulled her up from the love seat. "Julian, see if you can get Olivia to do more than pick at her food. I'm going to see Jana home. Good night."

"Good night," Julian called, his gaze on Olivia. "You really should eat something."

"I'm fine. Thank you for staying with me," she said.

His hand squeezed hers. "You've already thanked me a dozen times or more, and as I told you before, it's not necessary."

"But sitting with distraught mothers can't be how you usually spend your time."

"You're the only mother I've ever dated," he said, not quite sure why he revealed that about himself.

She frowned. "I'm honored and puzzled."

He shrugged carelessly. "It's just that a lot of single mothers are usually looking for husbands."

"And you were honest enough to know you weren't going to be around for the long haul."

She'd hit the nail on the head. "Something like that."

"I can see why you picked me then," she said. "I have no intention of marrying again."

Her words shouldn't have bothered him, but they did. "Just because Aaron broke your trust is no reason to think every man will."

"I think we've had this conversation. Thanks for coming." She came to her feet.

He didn't move. "We have. Complete with you trying to toss me out."

"And Griffin came to my rescue," she said, her voice trembling.

He came out of the chair, wrapping his arms around her. "Don't go there. Stay annoyed with me."

She almost smiled. "Which can be so easy to do."

His hand stroked her back. "Part of my charming bedside manner."

Olivia pushed out of his arms. "Are you really so horrible?"

"Used to be." His hand cupped her face. "But since a certain woman took me to task in the emergency room, I'm almost completely reformed."

"You needed it," she said.

He chuckled, hugging her. "You talk about Griffin being opinionated. You and Tyler are the same way." He gave her a quick kiss. "Griffin will come through this and figure out a way to stay up later, eat more junk food, and get that new game he wanted."

She bit her lip. "I planned on picking it up after church tomorrow."

Julian tsked. "Well, I certainly hope you don't plan on giving it to him until he's been home at least an hour."

"I was thinking of giving it to him at bedtime so he wouldn't remember being alone tonight," she said.

Julian sobered. "You're a fabulous mother, and if you think I'm leaving *you* tonight, you don't know me very well."

"Julian, I couldn't—" She trailed off and placed her head on his shoulder.

"If I didn't know how upset you are, I might revert to my old self and become angry that you thought I expected sex." He set her free and turned to stare down at the sofa. "Griffin says this turns into a bed. I thought we'd watch movies until you fell asleep. Then in the morning you can cook me breakfast."

She folded her arms. "Why can't you cook me breakfast?"

"Because I asked you first." He began taking the cushions from the sofa.

"I'll go get the linen."

He straightened. "What thread count?"

She grinned. "One thousand two hundred."

"You certainly know how to tempt a man."

"Don't I though," Olivia said, and headed for the stairs.

"You must really like Julian," Jana said as hand in hand she and Tyler slowly made their way to her apartment.

"He cares about Olivia and Griffin," Tyler answered.

She slanted a look at him. "Is that why you gave them time to be alone?"

"Yeah." He paused and looked back at the black Maserati at the curb. "I hope he doesn't make me regret trusting him."

Jana tugged him forward. "He just wants to be there for her."

"That's what I thought, but if I'm wrong . . ."

"Olivia is old enough to make her own decisions." Jana started up the stairs with Tyler slowly following.

"Sometimes women don't make the right decision when a good-looking man is involved."

Jana turned from opening the door. "If Olivia heard you insult her like that, she'd probably infect your precious computers with some super virus or spyware."

He shuddered and followed her into the house. "Don't even joke about something like that."

"I wasn't joking."

"You certainly know how to hurt a man."

Once she might have taken offense at such a statement. "Don't you forget it. You want iced tea or lemonade?"

"Lemonade." He plopped on the sofa. "How long do you think it will take for them to say good night?"

"I didn't get the impression Julian was in any hurry to leave."

"What?" Tyler paused in reaching for the remote. He'd talked Jana into letting him buy her a small television so they could watch movies together.

"He only left her side to go check on his patients at the hospital," Jana reminded him. "He's very perceptive. He realized that the more Olivia is alone, the more time she has to think of Griffin and get depressed. Julian doesn't want that to happen and he's there to comfort her."

"She has me."

Jana turned with the glasses of lemonade and rolled her eyes. "Tyler, come on."

He stared at her a few moments, then launched himself out of the chair. "He's dead meat."

"Tyler, come back here." She hurriedly sat the glasses down and caught up with him, her hand slipping behind the belt buckle of his jeans. "Don't you dare go over there and embarrass her with all she's going through."

"He's not taking advantage of Olivia," he said.

"Who says he is?" Jana asked. "There are good men left in the world."

He simply looked at her.

"Yes, I said it. I'm looking at one."

His smile was slow. "Hallelujah."

She let go when she wanted to tug him closer. "Don't get a big head."

"Wouldn't dream of it," he said, then started toward her.

Jana backed up a step. "Don't you want your lemonade?"

"I got something better in mind." He kept coming until their bodies touched. His hand settled on her hips, keeping her in place. "Since you don't want me to go back to the house, I have to keep busy doing something."

"Like what?"

"Why don't I show you?"

It was after twelve when Tyler left Jana. He hadn't wanted to leave her at all, but he's been worried about Olivia. Seeing Julian's car still there, Tyler's eyes narrowed, then he thought of what Jana had said and what Olivia was going through. If Julian could help her, Tyler would try to stay out of it. But if he was playing with his sister, then *he* was going to need a doctor.

Opening the front door, Tyler headed for the stairs, telling himself he was going to be sensible and an adult, but he didn't realize his hands were clenched into fists until he heard muted voices coming from the media room. He swiped a hand across his face. He didn't want to look if anything was going on, yet he didn't want to leave his sister to be taken advantage of.

Slowly, cautiously he went to the half-closed door, took a breath, then peered around the door. Olivia and Julian, both fully clothed, were on the sofa bed. Olivia had changed into sweats. She had her head on his shoulder, his arm was around her and they were watching a movie. He left as quietly as he had come.

Jana had been right. There were good men in the world and it looked like his sister had found one. Assured Olivia was all right, he left as quietly as he had come. There were also good women and he was going back to his.

18

Jana and Olivia cooked breakfast together. They ate on the terrace. Julian left soon afterwards to check on his patients in the hospital. Olivia, afraid that if she went to church she might miss Griffin's call, had stayed at home to prepare Griffin's favorite meal. Jana helped while Tyler worked on designing the computer program for his latest client.

It was after lunch when Tyler received the call he'd been waiting for. As soon as he hung up he went to find Olivia. She was in the kitchen grinding out noodles while Jana stirred the homemade pasta sauce.

"I know why Aaron wants Griffin so badly." Both women stopped what they were doing.

"The private investigator learned from one of the people working at Aaron's father's house that his father passed over Aaron and plans to leave the company to Griffin. The employee heard them arguing," Tyler said. "Aaron is an only child. He and his father aren't on good terms because Aaron wants to sell the business, but his father is adamantly against it. As guardian of Griffin, Aaron will have control of the company."

"I don't want the money," Olivia said. "I'll tell him as much when he brings Griffin back this afternoon."

"It's not that simple. According to the servant, Griffin has been entitled to a share of the profits since his birth," Tyler said. "You refused spousal support, but once Griffin was born he was a legal heir. His grandfather was giving Aaron the money to send, but he spent it. Griffin is due a sizable chunk of the company's assets, and considering they haven't been doing well since his grandfather's illness, there might not be that much left."

"Then that's it." Olivia said. "All we have to do is tell the judge."

"He'll deny it and probably turn it around as a reason for wanting Griffin, to ensure he has his inheritance," Tyler said. "Or say he invested the money to help Griffin and lost it in the stock market."

"You're right. He's sly and devious." Olivia swallowed. "I won't let him come anywhere near Griffin after today."

Tyler put his hand on her shoulder. "We'll do whatever it takes."

"This has been so much fun, Griffin, hasn't it?" his father asked as he sat across the limousine from him. "Soon you'll be with me to have more."

"Yes, sir," Griffin answered. He'd quickly learned his father didn't become impatient with him if he agreed with everything he said. Griffin had also been careful not to ask for seconds during breakfast or lunch.

"You'll tell your mother that, won't you?"

"Yes, sir." Looking out the window Griffin saw his street sign as the limo turned the corner. He began counting the houses.

The limo pulled up to the curb. Through the window Griffin saw his mother, Uncle Tyler, and Julian. Forgetting they couldn't see him, he waved.

"Don't forget, Griffin, you had a wonderful time."

"Yes, sir."

Opening the door, Aaron emerged from the vehicle. Griffin came out of the car in a flash. He didn't stop until he was in his mother's arms. He didn't care who saw him. He held her as tightly as she held him. They went into the house and Julian followed.

Aaron turned up his nose at the rudeness of Olivia and the man with her. Obviously he was as uncouth as she was. They could have been cordial enough to speak. If they had he could have learned the identity of the gorgeous man with her and tried to get a feel if he swung both ways. Perhaps it was for the best. Money first; pleasure later.

And when he had Griffin in his custody, all that pampering nonsense would cease. A good boys' school, preferably one as far away from him as possible, would help shape him up. As soon as he got home, he'd have his secretary do some research on the matter.

Tyler held out his hand. "My phone."

"I don't have it," Aaron told him. No matter how much money Tyler had, he remained unpolished.

Tyler got in his face. "Then you better find it or I'm going to press charges for theft."

Aaron almost laughed in his face. "You can't be serious."

"As a heart attack. The phone cost three hundred dollars. I have friends at the police department. Want to bet I can file a complaint and they arrest you before your plane leaves?" Tyler said with entirely too much glee in his voice for comfort.

Aaron's clenched his teeth. "I'll leave it at the hotel."

"Make sure you do. Or the police will be waiting for you when you return." Dismissing Aaron as if he were nothing, Tyler started for the house. Aaron's dislike for Tyler escalated. He knew the perfect way to take him down a peg or two.

"You're awfully nonchalant for a man who is interested in a woman who is known to crawl into the pants of any man—" Aaron stopped abruptly when Tyler whirled, fist clenched. Aaron stumbled back.

"Say another word and you'll be picking your teeth up off the ground."

Aaron opened his mouth, then shut it. He rushed back to the limo and climbed inside. He'd make them all pay.

Tyler didn't move until he felt his anger was under control. He'd only gone a few steps when he glanced to his left. Jana stood on the walkway coming from her apartment. From the stricken look on her face, he knew she'd heard Aaron.

Head bowed, she started back to her apartment. Tyler wished he had Aaron in front of him for five seconds. How much more could Jana take?

Jana knew he'd come.

She'd made him an offer he couldn't refuse. After overhearing Aaron, she'd taken a cab to a pay phone and called him. This time he'd taken her call.

Her father looked like a respected businessman in his tailored sports jacket and slacks. He had always made a point of never being out in public looking less than his best. Public perception meant a lot to him. Perhaps that's why she meant so little.

"You said on the phone you were ready to discuss leaving," he said the instant he slid into the booth across from her at the dimly lit restaurant where he insisted they meet. He wasn't taking a chance that they might be seen together.

"If you promise not to testify at Griffin's custody hearing," she said. "His mother loves him more than anything."

He tsked. "You can't tell me you care."

"Despite having grown up without love from either parent, I can recognize it."

His facial expression harshened. "You brought it on yourself."

"Did you ever stop and ask yourself why?" She braced her arms on the wooden table. "I'll tell you. It was because first I wanted my mother's love and thought if I was like her, she might pay more attention to me than she did to the latest fashion or her latest lover."

He started to rise. "I don't have to listen to this."

"You do if you want me to leave and never come back," she told him.

He sat. "Say it and get out of my life."

Once the words would have taken her to her knees. But she'd learned her opinion of herself mattered more than what her parents thought. Her mother had yet to call.

"Did you hear what you just said? To you, I'm too vile to even be in your presence. But did you ever make an effort to spend time with me? To try to teach me right from wrong? Encourage me? I'll tell you. Not once. Instead you ignored, then criticized, then shunned me. Not once did you do or say anything to let me know you cared when I was growing up."

"I was busy earning a living."

"Stop lying. At least be honest enough to admit the truth," she told him. "You hated my mother for trapping you into marriage, and that hatred spilled over to me. Neither of you wanted me. I tried to get Mother to love me by imitating her lifestyle. I thought if I acted out enough, you would pay attention to me. You never did."

"I've got the only family I ever want."

Her laugh was brittle. "So you have. I just hope neither of them turns their backs on you the way you have me. Good-bye, Thomas." Picking up her purse, she walked away, her eyes dry.

She expected to find the note from Tyler stuck under her door when she arrived home. He knew she'd heard Aaron and would be troubled when she didn't answer the door. No one had ever worried about her before. He was working on another project yet he was concerned about her. Putting her purse away, she went to the house and knocked on his door.

The door opened. Relief spread across Tyler's face. He pulled her into his arms. "Please tell me if you decide to go off again."

"I didn't mean to worry you," she said, hoping he didn't realize she hadn't answered him directly. She never wanted to lie to him.

"It took a lot of willpower not to go into your room and see if your suitcase was missing."

Somehow she'd gained his trust and his affection. "You about ready to take a break?"

Lifting his head, he stared down at her. Desire leaped in his eyes. "Julian took Olivia and Griffin to see a Disney movie."

Her hands went to the buttons of his shirt. She'd take every precious moment with him. They had to last a lifetime. "Perfect."

Julian had looked forward to the impromptu outing Tuesday afternoon with Olivia and Griffin, which didn't surprise him. He enjoyed challenging Griffin, trying to outwit him, being with him. The kid was smart and fun.

"I'm going to try and do something with this hair," Olivia said. They'd just come out of the wind tunnel. "I'll be back in a minute."

"May I have a soda while you're gone?" Griffin asked. "I'm thirsty."

Olivia leaned down to within an inch of his face. "No." Kissing him on the cheek, she went into the ladies' room.

Griffin turned to Julian. "I bet you're thirsty."

Julian smiled and put his arm around Griffin's shoulder without thinking and started for an empty bench. "You are not getting me in trouble with your mother."

"She can't stay mad at people for long," he said. "Uncle Tyler and my granddad are always telling her she's too soft-hearted."

"Probably, but that's what makes her such a wonderful woman and mother." Julian sat and stretched his long legs out in front of him. The corners of his mouth kicked up when Griffin tried to copy the pose. "She loves you very much."

Griffin drew his legs up. "I don't think my father does."

Julian's gaze went to the ladies' room. He needed help on this one.

"He was smiling when I first saw him, then I almost knocked him down. And when we went out to eat I got sick." Griffin turned and stared up at Julian with eyes exactly like his mother's and as wounded as when she had to let Griffin leave to visit his father. "Maybe he left because of me."

Julian's heart went out to Griffin. He recalled all too well his own doubts and insecurities about his father. "Griffin, you had nothing to do with your father leaving. Some marriages just don't work."

"That's what Mother said, but he didn't seem to like me much."

"Griffin," Julian placed his hand on the young boy's shoulder. "Fathers are supposed to love their children as much as mothers do, but it doesn't always happen. My father was in the military and was very strict with us and was often gone. My younger brother and I learned to stay out of his way on those brief furloughs home." He took a deep breath and let himself remember the good times and not the bad.

"My mother was as sweet and loving as your mother. Having her love made up for my father not loving me. It's not your fault or mine that our fathers aren't the way we'd like for them to be."

"Where's your mother?" Griffin asked.

"She died when I was sixteen, but I still remember her love. It's gotten me through some rough times."

Griffin leaned closer and whispered. "When I was scared the other night at the hotel with my father, I thought of my mother."

Julian hugged him. "We're blessed to have mothers who love and loved us." He looked up and saw Olivia coming toward him. Another blessing. He hadn't realized how much of one until he'd almost lost her.

Jana knew it wouldn't be easy. Knowing she was right wasn't any consolation. Each word of her resignation tore at her heart. Yet, there was a strange kind of comfort in that. She genuinely cared about people without expecting anything in return. She wasn't the heartless, bitter woman she once was. She had Olivia and Tyler to thank for that, for giving her a second chance.

Finished, she put the letter in her purse and placed her suitcase by the door. Her hand on the knob, she took one last look around the room. She'd had more happiness while living here than all the years she had foolishly wasted her life. Despite everything, she had found a measure of contentment here. She didn't know if it was possible anywhere else because Tyler wouldn't be there.

She had become one of those foolish people she'd always laughed at. She'd fallen in love. She'd never regret loving Tyler. It was probably one of the few unselfish acts she'd ever done. The other was leaving Olivia and Griffin as happy and secure as she had met them. Opening the door, she started for the house.

As usual, the front door was left open for her in the morning. That amount of trust and welcome meant more than she could ever say. Closing, then locking the door, she headed for the kitchen. Warm laughter welcomed her into the room. Tyler, Olivia, and Griffin were at the breakfast table and Wanda was at the stove. "Good morning."

A chorus of greetings welcomed her. She was wanted.

"Morning." Tyler immediately rose and came to her, kissing her on the cheek. "I was beginning to worry about you."

"Sorry." She took the chair he pulled out for her. She wasn't hungry, but she said her blessings, then placed her napkin in her lap.

"Pancakes all right, Jana?" Wanda asked.

"Just one or I won't be able to fit into any of my clothes," Jana managed.

"You look fine to me." Tyler looked at her over the rim of his coffee cup. "But then I'm prejudiced."

Jana tried to smile, but her facial muscles wouldn't work.

Tyler put his cup down. "What's the matter?"

"Nothing. I didn't sleep very much last night," she told him truthfully, then blushed at his slow grin. He hadn't left until nearly dawn.

"If you want to rest a bit before you come in, I'll go in by myself." Olivia smiled at Griffin. "You and Ann have been wonderful about me taking off with Griffin."

Jana looked at Griffin's happy face, saw the love shining in his mother's eyes. "We were both happy to do it."

"Still, I appreciate it." Olivia sipped her coffee.

Griffin chewed and swallowed his blueberry pancakes. "Julian is coming over tonight to teach me chess. I bet once I learn I'll beat him."

Olivia shook her head. "I honestly don't know if I should try and curb his self-confidence or not."

"It's not self-centered or vicious. Griffin is going to grow up to be a wonderful man. You've taught him what's important, what to value. You're the type of mother all children should have," she said, unable to keep the longing and regret from her quiet voice.

Suddenly aware that she had unwittingly drawn the attention of the adults, Jana busied herself adding cream and sugar to her coffee. They'd felt sorry for her long enough. So had she.

Under the table, she felt Tyler's hand gently touch her leg, reassuring her. For him, for the love she could never give him, she gave him the smile he waited patiently for. There would be time enough for tears later.

Jana took the excuse Olivia had given her and returned to her room instead of riding to work with her. That way she could take a cab to work and have her suitcase with her when she turned in her resignation so she wouldn't have to come back. If she did she knew she'd find Tyler waiting for her. He was as stubborn as he was loyal.

"Jana?"

Jana stopped pacing in the front room on hearing Tyler's voice. "Just a minute." Picking up the suitcase, she placed it in the closet in the bedroom. Tyler might become suspicious if the door was closed.

Rubbing her sweaty hands over her slacks, she opened the door. "Hi."

He stepped over the threshold, closing the door behind him, and pulled her into his arms, his warm lips finding hers. Her arms circled his neck, her body sank against his, and she let the kiss empty her mind, enjoying the hum of her body, the strength of his arms around her, the hard muscles.

"Hi," he finally said on lifting his head. "Now what's going on in that beautiful head of yours?"

He knew her so well, and liked her in spite of what he knew. He was both her salvation and her penitence. "You're an amazing man."

Puckers ran across his brow. "Was that meant to throw me off track?"

"Just stating a fact." Her thumb traced the strong line of his jaw, the sensual lower lip. "You have an amazing mouth, an amazing body."

Tyler's breathing quickened. "You're going to make me forget my good intentions if you keep that up."

"Let's see." Jana took the kiss she desperately wanted. There was a maelstrom of fire and burning desire from the moment their mouths touched.

Tyler's hand was hot on her skin: his fingers gentle and rough as he plucked at her nipple. They hardened even more.

Her hands went to his shirt. She wanted him. Her body was on fire.

He moaned. "If I didn't have to meet the team for a new installation, I'd take you back to bed."

"You can't be a few minutes late?" she asked, tugging at his shirt.

His laugh was rough. "It would be more than that and you know it. See you tonight." He sobered. "Tomorrow is the hearing. I'll be glad when this is all over. The judge has to rule in Olivia's favor."

"She will." Without her father's damaging testimony to harm Olivia's case, Griffin would remain where he belonged, with his mother.

"That's what we're all praying for." He kissed her again, then he was gone.

Shivering, Jana stared at the closed door. She was doing the right thing. She just hated that it hurt so much.

"I'm leaving." Jana handed the letter to Olivia shortly after the store opened and watched the stunned expression race across her face.

Olivia didn't even look at it. "Why? I thought you were happy here."

Jana swallowed. "It's better this way."

"How can you say that?" Olivia asked, suspicion in her eyes.

"My taxi is waiting," Jana said, tears stinging her throat. "I'll miss you."

"Then stay," Olivia said.

"I can't," Jana said, turning and going to the front door.

"Tyler won't let you walk out of his life," Olivia warned as she followed.

Jana stopped abruptly. "I'm not the right woman for him."

"Bull." Olivia turned her around. "You once accused me of being a coward and you were right. Who's the coward now?"

"Don't you think I'd stay if I could? I'd give anything to be able to erase my past, erase the things I've done." She gulped. "Tyler deserves a woman he doesn't have to be ashamed of or wonder how many of the men in a social gathering she's slept with."

"He also deserves a woman who'll love him. He deserves you."

Her throat too full to speak, Jana gave Olivia a quick hug, then hurried out the door, only to bump into Julian. The smile on his face died when he saw how upset Olivia was. "What's going on?"

"She resigned. Maybe you can talk some sense into her head." Olivia sniffled. "She won't listen to me."

"Come on." Taking Jana's arm he led her a wooden bench beneath a mature elm tree a short distance away from the store. "You picked the worst possible time to leave with the hearing tomorrow."

"I'm doing it to help." She glanced away. "My father won't testify if I leave town."

Julian cursed softly under his breath. "Do you know how much guilt this is going to put on Olivia's shoulders?"

Her head whipped back around. "I didn't tell her the reason."

"She'll figure it out," Julian said. "What about Tyler? He loves you."

The words pierced Jana's heart. "He cares, but he doesn't love me."

Julian tsked. "You're wrong. Or are you kidding yourself so you won't have to take the blame for hurting two people who helped you when no one else cared."

"I wouldn't do that. I love them," Jana cried.

"Then stay and prove it." Julian stood. "Tell your father to take a flying leap. He has his family and people who love him. He's leaving you with nothing. Your choice. Love or loneliness?"

Jana stared after him. "Why do you care?"

He turned. "Because I've come to know you, and I like the woman you've become. Others feel the same way. You can have a life here or you can keep running."

Jana briefly closed her eyes, then went to the parked taxi and got in.

Late that afternoon Tyler was back in his office and in the middle of imputting data when there was knock on his door. Since Wanda didn't disturb him unless it was important, he hit save, went to the door, and opened it.

Surprise, then alarm hit him on seeing Jana standing there, trembling, biting her lip. His heart almost stopped when he saw the suitcase by her feet. "You're not leaving me."

"No, I'm not." She launched herself into his arms. "I know you're busy, but I need you to come with me to see my father."

The bastard would only hurt her more. "Honey, maybe you should think about this."

Loosening her hold, Jana stepped back a fraction. "I have. I'm going to tell him I've changed my mind about leaving town so he won't testify, and assure him that he won't have to ever worry about me trying to contact him again."

"Not testify? You mean you're telling me you agreed to leave so he wouldn't testify?" he asked, his eyes growing cold.

"Yes, but I've changed my mind," Jana answered.

"Thank God," Tyler said, cupping her cheek. "I'm sorry. I know he hurt you again."

"Not as much as leaving you and Olivia. Julian made me see that."

"Julian?"

"I was leaving the store after turning in my resignation and bumped into him," she explained.

"I owe him. Let me get my keys." With the keys in one hand and Jana's in the other, they went to the garage. A trailer home pulled up and a good-looking older couple emerged.

"What great timing! I knew you'd make it," Tyler said, greeting his parents with a hug, then pulling Jana forward. "Mama and Daddy, I want you to meet a very special woman, Jana Franklin."

Jana very much wanted Tyler and Olivia's parents to like her. She was extremely nervous, but soon found that they were genuinely warm and as outgoing as their daughter. They were going to the store to see Olivia while Tyler took Jana to Frisco to see her father.

"You sure?" Tyler asked when he parked in front of her father's sprawling ranch house. Homes in the swank development started at two million dollars, then rose sharply in price.

"Positive."

He squeezed her hand and then released her. Jana went to the double recessed doors and rang the doorbell almost hidden by English ivy. The man she came to see answered. His eyes filled with anger when he saw Jana.

"I'm not leaving town, but you don't have to worry that I'll ever try to contact you again in any manner. If you're low enough to try and get back at me by testifying tomorrow, that will be on your conscience. I have people who care about me and I'm not giving that up. Good-bye."

Jana's father stood speechless in the doorway as she turned and went to Tyler waiting by the truck.

Tyler caught her hand again. "Well done."

"Could you do something else for me?"

"Anything," he answered.

"Take me to the store. I want my job back."

Olivia tried to be happy that her parents were there, but she couldn't stop worrying about tomorrow. She had yet to speak with Griffin about him having to talk to the judge. After dinner she excused herself and went out to the pool. Julian followed, sliding his arms around her from behind and pulling her to him.

"Tomorrow he'll come home with you."

"But will he stay? I've prayed, but I know God's answer isn't always the one we want to hear." Her voice trembled. "It's telling that he hasn't mentioned his father since he returned. Did you hear him tell my parents about you?"

Julian grunted. "Yeah. How badly he beat me."

Olivia turned around. "That's just it. He enjoys being with you."

"I feel the same." He kissed her forehead. "Of course I'm extra partial to his mother."

"Thank you for being here for us," she whispered.

"Where else would I be except here with you and Griffin?" The words were barely out of his mouth before he realized their implication.

"We appreciate it."

Julian didn't want her appreciation, he wanted, he needed her love. Instead of shock the realization brought a calming peace.

She stepped back. "I need to talk to Griffin about tomorrow." She kissed his cheek, then walked away.

Julian wanted to go after her, but she had enough to deal with. After the hearing tomorrow was time enough. With Griffin home, Julian hoped they'd have something else to celebrate.

The next day Olivia discovered that talking with Griffin wasn't as difficult as letting him go alone into the judge's chambers. "I'll be here when you come out," she told him, trying to smile.

"Your Honor, you should take into consideration that she may have influenced the boy," Aaron's lawyer said.

Judge Watkins cut him a look. "Are you presuming to tell me how to conduct this interview?"

"No. No," Aaron's lawyer quickly said.

"Good." She held her hand out to Griffin. "Griffin, we're going into my chambers. You have nothing to be afraid of."

He nodded and took her hand. At the door, he looked back at his mother. Julian was there as well.

"We'll go get pizza when this is over," Julian called.

Griffin wanted to smile, but he couldn't. His mother looked sad and his father looked angry. Tucking his head, he continued through the door.

"I want you to know that you can trust me," Judge Watkins told the boy. She sat on the sofa and patted the seat beside her. "I just want to ask you some questions. There are no right and wrong answers."

"Yes, ma'am." Griffin sat beside her. His teachers said the same thing and never meant it.

"How did the visit with your father go?" she asked.

"All right."

She smiled, reminding him of his teacher last year. He'd liked her. "Just all right? You mother told me how much you cared for your father."

"I do."

She leaned back. "What did you do?"

"We went to dinner at a pizza place, then went to his hotel and watched Disney movies." He kicked his feet. "I got myself ready for bed."

"You certainly are a big boy. You mother and father must be very proud."

"My mama is," he confided. "She and Uncle Tyler and my grandparents always come to awards assembly at my school."

"Your father might like to attend as well."

Griffin glanced up than lowered his head. "I don't think he likes me."

"Why?"

Lifting his head, Griffin told her about how he had made his father angry, how he called him a crybaby. "But that's all right because Julian told me that his father didn't like him very much, but his mother loved him so much and it made up for his father not loving him. My mother loves me a lot too."

"Julian is the man with your mother? The one who said you were going out for pizza?"

Griffin grinned. "We're dating."

She frowned. "We?"

"I get to go with them sometimes. We went to Six Flags the other day. Julian's cool."

"So you like Julian?"

His shoulders drooped. "I wish . . ."

"What?"

"That he was my father," whispered Griffin.

"I see. Griffin, you're a very fortunate young man. I want to talk with your parents while you stay with your grandparents and uncle." The judge stood and went to the door. "Everyone please come in. I've made my decision."

Cheers went up in the judge's chamber amid protests. "My decision is final. Permanent custody is awarded to Griffin's mother, Olivia Sanders. Mr. Sanders, you had your chance."

"I love my son!" Aaron yelled.

"According to the documents before me, your newfound love is a result of his being in line to inherit the family firm," she said with disapproval. "I only hope you learn to value him as much as his mother and his extended family does."

Without a word, Aaron left the court, his lawyer behind him.

"He's mine forever." Olivia rushed back outside to her son.

"You think you have room enough for me?" Julian asked.

Olivia turned to him. "What . . . what did you say?"

His arms circled her waist. "Will you marry me?"

"Oh, Julian. Yes!" She flew into his arms.

He held out his other arm for Griffin. "You too."

Griffin wrapped his arms around Julian as far as they would go. "Are we still going to get pizza?"

Everyone laughed as they piled out of the courthouse. They were coming down the steps when a black limousine pulled up at the curb. A uniformed driver jumped out and opened the door. Out stepped a tall, distinguished man with silver hair.

Beside Tyler Jana gasped. "What is it?"

The well-dressed man started up the steps, saw her and quickly went to her. "I found you at last."

"Frederick," Jana said, making the introductions. His family owned several oil tankers. He was one of the richest men in the country and one of the men who had begged her to stay. "What are you doing here?"

"I've come for you, of course." He caught her arm. "Come, the car is waiting." He'd already turned back when he felt resistance.

"She's not going anyplace with you," Tyler said, his voice hard.

"Do not be angry because I didn't take your calls," he said. "I was furious at you for leaving me, but I have come to my senses. I want you back."

"She's not going with you," Tyler said, his arm sliding possessively around Jana's slim waist.

Up went Frederick's aristocratic nose. He dismissed Tyler with a glance. "You'll want for nothing, Jana, my darling. I'll take an extended holiday and we can go to Saint-Tropez or Morocco or anyplace you desire."

"She's rather stay with me and be my wife," Tyler said bluntly, his face as harsh as his voice. No one was taking Jana away from him.

Jana gasped. She stared at Tyler. "You want to marry me?"

"I planned to ask you later. I love you." His face softened, his voice gentled.

Tears crested in her eyes. "I love you, too. So much it almost scares me." She turned to Frederick. "Nothing can compare to what I have here. Goodbye, Frederick."

"If you change—"

"I won't. This time it's forever." She gazed up at Tyler with love shining in her eyes. "Only this man will do."

To the cheering approval of his family, Tyler took Jana into his arms and kissed her. For him, only she would do.

Epilogue

Jana had thought her wedding day had been the happiest day of her life. She'd been wrong. Since then, each day with Tyler was more incredible than the one before.

Waiting for Tyler to finish working and come upstairs, she sat in bed with a forgotten book and stared at their wedding picture on the nightstand. Both of them were beaming. The "small" garden wedding six weeks ago had had a hundred well-wishers. The number swelled to over three hundred for their reception at Hotel ZaZa because Tyler was well respected and had so many friends. Many of those in attendance were now her friends, too. She was doubly blessed to have found Tyler and that, miraculously, he loved her.

Olivia's wedding was to be a more formal affair, and was scheduled to take place in two weeks. Afterward, Julian was moving in. Since Olivia and Tyler each had a separate wing in the three-story house, there was enough room for both families. *Family.* Jana hugged the book to her chest. At last she belonged, and had a family of her own.

The bedroom door opened. Tyler, a broad grin on his face, began unbuttoning his shirt before he was two steps inside their room. Laughing, she jumped out of bed and ran to him.

Kissing her, he picked her up. "You're going in the wrong direction."

She kissed, then nuzzled, the strong line of his jaw. "It got me in your arms faster."

"Point taken." He sat on the side of the bed with Jana in his arms and stared deeply into her eyes. "I love you, Jana Maxwell."

Her hands, palming his face, trembled as much as her body. "I'll never grow tired of hearing those words or take for granted how blessed I am. I love you, Tyler Maxwell, for now and for always."

"I know," he said, his voice deep and raspy just before his mouth covered hers.

Jana gave herself up to the rapture of loving Tyler, the first and only man she'd ever love unconditionally, the first and only man who knew her faults and loved her back the same way.

CPSIA information can be obtained
at www.ICGtesting.com
Printed in the USA
LVOW08s1939020217
523030LV00001B/67/P